THIS TRADE PAPERBACK ORIGINAL IS PUBLISHED BY
BRISK PRESS, WAPPINGERS FALLS, NY, 12590

SUBSTANTIVE EDIT BY: LYNDA SANDOVAL
COPY EDIT BY: AVERY BROOKS
COVER DESIGN BY: ANN MCMAN, TREEHOUSE STUDIO
AUTHOR PHOTO BY: WILLIAM BANKS
BOOK LAYOUT AND TYPESETTING BY: KELLY SMITH

FIRST PRINTING: MAY 2021

ISBN-13: 978-1-7343038-4-1

To Susie, this book may or may not
be about you, but it is definitely your fault.

Prologue

"State champs, state champs, state champs." The chant emanating from an unseen room guided her deeper into the sprawling house. She'd never been here before. She honestly wasn't even sure where "here" was. She'd seen the address on the group text, and she'd relayed it to the cab driver, but she didn't know exactly which of her teammates lived in the ostentatious McMansion. She had the right house, though, because the chant grew louder and faster as it crescendoed.

"State champs state champs state champs." The pace picked up so much speed the words ran together.

She wandered through a formal sitting room with white carpet and white furniture and white walls covered in black and white photographs. She had a brief awareness that those design choices might lead to some regrets by tomorrow morning, but then again, maybe not. These people clearly had enough money to pay for a refurbishment if the party got out of hand enough to do permanent damage. Would the party get that wild? She had no frame of reference for how wild a high school girls' fencing team could get, or how that compared to other high school parties, unless you counted the teen movies she'd been frantically watching ever since she'd passed the PG-13 threshold a few months ago.

"State champs!" The final iteration erupted into a primal shout. She was almost sad to have missed that wave, but there had been

1

others, and she expected there would be a few more over the course of the night.

She turned the corner to a more casual living space filled with approximately twenty girls standing on couches and coffee tables and holding sabers and red plastic cups. She smiled. Most people would've probably found the swords part jarring, but the cups caused the catch in her chest. Sword play had landed her here. The cups suggested she might be in over her head.

"Drink!" someone commanded, and as if to prove her point, everyone obeyed.

She scanned the crowd of familiar faces, subconsciously searching for a specific set of eyes, the ones she'd sought at every practice, on every bus ride, during every competition and celebration all year. They were rarely the exact same color, changing blue to green, or swirling with hints of gold, like the sky or tide, but they always pulled her in and held her close no matter their hue.

She caught a distinctive flash of blue amid the whirling colors, and her heart kicked her ribs in the way she'd learned to associate with Lauren.

"You should put on shoes or take off your socks." Lauren offered a hand to ease Val off a large wooden table in front of the TV. "If you're going to dance on the furniture with a foil in your hand, you definitely don't want to slip."

Val stared down at the cup and hilt she held as if weighing her options, then with a shrug, handed off the sword. "Fair, but tell me something, O captain, my captain."

"What?"

"Is it exhausting?"

Lauren smiled up at her. "What? Running through your mind all day?"

Several of the girls snickered, but Val shook her head. "Being the responsible one all the time."

"Always."

"You could just not," someone else called from across the room, but Jess couldn't tear her eyes off Lauren to see who.

"I could, but I wouldn't be me," Lauren admitted, then with a grin added, "and you wouldn't be a state champion."

"State champs," someone shouted, and the rest of the group took up the chant again.

Jess's chest expanded with a mix of pride and something else. She almost joined in, but she hadn't quite found her voice yet. Not like Lauren, who managed to be part of the group even as she also stood out in the crowd.

She'd known Lauren was special the first day in the gym when she'd lifted her fencing mask, her smooth, graceful features flushed after a bout. Something had rumbled to life inside her body in that moment like an earthquake summoned to shake her foundation.

She'd been noticing girls differently for almost a year by then, but her heart about stopped when Lauren shook out her long, brunette hair, chest rising and falling dramatically, lips parted in a smile. When their eyes had met, she'd known two things with a clarity she'd never felt before. One, she was definitely gay, and two, she was completely in love with Lauren Standish.

She hadn't known what to do with either of those deep understandings, but they'd filled her with a strength and energy that teetered on the tightrope between thrilling and terrifying. She channeled her newfound certainties and all uncertainties they inspired into a record-shattering fencing season.

She shouldn't have even made the team. It took a special allowance from both the school and New York State High School Fencing Association for someone so young to compete at the varsity level, but she'd charged in with a seriousness she'd never felt about anything until she had the chance to fight next to Lauren. Her presence amplified every one of Jess's emotions and made a game feel valiant somehow, like she might just be willing to get run through in order to prove herself worthy of that spot beside her.

But now the season had ended. They had a shiny trophy to show for their efforts, but it mattered to her only because it meant their names would be etched in bronze together after Lauren left for

3

college. She wasn't young enough or naive enough to believe they'd stay in touch, and someone like Lauren wouldn't ever come back to Buffalo. She shone too brightly for the rust belt.

The thought tinged her tongue with a bitter heat. She skirted the room, heading toward the open kitchen, keeping her eyes on Lauren right until the moment she had to examine her drink options. Cans and bottles floated in a large, stainless steel sink of icy water. On the counter, a huge silver bowl shimmered with a dark red punch. She couldn't even begin to imagine what the mix contained, but it smelled sweet and cool, so she grabbed a cup and a ladle of liquid courage.

She had the second scoop poised over the plastic in her hand when she became stomach-clenchingly aware the room had gone quiet. She froze, afraid to look up. Warmth blossomed across her face as she tried to avoid confirming her fears, but before the burn could spread, a gentle hand closed around hers.

"Hi Jess." Lauren's voice, low and close, caused the hair on the back of her neck to stand on end.

She allowed the cup to be taken and set the ladle back in the punch. "Hi."

"Who invited The Kid?" someone called.

She clenched her jaw against the moniker, part nickname, part blunt descriptor.

"I did." Val perked up. "She's on the team. She's a state champ!"

A mild cheer went up from the group, but the chant didn't take hold.

She glanced up, finally meeting Lauren's eyes with a silent prayer she wouldn't see pity there. She nearly buckled under her own relief when she met only affection.

"I'm glad you came," Lauren said.

"Yeah?"

Lauren threw one arm around her shoulder. "Of course. None of us would be here without you."

"Ah hell," Val laughed. "I'm going to get all choked up thinking about the way you took down that beast in the third round."

Excitement wound up around them again.

4

"You were all like, attack, counterattack, parry-riposte. And we were like, 'She's dead,' but then you roared back up, and step, hop, lunge." She replayed Jess's attack with her bare hand since Lauren had already confiscated her weapon.

"Blam!" someone shouted.

"Blam," a few others echoed.

"Someone get The Kid a drink!" Val shouted.

Lauren fished a can of Cherry Coke from the sink.

"Boo," Val called. "Come on, mom. She earned the real thing."

"She earned so much more than her first hangover." Lauren tugged Jess a little closer. "Come on."

"Where?" A stupid question. She didn't care where Lauren wanted her to go. She wanted to go there, too.

"Away from these wild banshees, so we can talk like civilized adults."

"Don't let her mother you, Kid," Val warned as Lauren steered her toward a large sliding glass door.

"I only mother you because you're not housebroken," Lauren shot back as she slid open the door, and a cool breeze hit them both in the chest. "I actually want to have a real conversation with Jess. Don't burn the place down while we're gone."

Then she shut the door on whatever smart retort Val intended to offer.

"Ugh." Lauren sagged against her side. "They aren't wrong, you know? They exhaust me."

Jess stood stock still, quietly thrilled her shoulders could bear the weight of Lauren's burden, like Atlas holding up her sky. "Why do you do it?"

"I don't know how not to. Or maybe I don't want to know how to stop." Lauren rolled her chin, so her hair brushed against Jess's cheek, rich with the silky scent of shea butter. "I guess I just love them, and I think it feels good to take care of people you care about."

She couldn't argue, as having Lauren lean on her was about the best thing she'd ever experienced.

"Do you want to put our feet in the pool?"

5

"Uh," she glanced across the patio, surprised a pool even had water in it in late April in Buffalo. "Sure."

Lauren released her and kicked off her Converse sneakers, then peeled away her socks. Jess followed, balancing on one foot, then the other, until they both stood barefoot on the cool concrete.

Lauren rolled up the cuffs of her jeans until they rested atop her smooth calves, and then dropping to sit on the pool ledge, sank her feet into the water.

Jess would've gladly jumped all the way in after her, but as her toes broke the surface, she sucked in a sharp breath.

"Too cold?" Lauren arched her eyebrows.

"No." Her teeth gave a little chatter.

Lauren rested a hand on her leg. "You're a terrible liar, Jess."

"No. I'm getting used to it." There had to be a heater of some sort, as the water was actually warmer than the air temperature, but they were wearing jeans and sweatshirts for a reason. "Either that or I'm going numb."

Lauren smiled even as she shook her head. "I love the cold. I forget other people don't."

"I do, too."

"No, you don't," Lauren said softly, "and you don't have to pretend you do. Not with the water, or the cold, or the alcohol."

They sat in silence for a moment, the pool light casting everything in a translucent kind of blue. The ripples on the water threw shimmering shadows across their bodies.

"I wasn't trying to impress anyone," she finally said.

"Good. You don't need to, 'cause you already have." Lauren paused until she met her eyes. "I can't believe you're only thirteen and you've already been to states. That's no small thing."

She shrugged. "I mean states was fun and all . . ."

"But?"

"But so was every other match, and practice, and everything else I got to do with you."

Lauren reached out and tousled her curls. "The feeling's mutual. This team is the best I've ever competed with."

"I didn't mean the rest of the team," Jess corrected, her voice lower than she'd ever heard it. "I meant you."

"Me?"

"You made me want to fence. I was just fooling around at the club until I met you."

She chuckled. "Your fooling around put you on the varsity team as a middle schooler."

"Yeah, but you made me fall in love with it. Fighting with you, working out with you, doing two-a-days in the gym, even the crazy-hard ones. You're such a good captain. You made me want to keep pushing even when I messed up or got tired. I wish I could always fence with you." The words all came out in a rush of honesty that sounded young even to her own ears, but Lauren didn't look embarrassed by the outburst.

"That might be the nicest thing anyone's ever said to me." Her chest rose, and the corner of her mouth did, too. "I love this sport so much, and I want to inspire other people to take up the saber, but I don't think I can take much credit for who you are with a weapon in your hand."

"You could. You're a really great teacher. You're better than any of our other coaches."

"Maybe I helped you tweak your grip or your lunge, but you have a fire when you take an on guard position that I didn't have anything to do with. I think you're either born with it in you or not."

Her heart gave another one of those deep bass thuds. "Sort of like being queer?"

Lauren eyed her more carefully than she ever had before, gaze flicking from her submerged feet, to her hands, and back to her face. "Something else we have in common?"

She nodded, her throat too constricted to speak. Apparently knowing something and saying it aloud felt different. Where the former had inspired strength, the latter left her bare, raw, and vulnerable in equal measure.

"Wow." Admiration mingled with affection in Lauren's voice.

"Wow?"

"You're thirteen and you just came out to me, all smooth and casual. You're impressive."

"Not really."

Lauren gave her leg a little squeeze. "Yes, really. You keep breaking the curve in everything you do."

"I haven't done anything about being queer yet. I just know that I am."

"The knowing is kind of the hardest part. I didn't know until right after I turned sixteen."

"But that was two years ago."

Lauren raised her eyebrows and pursed her lips as if trying to sort out a complicated math problem. "Doesn't feel that long."

"What's the best part?"

"Of being queer?"

She nodded and scooted closer, hoping she didn't seem too much like a kid anticipating story time.

Lauren bit her lower lip and pondered the question for a few seconds before her features lifted. "I think maybe it's like being part of a small club, like getting some inside, unspoken connection. Like do you remember when you made the fencing team? One day you weren't part of it, and then you were. Suddenly you have a cohort, something bigger than yourself. You belong to them, and they belong to you."

She frowned. "Oh."

"What do you mean 'Oh?' I thought that was a pretty good speech."

"No, it totally was," she agreed, letting the idea sink in.

"Then why do you sound so disappointed?"

"I'm not." She hoped the pool light wasn't bright enough to show the flush in her cheeks. "I guess I just sort of hoped the best part would be kissing girls."

Lauren threw back her head and laughed a bold shot of amusement that made Jess's skin so much warmer than the air or water should've allowed. In that moment she understood how someone could become addicted to something, anything that made them feel as good as that sound made her feel. "Well, I can't say I've kissed enough girls to get a comprehensive sample size, but from what I've experienced, you won't be disappointed on that front, either."

Her breath caught. "Yeah?"

"Yeah, but you don't have to take my word for it. I'm sure you'll have girls lined up around the block before long."

She snorted softly.

"Hey." Lauren's voice turned soft and serious. "I'm not kidding. You're already so far ahead of most people your age. You're already turning heads, and not just with a saber in your hand. Those red curls and those blue eyes and the little dimple in your chin—you're going to break so many hearts."

"I won't," she said sincerely. There was only one heart she wanted, and she would never break it. The desire to make that as clear to Lauren as she knew it deep inside herself built at her core and combusted. She couldn't speak or think or even breathe. She just leaned in, and catching Lauren's face in her hands, pulled their mouths together.

Lauren's lips were impossibly soft, but the breath she sucked in between them sounded sharp. She tasted like Cherry Coke and chocolate, and Jess wanted to slip deeper into her, but even in her lack of experience, her body recognized she wasn't being invited to do so.

Lauren hadn't wrenched away, but neither had she leaned in. The absence of any signal actually sent a pretty clear message, but she desperately didn't want the moment to end. Maybe it wouldn't. Her brain spun frantically with a million thoughts even as her nerve endings fritzed and fizzled. Maybe she could do something else, something better. She could still prove herself, if only she knew how.

Lauren's hand ran up her arm and closed around her shoulder. Gently, firmly, she squeezed the muscle there, and then eased them apart.

Jess kept her eyes closed as long as she reasonably could, doing everything in her power to cement the soft imprint of those lips, the caress of strong fingers, the scent of her shampoo into the

9

furthest reaches of her memory. When she finally allowed her lids to flutter open once more, Lauren smiled so beautifully her heart soared and shattered simultaneously.

So many emotions filled those kaleidoscope eyes, amusement, admiration, affection, and yet the missing piece overrode them all.

Attraction.

Lauren looked at her like one might view a super-adorable puppy. "See what I mean? Breaking curves and breaking hearts. I would've never dreamed to kiss a high school senior at thirteen. You're fearless, but you're also too smart for this. You understand the math and the law and the morality of why an eighteen-year-old kissing a thirteen-year-old is absolutely out of the question, right?"

The hit landed right in her pride, but the wound wasn't fatal, and she forged on. "I'll turn fourteen in August."

"And I'll be nineteen," Lauren said, her voice patient and kind. "You may hit some milestones faster than me, but the math will always be the same."

Frustration welled in her. "I can add."

"Hey," Lauren whispered, "I didn't mean to imply you couldn't, but you have to see the problem here."

"I don't. I'm not some dumb kid. I'm not." She clenched her fists and tried to calm down, but she wasn't great at that. She didn't even see why people cared so much about being calm or patient. "You said yourself, I'm advanced. I'm going to do great things. I know I can. I'm going to go places and do things so much bigger than some silly math problem. Those five years won't mean anything in the end."

Lauren gave her leg another little squeeze. "I believe you. I'm not arguing or underestimating you."

"You can't see past my age."

"I think I see past it better than you do, because I see so clearly that by the time you're old enough for the math not to matter, the milestones will. You're going to blow past me, Jessie."

"I won't. I'll never leave you behind."

10

"You will. You don't understand yet how amazing you are, and not just at fencing. Your mind is even faster than your hands. And that's saying a lot, because your hands are crazy fast." She bumped her shoulder with her own. "You're going to lead the team for years, and then you're going to go on to things that will make all of this feel small."

"Not you." The idea hurt her chest even more than Lauren pulling away from her kiss. "You'll never feel small to me. No matter what else I do, I'm going to come back and find you and ask you to go out with me."

Lauren laughed, but not in a way that made her feel silly. "You'll be able to blow me away by then."

"When?" A new hope rose in her chest. "When I graduate high school?"

"When you graduate high school, I'll have already graduated college."

She frowned. "When I graduate college, then?"

"Don't worry. By the time you're old enough to date me, you won't want to." Lauren reached out to tousle her curls once more, but this time Jess ducked away from the touch.

"I'm not dumb," she reiterated, her frustration edging into anger. "I know the odds are against me, but I don't care. I'm going to beat them. All of them. I'll prove everyone wrong, even you if I have to."

"Okay, okay." Lauren held up her hands and spoke in soothing tones. "I'm sorry. I didn't mean to imply what you're feeling isn't real or valid. I know you're a powerhouse. It's not that I don't have faith in you, it's that I have so much of it."

"Then tell me when." A hint of desperation crept into her voice. "If you mean that, then tell when you'll go out with me."

Lauren sighed as she gave some thought to the question.

Jess held her breath until it grew painful, but when Lauren's smile turned genuine, all the tension melted away. "Why don't you come find me when you're on your big Olympic run? I think I'd like to see that."

She nodded resolutely as a new dream sprang to life like a fire burning up her being. She understood Lauren probably thought she'd made a pretty safe bet, but the knowledge did nothing to dim the hope and resolve twisting in her now.

She extended her hand. "Make a pact."

"Jess . . ."

"No." She snapped, then caught herself and started again. "Don't patronize me. If you mean it, promise."

Lauren encircled her hand with her own: soft, strong, warm. Then she conveyed all the same things with her eyes as she met Jess's. "Okay. If you still want to go out with me when you're an Olympian, come find me. Deal?"

Her chest swelled and her jaw tightened as desire imbedded itself in steel and stone at her center. "Deal."

Chapter One

10 years later

How was it already nine o'clock on Thursday night? Lauren felt relatively certain it had only been eight o'clock on Tuesday a few hours ago, and yet several of her classes had seemed to run on for eons. Maybe the windowless bowels of the Nickle City Fencing Club managed to warp the space-time continuum. She turned off the overhead lights in the largest and oldest of their three gyms. The glow of the bulbs faded slowly until she could just barely make out the lines of tape along the shellacked floorboards.

She moved down a narrow hall lined with dull metal weapons, doing a quick scan to make sure none of her youth fencers had inadvertently, or perhaps jokingly made off with one of the club's sabers, foils, or epees.

Check, check, and check. With everything in place, she turned into a smaller rectangle of a room. It had fewer strips of tape on the floor, and exposed ductwork up above, lending a grittier feel as opposed to the all-purpose vibe of the first gym. No amount of antiseptic or air freshener had ever penetrated the omnipresent scent of sweat and scuffed rubber in the cramped confines, but at least its smaller size made it easier to check before closing up for the night.

As she worked back toward the main entrance, the hallway opened up into a small foyer and then a reception area. Along the far wall, a large picture window gave a direct view into their most refined fencing space. The view still carried a bit of novelty and sparked a hint of pride for her even after a year. In the silly, sentimental recesses of her brain, she thought of that view as her window to the future.

She shook her head. She didn't have the time or the energy to daydream about what other changes she'd like to make, and if that one window in five years of working here was any indication of things to come, she wouldn't have to worry about finding the energy anytime soon.

She reached through the door to the last gym and clicked off the lights quickly.

"Closing time," a familiar voice called from behind her. "Are all the scary women with swords gone for the night?"

Lauren laughed and turned to see her best friend's nose peeking through a tiny crack of the barely open front door. "We've been through this before. Women with swords aren't scary. They're sexy—all the danger and prowess and finesse with a sharp point. That shouldn't frighten you. It should turn you on."

"I don't see why it has to be an either/or sort of thing." Kristie eased the door open enough to step across the threshold, but still made a show of peeking around corners and through the viewing window until certain the coast was completely clear.

"It's just me here," Lauren said.

"And now me." Kristie hopped up to sit on the counter separating the reception area from the front desk. "What are we doing tonight?"

"Same thing we do every night, Pinky."

"World domination, Brain?"

"Try again."

Kristie scrunched up her face. "Cleaning fencing equipment?"

She nodded her confirmation.

"Ugh. Could we at least order some takeout?"

"That sounds amazing." Lauren's stomach growled its assent.

"One of my youth fencers got clipped through the glove tonight, so I spent my dinner break filing an incident report and contacting his mother. I haven't eaten anything since like two o'clock."

Kristie grimaced as if she found the idea painful. "I had a full supper before practice, but then I had practice, so I'm ready to eat again."

Lauren rolled her eyes at her friend's appetite and metabolism which worked together for both her fitness and her amusement. Of course, the three-hour hockey practices she ran all over town probably helped. Perhaps Lauren should've taken up hockey instead of fencing, but then again, fencing had always been more than enough to let her eat whatever she wanted without feeling sluggish until about two years ago. Maybe fencing wasn't the problem so much as her body approaching thirty years of wear and tear. The thought made her frown.

"Uh-oh." Kristie arched an eyebrow. "What grumpy thought did you have, and more importantly, will it end with me eating another chicken Caesar salad?"

She smiled at how well her friend could read her, or maybe how predictable she had become. "No, I'm tapped out on salads, too, but no more wings or burgers for a bit either. Sushi?"

Kristie shrugged, and her long, dark ponytail bobbed. "Sushi's fine if it comes with spring rolls."

"How about dumplings?"

"Sold!"

She turned and reached over the top of the reception desk to grab her phone when the sound of the door opening behind her caused her to freeze. She schooled her face into a neutrally pleasant expression before turning around to greet whatever kid or parent intended to tell her they'd forgotten something that would require her to scour the gyms again tonight.

When she straightened to face the interruption, though, her frustration fled in a rush. All conscious thought evaporated with it. Only raw recognition remained as the deepest part of her long-term memory swept her back on the whoosh of one sharp breath.

15

Red ringlet curls, sky blue eyes, a stubborn set of close, pointed lips drawn up in a short, shy smile. The features were all the same, and yet the woman who wore them bore less resemblance to the girl who'd last stood this close, than to the powerhouse whose likeness plastered various photos across the room.

Heartbeat hammering through her brain, Lauren glanced over her shoulder to check the display of Team USA memorabilia against the far wall to make sure the image hadn't come to life before her, but that poster hadn't shifted. She glanced back to the woman who'd followed her gaze, cheeks coloring as she recognized her mirror image held a place of honor in the space she now occupied in the flesh.

Neither of them spoke for the surreal set of ticking seconds it took for Lauren to find the simplest of words. "Hi Jess."

"Hi."

The voice was lower, smoother than it had been, but the essence of the simple greeting broke something inside her. Lauren opened her arms, and Jess stepped into the embrace. She didn't fold under her chin anymore, but rather rested hers on Lauren's shoulder, smelling of well-worn leather and an impending storm.

Lauren breathed her in, taking note of everything at once. The firm body, the soft wisp of her breath, the tender touch of a strong hand on the small of her back. This was Jess, and yet not the kid she'd known. This woman, already a tour de force in the fencing world, stood on the brink of so much more. Lauren clung to her tightly, the ferocity of her hug filled with all they'd been and everything the years in between represented for both of them. She laughed a little as the emotions overtook her and the absurdity began to seep in.

Jess laughed too, a low rumble that reverberated through Lauren's chest before she stepped back.

"What are you doing here?" she finally managed to ask.

"I came to see you."

"Me?" She laughed a little louder. "You?"

"Yeah. Me, you."

Lauren shook her head as if she'd said the silliest thing in the world, and her eyes landed on Kristie, who'd frozen atop the reception desk, mouth open. "Do you even know who this is?"

"No, but please, for the love of all things good and gay in the world, introduce me."

Lauren blinked away some of her shock and managed at least a little chagrin at her lack of social grace. "Yeah, sorry, Kristie Gallagher, meet Jess Kidman, one of my old teammates and the newest member of Team USA's Olympic saber fencing contingent."

"It's very, very nice to meet you, Jess," Kristie said as her eyes swept over Jess's long, lean form before she turned back to Lauren with a dramatic flair. "Why didn't you tell me you were friends with the super-hot fencing model on all the posters around here?"

"I haven't seen her in over a decade," Lauren said, then to Jess added, "and it's been a very busy decade. I'm so impressed with everything you've done. I cheered for you at Columbia and on the national team, and at worlds last year. I mean, none of it's surprising, but still so wonderful. And now the Olympics."

"The Olympics," Jess echoed and raised her eyebrows expectantly.

"You should be training. Oh my God, you only have a few months. Seriously, why are you in Buffalo?"

"We made a deal."

Now Lauren took her turn to arch an eyebrow.

Jessie frowned. "Please don't tell me you forgot."

She searched her memory, like rapidly clicking through a slideshow in the back of her brain. She had so many mental images of Jess, but they were all shrouded in the golden haze of youth.

"Your senior year, the party after we won the state championship, everyone was drinking." The seriousness of Jess's voice willed her to remember. "You took me out by the pool, away from the crowd, just the two of us."

"OMG." Kristie let out a giddy little squee. "It's just like a letter to Penthouse."

Lauren rolled her eyes at her friend. "She was thirteen."

"Whoa, senior year plus a thirteen-year-old equals jailbait. Right?"

A muscle in Jess's jaw twitched the same way it had that night, and the memories rushed back as the little tick softened something inside of Lauren the way it always had. "You were so brave and bold and serious. God, Jess, doesn't it feel like an eternity ago?"

She nodded slowly then took a deep breath. "Sometimes, but I'm here now. I've qualified for my first Olympics, and I don't see a ring on your finger, so unless you're with someone . . ." She glanced pointedly at Kristie.

Kristie held up both hands in a move of rapid surrender. "That's a big nope."

Jess grew less restrained, more confident in a way that hinted at so much more than she'd been willing to show before. She turned to face Lauren fully. "Then I'm ready for the date you promised me."

Lauren laughed, an incredulous shot of joy. "Seriously? You came all the way back to Buffalo in an Olympic year to tease me about a deal we made more than ten years ago?"

Jess shook her head so hard a red curl fell across her smooth brow. "I'm not teasing. You told me I could ask you again on my first Olympic run. This is me, roughly two months from the opening ceremonies, asking you to please, finally, go out with me."

Lauren could barely process the words, much less the swell of emotion they clearly carried for Jess. None of them made sense in this context. The context didn't even make sense. Jess represented both a blast from her past and a vibrant piece of the world Lauren never got to know. The idea she'd even remembered her would've been flattering, but to have her barge in and try to sweep her off her feet added up to something too surreal to fathom. The whole exchange would've felt farcical if not for those steady eyes burning with the same fire that bound them together in a different life. The heat of that fire held her cautiously back for fear of getting singed. "Do you have any idea how crazy this is?"

Jess gave her a little smile. "The thought has occurred to me over the last ten years."

"And yet, seriously, here you are, right now?"

"Seriously asking you to go to dinner with me tomorrow night, or any time really."

She ran her hands through her hair and glanced around once more, as if looking for the hidden cameras surely recording this prank. "I don't know."

Kristie groaned loudly.

Jess looked like she wanted to echo the sentiment. "Come on, Lauren."

"No, you come on." She began to pace, a nervous energy buzzing through her and tingling the tips of her fingers. This wasn't what she'd planned, not for tonight, not for any night. Her chest tightened. "You showed up at my place of employment after ten years with no warning. You didn't even call or email. You can't pressure me."

"I'm not trying to pressure you." Jess's voice dropped back into the low, almost grave tone she'd used when so much younger. "If you want out of our deal, I won't hold you to it, but in all the time I dreamed of this conversation, and all the times I worried I'd show up to find you married, or taken by someone else, it never once occurred to me you'd flat out break your promise because I didn't call ahead."

Her shoulders sagged. That wasn't what she'd meant. She didn't even know what she meant, but she didn't love being put on the spot, and she really didn't love the things Jess's sudden and very grown-up appearance did to her ability to think clearly. There was too much disconnect between the girl she'd once felt so comfortable with and the woman making her feel anything but comfortable now. Jess cut an imposing figure in her dark, low-slung jeans and her leather motorcycle jacket. The set of her jaw and shoulders conveyed the image of someone used to getting what she wanted, but the vulnerability in her eyes made it clear she didn't dare take this conversation for granted.

"Look," Jess straightened, then smiled once more before all her words poured out in one earnest rush. "I've missed you. I'd like to get to know you again. I wanted to catch up, and yes, maybe get another crack at kissing you, but only after a nice dinner, perhaps with a glass of wine, and more importantly, a couple hours of long-overdue conversation. Ultimately, I'm not going to hold you to a deal you made at eighteen years old, because I don't want to be held to who I was then either, but I'd like to go out with you in the present tense. Would you like to have dinner with me?"

Lauren stared at her. She couldn't even sort out the tangle of emotions surging in her, much less speak around them.

"Holy hell!" Kristie finally exclaimed into the awkward silence. "If you won't take her up on that offer, I will."

"Shut up, Kristie!" she snapped. "I need a minute to think."

"What's to think about? You haven't had a date in eons, and you were just saying 'women with swords are sexy' when a literal fucking Olympic swordswoman drops out of the sky looking hot enough to scorch the pavement and asks to buy you dinner."

Jess's satisfied smirk made her look older than she ever had in Lauren's presence. "I like her."

"Thank you." Kristie mirrored the cocky grin, and some of Lauren's tension faded.

"I really don't need the two of you on the same team."

"You could join the team, too." Kristie suggested. "Go out to dinner with my new, deliciously good-looking fencing friend here, and then come over to my house and tell me all the sultry details you've clearly withheld for the entirety of our friendship."

"Or just come to dinner," Jess offered.

"Okay." She threw her hands up in the air. "Yeah. Sure. Why not?"

Kristie gave a fist pump and Jess beamed, so she couldn't manage to feel anything other than happy, but even as her own smile spread, the nerves didn't disappear. They just got swept up into all the other emotions sparked by the understanding that what she'd agreed to encompassed so much more than dinner.

Jess's shoulders strained under her black tank top as a drop of sweat slipped from the tip of her nose onto her yoga mat. Every muscle in her core trembled with the effort of holding completely still as her obliques burned.

"Time?" She gritted through clenched teeth.

"Four minutes, thirty-five seconds," Haley said from the other end of their video connection.

She swore under her breath and tightened her glutes. Five-minute planks were always torture no matter how many times she did them, and she did them a lot. She never could tell, though, which bothered her more, the strain on her muscles or the mental fatigue of not moving for a whole five minutes.

"Almost there," Haley encouraged, not sounding nearly as taxed as Jess felt. "Five, four, three, two, one, up."

She sprang forward, feet landing between her hands, then launched herself upright before pouncing onto a box jump. Both her sneaker-clad feet landed with a unified thump that echoed through the weight room before she pushed off and back again. She coiled immediately and repeated the process nine more times in rapid succession.

"And out," Haley called. "Hydrate or die."

She gladly accepted the reprieve, grabbing her stainless steel water bottle and chugging to soothe her parched throat. She tried not to take note of the stunned stares of her fellow gym-goers. They clearly weren't used to Olympic-caliber workouts in the tiny mostly yoga-centered studio she'd dropped in on, and she wouldn't be sticking around long enough to explain herself.

"Take your pulse," Haley ordered. "And don't lie to me."

"Yes, mom." She held her fingers to her wrist and watched the seconds tick away on her smart watch, but the math only confirmed what she already knew. "Anaerobic."

Haley grinned at her through the laptop screen. "Well, I should freaking hope so, because if that workout didn't get your cold little heart pumping, I don't know what would."

"The workout is the same whether I do it in Manhattan or Buffalo."

"Maybe physically," Haley conceded, "but don't tell me you didn't spend the first three minutes of your plank thinking about your hot date tonight."

She didn't deny the charge. She'd thought of little else over the last twenty hours. How could she not? The way Lauren pulled her into that hug, flush against her body, had ignited her senses. She forced herself back to Haley's comment. "You don't know she's hot. She might be quite plain."

"I know you. And I know you wouldn't haul ass all the way across the state a week after being named to the Olympic team for someone who didn't set your body on fire at least as much as a good workout. Also, I internet stalked her."

"What? How?"

"Wasn't hard. There aren't many fencing instructors in Buffalo."

"I guess not."

"Have you ever stopped to wonder why that is?"

"Too much snow?"

"No. It's because all the good ones leave."

"She's a good one," Jess said defensively. "She went to Princeton on a full ride."

"Nine years ago. Which means she was pretty damn awesome at one point, but she's been out of the big leagues for longer than you've been in them."

"I don't care. It's not about credentials."

"Is it about her amazing ass? Because I saw a video, and it is a top-notch ass if you're into that sort of thing, which I know you are because you've had many a top-notch ass right here in New York. You did not have to shuffle on back to Buffalo to get a date."

She grabbed a towel, then flopped back onto the yoga mat. She couldn't argue with either point. Lauren had always had an amazing physique, and from the little Jess could process between her nerves, excitement, and relief, the girl she'd admired so many years ago had grown into a stunning woman. And yes, she'd had some personal experiences with enough women to draw a few favorable comparisons. She wasn't ashamed she hadn't exactly led a monastic lifestyle while waiting for her probationary period with Lauren to expire, but didn't that also prove she wasn't here out of desperation? "I've already told you. I waited more than ten years for this."

"Then, I don't see why you couldn't wait another three months until you're back from the games."

"I get that it sounds silly or even pathetic. Trust me. I spent years kicking myself for being so stupid, and then years throwing myself into every other woman I could find, but something made me feel like I needed to do this. Some people hit the big time and buy something extravagant. Some people make the cut and get the Olympic rings tattooed on their ass. For me, the culmination of the journey always meant Lauren."

She threw her arm over her head and tried to steady her breathing before going on. "Maybe I'm an idiot. Maybe we'll go out to dinner and I'll feel nothing. If that's the case, I'll close the book and come back to the city with renewed focus, but trust me, coming out here isn't the distraction you're afraid it is. It would've been a distraction if I hadn't."

Haley didn't respond, and Jess finally peeked out from under her arm to see if they'd lost their connection. When she did, she watched her teammate's expression soften. "Okay, fine. Go get this girl out of your system. I hope it's a terrible date, though, because almost everything about you not being here sucks."

"Almost everything?"

Haley grinned. "Well, there's a considerable upside to not having to smell you after a workout."

She turned her head toward her armpit and grimaced before she even caught a full whiff of herself. "Fair."

"I hope you have time for a long shower before your date tonight, or you might scare her off before you get through the hors d'oeuvres."

"Yeah, she doesn't get off work until like eight o'clock tonight." She glanced at her watch, and her stomach fluttered at the internal countdown telling her she still had four hours until the moment she'd waited for since middle school. Her heart rate picked up, and her hands trembled. She hopped back to her feet for fear if she didn't, her whole body might betray her. "You wanna go again?"

Haley shook her head. "Nope, tonight's fight night. I don't want to be in my legs."

"Ah, fight night," she sighed wistfully.

"There's a flight from Buffalo to JFK every hour. If you head to the airport now, you'll easily make it by ten tonight."

She shook her head. "For the first time in a long time, I have someplace I'd rather be."

Haley conceded. Anything or anyone that outranked fight night couldn't be argued with. "Fine. Go run some stairs, then sweep your girl off her feet, but you better be back here Tuesday or I'm coming after you, and while I'm in town I'm going to make your parents show me baby pictures."

Jess laughed. "I don't doubt it. I'll see you next week."

She powered down her laptop and shoved it into her backpack. Then slinging the straps over her shoulders, she headed toward the exit, but when she reached the stairs she'd come in on, instead of turning down them, she lowered her head and pushed off with explosive force.

She loved running stairs as much as she could love any exercise that didn't involve a saber in her hand. She loved the rhythm, the burn, the constant push of her toes against the concrete, the way it never gave, not even an inch. She also relished the imagery of going someplace better than spinning while standing still on a stationary bike or elliptical machine. And unlike a run on the track, on stairs, she worked steadily upward. Faster, higher, stronger, the Olympic motto doubled as her own mantra, what she strove for, what she chased, what she always knew she could achieve.

Come find me when you're on your big Olympic run. I think I'd like to see that. Lauren echoed through the ages, the way she always had. The words twisted in her chest, but her feet didn't falter. They never had. The only moment she'd ever doubted them came last night when Lauren seemed like she might say no, but she didn't.

She'd looked at Jess, those kaleidoscope eyes swirling with flecks of blue, green, and gold. There had been so many emotions there, but she'd read them clearly. She'd always read Lauren better than most, and in the years they'd spent apart, she'd learned more than her thirteen-year-old self could've ever imagined about the gamut of human experiences. Lauren was shocked and nervous, flattered and confused, but at no point had she been disinterested, and that was a start. More than a start, it presented a challenge, and she loved a challenge.

She'd never expected a woman like Lauren to fall into her arms or her bed, and honestly, a part of her would've been mildly disappointed if she had. The Lauren she knew was cautious, caring, steady, and secure in herself. From what she'd seen yesterday, none of that had changed. No, she'd never expected their reunion to be a fairytale formed in the mind of her thirteen-year-old fantasies, she'd only hoped the old bond would be enough to reopen the door between them. She felt confident the woman she'd become since then could handle things from there.

Lauren sat at the front desk watching the last group of adult fencers through the picture window. Normally she would've been in there with them on a Friday night, either as a referee or a sparring partner, but the club's owner, Enrico, had made one of his sporadic evening visits, which gave her the freedom to duck out and close the other two gymnasiums early. Now she only had to wait for the group to wrap up, and she might just make it out on time for once.

She tried not to look at the clock or worry about who would come through the doors when it struck eight. She refused to get worked up over a dinner with Jess. It would be silly to let herself be nervous about a reunion with The Kid, even if she absolutely wasn't a kid anymore. She also steadfastly refused to so much as glance at the poster of Jess across the room, or compare the girl from her memories to the woman who filled out her uniform or wore a cocky grin or moved with hands so . . . no.

This was Kristie's fault. She always had her mind in the gutter. Lauren wasn't that person, at least not with women she'd known in school. She shook off the unsettling lapse and refocused on her boss shouting in the other room. Something about someone's footwork, but she couldn't tell whose.

25

Enrico slouched back in his folding chair at the far-right corner of the gym, his long, silver hair cascading down his back in a loose ponytail, his dark Mediterranean features creased with time and years of scowling at young fencers who rarely rose to his exacting standards. He'd been a force in his days, and she was old enough to remember at least the tail end of them, but he'd long since let go of almost all of his expectations. Now, he mostly watched the adults, occasionally shouting a random instruction at someone who caught his eye or his ire. He reserved the lion's share of his energy for shooting the breeze with the cluster of middle-aged men who still revered him or lavishing compliments on women young enough to be his daughters. He was never wrong, but he certainly showed favorites.

She rolled her eyes and smiled as she clearly made out the word *bellissima*, and saw him kiss his fingers. That had clearly not been directed at any of the men.

She took a kind of comfort at being able to keep an eye on his antics as much as the other fencers. She would've loved a similar view into the other gyms. Maybe since they'd paid off the construction bill for the first viewing window she could talk to him about adding another one. Or cameras. Parents of the little ones would love a better view of lessons or competitions. They could wire a closed-circuit feed to a high-definition TV in the lobby. And, of course, if they were running wires, they might as well install some body cords in the other gyms, and—she halted her thoughts. They were too much, too far, and undoubtedly too expensive.

Where she saw potential, Enrico saw only dollar signs, and he didn't want to do anything that cut into his income. Scratch that. He didn't want to do anything, period.

Frustration knotted the muscles where neck met shoulders, and as she tried to roll out the tension, she inadvertently noticed the time. Twenty to eight. The adult league fencers had to be on their last scrimmage pairings by now. None of them would notice if she slipped into the locker room and changed. If she timed it right, she might even avoid arousing Enrico's suspicions, as he never stuck around long enough to risk being asked to help clean anything. With any luck he'd sneak out for the night before she snuck back in.

She headed down the hall and through the rusted old door to the locker room. They only had two small showers and bathroom stalls. The minuscule dressing area held a large floor-to-ceiling mirror and about twenty pale-blue lockers along the opposite wall, as well as a long, open rack for hanging fencing uniforms. There amid a row of bulky white jackets, her red and black sweater dress looked especially out of place. It felt even more awkward once she'd slipped it onto her body. She hadn't worn a dress since Val and Michael's wedding. How long ago had that been? Their daughter had just celebrated her first birthday, so probably two years ago. She didn't mind dresses. She just didn't have much occasion to get dressed up. Even her important days at work came with a uniform, and while it hadn't exactly been the eons as Kristie asserted since her last date, none of her more recent attempts at relationships had evolved into five-star restaurant territory. Most of them hadn't even moved past the food-truck stage.

She didn't let herself muse about the fact that Jess had already surpassed all of them when she'd texted to say she'd secured a reservation at 100 Acres. The restaurant was so far out of Lauren's normal fare she'd had to google it. She grimaced at how out of the loop she was and pulled on a pair of semi-sheer black tights, because no matter what her comfort level in the dress, late April wasn't bare-leg weather in Buffalo.

Besides, she wasn't trying to impress Jess by showing any expanse of skin. The idea almost made her laugh.

Jess.

The local kid who made it big came back for her.

She smiled as she had several times throughout the day, but she wasn't silly enough to believe she'd done anything to warrant the flattery. Jess didn't even know her. Then again, wasn't that what she wanted tonight? Surely learning how little there was worth knowing about the last ten years of her life would put an end to her little schoolgirl flight of fancy.

27

Still, it could be fun to have a nice night out with someone who'd had legitimate excitement in recent years. Jess surely had stories to tell. It wasn't every day a person got a brush with celebrity, and in her world, Jess had become about as big as it got. Between her impeccable fundamentals and her explosive speed, even people who didn't follow fencing closely found something compelling in her style.

Of course, her looks didn't hurt in the fame department either. How had Kristie described her? Hot enough to scorch pavement? She shook her head, not ready to indulge quite that much yet, but even with her more protective instincts still pulsing through her, she never found it hard to understand Jess's appeal to people outside the sport. She'd been the It girl of American saber competition for a couple of years, and Lauren had always enjoyed telling people she'd known her way back when. It might be nice to say she knew her now. Her stomach tightened, warning her not to wish for too much. She knew better than to let herself get carried away, so she pinned the little flutter of excitement on the prospect of engaging conversation and maybe a hint of nostalgia for a simpler time.

As if to punctuate that thought, the door to the locker room opened, and a sweaty, middle-aged woman came in all red-faced and blustery. "Oh good, there you are. The new guy from Erie just lost his cool and bent one of the club foils really bad."

She sighed. "And Enrico?"

"He said he had to go, and to find you."

"Yeah, seems on-brand for him." She sighed. "Just tell the guys to leave the foil on the desk. It's about time for you all to knock off."

She nodded. "It's been a bit of a pissing contest in there tonight anyway. The new guy and Chip spent most of the last hour pounding their chests. You should've come and put them both in their places."

She grinned at how appealing that sounded, then remembered to check her hair in the mirror, second guessing her choice to leave it down. Too late to change it now, and it wasn't like she knew how to put it up anyway, at least not for anything other than functionality under a fencing helmet.

"Hey," the woman said as if noticing her preoccupation with her own reflection. "You look really cute."

"Thanks."

"Hot date?"

She shook her head and hoped the flush in her cheeks looked like she was wearing blush. "Dinner with an old friend."

And that's how she resolved to think of the evening, she told herself on the way back to the desk, and again as the guys headed out, each of them doing a double take on their way past.

She reminded herself one more time there was no reason to feel any butterflies as a new set of headlights swept into the parking lot. She genuinely believed herself, right up until the moment Jess stepped through the door in tailor-made slacks, a snug charcoal sweater hugging her form, topped off with a smile that could've buckled a thousand knees.

"You look wonderful." Her eyes swept over Lauren's body, sparkling with pleasure and warming every place they touched. "Ready to go?"

She swallowed the truth, forcing it down her suddenly dry throat. "Absolutely."

Chapter Two

Jess drove through the city in her rented car. It had been years since she'd been back on this side of town, and she needed her GPS to guide her through the late-winter darkness.

"I haven't been near Delaware Park since high school," she admitted, to make conversation. "My parents bought a place on the lakeshore the year after I graduated."

"Nice."

"For them." She laughed. "A whole lot of good it did me. Can you imagine the summer parties I could've had if they'd bought it when I still lived there?"

"I can, and I imagine they could too, which is probably why they waited."

"Probably." She spotted a mammoth, castle-like structure looming ahead as the GPS announced their arrival. "Think we've found the right place?"

"If that's not a hotel, then someone has let capitalism run a little rampant in their life."

Jess snorted at Lauren's dry wit and warmed at the way she still used humor to break the ice. She'd been nervous and nostalgic driving to the club. She'd spent so many hours training there as a teen, the drive felt like a homecoming with some deeply implanted autopilot making the turns for her, but at no point had she been able to forget something very different waited for her in the familiar setting.

She and Lauren had overlapped in their training for only one year. Jess had left for college before Lauren returned, and while she'd been back to visit her parents at least once a year, those had always been whirlwind trips. She'd avoided the club, unprepared or unwilling to see Lauren until she could meet her as an equal. Tonight, she'd done so. She'd walked through the door with all the confidence one could muster when arriving to take their first love on a first date ten years after their first kiss, only to be taken totally aback by the sight of her in a dress.

Her mouth had turned into a desert. Time slowed, and her fingers tingled. Every ounce of speed and suave and good sense she'd cultivated in the intervening years had abandoned her. She hadn't exactly felt like an awkward teenager again, but close. Thankfully, Lauren hadn't seemed to notice or care, as she'd kept the light conversation going on neutral topics like the weather, directions, questions about Jess's recent travel. Now as they pulled up in front of the behemoth of a hotel, Jess was finally able to chat without feeling out of breath.

A valet approached the car and leaned down to the window. "Are you checking in?"

"No," she said quickly, "we've got dinner reservations."

The valet nodded and accepted the keys as she exited the car. "If you change your mind, simply dial the number on the ticket and we'll move it into the overnight lot."

Her cheeks warmed at all the implications of that possibility. "I'm sure we'll be fine. Thank you."

She jogged around and met Lauren on the passenger side, managing what she hoped was a chagrinned expression. "That got awkward quickly. I didn't mean to imply any expectations with dinner in a hotel."

Lauren laughed lightly. "Good, but for what it's worth, I didn't think about it either."

She might've felt a little disappointed by the admission if Lauren hadn't looped her arm through hers as they started up the stairs and into the lobby. The touch was casual, easy, like the way Lauren had always touched her, but it sparked something

31

akin to elation to have her close again. She hated to break the contact when the hostess led them right to their table.

"This place is beautiful." Lauren took her seat, her eyes scanning the dark accents of the long, dimly lit hall.

"It is," she agreed without even glancing at their surroundings. "Do you want to order some wine?"

"Sure. What kind do you like?"

"I don't drink while in training, but don't let that hold you back. I'm driving."

"Oh, I see how it is." Lauren's voice took on a teasing lilt. "You bring me to a hotel, then ply me with alcohol and your charm."

"My charm? What makes you think I have charm?"

"You were born with more charm in your little finger than most people have in their whole being."

She warmed at the compliment, even though it didn't fully land. "I don't know who you think you're on a date with. Do you have me confused with one of our other teammates? Val perhaps?"

Lauren's eyes danced with amusement. "Val is a lot of things, but charming isn't one of them. Brash, wild, over the top maybe. She's also married and pregnant for the second time."

"No kidding?"

"No kidding. She married Michael Adams. You probably didn't know him."

She shook her head. "What about Cara?"

"She lives in London now, still not married but climbing the corporate ladder. You don't keep in touch with any of our old team?"

"Not really. They were all so far ahead of me. I hear from people closer to my age sometimes though. Oh, remember Maxine? Her younger sister was a year older than me, and we fenced together through school, then against each other in the first round at nationals in Salt Lake City a couple years ago. We all went out to dinner together the night before."

"Be honest." Lauren leaned forward. "You all had a lovely time out on the town and then you brutalized her on the strip the next morning."

"Crushed her. So, I had a lovely time in both settings actually."

"You're such a shark."

She grinned enough to show her teeth, but the waitress arrived before she had a chance to respond.

"What can I offer you to drink?"

"I'll have a water," Jess said, then raised her eyebrow toward Lauren.

"Could I get a glass of pinot grigio?"

"Which one?"

Lauren grimaced. "It didn't occur to me there'd be more than one on the menu. How gauche of me."

"We have three of them."

"See, this is why I study the menu before I go places, but I didn't look at the wine menu."

Jess laughed. "Bring her one of the Domaine and one of the Hans, so she can compare the two."

"Very well."

"And since it seems she just tipped her hand about menu research, I think we're ready to order." She looked to Lauren for confirmation.

"You caught me. I've been thinking about the seared scallops all afternoon."

She turned back to the waitress. "There you have it, scallops for Ms. Standish, and I'll have the king salmon."

"I'll get those orders in for you." The waitress retreated, and she turned back to see those dynamic eyes studying her intently.

"You scoped the menu beforehand," Lauren said with mock accusation.

"So did you."

"I'm anal retentive. I always look before I leap. What's your excuse?"

"Could I go with 'I'm training, and I need to keep a strict diet?'"

"Is that the truth?"

"Part of it."

"What's the rest?"

Nerves pricked at her palms like they did before a big match, but she forged on. "I wanted to make sure they had enough menu items worthy of a first date with you."

Lauren stared at her, chest rising and falling on several silent breaths, before she smiled. "And you said you weren't charming. Tell me more about nationals. I haven't been since college."

She didn't miss the retreat to more neutral topics, but neither did Lauren seem displeased with the short foray into something more. She read body language better than most, and once upon a time she'd been more attuned to Lauren's cues than any others. A part of her wanted to stay on the more personal plane, but there was no tension in those shoulders, and she wouldn't be the one to put it there. "What do you want to know?"

"Who's the hardest person you've ever faced?"

"Hmm, physically? Probably Mariel Zagunis at my first national championship. She blew me off the strip. I'd never seen anything like her up to that point. I went home and immediately doubled my leg workouts."

"Did it work?"

"It didn't hurt. I came in second at nationals the next year, and won the year after that, though I'm not sure if I can fully credit the leg workouts as much as the confidence they helped inspire in me."

"You might be the only person I know who credits their confidence over their conditioning."

"Well, the two are closely linked, but confident fencers take risks."

"Then you must be the most confident fencer ever, judging from your style of attack."

Jess shrugged as warring reactions to the comment vied for her attention. "Sometimes."

Lauren searched her eyes. "Is that why you only said she was the toughest physically?"

"You caught that, huh?"

"Come on, don't leave me hanging. Who's the toughest mentally?"

Her jaw tightened, and she tried unsuccessfully to hide the steel in her voice. "Yelena Finko. The Russians are always torturous in a battle of wills, but she's such a mind screw. She just . . ." Her words devolved into something akin to a growl.

"Wow." Lauren's eyes widened and her lips parted, as if the ferocity of the response had taken her breath away.

Mercifully, the waitress returned with two glasses of wine. Jess had to physically resist the urge to snag one for herself and down it in one swallow. She hated Yelena's ability to get under her skin from a continent away, and she hated even more that she'd done so on a date with Lauren.

She took deep breaths in through her nose for four seconds, held it for four, and released it for four, but the breathing exercise fell flat as always. And yet, the sight of Lauren sipping first from one glass and then the other soothed her immensely. Jess enjoyed the way she scrunched up her mouth and looked skyward as if heaven might help her discern some difference in the drinks.

"What's the verdict?" she asked. "Do you have a preference?"

"I think this one is a little lighter." She pointed to the glass on her right. "And the other one is a little sweeter, but I can't remember which one is which label anymore."

"Does the label matter?"

"I guess not. I'm going to drink one with dinner and one with dessert."

She smiled. The last of the tension left her body at the reminder she was here, now, and Lauren wasn't planning to go anywhere for at least two more courses. "A very well-reasoned plan, and can I just say I'm inordinately pleased to hear there will be dessert?"

"Tell me about the club," Jess urged as their food arrived and they'd done an appropriate amount of gushing and chewing to warrant a return to civilized conversation.

"The club is . . . well, probably exactly the same as when you left."

"I find that hard to believe with you on staff." Jess angled her body forward attentively, and her green eyes carried an intense focus. "What've you been doing since you moved back to Buffalo?"

It didn't escape Lauren's notice that each time she tried to move the conversation to things further away, Jess deftly brought them back home. Her interest seemed too genuine to disregard, but Lauren didn't know how long she could hold it if Jess kept insisting on talking about the details of her daily existence. "I'm sure it all seems drab compared to the places you train and compete."

"I don't think so. A strip is a strip, and I noticed you have a new window through to the elite-league space. That's got to help with competitions and photography. Good marketing all around."

A flush of pleasure ran through her and spread so much warmer than the wine.

"What?" Jess watched her closely, her gaze as intent as ever. "Why the shy little smile?"

"The window was my idea."

"Of course. You've always had a mind for showcasing the sport."

"If only Enrico saw it the same way."

Jess scoffed. "Enrico's still hanging around?"

"Oh yeah. I mean he sits in his chair and bellows a couple times a week."

"I would've thought he would've handed everything over to you by now."

"He basically has," she admitted. "I'm in charge of everything but the finances."

"Oh, so you do all the work and get none of the freedom. Sounds about like him. Surely he can't hang on much longer."

She shrugged. "It's frustrating not to be able to put all my ideas into action, but I can't complain. I'm the first full-time employee he's ever had, and he has given me a lot of freedom as long as I don't spend any money. I set my own schedule, pick my own classes, run camps how I want, and work with whatever private clients I can find. I owe him a lot."

"Sounds like he owes you a lot too. I hope he realizes that when he decides to retire."

"Who knows. Every now and then he threatens to move back to Milan with his mother."

"He's got a mother?"

She laughed. "Apparently, and she's almost a hundred years old, so clearly he's got longevity in his genes, but I seriously doubt he has the drive left to execute an international move anymore, so I'll have to keep waiting."

Jess's eyes darkened with something akin to sadness. "Just waiting?"

She swirled the wine in her glass. Was that what she'd meant? "Maybe not *just* waiting."

"Then what else?" Jess pressed gently, relentless in her hopeful style of inquisition.

"Working. Teaching. Learning. Trying to pad my resume as an instructor, building up my savings, and biding my time."

"Until?"

"Until I can buy the club outright and rework it according to my own vision." She wasn't sure why she'd said it so bluntly. She didn't usually talk about the end game very often. She didn't even let herself think about long-term plans, choosing instead to focus on laying a foundation slowly, steadily.

"Now that"—Jess raised her glass enthusiastically—"sounds like a dream worth toasting to."

"Is it?"

"Your own club? Of course." Jess's grin turned a little lopsided. "I mean, I'd think securing a bright future for the next generation of a sport we both love, in the place where we learned to love it, would be quite the legacy. I suppose only you can decide if it's the one for you."

She raised her glass, marveling at the way Jess's approval helped ignite the spark she'd allowed to dim. "Actually, I think it is."

"Really?"

She nodded. "I love to bring people to the sport."

"And?"

"I love coaching, at least when I feel like I can do it well."

"You're still the best coach I've ever had."

Her face flushed again, not because she didn't believe the compliment, but because Jess so clearly did.

"And with free rein, there's no end to what you could do for fencing in Buffalo."

She bit her lip, not wanting to get too carried away in this conversation or in this woman, but she couldn't keep from adding, "I do have a lot of ideas, for someday anyway."

Jess clinked her glass. "Then, let's drink to that future."

She did drink to it, feeling better than she had in ages, and more comfortable too. Jess's confidence inspired her own. She probably should've worried more about that. They didn't even know each other. Aside from a love of fencing and an affinity for checking menus before visiting a restaurant, they didn't have much in common. Still, Jess was qualified to have informed views about fencing. She knew a thing or two about how a small club could serve as a springboard to bigger and better things, which made her more qualified to comment on her dreams than anyone else in Lauren's life. Maybe she was exactly the kind of person who could visualize the future Lauren had spent years envisioning. The thought gave her a thrill just as intimate as any touch.

"What are you thinking?" Jess asked after a few moments of quiet reflection.

"It's just been a long time since anyone showed any genuine interest in the club or my hopes for it."

Jess arched an expressive eyebrow up under her red curls as she took another bite of her salmon.

"That sounded bad. I mean, my mom's great, and she believes in me. Kristie does, too, in her own way, but they aren't fencers. They can't see what I see in the place."

"What about your students?"

"I love them, and I think they like me, but all they know is what they've seen at our club. None of them travel or compete at high levels, so it's hard for them to know what they don't know. And Enrico, he's . . . well, you've met him."

She smiled sadly. "Yeah."

"We do get some wonderful high school fencers every few years, and a couple of the college teams train at the club." She tried to bounce back onto more steady ground. "The collegiate fencers help keep me sharp tactically and physically, but we don't get to cultivate much in the way of long-term relationships. As soon as they graduate, they bolt for bigger and better cities or clubs."

Jess sat back and studied her again, and this time Lauren didn't look away. Not from her red lips, her smooth skin, the set of her strong shoulders, her eyes compassionate but probing. Did she understand the effect she had on women, or did the allure come so naturally she didn't notice? "I have to admit, I was surprised when I heard you came back here after Princeton."

The pain in her chest felt more like a knife than the dull ache she'd inured herself to over the years. For that split second, she wasn't sitting in a five-star restaurant across from an old friend. She was alone and confused and shrouded in darkness. Her expression must've given her away because Jess leaned forward as if she might have to catch her.

"It's fine. I'm fine." She took a long, steady sip of her wine to gather herself. The pain so rarely caught her off guard anymore. "Life, um, it surprised me, too. I didn't plan on working in a warehouse. That's certainly not what I got an Ivy League degree to do, but things . . ."

"We don't have to talk about it."

Her eyes welled with tears she thought she'd banished, or maybe they weren't what they used to be. Maybe this time they rose in her for the tenderness she saw in Jess's expression. She'd gotten so used to pity, but somehow Jess managed to convey something deeper without even saying a word. She reached across the table, wanting to pull her closer even as she closed that particular door. "Would you mind if we didn't?"

"Of course not." Jess intertwined their fingers atop the white tablecloth.

"It's not that I don't trust you. It's just, I'm having the best time I've had in a long time, and I'd like to hold on to that."

Jess squeezed her hand. "That's the best reason not to talk about something. It also sounds like a great reason to segue onto the topic of dessert. Are you going to tell me what you've already chosen, or should I guess?"

"Oh, you've got a one-in-five chance of guessing correctly."

"No, a stranger would have a one-in-five chance," Jess corrected, her voice dipping lower, smoother, more intimate, as she lifted her eyes under dark lashes. "I'm not a stranger, and you're having peach Bellini sorbet."

Her heart gave a little jump. "How did you know?"

Jess ran her thumb over the back of her hand. "It's sweet and elegant, like you. More importantly, you like the cold, even in winter."

This time her breath caught for much more pleasurable reasons, but she still couldn't find her voice, or maybe she didn't want to for fear that if she did, she'd tell Jess she wasn't sure she'd ever be able to feel cold in her presence.

"My dessert was sinful," Jess said, a faint hint of honey and chocolate still coating her tongue.

"It was certainly decadent," Lauren agreed as she polished off her sorbet. "What would your coaches say if they knew you'd eaten a slice of chocolate almond torte topped with raw honeycomb?"

"Well, I don't have a personal coach right now, and the Team USA coaches would probably encourage an extra anaerobic workout, but I'd remind them they aren't the boss of me."

"Aren't they?"

She laughed. "None of them have managed to be for very long. You said you followed my career. Haven't you heard my reputation for being a little rebellious in more than my style of combat?"

The corner of Lauren's mouth curled up. "I didn't need any rumor mill to tell me that, but yes, I noticed you'd gone through a couple of coaches since you left Columbia."

She nodded, a little impressed Lauren had not only paid attention, she'd also nailed down her last good working relationship with a coach.

"I started fencing with you and the team at school, and then went on to Columbia. I'd only been a fencer at school. I mean, of course I worked with pros at clubs along the way, always as part of a larger team, but when I graduated, it was just me."

"I wouldn't think you'd wilt under the glare of one-on-one attention."

Her natural defenses rose. "I don't think I've wilted."

Lauren laughed. "No. But I see you do chafe a little bit under scrutiny."

"Hey now."

"What? It's not unusual for elite athletes."

"I can handle scrutiny. I've had tons of it. Trust me, I live up to every challenge."

Lauren's beautiful lips curled up. "I don't doubt you. But why so many coaches then?"

"None of them challenged me, not in any meaningful way. More lunges, kettlebells, a different yoga routine, or footwork drills I could do in my sleep. They didn't ever manage to make me a better version of myself. They only tried to make me like someone else."

"I don't think anyone could make you into someone else."

Jess relaxed at the truth of the statement and the affection with which Lauren delivered it. "Maybe you could call Team USA and tell them they're wasting their time."

"Why do I get the feeling you already told them yourself?"

She pursed her lips before finally letting a small smile squeak out. "I have a good training regimen now. I work out with some other Olympic-bound fencers a couple of times a week. No one pushes me harder than I do, and yes, I'll make myself do a few extra flights of stairs to burn off the dessert when I get back into the gym on Sunday."

"Sunday?"

"I normally take it off to let my muscles recoup and my brain

41

have a bit of a break, too," she explained as the waitress brought the check, and she slipped her credit card into the folder. "But I'm traveling back to the city tomorrow, so I'm swapping my weekend workout days."

"You're leaving so soon?"

The hint of disappointment behind the question sparked a pair of dueling emotions. The prospect of disappointing Lauren constricted her chest, but the idea that Lauren may've hoped she'd stay longer caused her heart to feel a little lighter. "I only took a couple days off to see my parents, and of course, come hold you to an old promise."

"Of course." Lauren smiled, then sidestepped the larger implications. "I knew you needed to train, but I'm so glad you did hold me to my promise, Jess. This has been such a beautiful evening, and I'll always cherish it."

She didn't love the sense of summation in that sentence, or the way Lauren seemed to accept it as something prepackaged and ready to be filed under the heading of good memories. She'd come here fully aware this visit may very well be the end of a long emotional journey, but nothing about the hours they'd spent together felt like a conclusion. "I'll have a lot more time after the Olympics. I'll be back later in the summer, and I can stay for longer."

"I'm not sure you should plan on that," Lauren said. "I have no personal experience to go on, mind you, but I think Olympic medalists generally see an increased demand on their time."

She shook her head, not at the assumption she would medal at the Olympics, but at Lauren once again backing away from the idea that Jess would come back for her. She hadn't let it stand the first time, and she wasn't about to now. "You underestimated my resolve ten years ago. Do you really want to do it again?"

"Jess."

"Don't patronize me," she warned, but laughter brimmed in her voice.

"I wouldn't dare. You've proven yourself much more driven and stubborn than even your most frustrated coaches could've imagined. I know if you set your mind to something, you'll get it. I only meant to imply there's so much more on the horizon for you."

"I don't disagree." She leaned forward and held Lauren's gaze before adding, "I plan to shatter every expectation, even yours."

"I believe you."

"I'm not sure you do," she said matter-of-factly. She accepted her card back from the waitress, trading it for her valet check. "But that's okay. I survived ten years on a sliver of hope for tonight. A few months of knowing full well how right I was won't break me."

"How right you were?" Lauren rolled her eyes playfully. "You're a lot cockier than you were at thirteen. I mean, I'd seen it on the strip, but I guess I didn't expect to ever have it leveled at me."

She smiled at the realization that Lauren hadn't taken issue with the idea of her having been right, only her confidence about it. "I'm not cocky."

Lauren scoffed.

Jess rose and extended her hand, then waited for Lauren to take it before continuing. "I know what I want, and when I'm right. It doesn't matter if it's with coaches and opponents, or—"

"Women?"

"I wasn't going to say 'women.'"

"It's the truth, though, isn't it?" Lauren prodded without tensing up.

"I wasn't thinking of other women."

"It's fine if you were counting them among your reasons to feel self-assured. You don't have to deny anything for my benefit. I've heard all those rumors, too."

They strolled out into the chilly night air as the valet pulled her car around, but before Lauren could climb inside, Jess tugged her hand until they faced each other and then spoke the truth plainly. "I'm not denying there have been others over the years, but none of them shaped me the way you did. None of them held my attention, my attraction, my fascination the way you have. There's not a single one of them I would've offered to wait months for, much less years."

43

＊ ＊ ＊

They drove in companionable quiet for several minutes, Lauren's mind a whir of thoughts as her chest swirled with emotions. Part of her wanted to pinch herself to make sure this was real, but Jess was too perfect for her imagination to conjure on its own. Which, of course, also made her too good to last.

She stole glances of her as she drove, memorizing every detail, the ones she remembered and the ones that had changed over the years: the perfect way her hair fell in ringlets across her brow, the smooth plane of her cheek, the strength of her jaw. Her lips were a lush shade of maroon most women would pay dearly for if only someone could find a way to bottle it. Her hands on the steering wheel, they'd always worked wonders, but tonight as they'd held hers across the table, she felt in them the contrast of lightly calloused palms and soft, gentle fingers, a microcosm of the woman herself. And the way she made Lauren feel when she looked at her, as if she were the only woman she'd ever really seen.

She shook her head slightly. She had to stop. She couldn't get swept up. She'd sworn she wouldn't let herself think of tonight as anything more than one wonderful evening. Jess would go back to New York tomorrow, and despite what she'd said about returning, Lauren knew better than to let herself count on that. She didn't doubt Jess had the ability to sweep back into town three months down the road. If she wanted to, she would. She'd already proved she always got what she went after, but whatever brought her back this time was a holdover from a different time when they'd been different people. Tonight had proven neither one of them was the person they'd been by the pool years ago. They'd grown up. They'd traded roles in so many ways. They'd become two women on vastly divergent paths.

"Jess," she whispered into the darkness between streetlights.
"Yes?"
"I don't want you to come back for me."
"What?"

"I want you to go forward and let tonight be what it is."

Jess frowned. "What is it?"

"A beautiful, shining moment. The best of memories. A chance to get swept up in something bigger than both of us, without any guilt or remorse or obligation."

"What makes you think we'd feel those things if I came back?"

"Because you're destined for so much more. You told me so all those years ago. You said you were going to take the world by storm. I believed you then, and I believe you now."

Jess pulled the car into the parking lot of the fencing club and killed the engine, turning to face her more fully.

"Please don't look at me like I've let you down. I'm letting you go because I think you're amazing. There's nothing you can't do, and nobody you can't woo. You're not thirteen anymore. You don't have to wait any longer. Go do all the things."

"What things?"

"Train hard, win some medals, get endorsements, raise the profile of the sport, throw lavish parties, buy a Ferrari, but always *always* wear your seatbelt. Be powerful, be whimsical, live your best, most exciting life."

"What about you?"

"I don't want Ferraris, or even much excitement. Didn't you just hear me? I worry about fictional seatbelts. I work here." She waved her hand toward the warehouse. "I teach fencing to teens and frustrated housewives, and tonight you reminded me it's a pretty good gig. I adore you for that."

"But?" Jess asked, a new hardness to her voice.

"No 'buts.' It's an 'and' proposition," she explained. "I adore you, *and* I want to see you succeed in every possible way. As a fencer, as a woman, as a superstar, as a human being full of endless potential. You've fired coaches for trying to turn you into someone else. I want the opposite. I want you to become the best, fullest, most vibrant version of you."

"And it doesn't sound like I get much say in this." Her voice held none of the defiance it had the first time they'd had this conversation.

"You do. You get a say in all of it, except for a second date."
She sighed.

"Come on." Lauren nudged her. "Let's not end on a sad note. Walk me to the door, look me in the eye like I'll always mean something to you, and give me a kiss that'll make me regret letting you go."

Jess managed a strangled laugh. "No pressure there."

"I have faith in you." And she did. More than faith, she feared she was playing with fire by letting this woman get any deeper into her heart or allowing the evening to become any more magical. If Jess weren't leaving tomorrow, she might not have taken the risk, but even their impending distance did little to stem the buzz of anticipation as they drew near the door to the club.

She slipped her key into the lock and applied pressure until she heard it click, but before pushing down the lever, she surrendered to the anticipation building in her.

Turning slowly, her back to the wall, she met Jess's eyes. They were deep and serious, dark even in the amber halo of the floodlight above them. She bit her lower lip, no longer trusting herself not to offer more than she already had. This woman was too close in every way. Lauren had been so diligent all night, never letting herself forget who she was, who Jess was, who they'd always been, and who they would be going forward. She hadn't lost her perspective at any point, which made it all the more frightening to feel it slipping here at the end.

Maybe that was it, the end of a journey she hadn't known they'd been on. Years of longing filled Jess's expression, and Lauren only got to experience them in this one instant. The weight of the realization made the moment too heavy, too big to see around, to put into context. Jess in her space, in her world, in every breath she took. She was so vibrant, an unexpected shot of color in a gray world. The sheer magnitude of her presence made Lauren feel small by comparison, but not weak. It would be impossible to feel weak with the strength of the desire surging in her. It nearly lifted her off her feet, and she tipped forward into a kiss she never should have let herself want this badly.

Jess's lips offered the perfect paradox to complement the conflict that all but evaporated on contact. Soft and firm, confident and yielding, Jess managed to be everything she'd been throughout the course of the evening, only now all of those things at once. Lauren melted into her.

Starting slowly, Jess tested, a light brush, a gentle press, and treading carefully, she took hold of Lauren's hips. Her hands, strong and steady, should've helped anchor Lauren. Instead, they set her body alight. Parting her lips at the electric current of connection arcing through her, she opened more fully to Jess's mouth.

The kiss escalated on every level as she lost track of any reason why it shouldn't. She welcomed a little sweep of Jess's tongue and the growing pressure between them as their bodies pulled flush. Her hands were on Jess's face, tangled in curls, and flattened along the plane of her smooth cheek. This wasn't even their first kiss, but it felt like the first kiss she'd ever had like this.

Jess kissed like she did everything, fully, intently focused, attentive, and yet with something akin to abandon. Or maybe the abandon came from within herself, because in that moment she would've dropped everything, forgotten everything, left everything that had held her back in a pile of ash in the parking lot. A wave of fear welled up in her, on a flash of awareness that Jess could have whatever she wanted from her right here. All of the assuredness she'd displayed all night hadn't been empty bravado, but a simple statement of her own self-worth. Lauren's mind swam with those implications, even as her body continued to blur the boundaries between them.

She ran her own tongue across the hot curve of Jess's lower lip, tasting the hint of honey, or perhaps that's just how Jess tasted. Nothing could surprise her in a moment where she'd reacted to a kiss like this. But then Jess eased back, slowly but purposefully, and Lauren found she'd misjudged everything once again.

She blinked open her eyes as the light that seemed so low earlier now assaulted her overwrought senses. Her gaze settled on the lips that had just cracked her foundation. They were darker and fuller now, but slowly curled into a smile around the whispered words, "Thank you."

"Thank me?" she managed as she forced herself to meet Jess's eyes once more.

"For tonight. For the years of inspiration, for helping me fall in love with the thing that became my life." She laughed lightly. "For not shoving me into a pool when I tried to kiss you all those years ago."

She managed a smile of her own.

"Thank you for everything," Jess said. Then with a nod she turned and walked away.

Lauren watched her go, and feeling numbly for the latch of the door behind her, pushed it open and fell backward into the world she hadn't wanted to return to yet.

She didn't turn on the lights. She didn't want to see it. She didn't want to feel it close back in around her, which terrified her almost as much as the kiss. She didn't run from reality. She didn't let herself get carried away or have one-night stands or capitulate to fantasies. She never made rash decisions she may regret later. And at least that sense of self hadn't been shattered tonight, but she harbored no illusions that she'd been the one to uphold them. She would've let things go so much farther, and she didn't know if she should feel relieved or disappointed that Jess had been the one to pull away.

A chill ran through her, alone in the dark room, as she stopped her mind from wandering down the darker path of what might've happened if Jess hadn't respected a boundary she herself had been willing to blow past. Ultimately, it didn't matter, and there wouldn't be any more opportunity for it to happen again.

Chapter Three

Jess drove back through the city in the vague direction of her parents' home. The entire front of her body burned at every place it had touched Lauren's, but those sensations paled in comparison to the fire raging through her brain. Lauren had wanted her. She knew it the same way she knew what her opponents were thinking, and with the same level of instinctual certainty she knew how to move with a blade in her hand. It transcended explanation, and yet her actions, her words, the pleading in Lauren's voice told another story, one that rang equally true.

Lauren set her free.

Not rejected her, like she had last time. Though, maybe she really had been trying to do the same thing then and Jess had been too young or inexperienced to process the nuance. Maybe she'd believed in her this deeply all along, but in the moment when she'd begged her to become the best, fullest, most vibrant version of herself, she wanted that for Jess even more than she wanted Jess for herself.

She screamed into the silent interior of the rented sedan.

Pulling to the side of the road, she grabbed her phone, and snapped, "Siri, call Haley."

Three rings rattled through her ear, followed by her friend's voice. "Must not have been a great date if you're calling me before midnight."

49

"Uh." She wouldn't have put it that way. "It wasn't what I expected."

"I'm sorry. Really." Haley's voice turned sincere. "It would've been sweet if the whole first crush thing worked out, but you know you have so much awesomeness on your horizon, right? Now you can grab onto it with a clean conscience and a clear mind."

"About that."

"What about it?"

"I'm not going to make it back for leg day on Tuesday." She hadn't even made the decision until she said it aloud, but once she did, there was no going back.

"What?"

"I need to stay in Buffalo a little longer."

"How much longer?"

"I don't know."

"What happened?"

"I don't know."

"Are you staying for her?"

"I don't know."

"What the fuck?" Haley shouted. "What do you mean you don't know?"

"I mean, I don't know. And don't make me feel any worse about that," she begged. "Do you have any idea how hard it is for me not to know what's happening in my own brain? Have you met me? I always know."

"Okay, okay." Haley's voice lowered but still held a panicked edge. "Slow down. We'll figure it out."

"I'm trying."

"Just walk me back through the bout. Where did it go off the rails?"

"I thought everything went great. The conversation came easily. She's smart and stunning, witty and engaging. And she loves fencing, like all of it, not just the bouts, but what makes it work and the future of the sport. Hell, she even roasted me for firing coaches."

Haley gave a little snort of amusement.

"It felt so good to be with someone who really understood, you know, but when I said I could come back after the Olympics, she told me not to."

"I'm sorry, dude. How are you feeling?"

"Well in the moment, I couldn't feel anything other than empty. Not just disappointed or bummed out, but like a void."

"Not good."

"No." She rested her head on the steering wheel. "You know when you said I needed to get her out of my system?"

"Yeah."

"Well, for a second there, I did. And when she was gone, my pilot light went out too."

"You have other things in your system than this woman. You have a fire in you, Jess. What about the Olympics? You burn for those rings more than anyone I know. Those flames singed everything you've ever done."

"Flames she ignited years ago."

"Don't give her the power to douse them now."

"That's not what she's trying to do. God, she practically begged me." Lauren's voice rang through her ears. "She believes in me more than I believe in myself."

"You've never lacked for belief."

"That's not true. You've been there. You were at worlds."

Silence met her on the line this time.

"It doesn't matter," she finally said. "I know what I felt or what I didn't feel. Without her in front of me to charge toward, I blew a fuse, and the house went dark. Then she kissed me, and it felt like someone flipped all the breakers back on again."

"You sort of skipped the kissing you part," Haley mumbled. "Before or after she told you not to come back to Buffalo?"

"After."

Haley groaned.

"Yeah. An alarm went off in my brain like some horrible ghost of fencing future come to warn me, then leave me to wake up in a sweat with the realization that it'd just been a dream."

"She's going to distract you from your drive."

51

"She can't. She's not capable. She *is* the drive. She sets me alight."

"That's lust you're feeling."

"It's not." Her temper flared at being reduced to her baser instincts. She knew better, and she deserved better.

She had a vivid memory of the fireworks flashing behind her eyelids as their lips had met, but they'd also sparked in her chest when Lauren launched into her passionate speech about wanting her to succeed as a whole person. The echo of those words clung to her like a barb in her chest even now. It tugged at her almost painfully, pulling at memories and ripping at relationships both distant and recent. That feeling was what she'd been afraid to lose that night by the pool, and it's what she'd chased ever since. It's what she'd lacked in every coaching relationship since graduation, and what she'd craved when she stepped into Lauren's arms last night.

Their connection had always been laced with attraction. She'd known it then and confirmed it with a kiss, but just like her teenage self had been incapable of processing the nuance of Lauren's rebuff, she'd also been unable to grasp the depths of her own desire until this moment. Maybe she couldn't even put her finger to the pulse point now, but she had enough experience to recognize the complexity she hadn't back then.

Tonight had been confirmation of so much more than she'd come here looking for, confirmation of everything she'd tried to proclaim. She'd been right back then. She would do great things, but she'd found her strength, her sense of purpose only because Lauren had planted the seed and fed it with her little challenge.

Come back when you're on your big Olympic run.

Had she even wanted that dream until Lauren gave it voice?

"No," she said aloud.

"'No' what?" Haley's voice startled her. She'd forgotten she was still on the line, but a rush of gratitude surged through her at not having to say what came next to an empty car.

"She's always been intertwined with my drive, with my passion, with the fire inside me. She's pushed me forward all these years. It's always been her voice in my head."

Haley sighed. "You know that's not her job, right?"

Jess laughed, a short bubble rumbling up inside her. "Actually, it kind of is."

"What?"

"Her job. She's a fencing instructor. Driving fencers to be their best is totally her job."

"Yeah, but she's not *your* coach."

The little flame inside her flicked higher as a few more pieces of kindling caught inside her brain. Lauren had inspired her best at every turn. She'd known it since the first moment she'd seen her with a sword in her hand. She may have been young and confused then, but she wasn't dumb. And the ideas igniting inside her now might be rash, but she wasn't stupid.

"Dude," Haley warned. "She. Is. Not. Your. Coach."

"And why not? If I'd told you I'd gone anywhere else—"

"Not Buffalo, dude. Buffalo is a joke in the fencing world."

Jess gritted her teeth. "I'm from Buffalo. I have my roots here. I learned to fight here. And if I'd worked out in any other club and had some epiphany that set both my mind and body on fire, what would you say?"

"This isn't any club, or any woman. This is insanity."

"No. To walk away would be insanity. To let Lauren go right now would deprive me of the thing that's always made me better at exactly the moment I most need to be my best. I can't separate the passions in my life, and why would I want to?"

Giving voice to the fledgling inspiration gave it life. "I don't care if every other person in the world condemns me for it."

"Every person?"

"Even you, my friend."

"What about Lauren?" Haley asked. "Does she get any say at all?"

She had no quick comeback as the tip of that point lodged between her ribs.

"She asked you to leave." Haley twisted the blade.

Her resolve crashed into that stumbling block and brought her mental momentum to a shuddering halt.

Lauren wouldn't be happy about Jess throwing caution to the wind or invading her neatly ordered life. Then again, Lauren didn't exactly seem very happy in that neatly ordered life either. Jess had watched the sadness fill her eyes, and the worry crease her brow too many times over the course of the evening. She'd also felt her melt into the kiss like a woman who ached to come undone. The twin understandings warred within her, and as sure as she knew they stood in opposition to each other, she knew she didn't get to make that choice for someone else.

She was in charge of her career, her future, her drive, and she intended to take hold of them all from here on out, but whatever hint of heat their budding romance had revealed wasn't hers to wield, and honestly that might be for the best.

"You're not wrong," she finally said to Haley.

"There's a first."

"You've been right before."

"I meant you admitting it."

She rolled her eyes, but she wouldn't be pulled off topic. "Lauren isn't ready to be swept off her feet. If I come on too strong, she'll dig her heels in."

"Sounds like someone else I know."

"I have to focus on the common ground of fencing. I need to be a professional and approach her like one as well. I don't think it'll be hard to do. She's a good coach."

"You don't know that."

"She was born to be a good coach," she stressed. "I'll take my stand on that hill. I'm going to work and train and cultivate the fire."

"And not try to get into her pants?"

"And not try to get into her pants." Jess set her jaw against the way her body tried to rebel and forged on. "I'm here to get onto the podium first and foremost. I don't need any distractions to consume my energy or the raw emotions I need to carry me through the next few months."

"That sounds remarkably stable of you." Suspicion seeped through Haley's voice. "What gives?"

"Nothing," she said quickly. "I'm focusing on the steak and not the peas. I won't lie and say I'm not still attracted to Lauren. The kiss, oh Lord, the kiss about melted my bones, but the Olympics are the end game for the next few months. Trying to do anything else now would be playing with fire."

And if the kiss was any indication, the fire could consume them both. It carried a dangerous and unpredictable quality even a reckless woman who made her living playing with swords had to respect.

"Fencing brought us together. It can keep us moving forward. And we both need to move forward right now. If my personal life needs to fall on a few swords in the meantime, we both know I've had plenty of experience getting stabbed."

Saturdays were Lauren's only early mornings at the club. Her first lessons of the day for her youngest and most energetic little protégés started at 8:00, which meant she had to have her smallest foils and protective padding all laid out and ready to go by quarter 'til, which meant she had to be there, fully caffeinated by 7:30. She hadn't thought that through before agreeing to go out with Jess on a Friday night. Then again, she hadn't expected to lose as much sleep as she had.

She should've just called Kristie and spilled her guts as soon as she'd started staring into the void last night. Kristie would've gleefully listened to all her mangled emotions, but she hadn't been ready to share them yet. She hadn't been ready to share anything about the evening, or Jess. She'd been too overwhelmed to make sense of them, and even if she had, she wasn't sure she needed to give them voice. Doing so would make them too real, too concrete when it felt so much safer to relegate the entire experience to the realm of fantasy fodder. Of course, fantasy fodder didn't feel quite as safe while she lay sleepless in her bed all night.

At least if she'd called Kristie, she could've gotten everything off her chest and given her friend's exuberance the opportunity to exhaust her into sleep. Then again, if exhaustion were the answer, handing pointy weapons to a gym full of elementary school children would likely do the trick.

She smiled wearily and laid out tiny sets of gloves in a neat row on the gym floor, allowing herself to get lost in the rote mindlessness of the tasks ahead, followed by the hypervigilance of conducting class. Then she repeated the process with another, and another, and another until she worked her way from six-year-olds all the way through her middle schoolers.

By the time she'd sent them to clean up, she'd driven the date into the darkest recesses of her mind. She might've been able to keep it there, too, if she hadn't stepped out into the lobby and caught a glimpse of bright red curls through the large viewing window.

Her heart skittered almost to a stop, then jumpstarted with a mule kick to her ribs as Jess turned to reveal her flawless profile. Lauren took two steps toward her without even realizing she was moving, and then another two before she could regain control of her own reflexes. Jess pulled the iron in her veins like a magnet.

She wore a fencing jacket with a traditional high collar that drew attention to her strong jaw and porcelain complexion. The white palette provided a stark canvas for the bold splashes of color in her rich burgundy lips along with her cornflower eyes, and of course the red mop of curls that caught her attention in the first place. Color upon color, the contrast Jess provided to literally everything around her drove all shades of gray from Lauren's field of vision. She might've stared at her for an eternity, as if transfixed by any work of art, if not for the discordant clang of warning bells sounding inside her own skull.

Jess was supposed to be on a plane back to New York City and her Olympic dreams. She was supposed to be a safe and respectable distance away, not close enough to stir the tremor twitching in Lauren's stomach. She certainly wasn't supposed to be close enough to force her to confront how amazingly she filled out her fencing uniform, which of course meant she was wearing a fencing uniform as well, which also didn't add up to someone getting on an airplane anytime soon.

As if sensing her presence, or maybe the wash of conflicting emotions radiating in her general direction, Jess turned her head and met Lauren's gaze through the glass. Her lips curled into a smile, sweet and genuine, but more restrained than the ones she'd lavished on her the night before. They held each other's gaze for a suspended series of seconds until, with a slight incline of her head, Jess extended an invitation to join her.

And Lauren did.

She left a lobby full of preteens unattended around racks full of sabers without a second thought. This was a problem. Lauren sensed it building in her as she moved toward Jess. The lack of reason, the lack of restraint, the lack of control she felt around this woman shook something deep inside her, and she didn't like it, but she didn't resist it either.

"Lauren!" Enrico greeted her from his metal folding chair in the corner, but she couldn't manage to spare him a glance. "Look who's here to visit her old coach."

"Jess, what a surprise." It wasn't an accusation so much as a statement of fact.

"Honestly, no one's more surprised I ended up here again," Jess said, a hint of nervousness in her smooth voice.

"I might beg to differ if I thought it would do any good to enter into any sort of competition with you."

Enrico clapped his hands together. "Jessie is going to train here for a while."

"Is she?" The words squeaked out, through the crush of her diaphragm.

"I haven't decided yet," Jess corrected, "but I am looking for a new place to train, and some new people to train with. I know you're well aware of the unique challenges we'd both face, but I trust you as a person, I respect you as a professional, and, well, I came back hoping to have a discussion."

"Funny, you don't seem dressed for discussion." She shook her head, trying to dislodge the little tinge of pleasure at having Jess's trust and respect. "You look dressed to . . ."

Her voice trailed off. What had she intended to say? Dressed to impress? Because she did. Dressed to kill? Because she might if she stayed this close. Lauren's heart raced to drive home the possibility. No, she'd dressed to fence. She opened her mouth to correct herself, but Jess unsurprisingly beat her to the punch.

"'Work.' I'm dressed to work."

"Right. Because you get paid to fence."

"A little bit." Jess flushed. "I mean, I get paid a little bit. I fence a lot."

"If she fences here," Enrico cut back in, "money, press, people. Think about all your plans."

"My plans?" she sputtered. This was not part of her plans. Jess wasn't slow or steady or safe. She didn't fit into any of the neat and tidy five-year projections she'd allowed for herself. Nothing about Jess was neat or tidy, not the way she fought, not the way she kissed, not the way her mere proximity made Lauren feel woozy.

"Yes, think of everything you could do with all the new students and their money. The windows, the cameras, the big TV." Enrico used all her dreams against her, but no desire for technology could eclipse her desire for the control which had disintegrated the moment Jess's lips had touched hers.

"Don't." She held up her hand to him. "Don't try to bullshit me. Any new money coming into the club always goes straight into your pocket."

He laughed so hard he coughed a little. "This is true, so true, but this time I could make it a split. Some for me, some for you, some for improving the club."

She finally tore her eyes away from Jess to look at him. "What's different this time?"

He gave a little shrug and a sly grin. "Because I think Jessie is not really here to visit her old coach. Maybe if she doesn't get what she came for, we'll get no money at all."

She turned back to Jess, who'd been uncharacteristically quiet. "What did you come for, Jess?"

"I'm not sure yet."

She arched an eyebrow and waited.

58

"Maybe she's in town to find a new coach because she fired all the ones in Manhattan," Enrico offered.

"Could be," Jess admitted.

"Maybe she needs a change of scenery, or her mama's cooking."

"Both valid possibilities."

Lauren folded her arms across her chest.

"Maybe she needs to be near her friends right now."

"She has friends in the city." Lauren tried to forestall any emotional appeals.

"Maybe she needs to work out with a friend she can trust to be in her corner even when she has to face a Russian who keeps kicking her keister on the world stage, no?"

Jess winced and Lauren froze again. The little twitch in her jaw, the quick crease between her eyebrows, they triggered something deep and protective inside her, and she struggled to hold it at bay. She didn't appreciate being ambushed. She didn't make decisions on the spot. Ever. But especially when she didn't even understand all the details. She was about to say so when Jess preempted the assertion again.

"We don't have to make any long-term decisions today. You can take all the time you need."

"Not all the time," Enrico grumbled. "Two months until the Olympics is not a long time."

Jess shook her head. "It's enough time for me to find another option. If this isn't a good fit for either of us, I can find another way or go it alone, but I just thought maybe we could talk, if you'd be willing to hear me out."

"Of course she should hear you out!" Enrico exclaimed. "You are friends who need each other, and—"

"Stop," she snapped and then sighed. "Please stop. Of course I'll talk with you, Jess, but I need a minute alone, and then I need to talk to *you* without your cheering section or your manager or whatever else Enrico envisions himself as right now."

"I can go sit outside," he offered too quickly.

"So you can eavesdrop through the door?" She shook her head.

59

"You're going to sit right back down in your chair. I'm going to go catch my breath, and then in five minutes, Jess, you can meet me in the women's locker room. He knows better than to follow you in there."

"Perfectly reasonable." Jess kept her voice steady, but she rocked forward from heel to toe as if readying herself to charge forward, giving away her excitement and revealing she wasn't nearly as calm and collected as she'd tried to convey.

Was that why she'd been so quiet? Nervousness didn't track with the confident firebrand image she showed the rest of the world. Was this about the kiss? Surely not. She'd walked away last night. Why come back now? Did she really intend to train here as an excuse to continue what they'd started last night? Did she have any idea how much that would upend Lauren's world?

Jess and Enrico stared at the door for a long time after it closed behind Lauren, then she felt his hand fall heavily on her shoulder.

She turned to see his dark eyes full of questions she couldn't answer. Instead, she offered him the best smile she could muster. "I think that went pretty well."

He tutted his mix of disagreement and amusement.

"No. I mean it." She lied to both of them. "We caught her off guard, which isn't her favorite, but she stayed calm, and she made a plan."

"I thought you were good with the women." Enrico sidestepped back over to his chair and lowered himself into it. "I think those stories are exaggerated."

"What?" she laughed. "I can't believe you just said that. I am good with . . . I mean . . . Lauren isn't 'women.'"

"Slow *and* blind." He shook his head. "You are doomed."

"Stop. I know she's a woman, but not just any woman, which is beside the point." Her stomach twisted at the memory of how seeing her through the glass had stolen her breath so badly she hadn't been able to speak for entirely too long during the exchange while Enrico had spun wildly out of control. "She stayed calm."

He eyed her skeptically from under bushy eyebrows. "Calm is how a woman always seems when she is plotting how she intends to kill you, yes?"

"No. She agreed to hear me out, alone."

"Alone is easier for the murder."

She gave a nervous chuckle, but he didn't join her, and she didn't like his eyes on her in the silence. She wished Lauren had stayed. She wished she could've talked to her the way they'd talked last night. She wished she wore a watch. "Has it been five minutes yet?"

"Close enough," he said, then made a sign of the cross in her direction. "Go."

She rolled her eyes but obeyed, threading her way between a mess of teenage girls who were mostly too busy watching the boys or staring at their phones to pay her any mind. As she reached the locker room, she took a deep, steadying breath. She gave a fleeting thought to going back for her helmet in case Lauren did intend to kill her, but she shook it off and slowly pushed on the door enough to stick just her head inside.

Lauren leaned against a bank of lockers, arms still crossed, but her eyes distant and unfocused.

"Are you ready for me yet?"

She turned her head slowly, her lips pressed in a tight line as her gaze sharpened. "I'm not going to sleep with you, Jess."

The statement hit her like a roundhouse to the ribs, and she regretted not bringing her helmet after all. If nothing else, it would help hide her emotions. She'd become a professional at schooling her features over the years, but she hadn't adequately prepared to do so now.

"Wow." She stepped through the door and pressed it closed with her body weight. She'd expected resistance, but she wasn't used to starting with her back flat against a wall.

Lauren stepped forward, clearly sensing her advantage. "I thought I made myself clear last night."

She didn't agree with that assessment at all. Lauren had sent a mix of signals all night long, her mouth saying one thing, her body screaming another, but she knew enough to sense there was no victory in that angle.

"If you think throwing away your future for some sort of fling is going to impress me," Lauren continued, "you have the wrong woman."

Jess pushed off the door as the point missed its mark. "No, that's why I know I have the right woman. You refused to let me wreck myself or get distracted or derail my career over my stubborn pride. Do you know how long it's been since I've had that in my life?"

Lauren stopped, clearly caught off guard by the redirect. "No."

"You do. You're the one who brought it up last night. You pinpointed the exact moment I got reckless and defiant."

"You've always been reckless and defiant."

"Fair."

"What are you angling for here, Jess? You clearly want something, or you'd be gone by now. If it's not about last night, what is it?"

"It *is* about last night. It's about how you saw through my bravado about the other coaches. It's about the excitement in your voice when you talked about the future of fencing. It's about all the things you said in the car, about me being my best self."

"I meant those things."

"I know you did. You're the first person who has looked at me as a whole person in ages. Everyone else has broken me down to pieces. They see me for my feet or my hands, or for statistics to cut apart in a video room and reassemble on a metrics chart. Do you know what it's like to have my motivation divorced from my actions like a picture of myself being carved into puzzle pieces and scattered across a gym?"

Lauren's lips parted as a breath lifted her chest.

She inched forward with her right foot and followed with her left, the way she might if preparing to pounce. Lauren's eyes flicked to her feet, then up once more, a new awareness swirling in her. "And yeah—"

"What about the kiss, Jess?"

62

She stopped, and the tightness in her chest warned her from recklessness. "The kiss was . . ."

Lauren watched her carefully. "What?"

"The kiss was a lot of things," she admitted honestly. "Amazing and thrilling, and a terrifying reminder that neither of us are teenagers anymore."

Lauren sighed. "Yes."

"I won't lie to you. For the first time in a long time, I'm going to lay all my cards on the table. You could probably wreck me if you wanted to."

"I don't want to hurt you."

She laughed. "I've known that since I was a kid, but I'm not a kid anymore. I'm a grown woman who's pushing back against a crushing wave of opportunity and pressure and responsibility."

"Then why aren't you on a plane back to the city?"

A little smile tugged at her mouth. "Because I'm a grown woman with a crushing wave of opportunity, pressure, and responsibility crashing over me. For the first time in my life, I'm mature enough to realize I can't beat it back with brute force, and I can't do it alone."

Lauren's shoulder dropped.

"And you know, too, don't you?" She heard the old desperation to be understood cracking her voice again. "You know what it took for me to admit that, right?"

Lauren bit her lip and nodded.

"You're the first person in a long time who does. You're the first person who really sees me, all of me, and doesn't want to change any of it. You're the first person who's wanted to build me up without breaking me down first."

"Of course I want that for you, but I'm not even sure what you're asking, much less whether or not I'd be able to give it to you. I'm not a professional coach."

"Maybe you should be, or maybe you don't have to be. You said it yourself—I have a Team USA coach, and I don't have any more competitions between now and the Olympics. I need someone to train me, to push me, to help me not lose my mind over the next couple of months. There's so much swirling around me right now, the sponsors, the press, the Olympic officials. I need something, someone, I can trust to help me navigate it. We can work out the details along the way."

Lauren glanced around them at the lockers, the floor, the mirror, and let her hands fall heavily to her sides. "I don't work for Team USA. I don't work for Nike. I don't have connections at any talent agencies or marketing teams. I don't know what I could give you here."

"Can you give me more speeches like you gave me in the car last night?"

"Probably."

"Could you stay steady when I can't?"

"Yes."

"Even when I lose my temper and throw a saber at the wall or scream into the floor or pace around the gym roaring like a caged lion?"

Her pressed lips twitched as if she liked the idea. "Yes."

"Could you be on my team, by my side, have my best interests at heart even when I can't remember what they are myself?"

Her chest rose and fell again, but instead of backing away, she took one step closer and placed her palm flat on the spot where chest met shoulder. "Always."

Jess nodded. "Then I'm staying here."

"What about all the rest? What about the footwork and sparring partners and, and, and . . . the kiss?"

She wondered if Lauren could feel the kick her heart gave at the last item on the list. "I don't know."

"There are rules for coaching relationships. Even when there aren't official rules, there are still ethical concerns. If we're training together, close to each other for hours, touching, working, breathing the same air, what does that make us to each other now?"

She shifted under the sharp point behind the question pressing against her chest. "I don't have all those answers."

"That scares me," Lauren admitted.

"I know, but I also know I can trust you to set boundaries you think are fair and ethical."

"And I know I can trust you to push every one of them every chance you get."

She grinned. "Probably, but I also trust you to hold firm."

A little flash of gold in Lauren's eyes suggested she didn't have the same faith in herself, and Jess gritted her teeth against the urge to explore that impulse, before continuing, "We don't need to pin down labels right now. Can't we just consider this a probationary period and trust two consenting and caring adults to figure things out as they arise?"

Lauren gave Jess's shoulder a tight squeeze. "That's not my favorite way to do things, but if this is really about the fencing, about the training and what you need to move forward instead of diving back into our past, then I can try."

Jess's heart pressed against her rib cage at that confirmation of every instinct she'd ever had about this woman. "That's enough for now."

Chapter Four

"Wait, wait, wait." Kristie laughed so hard she nearly fell off the front porch. "I'm so confused."

"Yeah, me too." Lauren pinched the bridge of her nose trying to stop the pulse throbbing there.

"First of all, I love that. I'm confused all the damn time, but I so rarely get to see it on you. It's a little maddening how put together you are."

She rolled her eyes. "That's not helpful. Besides, you know what I was like a few years ago."

"I know what you went through, but I also know how you buckled down, how you lowered your head and worked yourself and everyone else back onto level ground. I know how you gritted your teeth and took deep breaths when any normal human would've screamed into the storm." Kristie's voice softened. "But I also know this isn't the same thing. Do you?"

She nodded slowly. Jess threatened a lot of things, her stability, her sense of self, maybe even her sanity, but she was made of pure light, a brilliant contrast to the darkness Lauren had only managed to trade for shades of gray.

"Okay, so Jess is different, and believe me, I get why she makes you feel a little unmoored, but I don't have any grasp on the details. I only asked what you wanted for lunch, and you unloaded on me."

She sighed and glanced around, grounding herself to the place and present tense. They stood on her mother's front porch. The cold air around them spit flecks of frozen mist. Kristie wore a Buffalo Beauts jersey, a Sabres stocking cap, and a pair of snow pants she'd probably thrown on over her favorite flannel pajama bottoms.

"I'm sorry. I should've let you get through the door first, but I haven't told my mom anything yet."

"It's cool. I'm the St. Bernard of hockey lesbians. We can sit outside, but I do need you to back up and start from the beginning of your story."

"Okay." She drew a shaky breath. "I got to work on Saturday and—"

"Start earlier."

"Fine, when she picked me up for the date on Friday—"

"Nope." Kristie lowered herself to the porch and dangled her legs over the side into the dead flower bed, then patted the spot beside her.

She tugged her coat a little so it covered the body parts about to come into contact with the cold floor, then settled in beside her. "I met Jess when she was thirteen and I was eighteen."

"Perfect," Kristie said. "Was she just like a mini version of who she is now, all fierce and fire-headed but scrunched into a tinier package?"

Her smile sparked in her chest. "Actually, yes."

"Good, keep going and don't skimp on the details."

And she didn't. She told her everything. The stories of who they'd been, and all they'd done, collecting threads she'd dropped along the way and weaving them back into the tapestry of the last few days, careful not to dwell too deeply on the ones she could no longer find in the tangle of those intervening years. She talked about their career paths, skimming the parts Kristie knew about hers, to get to the point where worlds had collided in front of her a couple of days ago, then swirling deeper into the hours that had flown by in Jess's company on their date. She made it all the way to the kiss before her friend interrupted again.

"Scale of one to ten, with one being the kiss she'd tried to give you as a tiny little baby baller, how did this kiss rate?"

She smiled in spite of the whispers of caution in the most central part of her personality. "Really good, like a nine."

"Wow, a nine on the first go round? Was that hard for you to admit?"

"A little."

"Well done. Now in the theme of honest self-reflection, tell me truthfully, did you shave off the one point because you didn't want to admit the kiss was really a ten and that terrifies you?"

She covered her face in her hands and mumbled "yes" into her palms.

"Oh, this is the best thing ever. She broke your internal scales."

She wanted to argue. Instead she pushed on with her story. "I was going to be okay. She was going back to New York."

"Wait. I need a conjunction for those two statements. Were you going to be okay *and* she was leaving? Were you going to be okay *but* she was going back to the city? Or were you going to be okay *because* she was leaving and taking all the temptation with her?"

"Um, option number three."

"Yeah, okay, that's what I thought. Please continue."

She did. She told her every heart-wrenching detail of Jess's unexpected appearance at the club, the pressure, her resentment born out of the reminder that she had so little control over any of this, the way Jess had let her back into the driver's seat only long enough to tie a little rope around her heart and then start to tug Lauren toward her.

"Whoa." Kristie injected a sizable dose of awe into the single word.

"Yup."

"Okay, that's a lot."

"So much."

"Let's deal with the easier aspect first."

She nodded.

"You're coaching an Olympic fencer."

Her shot of laughter sounded every bit as incredulous as she felt. "You think that's going to be easy?"

"You're good at fencing."

"And you're good at hockey. Could you just take over as head coach of the Sabres on a moment's notice?"

Her eyes lit up. "Oh, I have a few suggestions for them. I've shouted at their management on social media and from the cheap seats, but I'd kill for a shot to actually coach them."

She shook her head. "Of course you would, but I'm not you. At least I'm not anymore. Maybe when I was younger I dreamed of a responsibility like this."

"Just going to point out you are twenty-eight. Most people our age are still paying their dues, but you keep talking about yourself like you're over the hill. You still get to earn your place."

"Yeah, and before everything blew up, that's how I thought it would go. I thought I'd have the chance to earn a job like this over time. I thought I'd grow into the role, not be pushed off the cliff with two months to prove myself. I'm in so far over my head. This isn't high school states, it's the Olympics."

"So? What do you need to do?"

"I don't even know where to start. I should probably study and watch film and draw up competitor profiles and read exercise science journals."

"Okay, then do that."

She rolled her eyes. "You make it sound so easy."

"Not easy, but doable for you. You have this in you. Everyone can see it."

"Not everyone."

"I do. Jess does. And deep down I think you do, too. You wouldn't have agreed if she hadn't convinced you. And as far as I can tell, those are all the people who really matter."

She didn't shoot back right away. She wasn't sure she believed all of that, but the important parts rang true. Jess had convinced her she was the right person for the job, if not technically, at least mentally and emotionally, and she'd always been adamant those factors mattered every bit as much as the physical ones when it came to building fencing champions.

"Okay. I'm going to take your silence as you conceding my

69

points and call it a victory for me," Kristie said, then charged forward. "The bigger issue in this larger panic attack isn't that Jess is an Olympian. It's that you two totally have the hots for each other."

Her natural defenses flared once more. "You don't need to pile on any hyperbole here."

"Who's being hyperbolic?" Kristie laughed. "She's carried a torch for you for almost half of her life, and she used it to set you on fire with a single kiss."

She pinched the bridge of her nose again. The summary wasn't helpful, but neither was it false. "I sent her away. I told her to go."

"Yeah, because she scared the living crap out of you."

She didn't argue, which was as good as confirmation for her friend.

"You're going to have to deal with that. You can't be what she needs if you're scared of the things she makes you feel."

She gave a little shiver. It was warranted. They'd been sitting outside for an hour, and yet the chill spreading through her now worked from the inside out instead of the other way around. "I don't suppose there are any books or medical journals I could check out to help me process through those details, are there?"

"I might be able to suggest a few videos to give you ideas on what to do with her, but they definitely wouldn't be safe for work."

She shoved her. "You're not helping."

"I've found those things very helpful in past relationships, but sure, fine, you could find something else to anchor yourself to."

"Yeah." She knew the answer. It was the same as the earlier one. She needed to throw herself into the work. She needed to study and train and practice both of them into oblivion. She needed to focus on the things she could control, and the last few days had taught her she had no control over the feelings Jess sparked in her.

"Yeah?"

"It's the work, the fencing, the dream, and if we ever reach a point where that fails to exhaust us, then I'll just have to remind myself of the promise I made."

"Which one?"

"She asked me if I could be on her team, by her side, and have her best interests at heart even when she can't remember them for herself." She blew out a heavy breath as her pulse slowed, leadened by the weight of responsibility.

"Shit." Kristie stared at her. "What did you even say?"

"I promised her I always would, and I meant it. If that means taking the torch she passed and putting it on ice, then I'll find the strength to do so."

Kristie grimaced. "Do you have to totally douse it, though, or could you just maybe hold onto it for her for a while?"

She stared off into the thickening mist around them. "I guess we're about to find out."

Jess arrived at the Nickle City Fencing Academy along with the first light of dawn. It had been years since she'd been up at sunrise by choice, though to be fair, sunlight came later during a Buffalo spring than it did in most of the country.

She checked the dashboard clock on her mother's old Audi. 7:00. She yawned in spite of the little shiver of her anticipation, just another example of the mind-body disconnect she'd suffered over the last forty-eight hours. She'd spent the day before arranging to have the bulk of her fencing equipment and workout clothes shipped to Buffalo. Thankfully she always traveled with the basics, so she'd also taken a couple of hours to get those things settled in her parents' basement bedroom.

She grinned, thinking of her parents' mix of concern and elation at the idea of her moving back in with them. Thankfully, they'd been much easier to convince than Lauren. They didn't know what Lauren knew about the practicality of training or about the low thrum of arousal undercutting every one of Jess's intentions. Still, she'd had these conversations so many times over the last few days she'd memorized her key points and had even managed to internalize most of them. She didn't need specialized equipment other than the ones she traveled with all the time. She

71

could exercise anywhere. A saber worked the same way here as it did at the other end of the state. There were fewer distractions here.

Okay, maybe the last one wasn't completely true, a fact evidenced by the injection of adrenaline that coursed into her veins at the sight of Lauren's car pulling into the lot behind her.

They both got out at the same time and smiled a little nervously before heading toward the door together.

"You got here before I did," Lauren said. "I didn't peg you for promptness."

She scoffed, then admitted, "I'm not always. My social circle would say I'm not ever, but I take training seriously, and I figured you were the kind of person who's always on time."

"You're not wrong, but 'on time' at work for me usually comes a lot later on weekdays."

"We'll need to share our schedules. I don't want mine to override yours."

"We have lunch hour open gym a few days a week, but most of my work is on nights and weekends." Lauren unlocked the front door to their corner of the large warehouse and flipped on the lights.

"I remember those days." Jess stepped inside as the memories rushed back to her. "After-school extracurriculars, group lessons with my mom waiting in the car. Saturdays where my parents would drop me off and then go run their errands. I had to go to church on Sunday mornings, and then family lunches spent staring at the clock until this place opened at 2:00."

Lauren had begun the little tasks of opening up various rooms and turning the page of a large desk calendar from April to May, but her smile grew a little wistful. "I was on the same schedule a few years ahead of you. Then again, I'm pretty much on the same schedule these years too."

"I've shifted the times so most of my work happens during the days," Jess said. "Which keeps me in clubs at times when the kids aren't."

Lauren grabbed a notebook off the front desk and herded her

toward two of the four chairs in the lobby. "Tell me about your routine."

The setup felt a little too like a therapy session as Lauren took the seat directly across from her, crossed one leg over the other, and rested the notebook in her lap. "Walk me through a daily schedule for you."

"Well, it can change if I have an event or meeting of some sort, but on average I start with a low-impact workout, a lot of yoga, stretching, flexible strength, and warming up my core."

Lauren nodded, and a little strand of hair fell from its messy bun as she made some notes.

"Then a technical workout. Mostly foot and form drills. I like to put fundamentals ahead of bouts, because if I do it the other way around, I get a little carried away. Whereas, if I lay my foundation first, I set my intention for good muscle memory," she explained, then undercut her professionalism by adding, "in theory."

Lauren smiled as she scratched a few more notes.

"Then a cardio session before lunch, a run when I can, wind sprints or a stationary bike when I have to."

Lauren glanced up from under thick lashes. "Are you able to eat something substantial after working so hard?"

She laughed. "I never find it hard to eat."

Lauren's eyes flicked over her body in a way that made Jess's breath catch, but she merely said, "It seems to work for you."

Before Jess could formulate a witty response, Lauren returned to business mode. "What happens after lunch?"

"Video and a chance to cool down my body while I bring my mind up to speed. Sometimes I watch old bouts, sometimes opposition research, sometimes I watch my practice from earlier in the morning. If I'm super lazy, I play chess."

"Chess?" Lauren arched an eyebrow.

"Yeah, same muscles really. Analysis, anticipation, strategy, but unlike video, chess engages my competitive synapses. The main thing is for me to get sharp and process through details, plus I get to read someone else, which is my favorite part of the mental game."

"Hmm."

"What?"

"I don't know." Lauren's brow furrowed. "But I'm going to file that away for later."

For some reason the comment and the promise in it made the hair on the back of her neck stand on end.

"What do you do after chess?"

"One-on-one bouting for about an hour if I can, then we're usually coming to the point where the kids take over my training spaces, so I head to a weight room somewhere."

"What are your target areas?"

"Monday, Wednesday, Friday are core and light lifting. Tuesday, Thursday, and Saturdays are legs."

She watched Lauren nod again as if the answer met with her expectations or maybe even pleased her and felt a little prick of pride at not having fallen short of whatever fantasy standards people held of Olympic-caliber athletes.

"How do you usually spend your evenings?"

Jess opened her mouth, then stopped as Lauren's cheeks colored, and she worked to reel the comment back in. "I didn't mean, like socially. That sounded . . . I'm sorry, can I rephrase?"

She grinned at another little crack in the professional façade. "You don't have to. I know what you meant, but I actually do spend many of my evenings socially. I don't like to eat alone after a full day. I can get obsessed sometimes, and I need other people to bring me out of my own head. I'm an extrovert who spends a lot of time in a cage of my own making, and that's dangerous for my mental health."

"Has the mental health aspect been worse without a coach to process with?"

She clenched and unclenched her fists, and Lauren's eyes tracked down to them immediately. She didn't miss much, and Jess would probably do well not to try to sneak anything past her, especially if she insisted on those quick, surgical incision-like observations. "Yes."

Lauren set the pen down and studied her more fully. "Tell me about socially then."

74

She made a little wave of her hand. "Dinner with a friend, a Broadway show, some live music."

"Dates?" Lauren said the word without flinching.

Jess couldn't manage the same and shifted in her seat. "Sometimes. Less often recently."

"You're going to have a harder time filling the social void in Buffalo. And I agree, it's an important aspect of your personality. You were strongest as part of a team to push you and offer you more well-rounded outlets." The creases in Lauren's brow deepened. "We'll have to work on that."

"I don't expect you to become my social secretary or schedule my playdates."

Her mouth curled up in that understanding way. "No, I'm sure you can handle your little black book on your own, but I can't ignore your extroversion. You came to work with me because I wanted the best for you as a whole person. But looking at the other aspects of your routines, I think I can be present until the time when you would normally hit weights before I have to turn my attention to the club."

"I don't need you in the weight room with me. My friend Haley and I video conference for those workouts anyway."

"Haley Ivers?" Lauren's inflection rose more than a simple question warranted.

"You know her?"

"I know of her. She was three years behind me on the college circuit. I never faced her, but a couple of my younger teammates did." Lauren's voice stayed level but cool.

"What are you not saying?"

Now it was Lauren's turn to shift in her seat. "I'd heard the two of you were . . . close."

"Oh," Jess said.

"It's none of my business."

"No. I mean yes, it is. You're my coach, and you're my friend. Haley and I are close, but not romantically. There was one time after nationals, but years ago, nothing since then. She's really more into guys, and I'm more into, well, you."

Lauren blinked a few times before opening her mouth, then closing it again.

"Okay, so maybe I shared more information than I needed to there," Jess admitted.

"I have a feeling it's something we should both get used to if we're going to spend time together in a competitive pressure cooker for the foreseeable future." Lauren pushed up from her chair, adding, "And we will."

She nodded, not sure how Lauren felt about those prospects, but the warmth that hadn't dissipated at her core since the moment she'd seen Lauren this morning suggested she wasn't going to find their new proximity a hardship. A challenge, maybe, but not a hardship.

Lauren had sent Jess to change while she checked her email and then went to roll out two yoga mats in the big gym. They didn't have any specialized equipment in here, no wall cords or buzzers, and the strips were merely taped on the floor, but there were mirrors to check their form and plenty of space.

Judging from the way her body had coiled at the thought of Jess and Haley together, she needed all kinds of space. She didn't even know what to make of the additional information that Haley preferred guys. She felt a little better, maybe, but also a sense of awe that even women who weren't naturally inclined toward other women occasionally surrendered to Jess's charms. What hope had she of resisting? Especially if Jess kept being so honest about her own attraction.

She wanted them both to be open and vulnerable. They needed to if they were going to cement a coaching relationship in such a short window, and yet she'd practically vaulted out of her chair when Jess toed near the line she'd drawn in the sand. She hadn't expected the topic of training schedules to slip off the rails so quickly. Now she worried Jess had seen through her quick redirect.

Jess saw through a lot of things.

She stared down at the notebook she'd brought into the gym

with her. She'd written a rough sketch of her routine down the center of the page, but along the margins she'd squeezed in little asides about Jess's temperament. She noted her admission that she'd been lonely, and needed to process externally, the surprising reveal that she loved the mental and emotional aspects of training and competition as much as the physical side, and also played chess. She smiled at the idea. The press and publicists left those details out of her bios, probably because they didn't fit neatly into the advertising portrait they sold of her as a firecracker with a short fuse. She made another note to find a nice chessboard for the club.

The margins of the paper filled faster than the main page. She had the sense to realize that might be a warning sign. She couldn't live in the margins with Jess. She needed to walk a middle road, but before she had any chance to anchor her intentions, Jess pushed through the gym door in nothing but a pair of shorts and a black sports bra.

"Ready to get warmed up?" Jess asked.

She managed to bite her tongue to keep from saying she was already warm and headed toward hot. "Sure."

"Do you have a sound system in here?" Jess asked.

She nodded toward the old iPod port she'd rigged into some gym speakers a couple of years ago.

Jess sauntered over and pulled out her phone, either oblivious to the way her body caused Lauren's core temperature to rise faster than global climate change, or reveling in her ability to render Lauren's cognitive process utterly useless.

Her body could've gone into the fencing dictionary under "physique: prime form." She had the type of strong thighs that came only from eternities spent in lunge position. They were large by any standard, but muscled in a way that left little room for worthless societal standards, or maybe even moral standards, because Lauren defied anyone to keep their thoughts pure when looking at those legs. And the slope only got more slippery as those legs curled into tight glutes Lauren didn't even pretend not to inspect when Jess crouched down to plug in her playlist.

77

She barely managed to pull herself together just as Jess rose and turned toward her once more, though the view from the front was no less impressive. Her stomach was flat, save for cut grooves of her obliques forming c-curves through her ab complex. Her arms were lean and smoothly toned. Clearly she'd avoided upper body bulk in favor of a more sinewy kind of strength that would allow her to make minute movements quickly and unencumbered. It wasn't just sexy, it was also incredibly smart from a kinesthetic standpoint.

Lauren allowed herself a few more seconds to assess Jess's tightly strung shoulders, the smooth expanse of her chest, and the small swell of her breasts dipping into their tight constraints. None of those body parts were worth noting from a professional position, but professionalism didn't keep her from taking note of them as Jess centered herself on the mat.

Subtle strains of a few opening chords strummed through the speakers, shaking her out of the animal part of her brain with a jarring shock to her system. She couldn't remember the last time she'd let herself look at another woman with such blatant appreciation. She didn't know if she ever had, at least not since her teenage hormones had settled into the stability of adulthood. The edge of something unrestrained coursing under her skin unnerved her.

Jess managed to seem cool and almost languid as she lowered herself to the floor and eased onto her back. "Did you just want me to run through my normal warm-up today so you can get a baseline?"

"Please." She hoped the pleading didn't come through in that affirmation.

Jess's grin turned a little lopsided. "I don't normally do this with an audience. Any chance you'd like to join me on the mat?"

She bit her lip as she scanned the space left on Jess's yoga mat before her reasoning skills kicked back in and reminded her she had her own mat, so they didn't need to share. "Sure. I'll try to keep up. Yoga is probably a good speed for me."

Jess's mouth gave another little quick twitch, but for some

reason she schooled it like a kid trying to stifle a little joke, and started a series of cross-body stretches. Lauren followed along, groaning as her own stiff muscles demanded their due. Drawing knees to her chest, she took deep breaths and settled her mind.

She'd been knocked off balance the moment Jess stepped back into her life, and every moment after had been a windstorm of emotions. No one could blame her for being a little out of sorts, but all things considered, she hadn't lost her whole mind at any point yet. Well, maybe during the kiss, but she'd rebounded. And yes, there'd been a little lapse when Jess walked in half-dressed, but that would take some getting used to with anyone. While she wasn't the kind of coach who normally assessed her charges' physiques in quite so hungry a fashion, none of her other clients had professional-grade bodies.

Appreciation and attraction often pulled the same strings, and even if she'd seen a body like that on a man, she would've given it a nod of approval. The human form had inspired art for centuries, and Jess was certainly worthy of her fair share of oil paintings or sculptures in stone.

She straightened her right leg and brought her left knee all the way across her body to the mat for a delicious torsional stretch and settled on that explanation. She rolled back to center and switched legs. This time, as she angled her twist toward Jess, she kept her breathing slow and steady.

Yoga was good. Yoga was slow. Yoga gave her time to clear her head, inhaling clean and clear, exhaling confusion and clutter.

It had been ages since she'd trained the way she would've liked. Maybe she'd see her own improvements from having someone like Jess to ease her through her paces more often. As Jess tucked herself into a ball and rolled to sitting position, Lauren followed. Folding forward, they planted their hands on the mat and worked through a couple of sun salutation series, their breaths coming in companionable unison. Her heels sank lower with each downward dog as she settled into her own body rather than fixating on the one next to her. Confidence built with each fluid transition.

I can do this.

The song on the speakers ended and Jess stretched upward, then cast her a sideward glance. Lauren had only a second to register the hint of mischief in her eyes before the first rapid guitar riffs of AC/DC's "Thunderstruck" reverberated through the room.

"What is happening?" she asked over the intro of the iconic base beat.

Jess bounced her eyebrows playfully to the music. "Yoga?"

Then she dropped quickly into plank position and used the drum rhythm as a metronome to bring her knees in toward her elbows, alternating sides as she went.

"Come on, Standish," Jess called. "Get in on this."

She sighed and lowered herself down, but before she'd even caught up to Jess's pace, she shifted again. This time, modifying downward dog with one leg kicked high in the air, her back extending into one sharp, dramatic line before crunching her knee and swinging drastically down to her elbow, then cutting it across her body in an arching swoop. She ended with her opposite hip nearly touching the ground and her foot kicked wide to the underside of her completely still shoulders. It took Lauren several reps to even break down what Jess was doing, basically a full-rotation ellipse kick, all while balancing her entire body weight in an ab-crushing position inches from the ground. The move combined part plank, part horizontal plié, part roundhouse kick, and if that weren't enough, Jess kept a relentless pace. Up on the inhale, kick out on the exhale, and then back up again without pause, even when she flipped herself to the other side.

"What is happening?" Lauren asked again.

"Yoga," Jess repeated steadily as she kicked through once more.

"Doesn't look like yoga. Doesn't feel like yoga." The high, screaming vocals overhead added to her argument. "Doesn't sound like yoga."

Jess laughed and popped up into a side plank, her eyes bright as she looked at Lauren. "I don't really like to hold still."

"Okay." What did someone say to that? She'd thought they were easing in. She'd thought she was keeping up. She'd held no illusions she could pose much of a challenge to Jess on the strip, but she'd foolishly let herself believe she could handle a yoga-based core warm-up.

Again, her heart revved for all the wrong reasons, but now the arrhythmia didn't come with the pleasant flush of borderline inappropriate thoughts. The places her mind wandered while watching Jess now were steeped in fears of inadequacy.

Jess arched her back and fell into the full wheel, feet and hands on the mat behind her with every other part of her body bent into an upward-facing arch, and held everything aloft for a single breath before launching herself into a side plank on the opposite arm.

I cannot do that.

God, this woman was such a mental roller coaster. Between her sexual appeal frying Lauren's synapses and the physical exertion threatening to break her body, Jess would drive Lauren right up to the edge of all her capabilities. The prospect might not have been so unsettling if she didn't have the wherewithal to remember things were supposed to work the other way around. She was supposed to do the pushing. She was supposed to pull Jess forward. She was supposed to goad and tease and challenge her, but here was Jess with her mischievous grin and her flashing eyes, practically daring her to keep up.

Then, as if she hadn't already driven home her point, Jess flipped into an arcing back bend again, only this time she extended one of her arms off the mat and then let her pelvis drop, until her impressive glutes nearly hit the floor.

Something about the position seemed almost absurd, like a break dance move gone awry, and she had a flash of hope that this little show of style and stamina had met with an abrupt end. Surely there was no graceful place to go from there, and she found the prospect more than a little soothing against the burn of insufficiency that had scalded her a few seconds ago. She folded her arms across her chest as her worry ebbed and her curiosity expanded to fill the space it had occupied.

Jess must've noticed a change in her expression because she

froze, the hint of a smile starting to curl those lips, but not quite making it past a smirk. "What are you thinking, coach?"

"Nothing, just waiting."

"A feeling I know well."

"I thought you didn't like to hold still."

"Well, now that sounds a bit like a challenge." Jess's voice dropped low, and her eyes darkened.

"Maybe, but I can't seem to decide if I'd rather see if you have the fortitude to stay in that contortion, or the coordination to get out."

"Take all the time you need to make your decision." Jess stage yawned. "I can do this all day."

"Seriously?" She circled her now, making one slow, deliberate lap around her elongated body. Jess's eyes followed her as she went and Lauren could feel them on her the same way she'd felt the brush of her breath in the moment before they'd kissed. Jess was waiting on her, watching her, deferring to her. Coiled and poised to spring, undoubtedly, but deferential even in her own desire. Lauren had taken this explosive mind and body, the woman who refused to hold still, and suspended her in exquisite form, not by keeping up, or chasing, but by dropping back, by stepping away.

The sudden realization that Jess would bend to her will made her feel strong in a way she never had before. She's been on the verge of panic mere seconds ago with racing thoughts about how she'd never be able to keep up with Jess, but in an instant, she realized she didn't have to, at least not in the physical sense. She only needed to find a way to motivate Jess to keep up with her own abilities. She didn't need Jess to work with her, she needed Jess to work for her.

She breathed in deeply, slowly feeling her lungs expand in a way they hadn't been able to a minute ago. She could do this. She could make Jess work for her. She had before, and maybe, if what she'd said in the locker room two days ago had been true, Jess had always worked for her.

The thought made her shiver. She'd never asked for that kind of power over anyone, especially not a woman of Jess's potential, but as she completed her circle around the flexing form, she knew she could wield it. Or at least she could learn to wield it faster than she could learn to keep up with her mentally or physically, which meant Jess needed her to wield it. There was no use examining any other motivation, no reason to consider what stepping into power like that might mean for her own sense of self, or what kind of precedent it might set for them personally.

She gave a nod, more to herself than the woman beneath her, but Jess's smile, cocky and confident, served as confirmation.

"You ready?" Jess asked, a challenge in her low timbre.

She wasn't sure exactly what she was agreeing to, but for the first time, she believed she might be capable of figuring it out. "Let's see what you've got."

Jess thrust upward with her hips, and in a burst of kinetic fusion all her muscles followed, firing like rocket boosters to lift her off the ground. She landed upright, on the balls of her feet, the length of her mere inches from Lauren's body, and she had to school every reflex not to react to the show of force, or the proximity, or the Cheshire-cat grin of someone who knew exactly how impressive she was.

This time she saw past it all to the heart of a woman who wanted to impress *her*.

Chapter Five

"You want me to fire up the video?" Jess asked. She tried not to stare at Lauren, who'd knelt down beside her, offering a tempting eye angle down the front of her sweater. The view and its proximity caused her cheeks to warm and her heart to kick her ribs.

"Please," Lauren said without glancing up from her vigil of waiting for the popcorn bag to jump to life in the microwave below the front desk.

Jess settled into the folding chair next to her and surveyed the setup Lauren had rigged over the last four days. While they'd settled into a decent workout routine, video sessions had proved more challenging. First, they'd tried to watch video on her iPad, but it didn't have the size needed to show details, so they'd moved to the laptop, which at least let them control the speed and zoom in more easily, but it had still been too small. Today, Lauren had lugged in her larger desktop monitor and wired it as a mirror display. At least the picture would be bigger, but the ensemble took up the entire reception desk and seemed a lot more complex than the task should have warranted, which seemed to make Lauren a little self-conscious about the resources she lacked.

However, instead of second-guessing her choice to train in a lower-level facility without all the technical capabilities she'd grown used to, Jess saw the lengths Lauren was going through to make this work as further evidence she'd made the right call. Anyone could eventually find a way to study if they had the dedication to do so, and Lauren's commitment vastly outstripped anyone Jess had worked with in a long time. What's more, since she wasn't used to perfection, she didn't expect it out of Jess. Too many people in the fencing community had a hard time separating privilege from potential, and since so many of them were born with silver spoons in their mouths, they often devolved into tirades any time something didn't go their way. Lauren, on the other hand, let her lack of resources challenge her to be more proactive, more creative, and in a few short days she'd already begun to inspire the same in Jess.

For the first time in ages she'd begun to feel comfortable, confident, and in command while training. She liked the calm capability Lauren inspired in her so much she wasn't looking forward to what would come next.

"Okay, microwave popcorn isn't on your training diet, so this is all mine, right?" Lauren poured the entire bag into a plastic bowl while Jess pretended to fiddle with the video settings even though they didn't need it.

"Popcorn is a whole grain, so as far as snack foods go, it's actually perfect for me." She reached for the bowl, but Lauren snatched it away.

"But popcorn is my favorite," Lauren said, glancing toward the screen expectantly.

"I remember. You always used to buy the cheesy kind from the vending machines when we went on fencing trips in school," Jess said, then spun away from the monitor to snag a handful anyway.

Lauren pretended to be offended for a few seconds, her mouth open and her eyes incredulous, but she couldn't sustain the charade for long. "Fine, I'll share the popcorn."

"I know that, too. You never could hoard your snacks. Do you remember the time when you gave the other team your snacks and then we almost lost to them?"

"No. Not at all." She shook her head. "Do you remember everything from high school?"

"Nope." She popped a piece into her mouth. "Just everything

about that season with you. It was one of those formative years for me."

"Because you made the varsity team as a seventh grader?"

"I mean, not to brag or anything, but making the team was the least of my accomplishments. I also came out, kissed a superhot older woman, and won a state championship."

Lauren rolled her eyes. "I guess I should be honored you managed to remember my popcorn addiction amid all those high opinions of your own adolescent excellence."

"You really should," Jess agreed, tongue planted firmly in cheek. "Most women I've known would be wowed right out of their socks, and maybe a few other items of clothing as well."

Lauren paused, a piece of popcorn inches from her mouth as her expression turned almost pensive, and her chest rose noticeably higher on the next breath. "You are rather impressive. I can see where women wouldn't be able to resist your charms."

Her mouth went dry as Lauren leaned close enough for Jess to smell her perfume, something clean and subtle.

"I know I'm supposed to stay neutral and not ask you such personal questions while we are training"—she lowered her eyes under dark thick lashes—"but sometimes I just get so swept up in something you say, my mind wanders down paths that really aren't relevant."

"It's, uh, it's okay." She tried to sound cool, but her voice cracked.

"Is it? You don't mind me asking about you and all these women you allude to."

"No, not at all." Every muscle in her body tensed as Lauren leaned close and rested a hand on her knee. "Ask away."

"When you're with them, and you're telling them all those tales of your glory, do they all . . ." She stopped to catch her breath and wet her lower lip with the tip of her tongue. "Do they know you're full of shit?"

Jess about fell out of her chair. "Wh-what?"

Lauren laughed, pushing back into her own. "Do all those women know you're using your memories as a way to distract me

86

from making you review video of a tournament you don't want to relive?"

Her cheeks flamed as the realization burned through her lustful haze. Lauren had just juked her, and she'd fallen for it.

"You really are going to have to work harder if you want to distract me." Lauren popped a piece of popcorn into her mouth.

"I wasn't trying to distract you. I was having a nice stroll down memory lane."

"Save the reminiscing for off-hours, and let's get this show started."

Jess sighed and cued up the video, but as all the blood slowly returned to her brain, she had to admit being a little impressed with the way Lauren had just roasted her. Despite their shaky start and Lauren's early reticence about her new role, she hadn't held anything back. She also refused to let Jess get away with her standard redirects, which said a lot because she was usually damn good at pulling people off their own agendas and onto her own, a fact made evident by the first round of video that appeared on the screen.

The scene came from last year's world championships, and this homemade compilation would run from the first-round bout all the way to the semifinals. The muscles in her neck tightened in anticipation, and not the good kind.

Lauren didn't seem to have any similar misgivings as she ate her snack and watched Jess carve up her first opponent in short order.

Lauren gave a low whistle as the replay came to a close.

"Not much of a warm-up there," Jess admitted, but she enjoyed the awe in Lauren's eyes as she blew through several touches in quick succession.

"That was a mercy killing."

"I knew it would be a long day, so I just wanted to conserve energy."

"You conserving energy is still more overpowering than anyone I've ever faced."

She warmed at the compliment as the video shifted to her next

87

opponent. This one hadn't given her any more pause than the first, though Lauren leaned closer to the screen, and by extension closer to Jess.

"What's your vertical leap?"

"I box jump 48 inches every day, but I don't think I've maxed out. It's about control and thrust in the gym, and in competition, it's more about adrenaline and angle. Sometimes I get higher in a bout, but most of the time I won't need to."

Lauren nodded and Jess could practically hear the wheels turning in her brain as she eyed the third-round match with more precision focus. She must've seen something in the vertical leap, something worth pondering. Lauren saw everything. Jess had always been proud of possessing that skill herself, but she'd never given any thought to what it would feel like to have it directed at her, and now Lauren used it all day, every day.

Instead of trying keep up physically, Lauren studied. She observed, she analyzed, then adeptly converted those observations into running circles around her emotionally and intellectually. Jess appreciated the ways Lauren was earning her keep. She'd already seen the benefits on the mat and in the minutia of her footwork drills, but neither of those places laid her bare the way these videos were about to.

Her quarterfinals match flickered into focus on the screen, and the memories rushed back like a visceral gut punch. The scent of her own sweat stung her nostrils as she pulled on her helmet, and she paced her breath with an economy that anticipated a deficit. At the far end of the piste, Haley stepped into view. She saw it now as she had then, rather than as the third-party viewer the computer monitor tried to make her.

Even from a distance she could make out her dark eyes through the face mask screen most people would expect to obscure their ability to discern details. Her mind decelerated, making each step and flex feel deliberate. Through the dull thrum of blood moving through her ears, she heard the command, "*en garde*," and her reflexes took hold. Saber arm up, the other tucked automatically behind her back, and her feet shifted to match. She settled into a lunge that would've felt like a strain at any other point, but barely registered its complaints in relation to what would come next.

She met Haley's gaze as a spiral of thoughts floated untethered through her brain, but the one through line piercing them all was that one of them was about to end the other's dream.

"*Allez.*"

She took flight. She'd watched the tape enough times since then to verify what her body knew. There was no footwork to the first touch, or the second. Both times she merely levitated. The second blow caused Haley to stumble back, lifting her mask to stare as if she'd actually inflicted a wound. Jess didn't dare meet her eyes, knowing her friend would see that fear had driven her superhuman attack, but as soon as she acknowledged the truth within the dark recesses of her own brain, the spell shattered.

When they clashed again, Haley got her under her ribs, then across the right shoulder. The third time, she was on her heels in an instant, scrambling backward, blocking blow after blow at close range before she finally fell, flailing.

She screamed so loud several trainers moved toward her, but she sprang back to her feet and waved them off.

She couldn't survive on raw force anymore, and now Haley knew she was trying to. She had to clear her mind quickly. Haley had attacked three times in a row. Jess could counter or she could try to use the momentum against her. This time when the call came, she took a step back, only Haley hesitated too. They both deferred for a stutter of a step, but then Haley shot forward again. Only in the flash of indecision Jess had leaned back even more, putting her just a hair out of Haley's reach. The lack of contact upset the balance of her attack, and with a quick dodge Jess brought her saber down across the friend's extended arm, and they were even. Except they weren't. She'd misjudged Haley completely, and her indecision, not her action, saved her. What's more, now they both knew it.

Lauren gave a low whistle beside her, and Jess jumped. She'd forgotten she was there. She blinked herself out of her own head and back into the club to see those complex irises centered on her.

"You okay?"

She stared at her for a moment, trying dumbly to process the question. She wasn't sure which version of herself Lauren was questioning, the her on the screen before them, or the her reliving it. She didn't come to a conclusion before the video demanded their attention once more. This time the shout blaring through the speakers came from Haley.

Lauren turned to study the video. "What happened?"

"I drilled her in the side."

"Oh, well done, you."

She bit her tongue as Lauren's eyes narrowed at the screen.

Jess didn't have to look. She knew what she saw this time, and instead of reliving the next moments, she chose to watch Lauren watching them.

Buzzers sounded in rapid succession. Point after point ticked into place. The lion's share would land in her column, but all the grumbling came from her end of the strip as well.

"Jess," Lauren asked without turning to face her, "you care to break this down for me?"

She shrugged as she heard her own voice raised in frustration.

Lauren turned to her again. "Didn't you just win that point?"

"Only technically."

"You're up thirteen to nine."

"Wait for it."

She squeezed her eyes tightly shut, but doing so only turned the inside of her eyelids into a sort of mental projection screen. She watched the tip of her saber block Haley's, but before she could reset her own blade, it slipped down over the guard and onto her opponent's wrist. A buzzer sounded and she saw red everywhere, including on Haley's helmet.

The riser they fought atop shook under her stomps of rage.

"It's fourteen to nine."

"Yeah."

They reset and took up their starting positions, but this time when given the cue to proceed, she snapped to attention, blade raised but stock-still in front of her face. Haley jumped, then

90

faltered just as the tip of her saber landed right in the center of Jess's chest guard.

The crowd gasped and Haley lifted her helmet, shock crossing her face, followed quickly by a flash of silent fury.

"Do I get an explanation here, or do I have to guess?" Lauren asked.

Jess made a rolling motion with her hand, and Lauren allowed the replay to continue. She could still see the warning in Haley's eyes, and if she'd been a better person, she'd have heeded it. Instead, she resumed her starting form, then again deferred.

This time Haley didn't keep her displeasure to herself. "You do that one more time and I'll run you through."

She blew out a heavy breath both in real time and replay. "We're even."

"Helmets!" the referee called.

Haley shook her head but tugged her helmet down roughly. "I'm serious, Jess. You will pay hell."

"Yeah, I can't figure out why anyone would think there was something more than friendly competition between you two," Lauren mumbled.

She snorted, desperately wishing she could blame her ensuing meltdown on some romantic drama or sexual frustration. Instead, she kept her thoughts to herself and waited until the final point played out. The scoreboard would say she earned it, and with it the win, but for the rest of her life she would know she hadn't.

The sound of her wailing, "No!" reverberated through the computer speakers, but she could still feel it in her throat.

Lauren slapped off the computer, and Jess felt her eyes on her even before she managed to open her own.

"I'd heard stories," Lauren finally whispered, "but they didn't show that match online."

She gave a silent exhale of gratitude for that minor mercy.

"Can we talk?"

"Do we have to?"

"I'm just confused," Lauren said softly.

Jess nodded. She'd heard this all before, and she didn't really

91

want to rehash it again with Lauren, but she was mature enough to understand she owed her an explanation. She wasn't mature enough to be able to offer one gracefully. "I got pissed off, okay?"

"Okay." Lauren waited for more, but when no further explanation came, she nudged. "Could I tell you what I'm seeing here, and then maybe you can tell me where I go wrong?"

She thought for a moment, waiting for the usual scalding rage that accompanied pressure for explanations, but this time it didn't come, either because of the person doing the requesting or the new way the request had been made. She nodded her consent.

Lauren drew in a deep, slow breath. "You won the match with a progression that suggested you can out-strategize almost anyone."

A muscle twisted in her jaw, but before she could snap back, Lauren pressed on.

"You asserted dominance over the first few touches, then fell back enough to draw her into your space, but you let her in a little far, and she knocked you down. Instead of letting that rattle your confidence, you channeled it into a productive type of rage."

She snorted a little at the "productive" part, but Lauren's calm, steady voice had soothed enough of her frayed edges to keep the word from grating against them.

"But as you roared back into brute force, you lost your grip on the strategy you'd anchored yourself to, which made you erratic, but that's where I lose my grip on what happened internally." Lauren eyed her, visually urging her to step in. When she didn't, she offered up another gentle nudge. "You won the match, Jess."

"No, I didn't."

Lauren raised her eyebrow.

"I got lucky, or maybe Haley got unlucky, but I didn't win. I didn't earn those points. I didn't deserve at least three of those touches."

"Which is why you gave her two of them back," Lauren summarized, her voice filled with a blend of awe and understanding. "And you wanted to give her another one, but she got so mad, you stopped short."

"I owed her one more."

"Jess . . ."

"Don't." She growled a low warning that caused Lauren to sit back, widening the space between them. She missed her immediately, but she wouldn't accept pity she hadn't earned any more than she accepted points she didn't have a right to win. "Don't tell me people get lucky, or capitalizing on someone else's mistake is part of the sport. I didn't capitalize on her mistake. I got awarded touches for *my* mistakes."

Lauren nodded. "Keep going."

"I saw her coming. I had a plan. I didn't execute."

"Because you didn't need to."

"My hand slipped," she shouted, then winced at the violence in her own voice.

Lauren didn't so much as flinch though, and her steadiness inspired a bit of the same in her.

"I misjudged the situation so badly it rendered my plan void. She had me juked out of my shoes, and then when I did catch up mentally, I was still two steps behind my own fucking brain. Do you know how awful that is? It's like slamming on your brakes to avoid a collision only to find they don't work."

Lauren's expression remained completely neutral. She didn't offer any platitudes or counterpoints. She didn't back away or reach for her. She merely absorbed everything rushing out of Jess, and in doing so, created the perfect floodplain for all those emotions.

"I can't stand being slower physically than I am mentally, but I can't stand it the other way around either." Her voice broke. "God, do you know how fucking frustrating it is to see the opening, to know in the deepest, most animalistic part of my brain how to beat her, and still not be able to execute?"

Lauren nodded slowly. "You're too smart for your own sanity."

"I'm too smart for my weak-ass reflexes."

"Hey." Lauren interrupted for the first time. "You have every right to be upset, but let's not internalize anything toxic. You and I both know your reflexes are off the charts."

"The charts are made for mediocre people."

Lauren laughed.

"It's not funny." She hated the pouty way the words came out.

"The idea of you being mediocre is very funny." Lauren's eyes danced with genuine affection now. "The match was a lot of things, your frustration, your honor, your fear. They're all real and valid, but nothing there, nothing about *you*, has ever been mediocre."

The anger began to dissipate, breaking off in tiny grains like sand being washed away on a receding tide. She should've been relieved, but she didn't have any right to be. Nothing about the situation had changed except for the way Lauren saw it, which shouldn't have made any difference. It shouldn't have complicated anything to be understood, but it did. Without the rage that sustained her for so long to cover all her other emotions, she felt raw, exposed, vulnerable, and she didn't know if she was ready for either of them to see what other pieces of her might be left strewn along the beach in its absence.

Lauren was too close, she'd seen too much, she knew too much. Jess didn't want to go any further down that road, not with what she knew was still to come on the video compilation. She hopped up quickly. "I don't want to do this anymore today."

Lauren glanced at her watch, an unspoken reminder they hadn't completed the time they'd allotted for video review.

"I don't care," Jess snapped, then caught herself. "I know it's early, and I don't care."

Lauren nodded once more, still so steady and contained.

"I'm going to the gym now. I need to burn off steam."

"Okay." Lauren didn't hesitate.

Jess grabbed her keys off the desk and nothing else as she made her break for the door, but just as she pushed it open, Lauren called out lightly, "Dinner's at 8:30 if you can wait that long."

Her momentum faltered. "What?"

"I'd planned to order takeout tonight," Lauren continued breezily. "Maybe Thai food?"

Jess froze, confusion at the non sequitur jumbling all her other impulses.

"Kristie's coming over to entertain me while I eat and wipe

down the foils. It should be quite a rip-roaring way to spend a Friday night, but if you're not busy, I'd love to have you there."

The offer rattled around her brain as if trying to find a place to embed itself. Her fight-or-flight muscles pulsed, and intellectually, flight presented the safest option. This was the point when she ran, or at least the point where she'd run from all her other coaches, the moment they'd begun to peel back her layers in preparation of supplanting them with their own. But Lauren had already managed to dig deeper and faster than any of the others.

On all the screaming surface levels, the realization terrified her, and she still didn't bolt. In the stillness, another part emerged, one aching to stand under that complex gaze and not feel inadequate or childish, lacking. Part of her would enjoy a dinner with Lauren very much. That part of her craved easy, casual company with someone who didn't expect her to be something else. For the first time, that part of her overrode the other.

"I do like Thai food," she managed before the frustration fought to reassert itself. "But I don't like to talk about video time when it's not video time."

Lauren's smile returned. "Who does?"

"And video time is over?"

Lauren nodded. "For today."

She accepted the offer for what it was, a temporary reprieve, one that honored her boundaries and also Lauren's promise to hold steady when Jess flailed. She could've asked for more. She could've pushed for better terms. She could've made new demands. Only for the first time in ages, she didn't want to.

"I'll see you at 8:30."

Lauren sat in the same spot where Jess had left her earlier. She hadn't been there for five hours. She'd done plenty of other things in between, lessons, registrations, equipment maintenance. She'd even replaced one of the fluorescent bulbs in the men's locker room, but between each task, she'd returned to this spot to ponder what had happened here this afternoon.

She had some better understanding now of what drove Jess to extremes during the quarterfinal they'd analyzed. She didn't agree with the ways Jess had conceptualized her actions, but at least she understood them. She still didn't have a clear grasp on why Jess had been so upset here and now. She'd reacted like a wounded animal, not the cocky, confident woman who regularly thrived in high-pressure situations. The anger made a certain amount of sense. The other emotions she'd been able to parse out in those final moments, the fear, the skittishness, the shame, didn't add up.

She shook her head. She wasn't going to get any answers tonight. She'd promised not to even look for them, and she intended to keep her word. There was a danger in letting Jess's volatile nature subsume her own inner peace, and she'd already danced close enough to that line by inviting her to dinner tonight. Despite her earlier commitment to playing on their personal connection as motivation, she hadn't really thought through the invitation when she'd issued it. She felt only an unfathomable need to reach out to her as she ran, and instead of grabbing hold of her physically, she'd latched onto the memory of Jess saying she hated to eat alone.

The offer came out of her mouth before her brain caught up with her empathy and sounded the alarm that being alone with Jess, at night with both of their emotions running hot, might present a new set of issues she was unequipped to handle. Memories of the first dinner they'd shared and the kiss that came afterward assaulted her mind's eye, and she'd quickly inserted Kristie as a buffer.

As if on cue, her best friend bounded through the front door. "Hey, is the supermodel Olympian here yet?"

Okay, so maybe Kristie hadn't been the best buffer option. Lauren probably should've picked a more neutral partner to act as chaperone, but this was all she'd been able to come up with in the moment. "No, you beat her."

"Oh good. I'm glad I can tell people I beat an Olympian at something in my life." Kristie chuckled at her own joke, then eyed Lauren's outfit. "Are you going to change clothes?"

She glanced down at her yoga pants and plain, white, long-sleeve T-shirt. "No."

"Bold choice."

"You're wearing a hockey jersey and jeans."

"I just came from practice."

"So did I," she shot back.

"But now you're on a date."

"This isn't a date. If it were, I wouldn't have invited you."

"Yeah, there's your first mistake, but it's not too late for you to do something about your helmet hair."

"Seriously?"

Kristie grimaced. "I mean that in the best way."

"What's the best way for someone to have helmet hair?"

"You know, like you've had a helmet on, not your actual hair looking like a helmet, but let's focus on the fact that you still have time to fix it. I'll keep her busy if she gets here before you get back."

"That's a horrifying thought," she said, but even as she tried to convey the absurdity of this conversation with her voice and facial expression, she grabbed a hair tie from the top drawer of her desk and smoothed her hair before twisting it into a ponytail. "And I expect you to be on your best behavior tonight."

"Again, I think you may have invited the wrong friend."

"We had a rough afternoon." She injected some seriousness into her tone. "And we're not allowed to talk about it, but I want tonight to be a low-pressure situation. I need to hit the reset button."

"Okay, but like are we hitting it for you, or her?"

She pressed her lips together and considered the options. She'd not yet settled on one before Kristie offered up a better choice.

"Both?"

She gave one resolute nod. "Both."

"Good to have that settled, 'cause she's here."

"Fine." She ignored the way her heart rate ticked up into the aerobic zone. "We're having dinner with friends. Don't make it weird."

"Got it, no weirdness. I can be totally unweird."

The response didn't exactly inspire confidence, but as Jess came through the door and flashed one of her most magnetic smiles, it was hard to feel any sort of apprehension.

Things went smoother than she could've expected from there. Jess had clearly stowed her earlier anguish in a way that made Lauren wonder how much practice she'd had doing so. And despite her initial concerns, Kristie did manage to hold a conversation, not just like a normal person, but as an actual interested party.

She drew Jess into trading competition stories and a few borderline inappropriate jokes about scoring. Dinner arrived and they ate in companionable chatter, take-out containers spread across the beat-up coffee table she'd snagged at a yard sale years ago, all of them sitting cross-legged on the floor, the cleanliness of which she chose not to think about.

As digestion set in, Lauren collected some polishing rags and an armful of youth foils from the racks along the wall, then began the never-ending battle against rust.

Without comment, Jess snagged one of the rags and pulled a foil into her lap as well.

The conversation continued amiably for a couple more minutes before Kristie pointed to the weapons in each of their hands, and asked, "That's something you both do without even thinking about it, isn't it? You're not even plotting murder while you shine up your shivs."

Jess laughed. "What?"

"You're both stroking implements of bodily harm like it's not ominous at all."

"I'm not sure a foil counts as a dangerous weapon. Only the point is sharp." She pressed her finger to the tip before adding, "And even that's debatable in the face of communal club gear."

"Hey now," Lauren jumped in, "I keep the club gear in great shape. These are for children who I don't trust around foils sharp enough to pierce the skin of a peach."

"Fair," Jess said before turning back to Kristie. "Which weapon do you use?"

"Weapons are a big ole nope. I'm a pacifist."

Now it was Lauren's turn to scoff. "Pacifist? The last time I came to one of your hockey games, you had your gloves off and were wailing on some poor woman before the end of the first period."

"Yeah, I use fisticuffs like a civilized human. I didn't try to impale her like you homicidal maniacs."

"Wait." Jess paused her polishing. "You don't fence at all?"

"She's terrified of women with swords," Lauren explained, "and honestly if you'd met some of her ex-girlfriends, you'd probably affirm the fear."

"No lie there," Kristie agreed.

"But you're best friends with the best fencing teacher I've ever met."

Lauren warmed at the vehemence of the description.

"How have you managed to hold out against the greatest fencing ambassador Buffalo's ever had?"

"It's really not hard. I've just never felt an overwhelming desire to take up a hobby that involves getting stabbed repeatedly."

Jess laughed, deeply, genuinely, causing the remaining tension to slip from Lauren's shoulders. "But if you're good, you get stabbed a lot less, and you actually get to stab everyone else."

"Still not an appealing ratio. I like to spend my little free time on interests where no one gets stabbed, like, ever."

Jess regarded her with a curious expression that made Lauren suspect she'd never once considered the appeal of non-stabbing activities until this moment. The look was equal parts amusement and utter innocence. Some of the boundaries she'd clung to softened.

"But fencing is fun." Jess pleaded her case with the sort of shock and bluster of someone who'd just been charged with explaining the benefits of breathing. "You just have to."

"And yet I've lived thirty years without it."

"No, you've survived maybe, but like staying alive without art, or fine wine, or, or, sex, I'm not sure you can call that living."

"Well, I've had sex with women and—"

"And after the first time, didn't it feel like you could see colors

99

that had only been shades of gray before? Didn't you hear notes you'd never heard before? Didn't it restructure your very DNA and reorient your basic building blocks toward a new sense of purpose?"

"Fuck, first I thought we were just arguing about sports, but now I feel like I'm being asked to admit you're better at sex than I am." Kristie turned to Lauren for help, but she had none to offer, not after Jess's little speech turned her mental matter to mush. She only managed to hope she wasn't radiating arousal when Jess turned to her as well.

"How have you never gotten your best friend into a set of whites?"

"I've never really tried very hard."

"Why?"

"I figured she'd try fencing if I try hockey, and I have about as much desire to stand atop razor blades on a sheet of ice as she has to be stabbed repeatedly."

"I love hockey," Jess said quickly. "I played for years until I started to specialize in fencing."

"Of course you did," Lauren grumbled with a hint of teasing. "You fence like someone who has experience crashing into things."

Jess ignored the observation and homed in on Kristie again. "I actually still skate a bit during the winter. It's great for balance, core strength, and cardio. I'd love to work out together sometime."

"That would rock," Kristie agreed quickly. "I can get ice time pretty much any afternoon."

"Skating's an awfully big risk this close to the Olympics." Lauren cut back in.

"Not when you've got my skills." Jess injected some of the cockiness she'd lost earlier in the day. "Injury is always a risk when training for a combat sport, but skating won't be any harder on my ankles than the footwork drills, and the chance of falling is no more present than running stairs or box jumps."

"Also," Kristie added, "not as dangerous as playing with actual swords."

Jess laughed. "Fair point."

"Heh." Kristie grinned. "Point. I get it. Swords have points."

Lauren rolled her eyes, a little surprised she wasn't putting up more of a fight, and made a mental note to examine how Jess's mood affected hers as soon as she got a chance to think more clearly.

"It's settled." Jess set her foil on the table and hopped to her feet. "We'll set up some ice time in coming weeks, but only if you let us give you a fencing lesson right now."

Lauren shook her head and relaxed a little, feeling safer about Jess's ankles already, since there was zero chance Kristie would agree.

Kristie stood up a little less gracefully than Jess had, but when she did, she extended her hand and said, "You've got yourself a deal."

"You're such a traitor," Lauren said to Kristie as Jess led her into the Elites' gym. "We've been friends for five years, and you've never once set foot through those doors. Jess has been back less than two weeks, and here you are."

Jess smiled, hearing the humor in her voice again. She'd been so worried when she returned after her earlier meltdown that things would be different between them somehow. Maybe Lauren would hold her at arm's length or walk on eggshells around her, but the opposite had been true. As the night went on, they'd slipped into an easy comfort they hadn't shared since their date. She felt a wash of gratitude to Kristie for giving her a chance to stay in that comfort zone a little longer.

Jess had changed into the whites she'd left behind earlier, and she carried another pile of clothing for Kristie, who'd stripped down to a T-shirt and boxer shorts.

"All right." Jess set everything on the floor. "The first things are pretty explanatory. Knickers or pants. We call them whites because, well, they're white."

"Why are they white?" Kristie asked like a little kid on the first day of class.

"It's because there used to be red chalk on the tips of the blades to see who'd touched who, like drawing blood," Lauren explained.

Jess grinned, unsurprised Lauren had that information in her large database of fencing knowledge. "Cool."

"Cool?" Kristie asked as she pulled on the pants and snugged up the suspenders. "Stabby McStabberson is glad to confirm this is a blood sport?"

"No more blood," Lauren corrected.

"Usually," Jess added with a cheeky grin, "but just in case, here's your chest protector."

Kristie's mouth dropped as Jess held up a solid white plate with two round cups near the center. "Is that a boob plaster?"

"Pretty much." Jess handed over the white breastplate. "It's made from polyurethane, which makes it flexible enough to let it twist a bit, but it's still virtually impossible to crack."

"Is it too late to back out?"

"Totally, put it on over your sports bra and pretend you're Wonder Woman."

Lauren laughed lightly. The sound made Jess wish she'd worked up a whole comedic routine around this process. Instead, she helped Kristie fasten the back straps on the chest protector, then handed her the next layer. "This is your plastron."

Kristie held up the undershirt. "Uh, I think one of the arms fell off this one."

"That's for your free arm. It's not as important to cover as the one holding the weapon. "You're right-handed, no?"

"I am, but I'm also fond of my left arm as well. Shouldn't we protect them both rather than play favorites?"

"Don't worry. We have more layers to protect you."

"You know what else would protect me?" Kristie asked, then plowed forward. "Not stabbing me."

"Or you could just put on more layers." Jess continued to dress her.

"So many layers," Lauren echoed.

"Don't you swelter underneath it all?" Kristie sniffed the plastron and grimaced.

"Yes." They both groaned in unison, then shared a quick smile.

"The final cover for your torso is the jacket." Jess held it up for her. "It should be snug enough not to blouse and create a bigger target, but not so tight it restricts movement."

Kristie slipped her arms into the sleeves and tugged up the cross-body zipper.

"Great, now fasten your gorget."

"My goujon?" Kristie tried out the word with nothing resembling success.

"The collar," Lauren said. "It's what protects you from getting stabbed in the neck."

"Holy shit, please don't stab me in the neck."

Jess laughed again. "That almost never happens."

"Almost?" Kristie whimpered.

Jess ignored her and dropped to her knees to help fasten the straps dangling from the bottom of the jacket between her legs.

"Do you how long it's been since a woman got on her knees in front of me?" Kristie joked, a hint of nervousness still tinging her voice. "I just never thought that when it happened again, she'd be fastening my adult diaper."

"It's not a diaper," Lauren said.

"It looks like one, and honestly if you stab me anywhere near the body parts it's covering, I might end up needing an adult diaper. So, I don't think it's a bad idea."

"For the love of God, put a helmet on her," Lauren grumbled good-naturedly.

Kristie accepted it eagerly and didn't need any instructions on how to pull it over her head with the mask facing forward. "You can actually see a lot better in these things than I thought. They look so dark from far away, but the mesh is actually pretty fine up close."

"Clear enough for your opponents to see the whites of your eyes," Jess said as she tugged on her own helmet. "So, don't show an ounce of fear."

"How am I doing?"

"Terrible." Lauren tossed her a thick glove with a cuff that would extend at least halfway up her forearm.

Kristie pulled it on. "Where's the other one?"

"You only need one."

"I thought we already covered the fact that I like both my hands."

"Then keep the other one behind your back." Lauren suggested as she placed a hand on Kristie's back and directed her toward the middle of the room.

Jess followed with only a fleeting notion of how much she might enjoy having Lauren's hand on the small of her own back.

"Okay, stand over here on the piste," Lauren motioned to the metal runway-style strip atop the gym floor

"Stand on the pissy, got it."

"Piste," Lauren corrected. "Or you can call it a strip."

"Stripping sounds so much nicer in the moment," Kristie said, then turned to Jess. "Am I right?"

"Well, you're not wrong, but naked women aside, fencing is like a close second."

"Your value set is terrible."

Jess grinned so hard her cheeks hurt. She couldn't remember the last time she'd had this much fun in a lesson, but it also didn't escape her notice that Lauren had taken over the session as she angled Kristie's body with her right foot and hand forward, and her left foot to the back.

"Now bend your knees so they're right over the tips of your toes," she instructed, and both fencers obeyed.

Lauren picked up two sabers and handed one to each of them. "Kristie, there are three weapons in modern fencing, the epee, the foil, and the saber. Each one comes with its own set of rules, and each one has different advantages."

"Glad it's not complicated." Kristie accepted her weapon and wriggled it around in her gloved hand.

"Don't worry about the other weapons." Jess lifted her own saber into a ready position. "You've got a saber there. It's superior."

"They all have their advantages," Lauren repeated diplomatically.

Jess shrugged. "The saber has a point and a blade. You can strike with either of them. Also, the target area is clear-cut. Anything above the waist is fair game."

"No stabbing below the belt." Kristie nodded under her helmet. "There's the first rule I've liked in the whole scenario."

"Lift up your weapon, and you're in the on guard position, which is how you would start, but normally the referee would ask if you were ready first."

"What if I said no?"

"That's why I went straight to on guard," Lauren said, "which you're in, so now when I say 'go,' you will try to touch any part of Jess from the waist up, with any part of your saber before she can do the same to you."

Kristie made the sign of the cross with her saber hilt and raised her blade.

"Go!"

Jess had to fight every natural instinct and all her operant conditioning not to launch herself at the woman in front of her. Instead, she merely flicked her hand a fraction of an inch and parried Kristie's tentative attack. The second pass took even less effort. Kristie regrouped and this time came at her hard enough that Jess at least had to brace herself a bit to absorb the blow before swatting her away like a persistent fly.

The move threw Kristie off balance enough that Jess could've landed about seven touches before she managed to stand up again, and another five or six before she stepped back. It took actual physical restraint, the kind that made her muscles ache, not to pounce on all the exposed surface area.

"No, no," Lauren called. "Don't cross your feet. Scoot forward, right foot first, then bring in your left one to match it."

"I don't want to get closer to her," Kristie shouted. "How do I reverse?"

"Step back with your left foot, and then follow with your right," Lauren explained, then quickly added, "but don't. She hasn't even attacked you yet. She's just standing still."

"I can feel her building up to something," Kristie argued. "I see it in her disconcertingly beautiful eyes. There's a feral animal itching to bite."

She grinned, both at the compliment and the accuracy of Kristie's assessment.

The pressure mounted in her to lunge, slashing for the proverbial jugular. It had been two weeks since she'd really let go with an unrestrained barrage of attacks. She and Lauren had sparred of course, but always during drills, always working on one tiny bit of minutia, the set of her fingers, the slide of her foot, a weak defensive position. At least with Lauren, her mind had been fully engaged, and that presented its own sort of challenge, but here with a saber in hand and an easy target in view, some wild instinct clawed at her decorum. If Kristie had merely given her half a reason, she would've grabbed hold like a life preserver.

"Can I get a running start?" Kristie asked.

"No," Lauren said at the same time Jess said, "Sure."

Kristie clearly preferred Jess's response and took several rapid steps back, but she must've taken Lauren's lesson to heart because she did so by inching her left foot back one scoot at a time, before bringing the other foot to follow.

"Hey, that wasn't bad!" Jess said. "Do it again."

Kristie seemed all too happy to agree and kept on scuttling all the way to the wall.

Jess's vision formed a tunnel. It hadn't taken much. The mere hint of legitimate fencing movement was enough.

"She's ready," Jess proclaimed, reaching for a set of cords, the only item of clothing left in her original pile.

"What?" the others both asked.

"We're ready to fight. Get her in a lamé."

"Jess." Lauren's voice immediately dropped into its most placating register. "She hasn't even learned to lunge yet."

"She's athletic. She'll learn on the go. She can have a running start. Or how about a 15-1 ratio on points?"

"Fifteen to one?" Kristie asked. "I only have to touch you once before you stab me fifteen times?"

Jess nodded.

106

"Sounds fair," Kristie said, turning to face her. "Horrible, really, but fair."

Lauren didn't even look at her friend. Her eyes were fixed on Jess and filled with concern, the same way they'd been earlier in the day. "Why? Just tell me why?"

She gritted her teeth against the emotions pushing up through her throat. She couldn't explain, she didn't know how, and even if she did, she wasn't sure it would make sense to anyone else in the world, but she respected Lauren enough to give her everything she was able to give, and said, "I need it."

Lauren stood still, steady, quiet, connected to her through their shared gaze, until finally she smiled slightly. "Okay, let's go."

The whoosh of relief nearly buckled Jess's knees, but she rebounded with a leap and spin toward the remainder of her gear, not sure exactly what had inspired the burst of energy—the prospect of a fight, or the fact that for the first time in a long time, she hadn't had to fight the person who mattered most.

"Are you kidding me? You want me to put on another layer of clothing?" Kristie's voice took on an incredulous edge. I'm already wrapped up like some sweaty Michelin man!"

"This is the last one, and it's lightweight," Lauren explained as she tugged the lamé over her friend's head. "It's electric, and once I plug you in, it'll be connected to the scoring system."

"It's what? Did you say electric? As in like 'electric chair?'"

She rolled her eyes. "Not quite. It's more like the game Operation. It's a small, open circuit. If Jess touches any part of this with her metal saber, it will close the circuit, and a buzzer will go off."

"Can you go back to the part where you plug me in?"

Lauren turned her around and grabbed the cord hanging off the back of the metallic shirt. "Here, this clips into an extendable reel in the floor so you can move up and down the strip freely.

Kristie eyed the extension cord Lauren pulled from the wall and plugged into the lamé. "It's like one of those retractable dog leashes."

"Yes." Lauren stole another glance at Jess, who'd already completed all her steps and now paced at the far end of the strip. She wished she could put *her* on an actual leash. She got the sense Jess would bolt or lunge as soon as she had the chance, and while she didn't fear for Kristie's safety, she did worry about the pent-up aggression she saw swimming behind those blue eyes. Why hadn't she done more to dispel it through the week? She'd been so focused on the video and the footwork and inspiration. She'd exhausted herself trying not to drop any detail, but in doing so, had she failed to see the bigger picture of what Jess needed?

She shook her head. Of course she had. She scrambled to keep up with this woman on every level. Jess had been a maelstrom of emotions all week, and she'd pulled Lauren along with her. The ride was just getting started, though, and she suspected they had several more barrel rolls to come.

"Am I ready?" Kristie's voice drew her back.

She wasn't sure either of them could ever actually be ready for what was about to happen, but she chose to focus on the things she could control. "There's one more little cord on your sleeve to connect your saber hilt to an electrical current."

"Right, because it's not enough to just stab someone. You have to add an electrical current to the mix as well. I should've called you Stabby McSparky."

"You'll be fine."

Kristie eyed Jess skeptically. "Do you think I have a chance to score a point?"

Lauren glanced over at Jess as she prowled her small square of the strip, eyes flashing, fists clenched.

"Not at all. She's going to pummel you, but you won't die or anything." Then, hoping to forestall any more argument, she shoved Kristie onto the strip, feeling very much as though she'd just thrown her best friend to the lions.

What happened next was a blur. It wasn't uncommon for newbies to be disoriented by the speed and close confines of the sport, but Lauren had been watching high-level fencing for nearly two decades, and even she could barely make out the whir of limbs and equipment. Jess attacked and Kristie cowered. Then Kristie attacked, Jess counterattacked, and Kristie cowered. Then, for something different, Jess attacked so fast Kristie didn't even get a chance to cower. One time, Kristie tried her theory of getting a running start, which of course Jess easily sidestepped, bringing her saber down neatly across the top of Kristie's skull as she sprawled across the far end of the strip.

It was like watching a series of car crashes in real time, or worse, fast-forward, because Jess's reflexes were more agile than any sportscar Lauren had ever seen.

"What's the score?" Kristie gasped, stumbling back to her own end of the strip with all the grace of a prize fighter who'd sustained too many blows to the head.

"Twelve to zero."

"Great," Kristie panted.

"Is it?"

"Yeah, means we're almost done." She clutched the front of Lauren's long sleeve T-shirt and pulled herself up. "I'm so sorry for every time I made fun of your sport. I thought hockey was exhausting. I know what it's like to charge the goal with everything I have over and over, but I've never once imagined what it would be like if the goalie had a sword."

She laughed. She probably shouldn't have, but the joy shook her shoulders all the way down to her core. Jess had not only convinced her most anti-fencing friend to try the sport, she'd broken first her resistance, then her will, and replaced them with a considerable amount of awe.

Lauren turned to the woman waiting, poised and full of prowess across the room. She tucked her helmet under her sword arm as she ran her fingers through her mop of red curls, damp only with the slightest sheen of sweat. She wasn't even breathing hard, and the pink on her cheeks clearly stemmed from amusement rather than exertion. Her eyes sparkled with mischief as they swept over Lauren, then darkened as something else crept in, or maybe reflected emotion Lauren hadn't quite meant to convey.

She hadn't even known she'd been missing something like this in her life. She'd forgotten what it felt like to be close to someone who loved this sport as much as she had at one point. She hadn't even remembered how thrilling it could be to revere someone who stood beside you and have them look at you the same way.

"What can I do, coach?" Kristie called her back by pleading to her better angels.

"You know what?" she asked. "You're just not going to beat her at her game. Not ever."

"Sure, great, super helpful. Just lose the game? Sounds like a valid plan."

"That's not what I said." Lauren shook her head. "Play your game."

"I didn't bring my hockey stick."

"You've got a stick in your hand. Just hit her with a slap shot."

She didn't wait for any more questions. With one hand on Kristie's shoulder and one on her back she forcibly propped her up and propelled her toward Jess, before shouting, "Ready? On guard."

Jess fell into position as if Pavlov had just rung a bell.

Kristie did her best, which had to count for something.

"Go!"

Jess lunged, but this time Kristie fell back, not in the fencing form they'd tried to teach her, but with a weird, slipping push-off that propelled her just out of the range of Jess's reach. The move clearly caught everyone off guard, and Jess hopped back to regain her footing, but as she did, Kristie lowered her weapon until the tip almost touched the strip off to her right side. Then, as she pushed forward with the same sideways foot kick she'd used to back up, she brought her ungloved hand forward to clasp over the other and swung in a wide uppercut.

Jess's eyes went wide behind her mask as she shot her saber across her body. Their blades collided with a clang, but Kristie had momentum on her side. She pushed upward along the blade, over the hilt, and in a fraction of a second, clipped the sleeve of Jess's lamé just before Jess's blade found its own mark along her ribs.

110

Both buzzers sounded simultaneously, but Jess knew what Kristie didn't. She threw off her helmet and dropped her saber in one fluid motion as she let loose a ferocious roar that devolved into a peel of crazy laugher.

"What?" Kristie shouted. "What happened?"

"You won," Lauren said, frozen solid by her own shock.

"She stabbed me." Kristie stared blankly as she rubbed her side.

"You had right-of-way." Jess shouted as she spun in a circle.

"What does that mean?" Kristie shouted back, her excitement growing even though she clearly didn't understand why.

"Don't worry about the finer points right now," Jess said coming toward her. "We both got a touch, but you got a better one. You won the point."

"I got you?" Kristie sounded more stunned than anyone.

"You got me!" Jess wrapped her in a bear hug, lifted her off the ground, and shook her.

"And you're happy about that?" Kristie asked as Jess finally dropped her back onto the strip.

Lauren felt a rush of gratitude that Kristie had the where-withal to ask because she still couldn't manage to speak. The sight of Jess exuberant, flushed and smiling, twisted something deep inside her.

"Yes. You challenged me. You caught me off guard. You made me think and flex and react. Do you know how good that feels?"

"I thought you were, like, a hypercompetitive person."

"I am." Jess's laugher still rattled in her voice. "I want to win every time, but I can't unless I'm ready for everything. I wasn't ready for that, whatever that was."

Kristie puffed up her chest and removed her helmet. "That was my slap shot."

"Well it's terrible, so terrible my brain couldn't even process what to do. No legitimate fencer would ever move like that, and you sort of broke the rules by bringing your other hand around. Also, I could've cut your fingers off."

Kristie's complexion paled as the last comment sank in.

"But you're a boss," Jess continued excitedly. "You risked your limbs to win a point. I don't care about the rules. I'm so geeking out on you right now."

"Really? I'm a little nauseated."

Jess grabbed her by her shoulder. "Want to try again?"

"No!" Lauren found her voice.

They both turned to stare at her like they'd forgotten she was there, and she couldn't blame them. She hadn't really been there, not in the way she needed to be. The realization felt like a fist around her heart.

"I'm sorry," she said, her words thick with emotion.

"Why?" Jess asked. "This was awesome."

"It shouldn't have been." She shook her head. "You shouldn't have to carve up Kristie for kicks. You shouldn't be amped up over a 14-1 score. You shouldn't need the cheap thrill of getting hit with a slap shot."

"Hey," Kristie pouted, "I have a really good slap shot."

Jess's eyes softened and her shoulders dropped. "I got a little carried away."

"It's okay," Lauren said.

"It's not. You're right. I shouldn't have unloaded on her. I'm not really good at boundaries, or restraint." She managed a little self-deprecating grin. "But I didn't mean to beat up your friend. I just, I missed fight night two weeks in a row."

"What's fight night?" Kristie cut back in excitedly. "Or is the first rule of fight night that you can't talk about fight night?"

"It's nothing. It's just a thing we do in New York to blow off steam. It's like open bouting mixed with, well, yeah, fight club." She shrugged and stepped closer to Lauren, a heartbreaking sincerity in her eyes. "This is not fight night, and I shouldn't have let myself get swept up."

Lauren choked back the emotions tinged in her own insecurity for fear they would feed Jess's. She stepped closer, close enough to feel the heat pouring off her in waves. "You didn't do anything wrong."

"I pulled on my helmet, and something primal just took over. I lost all sense of situation and place, and, and—" Jess sighed. "I'm sorry."

"Don't." Lauren cupped her face in her hands, her fingertips burning against flushed skin as she stared into those eyes. They would figure this out. She would do better for this woman. She didn't know how, but she did know which point she desperately needed to drive home in this moment. "Don't you ever apologize for being a champion."

Chapter Six

Lauren had been busy with the little kids' lessons at the club all Saturday, so Jess put in her time in the gym and spent the afternoon trying to do mindfulness and visualization exercises in her parents' basement like she was fourteen again. She fully expected to spend her night watching *The Great British Bake Off* with her mother, and she thought she'd made her peace with that, but when she received a text from Lauren telling her to be at the club at 9:00 sharp, she practically levitated off the couch.

She'd pressed for more details, but all she got out of Lauren was a cryptic, "Show up suited up and well-hydrated."

When she asked, "What for?"

Lauren shot back, "Where's your sense of adventure, Stabby McStabberson?"

Feeling both the thrill of anticipation and the scrape of a challenge, she pulled into the parking lot of the club well after dark. The place should've been deserted hours ago. Instead, there were multiple cars around her and a strip of light flooding out from the open door.

She heard the excited chatter of voices even before she stepped across the threshold and found a slew of people milling about in the lobby. She had just a moment to let the energy of the crowd sharpen her senses before they noticed her presence and fell silent.

Several of them glanced from her in real life to the posters of her on the wall and then to each other as if to make sure everyone else saw the same thing. She scanned the faces turned toward her in a blend of surprise and expectation, as if somehow, she'd been the one to summon them. Aside from Kristie, who leaned against the back wall in her standard hockey jersey, everyone else wore whites with their club emblems on their knickers.

She recognized the crest of a local private university on several young men and a couple of women. She spotted a couple wearing the insignia of her own high school, one on a young woman who looked remarkably like one of her old teammates. A younger sibling? Her mind catalogued details even before she fully understood exactly how she intended to use them. A dark-haired woman by the desk wore the emblem of a world-class club in Rochester, while the two younger women and one lanky boy beside them looked to her for cues. A coach and three prized pupils. She met all their eyes in turn, not shying away from the questions there, but also refusing to answer them. It didn't matter that she didn't have any answers. She liked them thinking she did. Still, as she worked her way through the room, she found herself searching for the eyes she'd always sought when she entered this space, and finally found them as Lauren stepped through the door from the Elites' fencing gym.

She had her long hair pulled back in a low ponytail and wore her whites snugged all the way up to her chin. The high collar accentuated her regal bone structure and made the blues and greens of her eyes stand out against the otherwise stark palette. Jess wouldn't have thought it possible for her to be this sexy while wearing *more* clothes than usual. Things tended to work the other way around, but Lauren exuded a command that tinged the air with something electric.

She winked at Jess, sending a flutter through her stomach at the passage of something private between them. Then, squaring her shoulders, she let fly a sharp whistle.

Several people jumped, and a skitter of nervous laughter

rumbled through the room, but she cut an impressive-enough figure to captivate all the attention that had previously been centered on Jess. Lauren surveyed the crowd for a few seconds, her helmet tucked under her arm, and her hip cocked to the side with a confidently sullen stance.

"Welcome to fight night," she declared in a commanding voice. "You're all here because you belong here, and that's all I'm going to say about credentials or clubs."

She strode toward the center of the room and snagged a cell phone right out of the hand of one of the young coeds. She held it up for everyone to see, then dropped it into her helmet. "The first rule of fight night is 'no talking about fight night.'"

A few people exchanged nervous glances, but she continued, "I'm going to pass the hat, and everyone who wants to stay will hand over their phones. My friend Kristie won't be fencing today. She'll keep them safe until you're ready to collect them again on your way out. If you can't live with that, you're welcome to go now."

She paused for a beat as if waiting for an argument, but apparently no one in the room was moronic enough to challenge her authority, or at least their curiosity got the better of them, so, with a nod, she passed the helmet to the person next to her.

"We're here for open bouting. Standard rules, no refs, no replays, no whining." Lauren laid out her plans. "We'll break into groups across three gyms and run up the ladder. You win, you move up. You lose you go down a rung. The top rung is the center strip in the Elites' gym. You lose there, you go all the way back to the bottom of the pile and start climbing again."

Several people shifted in their seat as excitement grew, but only one of the young men was brave enough to ask the question on everyone's mind. Clearing his throat, he pointed to Jess. "What's she going to be doing?"

Lauren's smile spread. "She's going to stand atop the ladder and kick your ass all the way back down."

Jess grinned, her confidence rising like a hot-air balloon ready to take flight. She loved everything about this, but more than anything, she loved being a part of Lauren's plans. She wanted to throw logs on the fire Lauren had stoked. She wanted to prove herself worthy of this gift. "The first ass-kicking is free, the second one becomes a fundraiser for the club's new, big-screen TV."

"How much?" one of the older guys in an insignia from the home club asked.

She shrugged, doing the math on the fly. "Sliding scale. You can do a flat fee depending on what you can afford, or make a pledge per every point I land on you, but the stingier you are, the harder I'll stab you."

Kristie laughed in the back of the room. "If I were you, I'd pay generously."

She turned back to Lauren, checking to see if she had anything to add, but instead she found those eyes swirling with emotions she couldn't read. Pleasure? Surprise? Amusement? Maybe all of that and more.

"You heard the woman," Lauren finally called. "Let's go."

Lauren needed to make the rounds. She wanted to be a good hostess. She wanted to check on her younger fencers and see how they were holding up against the best the other clubs had to offer. She really should visit the other two gyms to make sure things were running as smoothly as they were at the upper level. Those spaces didn't have the electrical systems this one did, which would make them rife for disputes or outright conflict. She should be there to set a consistent tone. And yet as she patrolled the perimeter of the Elites' gym, she couldn't tear her eyes off the woman at the center of everything.

Jess flew through opponents one after another, slicing them up and making short work of the attacks that no doubt led to success with everyone else they'd ever faced. Challengers fell in droves, and the only time Jess ever took a break was when she worked too fast for her feeder strips and didn't have anyone else to face. Her dominance wasn't as surprising as the myriad of ways

117

she asserted it. She could beat anyone at their own game, meeting the men with raw power, and using finesse against the women. She fenced with gusto, blazing fast and blurringly complex against most of them, but as she stepped onto the strip against the top instructor in the region, she slowed, giving way to a cerebral element of paced counterattacks with textbook ripostes.

Lauren fought the urge to go a little swoony watching her work, and all those emotions only expanded when Jess would lift her helmet, shaking out her wild curls, and laugh in exultation. She was raw light and skill with an almost elemental charisma she could only process on a visceral level.

She must not have processed it well though, because as she took her next step, she walked right into a hockey jersey.

"Easy there, Juliet." Kristie caught her arm and kept her from wobbling into the path of two opposing fencers. "Don't get so absorbed in Romeo you walk right off your balcony."

She rolled her eyes at the absurdity of the allusion, but that didn't keep her face from flaming at its accuracy. "I'm not that bad."

"No, not at all." Kristie snorted. "I mean you may have drooled a little, but everyone is so absorbed in either their own swordplay or hers, I don't think anyone else noticed."

She let some of her embarrassment slip from her shoulders. "It's just so hard not to stare at her."

"Is it her chiseled chin? Those muscular shoulders? The epic ass that makes a person want to just grab and pull toward—"

"No." She couldn't let that line of imagery go any further if she wanted to save her brain from utter incineration. "I meant the way she fences."

"Oh," Kristie frowned. "I can't really tell what she's doing because she does it so much faster than everyone else. Honestly, they all look like they're just stabbing each other simultaneously. I don't know how you can even tell who won."

"You're not wrong." Lauren managed to set her lust on the back burner and slip into teaching mode. She'd spent years explaining this sport to people, and she felt a little rush of gratitude at being able to fall back on such a well-tread topic now. "Remember when I explained how the blade touching the metal in a fencer's lamé closes the electrical circuit and triggers the buzzer to signify someone had landed a touch?"

"Yes, Sparky, I remember getting lit up like a Christmas tree multiple times."

"In a one-sided matchup like yours, that's all you need. But in more competitive bouts, most of the time both fencers will land some kind of touch on a majority of their passes. If it's really blatant who got hit first, that can factor into points, but more often than not the decision comes down to priority, or who earns the right-of-way."

"Pedestrians have the right-of-way."

"Only in crosswalks, smart-ass, but you're not totally off base in connecting the rules of the strip to the rules of the road. There's an elaborate taxonomy, especially in saber, which allows hits from multiple parts of the weapon and gets blindingly fast," Lauren explained. "At the highest level of competition, there are at least two referees, one on the floor, and one on video review to help sort out the finer points in seemingly even attacks."

"Is there like a CliffsNotes version, something short of me having to earn a master's degree in fencing, but still lets me understand at least a little bit of who's winning?"

She nodded enthusiastically. "I've waited our whole friendship for you to ask that question."

"Don't get drunk on your new power. Give me the bare-bones basics."

"Okay, an attack is the easiest and most common method to establish right-of-way." Lauren turned to the center strip. "Watch Jess. It won't take more than a minute to see her attack."

As if on cue, Jess barely inched her feet in two quick steps before springing forward into a classic attack lunge. The other woman had no choice but to flail a bit as she fell back.

"See," Lauren continued, "it's not hard to tell there who's on the offensive and who's merely trying to fend them off."

Kristie let out a low whistle. "No shit. I take it the person who looked like she launched herself out of a cannon had right-of-way."

"Exactly. Another common factor would be if Jess had somehow missed."

"Not bloody likely in my experience," Kristie grumbled good-naturedly.

"But, just for the sake of argument, say she went for the big attack lunge and her opponent jumped out of range or sidestepped her saber. Right-of-way would shift. The same would be true if she blocked Jess's blade with her own, which is called a parry."

"I've heard of parries before," Kristie said excitedly. "Like thrust and parry."

"I'm going to ignore any jokes you're about to make about thrusting—"

"Oh, come on, not even one?"

"And move on to what comes after the parry, which is called a riposte. It's when you block your opponent's blade successfully and then hit them with yours, which generally gives you right-of-way, no matter which direction you're moving."

"I'm not listening anymore," Kristie admitted. "I'm still thinking about thrusting."

Lauren rolled her eyes but couldn't contain her smile. She'd have to keep making baby steps on conveying the finer details of the sport, but for the first time in a long time, she now had two friends in her life who would at least indulge the conversations to varying degrees. Tonight, that felt like an embarrassment of riches. She let herself soak up the glory of a full club.

Buzzers sounded all around them, people shouted in excitement or frustration, feet scuffed against the floor, and blades clanged in combat. She couldn't remember the last time she'd had this many people all working this hard across the entirety of the club. The heat of exertion permeated the air and the electricity in the room flowed from so much more than the electronic scoring system.

She'd missed this atmosphere more than she'd ever let herself admit over the last few years, and she suffered a little wave of fear that she shouldn't even admit it to herself now. None of this was permanent. They would all be gone in the morning, and when Jess left, many of them would not return.

Not like this, not en masse, not for her.

Jess roared above the crowd, pulling her from thoughts she was all too eager to release.

She turned to see her tuck her helmet under her left arm and bound forward with her hand extended to the young man she'd clearly just walloped. The poor guy, one of the protégées from the Rochester club, looked like he'd been put through the spin cycle on a washing machine, but Jess grabbed and shook his hand voraciously. "You were better on the counterattack this time."

"Was I?"

"Sure." She slapped him on the back. "Next time vary your foot speed, not just between different points, but within them. Don't ever let me get into a rhythm. If I can time your feet, I can time your lunge, and it only takes me about two steps to time your feet when you use the same pace the whole time."

The guy nodded sagely.

"Now go back to the bottom rung and practice on the way up, so you'll be ready next time."

He sagged. "I don't know if I have a next time in me."

"If you don't try, you'll regret it tomorrow," Jess said matter-of-factly, then turned away from him and shouted, "Next!"

One of the older college boys sprang forward, and she recognized him as Tommy Milton, who'd been the top fencer for a private school three years running. Jess must've recognized him from an earlier bout as well because she smiled broadly as he approached.

"Back for more beatings?" she taunted jovially. "What'll it cost you this time?"

"How about five bucks a point you land on me, minus what I land on you."

"So, that'll be $75," Jess asserted confidently. "You're not letting your mouth make a bet your blade can't cash, are you?"

Tommy held up a wad of money. "It's all my beer money for

two weeks, but this is better than any party I've ever been to in Buffalo, so why not?"

Jess laughed heartily. "Don't worry, I'll give you your money's worth."

And then she did. She teased and toyed and danced with him, drawing him in, then pushing him back the way a cat might play with a mouse before cutting it open.

Lauren had hoped the unpredictability of the less refined fencers might knock her off balance, and occasionally they seemed to do so for a point or two, but she only laughed and made such beautiful adjustments so quickly she would've appeared almost prophetic to an untrained observer. The same move never surprised her twice. She seemingly possessed an almost superhuman physical and mental recall.

Tommy might've actually kept up with her physically, but as Jess parried his blade time and time again, he faltered mentally much faster than athletically.

"It's like she can sense his next three moves when he can only react to hers." Kristie finally said, a hint of awe in her voice.

"She can." Lauren returned the sentiment, knowing enough of the nuances of the sport to add to her friend's observation. "She's playing chess. See how she just pulled him off balance? Now she's going to let him stumble right into her hand."

Tommy tried to surge forward, but in his eagerness he'd overextended. He had to jump back with renewed force in order to protect himself, and when he did, Jess charged, her feet scooting with speed that made the individual movements indiscernible and her trajectory reminiscent of a freight train. Tommy could only retreat and retreat and retreat, until he stepped all the way back off the piste. The move threw him even further out of control, and he had to drop his saber to catch himself on the back wall.

Then Jess lunged, the tip of her weapon hitting him square in the chest, pinning him upright and ending the fight entirely.

"Checkmate," Lauren whispered.

The poor guy looked visibly shaken, but to his credit he merely fished in his pocket, extracted the money, and held it out to her as if paying his own ransom.

Jess laughed, and Kristie joined her. She jogged over to relieve the boy of his cash and dropped it into the helmet she still carried with her.

"How much money do you need for the TV?" she asked as she rejoined Lauren once more.

"I have no idea."

"I thought this whole thing was your baby."

"It was," she said, then with a mystified smile added, "until Jess walked in. I didn't even tell her the plan beforehand. She arrived completely unaware, and yet she not only went with it, she took all of two minutes to raise the stakes."

Kristie grinned. "Sounds about on par for her. She lives just like she fences."

Lauren didn't respond. She didn't feel the need to add anything to the truth of the statement, but as she watched Jess jump deftly over another opponent's low lunge and bring her blade down across his shoulder, she couldn't help but wonder what chance that left her of resisting those qualities in any area of their relationship.

Jess downed a healthy swig of water and paced in a circle, trying to keep the lactic acid from settling into her muscles. "Next!"

"No next," Kristie called.

"What do you mean?" She inspected the connections between her cords and her saber hilt. "I'm ready to go again."

"You're out of opponents." Kristie punched Jess in the shoulder. "Well done. You sliced them all open until their blood and money both flowed like wine."

"Everyone's gone?" Jess glanced around the gym and then out to the lobby, but found the entire place empty.

"Yeah dude, you vanquished them, and they've all scattered to the winds."

"Ugh, sounds like someone has been watching *Vikings* again,"

Lauren said as she pushed back through the door, "but she's right. Even the boys from the college just crawled out of here."

"Already?" She blinked a few times and shook her head, wondering when she'd last been aware of her surroundings with any acuity.

"Already?" Kristie yawned. "It's almost one o'clock in the morning."

"What?" She laughed, then looked to Lauren for confirmation.

Lauren nodded as she leaned her shoulder up against a wall, but she didn't look any more tired than Jess felt. Her eyes still carried all the same color and focus they had when the night began, and Jess still found them absolutely fascinating.

"Not kidding, and not going to be able to stay awake much longer," Kristie confirmed. She held out the helmet she'd clung to all night. "Who wants the big bucket of money?"

Jess waived to Lauren. "It's hers. She earned it tonight."

Lauren laughed lightly. "I don't think we have the same definition of earning something, but I'll take it on behalf of the club."

"You did earn it," Jess protested. "This whole thing was your brainchild."

"All of it but the money."

"Hey!" Kristie cut back in. "How about you both earned it, and you both want it to go to the club."

"You're right." Lauren took the helmet and hugged her best friend. "You were awesome tonight. Thanks for all your help."

"Yeah, thank you," Jess added with a fist bump. "I'm glad you overcame your fear of women with swords enough to jump in on a fight night."

"I actually had a great time—" she yawned again "—but you crazy sword ladies wore me out. I want to stumble home and drag my sorry ass into my lonely bed."

"Go." Lauren stepped back.

"I'll call you tomorrow afternoon," Kristie called on her way out. "I wanna go TV shopping."

Lauren watched her leave, but Jess watched Lauren, the curve of her neck, the curl of her lips, the way her hair fell across her shoulders in a wave of contrast to the white jacket she'd allowed to loosen around her collar.

Lauren finally glanced back and caught her staring. "What are you thinking?"

"Don't ask questions you don't want the answer to."

"I do want to know."

"I was thinking about how beautiful you are in your whites. It was true when you were eighteen, and it's even more true today."

Lauren's breath caught audibly. "Jess . . ."

"You said you wanted to know."

"I thought you were thinking about fencing."

She gave a little shrug. "You and fencing have always been connected for me. Tonight didn't do anything to lessen the association."

"Tonight was really your idea," Lauren said. "You told Kristie about fight night and you just made it sound like it was your version of Christmas or your birthday party."

"It is. And you gave me the best present, one I didn't even know I needed." Her voice rose with the excitement buzzing through her. "I've been so focused on the work and the drills and the video review and the press requests, and I want to be good at all of it. I want it so bad I could scream, but I also just want to fight, you know?"

"It is a combat sport."

"It is!" She gave a little jump. "And there's ways to emulate parts of it, right? You can work your mind or your body or your technique in practice, but it's like stripping the parts off a robot to see how the individual gears turn. It's important to know about the pieces, but you can't see the sum of them until you put them all together. Tonight, you let me do that."

"I'm sorry I didn't offer you the chance sooner."

"Don't." She stepped closer. "Please don't apologize when I'm trying to thank you. You did a great thing, something you saw I needed before I did, and you provided it without asking. Let me be grateful."

"Okay." Lauren placed a hand on her shoulder and squeezed

125

tightly. "You're welcome. The pleasure was mine, though, really. I loved seeing the place full. I loved the atmosphere of excited people. I loved the passion you inspired in us all, and I loved watching you in your element. You were magnificent, and you earned your off day tomorrow, or well, I guess now it's today."

"Oh yeah, it's Sunday. We don't have to wake up early."

"We don't. And after the workout you had tonight, I hope you sleep long and hard."

That thought sounded amazing, and yet untenable given the rapid beat of her own pulse still pounding through her ears.

"What?"

"Nothing." She stepped back.

"Don't you pull away. You made me stop undercutting myself, now you owe me the same. Why did you make a face when I told you to sleep?"

"It's not a big deal. I'm just too amped right now. It'll wear off in a couple hours."

"A couple hours? I don't even know how you're still upright."

"It's not my body. It's my brain," she admitted. "As long as my mind has the ability to spin, it'll keep shooting adrenaline straight to my core. I'm used to it, happens every time I have a tournament that doesn't max me out mentally."

"What do you need?" Lauren asked, her eyes as soft as her voice.

"I'm fine."

"I want to help, Jess."

"Really. I'll be okay. You already did so much for me tonight, and it's late."

Lauren stepped closer again. "You asked me to be steady and firm. I promised I would. I'm not Cinderella. My promises don't turn into pumpkins at midnight."

She cracked a smile. "You're serious, aren't you? You really care about my wind-down?"

"I care about you. All of you."

The energy that had coursed through her for hours began to crackle. "Then fence me."

126

"What?"

"You against me."

"How will that help? You've been fencing for hours, and you're still raring to go."

"I told you. I haven't faced anyone who really challenged me mentally."

"What makes you think I'd be any different?"

"You've always made me think about things differently," she said sincerely. "Hell, you're the one who taught me to think this way in the first place, and you're still doing it. The video sessions with you push me in ways no other coach ever has. You're fundamentally different from anyone else I've ever worked with."

Lauren's cheeks flushed with either embarrassment or pride, but Jess didn't back down from the extravagant truth of her assessment.

"Give me a minute to think."

"Take all the time you need," Jess offered, then undercut the comment by bouncing up onto her tiptoes like an excited child.

"Different," Lauren mumbled. "Mentally exhausting, challenge, different, um, okay, okay, okay. Left-handed."

"What?"

"I'll fence you, but you have to fence left-handed."

She laughed. "I haven't tried to fence left-handed since high school, and even then, just as a joke."

"Good," Lauren picked up her helmet. "Maybe I stand a chance of wearing you out."

"Yeah, but I . . ." She stopped. Why was she arguing? Lauren had found a way to give her everything she asked her for and managed to inject a little fun into the exercise. "Actually, yeah, let's do this."

Jess had to grab a left-handed glove and jacket, then they both connected their lamés to the cords. They were back on the strip in no time, and her heart gave a little jump at the chance to stare into Lauren's dynamic eyes behind the mask one more time. They'd been working together night and day, but the intimacy of facing off competitively couldn't be replicated in another area, at least not one where they both remained fully clothed.

She smiled to herself and settled into her on guard position.

"Nope," Lauren said playfully.

"What? Oh." She grimaced and realized it had taken her less than a minute to forget she was doing this left-handed. She switched her saber to her other hand. For some reason, it felt heavier there, clunky and awkward.

"Now the feet," Lauren instructed.

She glanced down at her own sneaker-clad feet, the confusion taking a little longer to dispel this time.

"You can't lead with your right foot if you're attacking with your left hand."

"Huh," she made a little sound that combined her amusement with her awkwardness. "I didn't think this through."

"Therein lies the point. You'll have to think through things you've always taken for granted."

"I've faced tons of lefties. I know what it's supposed to look like," she said more to herself than to Lauren, but then she thought about the idea of brushing her teeth left-handed or signing her name left-handed and laughed again. "Why is this so complicated?"

"You're asking your brain to rewire itself. You'll have to work at it."

"And you're enjoying this already, aren't you?"

"Immensely," Lauren admitted with a grin. "Let's go."

Then she lunged, lightly tapping Jess with the tip of her saber.

"Hey, I wasn't ready."

"Ready now?"

"Um." She shifted the hilt in her hand, trying to convince herself her fingers weren't on the wrong side. "Maybe."

"Go," Lauren said, then swatted her effortlessly again.

"Gah!" she shouted. "I told my body to move, but it just didn't."

Lauren laughed. "This is fun."

"I'm not sure it is!"

Lauren paused just long enough for her to get back into a starting position before saying, "Go."

This time she didn't attack immediately. She reached out, flexing her wrist in a small motion, directly angled to Jess's center, and Jess managed to bat it away in a clumsy motion that took more effort and time than it should have. Still, a little pilot light of recognition flickered to life somewhere in the recesses of her brain. The click of their blades added another sensory cue for her to internalize, but then without thinking, she brought her right foot in front of her left.

The moment she literally stepped out of line, Lauren slapped her in the side and declared. "My point."

"Damn," she cursed, but there was laughter behind the frustration. "Okay, I'm getting better. Let's go again."

"Ready?" Lauren asked.

She settled back into the unfamiliar position.

"Go," Jess called on her own this time and immediately slid her left foot forward. The right one didn't step so much as drag behind her, but it was a genuine move in the right direction. She repeated the movement again, with slightly less friction, only passingly aware Lauren could've attacked seven times by now, but when she did, Jess was ready with another block.

"Oh, someone's a quick learner."

She sucked in a deep gulp of air and realized she'd been holding her breath as she tried to make her muscles obey new commands. Still, they had in fact obeyed, and Lauren's approval only bolstered her sense of purpose. "I've been told I've got good hands."

Lauren brought her saber around to swat her across the side of her helmet. "My point."

"What was that for?"

"For being cocky enough to talk smack while you're basically using training wheels."

She laughed and shook her head. "Not for long."

They reset one more time, and this time she'd already cued up her first couple of muscle memories. She pushed forward with

129

the left leg and extended her arm. While she missed, something about her position found a more instinctual mark.

"You almost looked natural," Lauren said, a new wariness in her tone.

"I told you, I'm quick." She demonstrated her point a few more times. The first improvements came with her hand, which took less effort to adjust than her footwork, but eventually that came around to something resembling actual competitive movement. Finally, she freed up enough head space to breathe, see, and lunge all at the same time.

"Oh, nice try," Lauren said as she barely managed to dodge an aggressive attack. Then she counterattacked, and Jess managed to parry before running out of plans. Lauren took a beat, then surged again, kicking up into an acrobatic lunge of her own. She caught Jess right under the sternum.

Jess growled. "If my brain could sweat, right now my skull would be drenched."

"Are you feeling fatigued yet?"

"I'm getting there, but don't think I'm so fried I didn't take note of your professional-grade attack."

"It's easier when your opponent is physically hobbled and mentally shot."

"Stop cutting yourself down," Jess said quickly. "Your lunge is beautiful."

Lauren shook her head. "I'm a little rusty."

"You're not. Or if you are, I don't want to face you polished. Your body was built for this. You're all long lines and lithe muscle. You're grace to my power."

"I wouldn't discount your grace. You're smooth, and not just in the way you're coming on to me right now."

"I'm not coming on to you," Jess said, then thought out the statement when perhaps she should've done those things in the opposite order. "I mean, maybe I am, but only because it's so natural. You've been magnificent today. How am I not supposed to be drawn to you?"

"You're supposed to keep fencing. First and foremost."

"What if the fencing only makes you more alluring?"

Lauren snorted softly. "Then I'll have to enforce some boundaries with the tip of my saber."

Jess's smile grew at the thought of anyone using a blade to hold her at bay, but she wouldn't win this point with her mouth, so she bent her knees and lifted her weapon. "Ready?"

Lauren mirrored her movements and said, "Go."

Jess sprang forward with enough raw force to knock Lauren back a couple of steps. She swung more than lunged, not trusting her feet to keep up with her desire. Lauren blocked her attack and countered with one of her own, but Jess merely reacted, which brought its own sort of victory.

She parried successfully, but Lauren gained the right-of-way quickly, and the tide shifted to surge behind her. Jess fell back, one step, two steps, three steps. She had to get a grip, or Lauren would have her against the wall in an instant.

"Shit," she muttered as she barely blocked the onslaught, but before she could regroup, Lauren nearly hit her on the riposte.

She had no choice but to stumble back as her footwork failed her again, but their proximity allowed her to clearly read a spark of something predatory flash through kaleidoscope eyes. Lauren wasn't just fencing. She was fighting. She scrambled and scraped, not against Jess but against herself. Lauren's motivations were so much more complex than her coaching style would allow her to admit. She was literally using her saber to hold them in check.

Was that really necessary? Lauren lunged again, indicating she seemed to think it was. This time, when Jess knocked her back, she didn't follow her, allowing some space to spread between them. If Lauren were merely trying to defend herself or her boundaries, she had nothing to fear from a distance, but she didn't accept the reprieve. She drew forward, closer, arm extended and eyes intense, in an emotional tug-of-war.

Jess repelled her once more, but again merely held her ground rather than giving or taking. She wouldn't push this woman. Not here, not now. Lauren would come for her or she wouldn't. Did she feel the heat as their bodies got close enough to clash? Letting an opponent into her space was a dangerous proposition, but Jess wasn't afraid of getting hit. A sense of certainty settled over her. This had never been a game, not for her, and never with Lauren.

Their blades crossed again, and this time instead of pushing her away, Jess softened her elbow, allowing Lauren to lean in. It wasn't a good fencing move, but at this point, the fencing was a mere metaphor. Lauren stayed both close and armed to a sharp point. The back-and-forth had all but disappeared as they fended each other off less fervently at close range, but neither of them were able or willing to end it.

Did Lauren want her to? Did she sense the stakes? Did she understand that breaking the plane between them would allow for a crack in the wall she fought to hold in place? Jess wanted to know the answer even more than she wanted to win, so she stepped back once more, drawing Lauren up against her even as the wall loomed at her back. How far would she go? Close enough to feel the brush of her breath through her mask? Close enough to see her pupils expand? Close enough to step across the line she'd drawn in the sand with her sword?

Close enough for the two of them to merely lean onto the sharp side of the blades between them?

Lights flashed and both sets of warning bells sounded as their bodies brushed together around the blades between them, but Jess could hardly hear anything over the sound of her own heartbeat. Keeping the weapons pinned harmlessly, she reached across the inches of electrically charged space and lifted Lauren's helmet. She let it clatter to the floor. Lauren didn't so much as tremble as she lifted Jess's mask in turn.

Then they collided in the only way they hadn't allowed for tonight.

Lauren's mouth met hers with all the force they'd failed to land with their sabers. Sharp, hot, strong, she let herself revel in the things she'd fought before surrendering. Shaking off gloves, they clutched one another, fists of knotted desire twisting jackets,

132

sleeves, and the sweat-dampened strands of hair cascading down Lauren's back.

Lauren's mouth tasted cool compared to the sweltering heat scorching Jess in every other part of her being, and she wanted to dive into that pool. She swept her tongue against her lips, and Lauren opened to her, inviting her in and urging her on. They stole each other's air, breathing out as the other breathed in. They broke away only far enough to send the blades pinned between them sliding to the floor, more connections to combat snapping as they began to move in concert.

Jess surged forward again, hungry to transition into a full-contact kind of sport, and Lauren absorbed the press of her body. Then Lauren took things a step further by taking an actual step forward, pinning Jess to the wall with the full weight of her need.

They didn't battle for position this time, both of them accepting the other and adding to the fire building between them. Lauren sucked Jess's bottom lip and raked her teeth across the slick skin before Jess slid to kiss the corner of her lip, her cheek, her jaw. Lauren exhaled and threw her head back, exposing the graceful arc of her throat. Cradling Lauren's head in her hands, Jess ran her tongue down to taste the salt of exertion and the sweetness of surrender all the way to the high collar of her jacket. So strange that she'd found this feature sexy earlier only to see it as a wasteful impediment now.

Her mind swam with the impulse to shred any barrier between them and a deep longing to make the most of every inch of skin already available to her before racing on toward more. The latter won out. Working back up her throat, Jess slid her tongue along the groove between neck and jaw all the way to Lauren's ear.

Lauren lifted her head again and inclined her chin to capture Jess's mouth once more. She moaned into the kiss and clung to Jess's hips with both hands, either to hold herself steady, or hold her close. Jess wouldn't complain about anything that ended with Lauren's fingers clutching any part of her, but the latter motivation was unwarranted, and the former might have involved some misplaced faith in her athletic ability. Sure, she'd been able to compete at an Olympic caliber for hours on end, but no one who'd stood opposite her tonight had Lauren's ability to turn her iron will into a molten puddle.

She felt like she may just slip right out of herself at the exquisite press of Lauren's mouth against hers. She could come undone for this woman. No, not *could* as in some hypothetical future. She was melting for her right now. Ready and willing to lose herself, her dreams, her plans, her purpose, too, if only this kiss would never end.

The thought worked its way into her muddled brain, trying to clang a cymbal of alarm, but it sounded dull and small amid all the other sensations vying for control of her synapses.

Lauren was kissing her.

Lauren.

Her breath caught sharply as the realization flashed white behind her eyelids, and she fluttered them open.

"What is it?" Lauren mumbled against her mouth.

"You." It was the only thought she could muster.

Her lips curled as she kissed her cheek. "Me?"

"Yes." The word sounded plaintive, both affirmation and plea. "Lauren."

"Jess," Lauren whispered, then slowed, "oh Jess."

Her chest tightened. She'd waited so much of her life to hear her own name on Lauren's lips like this, and yet she also heard the echoes of the past curling up from their collective memory, poised to drag them back.

Lauren rested her forehead on Jess's and sighed dreamily.

"This is going to complicate things, isn't it?" Jess asked.

She nodded slightly. "Undoubtedly."

"Can we add it to the pile of things we're going to have to talk about eventually, but not tonight?"

"That list is getting long."

She didn't try to argue. "Too long to start on at two o'clock on a Sunday morning."

Lauren pressed her lips together, then quickly pressed them to Jess's before she stepped back. "Fair point."

"I'm glad I managed to score at least one tonight."

Lauren shook her head and smiled. "I think you scored a couple of pretty big ones."

The sweet, dreamy, playful tone of the comment defused the tension that had been building in her since the kiss, and she managed to find her grin again. "Yeah, I guess I won all the ones that really mattered for the moment."

Chapter Seven

"Are you sure this is the one?" Lauren asked as she stared at the mammoth television on the showroom floor. She and Kristie had been to four different stores, examined at least twenty-five TVs, and compared hundreds of specs, but she still wasn't certain what mattered most in the abstract triangle of size, resolution, and price. At least her budget was finite, and not meager. Jess had raked in a boatload of cash, and Lauren suspected she might have thrown in her own contribution as well. Still, she wanted something big enough to be seen clearly from anywhere in the lobby, and yet high definition enough to show the minute movement of Olympic-caliber fencing.

"I think it's more than big enough for the space you have, and the resolution is bangin'."

She surveyed the screen once more and couldn't argue about the picture quality. The television currently showed a tennis match, and the image was so clear she could make out individual beads of sweat on Destiny Larsen's face.

"Okay. Yeah." She turned to the young salesman "We'll take this one."

He clapped his hands together, no doubt feeling the thrill of his commission. "Awesome. I'll have them bring one out to your car while I get you rung up at the register. Are you interested in signing up for our in-store Visa card today?"

"No, we've got cash." As if to prove her point, she fished the large wad of bills from the shoulder bag she'd clung tightly to all day long.

The salesman's eyebrows shot up, but he managed to exert enough professionalism not to comment. Lord only knew what he thought as he scanned the TV tag and counted out the bills into the register. He probably suspected illegal activity, and she thought about offering up the truth, but she wasn't sure if explaining they'd won it all at a secret midnight sword-fighting ring would've helped the situation.

So, she merely laid down some extra cash for the extended warranty and accident protection plan without specifying she needed protection from preteens with a variety of sharp weapons.

Then, she and Kristie walked out to the parking lot to supervise the two store employees who were loading their new behemoth into the back of Kristie's Subaru Forester.

"Wow," Lauren said, "even with two guys pushing, they can barely get it into your trunk."

Kristie snickered. "That's what she said."

Lauren rolled her eyes.

"Come on." Kristie bumped her shoulder. "That's a good one."

"I set you up well enough."

"And I appreciate your contribution," Kristie said as the guys closed the trunk and gave them the thumbs up.

They climbed inside and glanced back at their purchase, then at each other. Kristie smiled broadly, but Lauren only managed a nod of satisfaction.

"Okay," Kristie said seriously. "What gives?"

"Nothing. Let's get it back to the club."

"No, come on. You should be happier about this."

"I am happy."

"Only in the restrained, businessy, one-more-thing-checked-off-your-to-do-list sort of way, not in the 'Holy fuck, I'm one step closer to building my dream club' sort of way."

She sighed. "I'm under a lot of pressure."

"Yeah, and you're living up to it. You're training the shit out of an Olympian, you're upping the profile of the club, you're flush with cash for new tech. You're winning every one of your responsibilities."

The last declaration twisted like a tiny knife in her chest. "Maybe not all of them."

Kristie eyed her suspiciously. "What don't I know about?"

"Something happened after you left last night."

"Something awesome, or something awful?"

"Maybe both." She grimaced. "Probably both."

"Spill," Kristie commanded.

"I kissed her."

There, she'd said it. Not the whole story, but certainly the whole truth, because nothing that happened before or after carried the same weight as the moment when she pressed her lips to Jess's.

"Wow," Kristie finally said. "You kissed her. Not the other way around?"

She nodded.

"I'm going to need you to tell me all the things."

She opened her mouth, but she didn't even know where to start. She couldn't possibly explain to someone else what it did to her to watch Jess work, grow, respond to every challenge she had to give, all while looking at her as if she were some sort of stunning superhero.

Thankfully, she didn't have to, because the shrill ring of her phone shattered her haze. Without even checking the caller ID, she snatched it up and accepted the call, absolutely ready to buy whatever the person on the other end of the line was selling.

"Hello?"

"Hello, is this Ms. Lauren Standish?"

"Yes. May I ask who's calling?"

"Hello Ms. Standish, this is Abbey Handler from NBC Sports. I'm calling because the network is doing a story on the youngest Olympic athletes in their various sports, and we heard Jess Kidman is currently working out at your club."

Jess had told her there might be requests for press. That didn't mean she knew how much she was supposed to give away. "She is."

"And we're told the two of you were teammates back in high school."

"We were."

"This is really perfect for our angle." The woman oozed excitement.

"What angle is that?"

"We'd love to come visit the week after next and get some shots of your facilities and the training routines, sort of a before segment to contrast those humble beginnings with some footage we will shoot at the games and maybe, if all goes well, a follow-up piece about how Ms. Kidman's success and higher profile changed her life."

"Oh." Lauren said. Not her most articulate response, but it was all she could manage around the tightening in her throat.

"Would it be okay if we came mid-week, with one reporter and one cameraperson? We'd love to spend a few hours shooting video and chatting with you and any other coaches or former teammates who will be able to talk about knowing Ms. Kidman before she got famous."

"Sure. That'd be great." She managed to say the words, but failed to inject the corresponding emotions into her voice.

"Thank you. We'll be in touch when we make our travel plans."

"Thanks." She ended the call and turned to Kristie. "It was NBC Sports."

"Are you serious?"

She nodded.

"Holy fuck, my best friend gets calls from NBC Sports."

"Not because of anything I've done. They want to talk to someone who knew Jess in her humble beginnings, so they can contrast that during the games when she leaves all of this behind."

"Oh," Kristie got the point. "I take it now isn't a great time to go back to talking about the kiss?"

She shook her head.

"Okay, fine. I'll drop it as soon as you just confirm it was a good kiss."

She leaned her head back on the seat of the car and stared up at the roof. "So much better than good. It was amazing, mind melting, and, and I don't even know what comes after mind melting, but whatever it is, the kiss was that."

"Wow. So, she's everything she appears to be and more?"

"So much more. I just can't resist her. I tried. God, I tried, but I barely made it two weeks without falling into her. And I would've just kept on falling last night if she hadn't pulled back and looked at me with those deep blue eyes and whispered my name with the same reverence she had when she was thirteen years old."

Kristie winced. "Oh no."

"Yeah. It just reminded me of all the things I've promised her, then and now."

"Okay, the 'now' stuff is valid, but I'm not sure the 'back then' stuff needs to surge up again. You know she's not a kid anymore."

"No, she made that abundantly clear with the contrast she provided last night. She kissed me when she was thirteen, and this was definitely different. She's a full-grown woman with all the skills and the talents she always wanted to develop."

Kristie slapped the steering wheel. "That's very good."

Lauren rolled her head to the side in a little swoon. "So. Very. Good. Like, by-far-the-best-I've-ever-had good, which is very, very bad."

"Is it, though?"

"Yes!" she shouted. "She asked me to be steady and stable. I do not feel either of those things right now. What am I even doing with her?"

"I think that's up to you."

"I'm not sure it is. I want to be a good friend. I was willing to be a coach if that's what she needed, or at least try anyway."

"And you are." Kristie pushed back excitedly. "I'm not even a fencer, but fight night was amazeballs. You put her in her element.

140

You challenged her and affirmed her, and she was so damn happy. You said she hasn't been happy with a coach in a long time."

"Because she didn't trust them. They pinned their own desires on her. They made her bend to their will."

Kristie laughed. "I can't imagine anyone being able to railroad her. How'd that work out for them?"

"Not great. And I promised I wouldn't do the same thing," she said. "I also knew I couldn't push her physically. I needed to capitalize on this energy between us, so I tried to walk this line between professional and personal motivation. I let her get too close. I told myself I could play this game that would keep her on edge without letting her fall, but then *I* fell."

"You didn't fall."

"I did. And hard. One minute, I'm trying to push her mentally, then I was pushing her technically, and then I'd pushed her up against the wall."

"Hot."

"Yeah, it was, and if she were some woman I'd met at another club or a competition, I would've let her sweep me right off my feet." She shuddered at the memory of Jess's hands on her body and how she'd ached to feel them on her skin. "I was that far gone, but this isn't some woman. This is Jess."

Kristie held up her hand as if asking the teacher for permission to speak.

"What?"

"I'd like to point out Jess is a woman."

"You know what I mean."

"I'm not sure I do."

"I have a responsibility to her." Her voice cracked a little under the weight of that burden.

Kristie's eyes softened. "You have a shared responsibility to each other."

"It's not equal. It's never going to be equal." Her heart gave a dull throb. "She looks at me like I'm some kind of miracle, but sooner or later she's going to realize I'm just ordinary."

"Come on, don't undercut yourself."

"She said the same thing, but I'm not beating myself up. I'm really proud of the things I've learned and accomplished in a couple of whirlwind weeks. I'm thrilled with how fight night turned out. I love having a ginormous TV in the back of the car right now. I love that there's going to be an NBC video crew visiting the club, and I'm going to make the most of everything I can, but I can't let myself be deluded into thinking any of this will last past July, because it just won't. This isn't my life. It's hers and she's going to move on."

"Have you told her any of that?"

"No!"

"Why?"

"Because I can't let this moment be about me and my needs or fears. I can't let her even think about anything other than the Olympics. I promised to keep her focused and centered." She sighed as the energy started to leech out of her. "I care about her too much to let her burden herself with promises that will encumber a life she can't even imagine yet."

"What makes you think she can't imagine it?" Kristie asked, a new seriousness to her tone.

"You said it yourself, she lives like she fences." She laughed a little at the image, though she didn't find the implications funny. "When she wants something, she charges in full force, but she doesn't think about what happens after she wins. She lives for the next fight. She's not the kind of person who settles down with the white picket fence and teaches kids' classes at the local gym. If I tried to make her that person, then she'd end up bored and restless and resenting me the same way she resented all the coaches who tried to rein her in."

Kristie stared at her, biting her lip as if trying to hold something in. Kristie wasn't exactly known for her restraint, so if she was actively trying not to say something, it must've been bad. But the thought of something that bad could only lead to one place, and she struggled to fend off the realization even as it formed.

"This isn't about my dad."

142

Kristie's mouth twisted.

"It's not."

Kristie raised her hands in surrender. "I didn't say it was."

"But you thought it."

"And you haven't?"

"No," she said honestly, but now she wondered why.

She'd danced all around it ever since Jess had returned. All the fears about not being able to keep up, the ways she'd clung to the lack of permanence as her main defense, the ways she'd held her heart back, guarding it even at the point of a sword for as long as she could. Those were all lessons learned though trauma.

She hadn't thought about it because she hadn't let herself. But just like the kiss had broken down some wall she wasn't sure she was capable of rebuilding, this realization released something wildly uncontrollable inside her. She pressed her hands to her eyes and tried to take deep, soothing breaths. She could calm down. She could find her feet and put one of them in front of the other. She could pack up all those horrible thoughts and heartbreaks and put them in with all the other burdens she'd learned to carry, but she could never, ever set them fully aside.

She knew those things in the deepest part of her consciousness. What she didn't know was where that left her and Jess.

Jess resisted every urge to text or call Lauren on Sunday, and the will not to act actually took more out of her than any workout ever had. Still, as she arrived at the club on Monday morning, she wasn't as eager to burst through the doors as she would've thought.

There were big conversations ahead. Lauren had made that clear on multiple occasions and multiple topics, all of which seemed to carry a Monday deadline. They had to return to the video session she'd set aside. She didn't like it, but she got it, and she'd had enough time to refortify her emotions, right up to the point Lauren had kissed her. Then every ounce of fortitude fizzled and fried. Her brain and heart immediately diverted all their resources to processing every detail of Lauren's body against hers. She didn't delude herself into thinking that conversation would be easy either. She'd seen the worry in Lauren's eyes when they broke apart, and on some level, she shared those concerns, but with their chemistry, a shared desire to make it work, and an iron will to face whatever came head on, she felt relatively certain she could handle that conversation today.

What she couldn't do with the same self-assuredness was have both conversations at once, *and* train at a high level, *and* respect whatever boundaries Lauren would surely try to set while preparing to face a press onslaught. Something would have to give, and she hated concessions with the same passion she hated to lose a point on the strip.

With that happy thought, she pushed through the front door and glanced around. Lauren wasn't waiting there for her, but she still had all the video equipment out on the desk as a reminder of things to come. Jess wandered down the hall and pushed open the door to the locker room, finding it empty as well. Leaving her bag behind, she headed for the big gym and pushed open the door to find Lauren already sitting on her yoga mat. She'd crossed her legs and rested a hand atop each knee. Eyes closed, lips parted, the beauty of her serene features stole Jess's breath from her lungs.

The want lanced through her, hot, sharp, and tasting of metal. She'd known desire before, and she'd bowed to lust more times than she cared to remember, but the feelings surging in her now commanded all her senses and curled into her core. She wanted this woman in a way she'd never wanted anything in her life, and not just physically. She wanted to be close to her in every way, to soak up the warmth and peace she exuded and to offer her something in return, but in the face of her splendor she wasn't at all sure what that would be.

As if she sensed Jess's need, Lauren's eyes fluttered open, bright and more blue than green in this moment.

"Good morning," she said with a subtle smile. "Care to join me in my mindfulness exercises?"

"Sure." Mindfulness exercises weren't exactly her favorite, but she didn't hate them, and even if she had, she still would've said yes to an offer to join Lauren in almost anything that fell short of a murder-suicide pact.

Taking the same position on her own mat, she timed a few deep, even breaths to settle in, and tried to bring her emotional levels closer to a normal functioning range before turning to Lauren. "What are we visualizing today?"

"Let's start with an easy one. How about you on the podium six weeks from now."

Jess chuckled. "An Olympic medal is your idea of an easy jumping-off point? Sure, makes sense coming from you."

"Me? I meant easy for you to visualize, because I assumed you'd been doing it your whole life."

"Not my whole life, only since I was thirteen."

"When you made the varsity team?"

She shook her head and closed her eyes, not picturing the podium, but rather the moment she'd begun to chase it. The memory always came shrouded in the blue light of the pool. She shivered as the cold pricked at her submerged feet, and her chest tightened with the tension born of emotions still every bit as conflicted as they'd been that night. "I didn't start dreaming of the podium until you told me to."

Lauren drew in a sharp breath, but Jess didn't open her eyes to check her expression. She was still deep in her daydream.

"You had your hair in a messy bun, but the shorter strands in the front had all fallen down, and your lips were a little darker than usual because you'd had a bit of the punch before you settled on Cherry Coke instead."

"How do you remember that?"

"Because I've relived it a million times. When you pulled away from me, you pulled my heart on a string along behind you, and right out of my chest."

"Jess."

She kept completely still and entrenched in the visualization. "But when you said I could come back for you when I made the

Olympic team, you handed my heart back to me. You gave me something to patch it into place until I was ready to hand it off again."

She took a deep breath in through her nose and held it, stretching her lungs and pressing out from her chest until the image changed. This time she stood atop a white box and bowed her head for someone to slip a ribbon around her neck. She could feel the weight of the medal tugging as she rose again, but in the dreams, she never looked down to check its color. Instead, she scanned the generic faces in the crowd, all of them blurry and nondescript, always empty and aimless in their stares, only this time, she broke the trend and the trance by opening her eyes and meeting the ones she'd always searched for.

Lauren stared at her, a haze of gold now mixing with the green in her gaze. "We need to talk."

In her voice, Jess heard all the kindness and patience that had haunted her for years. Lauren wasn't meeting her in the middle like an equal. She was rising above. She was taking the high road and exerting all the nobility of her nature. Jess's stomach roiled the same way it had the first time she'd heard the tone. She couldn't take it again. Not after all the years, not after all the work, and certainly not after the way Lauren had kissed her over the weekend. She wasn't a kid anymore, and she refused to sit helplessly while Lauren issued the gentle brush-off clearly poised on her lips.

"Actually, I wanted to talk to you, too." She interrupted, not because she'd thought through what came next, but because she simply couldn't accept what Lauren thought should come next.

"Oh?"

"Yeah." She stalled, trying to give her mind time to process something other than the pain of her first heartbreak. She pressed the heel of her hand to her chest as if she could somehow hold her heart in place this time. God, why did it have to still feel this way? Why couldn't she find another way? Or at least hold onto the way she'd sustained herself for years.

She nodded as the thought took root. She was so close to the pinnacle she'd promised to reach for this woman. That path led her back here, and kept her here, but the same path also pulled her forward. Lauren had set her feet on it in the first place. She wouldn't push her off it now, not for any reason, even the boundaries they both failed to enforce. "I have some fencing stuff I need to do."

Lauren's eyebrows shot up. "Fencing stuff?"

She grimaced. Okay, so maybe not her most articulate redirect, but it had at least drawn Lauren's attention away from whatever heavy verdict she'd been poised to deliver. "I have to take a couple of days and go back to New York for some things."

"Fencing things?" Lauren asked, a hint of amusement in her voice.

"Actually, yes. Meetings, and Team USA scheduling . . . um scheduling . . . official press stuff, and oh, sponsors."

Lauren pressed her lips together as she rambled, but Jess kept on digging until she hit something that felt a little like solid ground. "I have to make an appearance with a couple of sponsors and maybe pick up one or two new ones."

Lauren's expression screamed skepticism. "I didn't know fencing sponsors were even a thing."

Jess laughed a little squeak of a sound. "Yeah, well they don't exactly pay the bills, okay? But I've done some ads for a neighborhood gym, and I've done some modeling jobs for a small sportswear company you've probably never heard of."

"Modeling?" Lauren asked, then let her eyes drift unapologetically over Jess's body before nodding. "Okay, seems legit."

Jess's face warmed under the blatant appraisal, and it took everything she had not to lean forward and capture Lauren's mouth once more. She suspected she'd get away with doing so for a few minutes that would ultimately lead her back to the conversation she was scrambling to avoid.

"Besides"—she forced herself to push forward—"my stipend ends after the games. I need to drum up some good press beforehand if I want to make enough money to cover my travel and still eat."

Lauren wavered. "I know enough to know they don't pay you a living wage."

She snorted. "They don't even pay me enough to cover my basic fencing expenses. I'm lucky my family has the means to help me, but I'd rather not live in my parents' basement until I retire."

Lauren finally cracked a little smile, even as she shook her head. "The timing's not great for your training regimen."

"I know, and I hate that," she admitted, trying to cling to the excuses she was currently feeding them both instead of the fear that gripped her moments earlier. "But the sports world only pays a sliver of attention to fencing once every four years, so if I want to drum up any sort of press, now is pretty much my only chance."

Lauren's smile grew grudgingly. "I assume you also got a call from NBC Sports this weekend?"

She nodded. "And one from *Teen Vogue*."

"*Teen Vogue*?" A hint of amusement crept into her voice.

"Hey now," Jess cut her off. "*Teen Vogue* is a political force, and it's not just for teenagers. They've done feature stories on politicians and environmentalists and Serena Williams, and—"

"Okay." Lauren returned to her placating tone. "I wasn't knocking *Teen Vogue*. I just never thought of you in a fashion magazine."

"They're doing a story on queer and feminist athletes." Jess tried not to sound too defensive. "But I could totally pull off a fashion spread."

"I know you could," Lauren said quickly. "Apparently you already have modeling experience I didn't know about, but just like I told you when I took this job, I want you to do all the things and live all your dreams. I just want you to also fence at your highest level, and I don't want anything to get in your way."

"Oh." Jess heard the hint of their original topic creep back in. "Nothing's distracting me from fencing."

Lauren stared at her as if trying to decide how much further to push her point.

"I promise," she said solemnly.

"How long will you be gone?"

She tried not to let her uncertainty show. She hadn't actually thought any of this through before starting the conversation. "I should probably head out tomorrow. I can work out in my normal gym and do some bouts with Haley, then fly back on Sunday so I don't miss another workout."

"We'll only have a couple of days of legitimate training before the camera crew comes to town."

"Then we'll have to buckle down and really focus for those two days."

Lauren seemed to think for a few seconds before she nodded. "Okay. I trust you. How can I help?"

"I'd hoped to have the new big-screen TV on the wall today, but apparently we need a stud finder and construction-grade screws for the mount."

Jess grinned. "Well, now, that sounds epic. I can't wait to see it when I get back to town."

"Kristie's already planning our Olympic viewing party for when you compete, but it'll be nice to have all our video sessions in high definition from here on out."

Jess grimaced.

"What?"

"About today's video session . . ."

Lauren read her expression just as she noticed the gym bag slung over her shoulder. "No."

"I'm sorry."

"You can't buzz out on this, Jess. I know you're afraid of what I'm about to see."

"I'm not afraid," Jess snapped as a flicker of fire flashed through her eyes, but she doused it before Lauren got to see how it would spread. "I mean, I've seen it all before, multiple times, and I've still got so much to do before I leave tomorrow morning. I'm also going to miss leg day while I'm traveling, and yesterday was an off day. I really need an extra gym session more than I need to see the same video for the hundredth time."

"But I haven't seen it."

"Go ahead without me."

"I want to see it *with* you," Lauren pushed. "I don't want to have to guess what you're feeling."

Jess gave a bitter laugh. "Don't worry. I made my feelings abundantly clear. Honestly, it's probably better for you to watch it alone first. You can see it with clear eyes. I can't."

"But, I can't do anything with my observations if you're not willing to stay present and engage with me."

"I promise I want to hear all of your observations, and I'll engage them with everything I have in me after I come back."

She pursed her lips, not knowing what to do. Her instincts told her Jess was running away from something and had been all morning, but she didn't know enough about the upper echelons of international fencing to be sure. She hated not knowing enough to call bullshit on this sudden trip back to New York. She also hated the way a part of her was grateful for the cognitive and physical distance it would offer. All the different instincts warred within her, and in her indecision, she deferred to Jess. "Okay. We'll talk about it when you get back."

"Thanks." Jess took two steps toward the door before stopping to meet her eyes one more time.

"What is it?" she asked, a hint of hope rising in her chest.

"It's um, nothing." She shook her head. "I mean, it's not nothing. It's just . . . I know I'm not always easy to work with."

Her heart melted a little. "You're not, but you're worth it."

Her smile turned a little shy, and the kid who'd had her heart broken showed through for just a second. "Could I, I mean, would you like me to text you or something, when I'm in the city?"

"If you're not too busy taking the place by storm." Lauren smiled in spite of all the emotions still tugging at her core. "I'd love to hear how things are going."

Jess nodded, then glanced at the door and back to her as if she didn't quite want to go but wasn't ready to stay. Lauren knew the battle well, but she wouldn't let her stay for the wrong reason, so she injected a little pep into her voice and said, "See you next week."

"Yeah." Jess's forced smile didn't reach her eyes. "See you soon." Then she was gone.

Lauren sat in the silence. She'd worked alone in this club every afternoon for more than five years without feeling lonely. There was no logical reason for her to do so now. Jess hadn't even been back in her life for a full three weeks. Surely that wasn't long enough to feel like a fixture. No, nothing about Jess's presence ever felt fixed, and her abrupt departure offered the most fitting reminder of how temporary this all was. They had a finite amount of time together and a very specific job to do. She'd actually started today planning to remind Jess of that very idea. She smiled at the way Jess had turned her own talk back on her. She shouldn't have been surprised. Jess always stayed two or three steps ahead of everyone else in the room.

With that thought, she turned toward the video equipment in front of her. At least the reprieve would allow her to catch up with Jess in a few key areas while she was out of town.

She pressed play on the video they'd paused last week and watched the coverage switch to the semifinals at worlds.

Jess stepped onto the strip to the right of the screen, and at the other end, Yelena Finko strode confidently into place. They went through the obligatory introduction speech from the floor referee, then took their positions.

Much like the previous matches, both women launched fast and ferocious, each trying to establish dominance, but unlike the other bouts, Jess didn't win all of those early forays. She was still faster out of the box, but Yelena's counterattack wasn't as easily rebuffed.

After a couple of attempts, Jess changed gears and parried before she let herself lunge. The defensive track worked the first time, then not again, and Yelena scored three points in quick succession.

Every part of Jess's demeanor changed. She curled in on herself. She wasn't roaring or raving the way she had against Haley. She kept her helmet on. She rolled her shoulders and hung her head. Then she shook out her limbs and set her feet again.

This time, she tried to push Yelena back in a measured advance. They extended the point with a flurry of blocks and ripostes before Jess kicked forward into the most beautiful lunge, but in the second before her front foot landed, Yelena struck her in the arm with the tip of her saber. Jess didn't even land a touch.

There was no reason Jess should've lost the point. She was faster, she was smarter, and her technical form was infinitely superior. Jess knew it, too, as she hopped up and stalked down the strip. She grumbled loudly now, and began to gesture with her free hand, though she didn't seem to be talking to anyone other than herself.

She reset and went again, much to the same result. This time she didn't even get her front foot off the ground on the lunge before she got hit on her sword arm, and the touch finally drew the scream she'd clearly been holding in. She jumped and came down hard, smacking her saber against the ground, earning her a comment from the ref. Lauren didn't know if she should feel the burn of empathy from seeing Jess lose her mind, or if her hope should rebound at the display of the fight still burning in her.

They reset and clashed again, and this time it was like the two of them had choreographed the fight scene together and mutually agreed Yelena would win. She moved in a perfect mirror to Jess's attack, anticipating her at every step to the point where she almost came across as omniscient or at least psychic.

Jess tried everything, every strategy, every attack in the book, and she executed every one of them to perfection. She wasn't melting down. She was upset, but she wasn't falling apart. If anything, she became more textbook in her approach. She still fought with a flurry of skill and grace most fencers would kill for, but the more measured and meticulous Jess became, the more anticipatory Yelena's reactions seemed.

Until finally Jess lost it. Out of options and out of her mind, she went into a full freak-out mode that made her match with Haley look like a ballet. She raged, growing wild and erratic for a few points. She managed to land a couple of points before Yelena caught up to some unseen pattern in her madness and met her brutality with deft counterattacks akin to swatting away an aggressive insect. The last blow came straight to her chest with enough force to kick Jess back a few steps.

Lauren winced at both the hit and the way Jess sagged. As she finally took off her helmet and accepted a drink of water, her beautiful facial features were dark and sullen in a way she'd never seen before. It was almost like Jess wasn't even behind those familiar eyes. She wiped the back of her hand across chapped lips, and as the camera zoomed in on her, Lauren thought she saw her fingers tremble.

It didn't make sense.

None of this made sense. It might have been understandable if Jess had shown herself to be a sore loser. Lauren might be able to write off the lack of confidence, the extinguished fire, the emptiness behind usually bright eyes. But the woman on the screen wasn't the woman who'd refused to take points she hadn't earned in her previous match. She wasn't the woman who cheered when Kristie scored her first point at her expense or the woman who effusively praised any fencer who scored a point on her on Saturday night. Most painfully, she wasn't the woman who'd taken a drubbing left-handed with a growth mindset so beautiful, it drove Lauren to break every boundary between them.

Jess had lost plenty of tournaments over the years, and she'd lost more than a handful of points in each match leading to this one. None of them had broken her. Why had other opponents fueled her fire to improve while this fight with Yelena extinguished it?

She watched the last few points again, struggling against her own desire to take Jess into her arms, to hold her, to shake her, to beg her to go back to being that brash and brazen competitor who burned with righteous indignation against Haley.

Then the contrast hit her.

When they'd watched the last match, Jess said the only thing worse than being mentally faster than her physical skill was the other way around.

Lauren had responded that Jess was too smart for her own sanity, but as she rewatched the end of the slaughter, she realized that's exactly what she'd witnessed. Jess was the stronger fencer physically, technically, and reflexively, but The Kid who'd burned through anyone who ever stood in her way was getting burned mentally for the first time in her life.

"The prodigal returns," Haley declared as Jess pushed through the door to the gym where they trained. The place smelled of sweat and the bagel shop below it on the street level. A couple of people looked up from the varied chaos of cardio machines, but none of them held her interest other than her best friend, who vaulted off a stationary bike at the sight of her.

Jess threw her arms wide. "Tell me how much you've missed me."

"Dude, so fucking much." Haley wrapped her in a hug and squeezed her so hard one of her vertebrae gave a happy little pop of relief. "This place has been so boring without you."

"Ha! You're the only person who could find the city that never sleeps boring."

"Well, it's not like I've seen the city lately. Without you here to drag me out, I've been to the gym, the club, and my own bed."

"Alone?" Jess pulled back and arched an eyebrow.

Haley cracked a smile. "Mostly."

She gave her a playful shove. "I thought so."

"No, seriously though, it's been almost entirely all work and very little play. Everyone's pushing here. There's no joy in Mudville. Everyone's tense, everyone's putting in the extra hours, everyone's ready to snap. They think Oren might have given himself a stress fracture."

154

She grimaced at both the injury and the impact it could have for the top male foil fencer this close to the games.

"Oh, and Ansel's here, always."

"You could've led with that, and then you wouldn't have had to tell me anything about anyone's stress levels." She glanced over her shoulder to make sure the Team USA coach wasn't actually within earshot. "Is it too late for me to shuffle back to Buffalo?"

"No." Haley grabbed her around the wrist. "Don't ever go back to Buffalo. Don't leave me here alone."

She laughed. "I'm here until Sunday, so you better get your fill of me before then."

"Seriously?" Haley stared at her with dark eyes, not quite able to hide the shadows of abandonment and betrayal. "You're not going to finish up training here with us?"

"I can't. I don't have a coach here."

"I told you Ansel's here now."

"Ansel's an asshole."

"But he's our asshole."

"No, he's *your* asshole." She shook her head. "I'll work with him for the team competition, but Lauren's my personal coach for right now."

"Then why did you leave her back in Buffalo to come here five weeks out from the games?"

She sighed. "It's complicated."

"Uh-oh," Haley said, "I'm going to need this story."

"I'm not sure I can tell it in an orderly fashion."

"Then let's get on the treadmills and you can tell it in a disorderly fashion."

She nodded slowly. She hadn't intended to dump all her conflicting emotions about Lauren on her friend, who was under every bit as much pressure, but at least Haley understood the stakes in a way few others did. "Yeah, I think I might need that."

"Okay, then toss your stuff in your locker, and—"

"Kidman!" A voice boomed from across the room.

"Shit," she whispered before plastering the politest smile she could muster on her face, and turning toward the coach. "Hello, Ansel."

"Where have you been?" he demanded as he wove his way between treadmills and ellipticals, his shoulder-length blonde hair wafting on the breeze of his blustery approach.

"Um, Buffalo."

"Why?"

"Because I train there."

"Why?"

"Because my coach lives there."

His blonde eyebrows furrowed together. "There are no internationally qualified coaches in Buffalo."

"I'd argue with you, but we both know how well that ends, so let's skip to the part where we go on about our own business."

He frowned. "Fine, but your coach is my business at least a little bit if he'll be traveling with the Team USA contingent to the games."

"Why, did you all have a sudden change of heart and decide to pay for everyone?"

He laughed as if she'd just made a legitimately funny joke instead of landing a little dig. "We have a limited number of floor passes for the individual competition rounds. If your coach isn't approved by our various Olympic committees far enough in advance, he won't have the credentials to coach you during your bouts."

"Is that a threat?"

"No," he snapped, then lowered his voice. "I'm not holding a grudge. I'm a national coach. I have no reason to work against the success of any American fencer."

"No reason at all?"

"Jess, grow up. We disagreed, you moved on, and neither one of us misses the other, but the more medals we take home, the better I look. I'm not going to get into a pissing contest over floor passes, but I can't hand them out like candy."

She eyed him skeptically. That sounded too reasonable for his brand. Maybe he'd really moved on, or maybe he'd merely had more practice bullshitting over the last few months.

He sighed. "This is the highest level of international competition. There are security concerns you can't even fathom."

"Must be hard to use metal detectors when everyone has a sword, or is it one of those things where the only thing that can stop a bad guy with a sword is a good guy with a sword?" She glanced to Haley, who coughed to hide a snicker.

"I'm not playing around, Kidman." Some of his normal testiness returned. "We have to run everyone through a security clearance, and even then, we have limited space. Every country wants to send fifteen athletes, and every athlete wants to bring a coach, a nutritionist, a physio, both their parents, and their little brother."

"Oh, both my parents are coming," she offered, probably unhelpfully.

"Great, we can get them tickets to be in the stands, but no one gets a floor pass unless they're approved in advance."

"Fine."

He stared at her expectantly. "Fine, what?"

"Fine, I'll talk to my coach."

"Talk to him about what? What's to talk about? Just give me his information, and I'll see what I can do about getting him approved."

"Lauren."

Ansel pulled out his phone. "What Lauren? Oh, is it Michael St. Laurent?"

"No, Lauren's *her* first name," she elaborated. "Her name is Lauren Standish."

"Her name is Lauren Standish." He repeated the sentence as he lowered his phone. "And she's out of Buffalo?"

"By way of Princeton."

He gave a grudging nod. "I thought I knew everyone who coached at Princeton."

"She didn't coach for them. She fenced for Princeton, but she's been coaching since graduation."

He frowned again. "And you plan to bring her onto the floor at the Olympics with you?"

She lifted her chin defiantly. "Absolutely."

He stared at her a few seconds too long, then finally looked to Haley as if she might cue him into whether or not this was all some sort of elaborate practical joke. She only shrugged and then glanced out the window as if finding some engaging distraction just across the street.

He finally turned back to Jess. "Is no one going to address the elephant in the room?"

"What's that?"

"Are you really going to make me say this?" he asked, and when they didn't let him off the hook, he crossed his arms over his chest. "Fine, go ahead and paint me as a sexist pig if you want to, but no woman has ever coached for any Team USA fencer at the Olympics. And you want to break that barrier with some no-name first-timer from Buffalo? Come on, Jess, it's reckless, even by your standards."

Jess opened her mouth to hit him with a quick comeback, but she didn't have one. She hadn't thought about Lauren breaking any barriers. She hadn't thought about Lauren at the Olympics at all, and obviously she should have, but they'd had so many other things to deal with along the way. They'd only been working together for a couple of weeks, and yeah, they'd agreed to talk about things as they came up, but they hadn't talked about this, and she internally kicked herself for dodging so many conversations lately. She should've thought of all this before now, but she hadn't, and she sure as hell wasn't going to admit that to Ansel of all people.

"Look, she's my current coach. I can't help it if she has a vagina. So do I, and so does every person I'll be facing."

He shook his head. "Fine, if you want to pretend that's all this is, I'm not going to be the bad guy. I'll send her name up the chain, but this could be a shitstorm, and you're smart enough to figure out why."

Lauren sat at the kitchen table staring numbly into her Cheerios.

"Honey, are you okay?" her mom asked as she shuffled into the room in her bathrobe and slippers.

She glanced up. "Yeah. Why?"

"Your cereal's gone soggy." Her mom poured herself a cup of coffee from the pot Lauren had brewed but not touched, then sat down beside her. "Are you sure you're getting enough sleep?"

"I'm fine."

"I thought with Jess out of town, you'd get a bit of a break, but you've been up before me every day this week, and when I got home last night, your light was still on."

"You should've come in. I wanted to hear about your date."

"I didn't know if you were studying or just fell asleep while studying."

"I never fall asleep while studying, not even in college, and I was getting a lot less sleep then."

"I don't even want to know what you got up to at that fancy school of yours, then, because it seems like you're running yourself ragged these days, and honestly I'm not even sure I understand what you're doing."

She gave a humorless laugh. "That makes two of us."

She'd spent hours on end over the last few days watching video until her eyes burned. At first, she'd feared Yelena had somehow gotten a read on Jess's movements. If Jess had a tick, or even a pattern, to her attacks, it would function like a baseball player tipping pitches or a poker player with a tell, but Lauren couldn't find any patterns in Jess's behavior, none at all, and certainly not enough of them for Yelena to predict multiple scenarios with such accuracy. Jess was smart. She varied her attacks. She was flawless. Even with the benefit of replay, slow motion, and years' worth of footage, Lauren couldn't find a hint of repetition.

"I'm missing something."

Her mom glanced around quickly at the table, the floor, under the fencing book she'd left open on the table. "Wait, what is it? An earring? Your pen?"

"Sorry." She shook her head. "I didn't mean to say that out loud. I'm just looking for something I can't find in my brain."

Her mother smiled at her sweetly. "I know the feeling well, but if anyone can do it, it's you."

She sighed.

"What?" her mom asked. "You don't believe me?"

"No, I don't. I've been at this for days, and I'm no closer to finding an answer." She understood now all the emotions she'd seen Jess work through on video. The realization of what was happening, the frustration of processing various solutions only to have them all thwarted, the anger at coming up short, the dejection of understanding you were out of time and out of options, the defeat of knowing you should've been able to win, but you still couldn't.

"Honey." Her mom reached across the table and took her hand. "You need to give yourself some time."

"I don't have time. Jess doesn't have time. We've barely got five weeks left, and even if I knew what I needed to do, which I don't, I'm not sure I'd have enough time and knowledge and ability to actually do what needs to be done. I'm stuck on square one, and Jess will be home in two days."

"Then meet her in two days." She squeezed her fingers. "Work through one day, one problem, one frustration."

"I'm not sure that'll be enough in the long run."

"I was never sure either," she said softly, her eyes filling with a thin sheen of tears. "When everything happened with your father, I didn't think I could survive, and some days I didn't even want to."

"Mom," she whispered, "don't say that."

"It's the truth, or it was, but it's not anymore. You pulled me through. You stepped up. You faced every challenge, and I'm not just talking about the money or the house or the lawyers. I mean all of my despair, all of my rage, all of my anguish, and every emotion too complex to name."

"I felt the same things."

"Which makes what you did even more impressive, love." She gave a sad smile. "I'm still a little embarrassed you had to be the one to parent me in the worst moments of my life. I know it should've been the other way around, but I'm so incredibly proud of the fact that you were able to."

"I love you."

"Your love is your strength. It's unwavering. It's inspirational. And, while I think part of it is just innate, I will admit I'm proud to think maybe it came from me."

A wave of bitterness coated her tongue. "Well, it didn't come from Dad."

"We don't need to go back there. I only mentioned it to say that when I looked at you, even at my lowest point, I thought maybe life wasn't a waste if you were still trudging on. You still believed we could do something good, something worth slogging through hell for, and you made me believe it, too. I am so proud to have raised you to be the kind of woman I wasn't able to be."

"No, you're totally that woman. You made it through." Her voice gathered a bit of command. "You went out on a date last night, one you haven't rushed to share any horror stories about, which makes me think it went pretty well."

Her mother's cheeks flushed. "Can we just say I'm guardedly optimistic and focus on the fact that you're coaching an Olympian?"

Her confidence faltered a bit. "I'm trying. I'm doing my best."

"Then you'll be the best. When you care about something, you always find a way."

She nodded. While she certainly appreciated the dose of perspective, she wished she could share her mother's faith in her ability to overcome anything. Yes, she cared about fencing, and she cared about coaching, and most of all, she cared about Jess in all the ways that accentuated their shared dreams, and in ways beyond where she should. A little shiver raced up her spine as memories of pushing Jess up against the wall flooded her senses in a visceral reminder of all the ways she'd let herself care too much. No, if simply wanting to be enough for someone actually led to being able to give them what they needed, she'd have a million brilliant solutions by now.

But she didn't, which only reaffirmed what she'd known for years: loving something or someone wasn't always enough to make you what they wanted or needed in return.

✳ ✳ ✳

"Shit." Haley pulled off her helmet and shook out her jet-black hair. "I was kind of hoping you'd gotten worse while you were away."

"Sorry to disappoint," Jess laughed.

"You're not. You're not sorry at all." Haley unplugged her saber and set it aside before picking up her water bottle. "I think you've actually gotten a little better on your low lunge. How's that possible?"

"I've been fencing really short people in Buffalo. Tiny, tiny children, really."

"Makes sense, because anyone who gets old enough to drive doesn't stick around there for long."

Jess raised her sword into an offensive position, and Haley jumped off the strip. "Whoa, killer, don't ever point that thing at me unless I'm in full protective gear."

"That's what she said," Jess shot back.

"Nice!" Haley laughed. "I've missed you. No one else pushes me like this while also managing to be a real smart-ass in the process."

"Then, maybe you should come to Buffalo."

"Maybe you should stay here."

"Sorry, also not sorry, about not staying here with Ansel all over my ass for the next five weeks."

"Well really, it's only like three weeks."

She paused, her water bottle inches from her lips, as she visualized the calendar in her mind. She was relatively certain she hadn't lost two weeks of her life.

"Dude, we're supposed to be at the onsite training center three weeks before the opening ceremonies."

"Onsite training center." She repeated the words as if struggling to translate them from a foreign language.

"We went over this. It was the day they made the announcement about the Olympic team. At nationals." Haley stared at her as if she might be a little stupid. "Have you even looked at the plane tickets we all bought?"

162

"I gave someone money for a plane ticket. We're flying out of JFK. I got a window seat."

"Very fucking helpful to know you have a window seat without knowing what flight you're on," Haley snapped. "This is why you need to be here. You're completely out of the loop, and you have no support team. You haven't done any concrete planning for a month, have you?"

"I didn't think I needed to do more planning. I got a plane ticket. We rented an apartment near the fencing center. I paid my share. I didn't think I needed to worry about flight schedules and packing checklists for weeks."

"Well, it's just three weeks."

Her palms started to sweat, but she tried to keep her voice low. "Okay, three weeks. Plenty of time. I just need to talk to Lauren about some details."

"What kind of details?" Haley asked suspiciously. "Does she think she's just going to show up at the Olympics the day of the individual competition."

"I don't know."

"What do you mean you don't know?"

"We haven't discussed it yet."

"You haven't discussed her travel details?"

"We haven't discussed whether or not she's coming with me."

Haley's eyes narrowed. "You mean, like with you on the same flight as the rest of us?"

"Yeah." She took another sip of water, hoping it might cool her whirring brain. "But also, maybe, whether or not she's coming at all."

"What?" Haley exploded. Several other fencers turned to look at them, which was saying a lot, because fencers who trained in busy gyms weren't easily distracted by people shouting.

"Shhh," Jess commanded. "Lower your voice. Do you want Ansel to hear you?"

"Actually, I kind of do," Haley said gravely. "I think he needs to hear this. You're in over your head, or maybe you've lost your head for this woman, but this is your first Olympics. You can't wing this shit. You need someone who knows what they're doing to navigate so many land mines."

"I can navigate them. I've been fencing my whole life. I know the system."

"Not like this you don't." Haley shook her head. "I was there last time. You weren't. Trust me, you've never seen a field like this, not anywhere. And it's not like the old days where you could pay off a ref to give you a fair shake. They're all randomized now. You never know who you're going to get until you're on the floor. You need a coach who knows these guys inside and out."

"A coach like Ansel?" She practically sneered.

"Pull your head out of your ass for a minute. You know I'm right. He's a fucking terrorist to train with, but I keep him around because he's also a crazy-ass bomber during the matches. He knows every ref in the sport, and he's not afraid to threaten their mothers if they blow a call against me. He doesn't get railroaded by the old-boys club because he *is* one of the old boys."

"It's bullshit," Jess finally snapped back. "Sexist bullshit."

"Of course it is," Haley said emphatically. "This is still a fundamentally sexist community, but we don't exactly have a lot to fight back with. The guys who're coaching and reffing right now have been in saber for forty years, and women have only been at the big table since 2004."

She didn't argue. She knew all this, at least in theory. When they were born, women hadn't even been allowed in the discipline at the Olympic level. Supposedly that's why there hadn't been a female coach. They were still fighting upstream against hundreds of years of male voices telling them they didn't belong. And now that they'd finally let them in the room, they were telling them it wasn't their fault none of the women were qualified to coach a sport they'd barely let them play.

"Look." Haley softened. "I didn't say anything about Lauren coaching you at the Olympics in front of Ansel because, in my heart, I want some woman to shatter the glass ceiling. I want to tell every condescending man in this sport to choke on their patronizing platitudes, but could we maybe start planning a little

164

better rather than springing it on some unsuspecting youth coach weeks before the biggest event in the world?"

Her chest constricted. "What am I supposed to do? Just give up on her? Just accept the status quo and never do anything to make this better?"

"Not forever," Haley said. "You're young. You've got time. Buckle down and do whatever it takes to give yourself the best chance to win right now."

"And leave Lauren behind?"

"I didn't say that. I only meant that once you establish yourself, you'll have four more years to bring her up with you. You can work up the ladder together. Teach her the international circuit, then next time, when she's really ready, you can shatter the glass without having to worry that the hit to the system could flatten both of your careers in the process.

She wasn't wrong. Jess saw the wisdom of the plan, but understanding something didn't stop her from hating it with a ferocity that tinged the back of her eyelids white. And it wasn't that she didn't love the idea of another four years of her and Lauren taking the world by storm side by side. No, what she hated most was having no idea if Lauren would even be in her life in four months, let alone four years from now.

"Damn." Jess followed the curse with a laugh that rumbled across Lauren's raw nerves.

"My point." Lauren called, though her singsong voice didn't convey any of her own surprise. Jess had managed to land a graceful touch with the tip of her saber dead center in Lauren's chest on the most beautiful lunge. Lauren, on the other hand, must've managed to barely nick Jess's sleeve. She was only sure she'd made contact at all because both buzzers sounded simultaneously. No ref in their right mind would've awarded her the point in a real competition, but they were playing a game meant to bend the odds in Lauren's favor. Any time she landed a touch, she took the point, even if Jess landed a better one.

"Fine," Jess said grudgingly, "but only because I'm working on defense today."

"Well, isn't that lucky? I happen to be working on offense."

"That's not luck." Jess laughed again. "We didn't pull this game out of a hat. You picked it and then rigged it to your advantage. That's called stacking the deck."

"Are you going to bellyache about it, or are you going to get better at fending me off?" Lauren prodded, enjoying the teasing banter even as a part of her still worried about what undercurrents they were using the humor to cover.

Jess smirked behind her mask. "I haven't decided yet. I'm not sure fending you off is a skill I actually want to master."

Lauren should've had a better comeback, or any comeback really. Instead, she turned around and checked her cords to keep Jess from seeing her smile. She didn't want to encourage comments like those but felt powerless to stop them, or to stop her body from reacting to them. Only a couple of weeks ago, she'd foolishly believed she could use their attraction to her advantage, to focus it, to drive them. Now she understood that, while those impulses still rang true, she'd been foolish to think she could control them.

And still, she'd been grinning like an idiot ever since Jess walked back through the door that morning. She'd spent nearly a week worried about what she'd do when she came back and wondering how she could face her without having come to any meaningful conclusion about any of the conflicts clouding their conversations before Jess had left. They hadn't talked about the kiss, the terms of their personal or professional relationships, or the fact that she'd completely failed to formulate any sort of plan on how to address the video review Jess had steadfastly avoided. Actually, she couldn't blame all the avoidance on Jess anymore, as she'd allowed her to dodge the topic in favor of a second technical workout. She should've pushed, but she couldn't bring herself to rain on their reunion by admitting how ashamed she was of her own lack of insight.

Jess seemed so happy, and it would be easy for Lauren to pretend the joy had merely rubbed off on her, but in reality, much of her own happiness stemmed from having her back. She reminded herself they had hard, serious work ahead, and they needed to focus. She shouldn't have let herself miss Jess's exuberant energy, the low rumble of her laugh, or the way that cocky smile sent a skitter of attraction through her veins.

"Ready?" Jess asked from behind her, but Lauren barely heard the question above all the warning bells sounding in her brain.

She had to stop letting her mind wander down those paths. They all ended in her heartbreak. If she'd missed Jess this much over one week, how was she supposed to feel when she was gone for good? She couldn't let herself forget Jess would leave soon, even if it meant digging the tip of that sword a little deeper into her heart. "Actually, do you mind if we take a breather and talk through a rough sketch of the next few weeks?"

Jess frowned. "Right now?"

"It doesn't have to take long, but I want to make sure we're both on the same page about what needs to be done before you head out. Also, what day do you actually head out, so I can get the details on my calendar and work backward from there?"

"Sure." Jess tipped up her helmet, her pink cheeks accentuating the blue of her eyes in a way that made Lauren's mind wander from the professional path she needed to drag them back onto. "I guess now's as good a time as any to mention I talked to several representatives from the national team in the city."

A subtle edge of uncertainty in Jess's voice caught her ear and pulled at her heart. "And?"

"Turns out I'm really supposed to leave for the Olympics a couple of weeks before the opening ceremonies."

"A couple of weeks?"

Jess nodded, a curl falling across her forehead. "Two weeks from today actually."

"Oh." Her heart gave a painful flop.

"Apparently, I knew this when I made my travel arrangements, but it slipped my mind. I asked around to see if it was a big deal, and it kind of is. The people in charge built, like, this whole training center to simulate the real competition arena, and going early helps with the jet lag of being on the opposite side of the globe. Also allows people to network and do research."

Jess kept rambling, and Lauren got the sense she'd continue to do so until someone stopped her, but it still took almost a full minute before she could force air out of her rapidly constricting chest, much less form a complete sentence. "Makes a lot of sense."

"Really?"

"Of course. These people have dedicated their entire careers to preparing Olympic athletes. I suspect they have the lead-up to the games down to a science."

"Yeah." Jess shrugged. "It sounds like it."

"Yeah," she repeated dumbly as she kept turning the idea over in her mind. On one hand, the new schedule would alleviate so many of her worries about not being able to be good enough for Jess in these final weeks, and while she would've loved to be the person who provided her with the things she needed most in the moments when she needed them the most, she didn't have the answers or experience to guide Jess through what came next. A part of her felt an almost knee-buckling level of relief someone else could not only offer Jess the things Lauren lacked, but had already made provisions to do so.

Sadly, that part of her wasn't strong enough to eclipse the part that felt nearly despondent at the realization they had roughly two weeks left together. Two weeks of feeding off the exhilaration. Two weeks of feeling the combined heat of their bodies. Two weeks of shared purpose. And then, emptiness.

"Come with me," Jess blurted into the silence.

"What?"

"Come with me to the Olympics. To the training center. To all of it." Jess said it all in a rush, then added a hopeful, "Please?"

"You know that's impossible. I can't leave the club for weeks. No one else works here."

"Make Enrico work. He owns the place."

She laughed. "And how many times have you seen him here?"

"Then, shut down for a couple weeks. Parents will understand.

Hell, they'll be thrilled to say their fourth-grader's fencing coach is on the floor at the Olympic Games. Think about the doors that could open for you."

She didn't think about it. She couldn't let herself. "Even if it were possible to leave my entire life for weeks, I couldn't go on such short notice. How would I even get a place to stay? God, I don't even know what flights halfway around the world cost, but I sure as hell know I don't have it in my budget."

"It's the fencer's responsibility to pay for their coach's travel. I can—"

"No!" She held up her hand. "You already told me you're scraping up modeling jobs and small business endorsements to stay out of your parents' basement. You don't have the cash to throw at international flights and weeks in hotels on two weeks' notice, and it's too late to secure other funding."

"My parents would—"

"I'm not asking your mom and dad for money. Jess, this is insane."

"It's not. You're my coach."

"You have a national coach."

"I gave him your name. I requested a floor pass, and I know I should've talked to you first, but I had to make a decision in the moment."

"A floor pass?" Lauren's heart hammered over the sound of her words. "Are you out of your mind?"

"No. I need a coach there with me."

"Then get a real one!" She threw her hands up in the air and let them fall back to her sides as if they were made of lead. She'd let herself get pulled into this whole absurd situation because she didn't want to let Jess down, but if she went to the Olympics with her, if she pretended to know things she didn't, or pretended she was capable of things she wasn't, she would let her down spectacularly. "I never agreed to any of this. You wanted someone to help train you, someone to watch videos and make observations and hold you accountable."

"And you have," Jess shot back, "better than anyone ever has.

Even Haley said she saw improvements in my technical attacks, and I haven't had any meltdowns."

Lauren arched an eyebrow.

"Okay, maybe I had a little meltdown about the video, but you handled it. You pulled me back in and gave me fight night. You keep me calm and focused and present. That counts more than experience or connections. I need someone I can trust in my corner. I want you beside me when I'm on the biggest stage of my life."

It felt like she'd put a crack in Lauren's rib cage and was slowly pulling it apart to get to her heart. She had to fight now not to get swept up into the whirlwind of emotions swirling around them both. "I'm so honored you want me there, but you need someone else. Someone who's been there before and knows what they are doing. I only know just enough to be certain I'm not that person."

"You could be."

"I couldn't," she said firmly, no matter how much she wanted the truth to be different. "I barely made it onto the international level as a fencer in college, but I did get there just long enough to know I'd jumped in over my head."

"It's not that different from fencing nationally."

"The unwritten rules are all different!"

Jess finally laughed a little. "Okay, so maybe the officials are a little more lax with how they enforce certain things, and there's sort of an informal bro code at times, but the rules themselves are fundamentally the same. Honestly, once you know how to work the system, you can play it to your advantage."

"But I *don't* know that system, much less how to game it for you, and maybe someday I could figure it out with enough time or practice, but not in the two weeks leading up to the Olympics."

"We'll figure it out as we go, right?"

She shook her head sadly. "I love that you believe that. I even love that you made me believe it for a while. This has been the ride of my life, and I'm going to spend every remaining minute trying to live up to the promises I made to be here for you while you train. I hope you know I'm giving you the very best I have in me, but I never said anything about coaching you from the floor at the Olympics."

"But—"

"It's not going to happen." She couldn't let her keep talking. She couldn't let Jess push her eternal optimism into her head or heart. Neither one of them could afford to go any further down this path, because she didn't have the strength to pull them back again. She hadn't been able to set or hold a boundary with this woman for weeks, but she had to do so right now, for both of them. "If you'd told me what you wanted weeks ago, I would've sent you on your way right then and there. If you need to find someone else now, then we can wrap up."

"No." A hint of desperation cracked Jess's voice, and in it, Lauren heard their younger selves the night Jess had offered to do anything just to have another chance with her. "No. I want to train here with you."

"What about the games?"

A small muscle in her jaw twitched. "I'll use Ansel."

She raised an eyebrow.

"It's fine." Jess gritted her teeth for a second, then continued. "We know each other. He's been with me enough to know he can't coach me. He'll just scream at the refs."

"And that's enough for you?"

The corners of her mouth curled up without actually becoming a smile. "I'm grateful for whatever you can give me."

She didn't believe her. She suspected neither of them did, but that was one more vote in favor of Jess leaving early. The proverbial ripping off the Band-Aid. As much as it would hurt to lose her now, it would be infinitely worse to let herself believe in something better and then come up short when it really mattered.

∗ ∗ ∗

171

"Excellent!" the reporter declared with enthusiasm befitting someone who'd been straight up guzzling coffee since she arrived four hours ago. When she'd walked in carrying multiple cups, Jess had expected her to offer one to each of them and worried she might seem snobby if she had to explain she didn't consume caffeine while training because it made her jittery enough not to be trusted with a weapon in her hand. Her worries about polite decorum were unfounded, though, as the reporter, Avery something-or-other, kept all the cups for her herself and consumed one after another like some sort of junky with a bladder of steel.

Jess felt a little extra zip of pep just watching her bounce around the Elites' gym, her dark eyes wide and her smile the sort of plastered-on version so many TV personalities had perfected, only she didn't point it at everyone equally, instead choosing to save her best press persona for Lauren.

"The first time you did the drill, I couldn't tell what was happening at all," Avery continued exuberantly, "but after your explanations, everything makes more sense. It's almost like you have practice teaching people about fencing."

Lauren smiled brightly enough to keep Jess from rolling her eyes. Of course Lauren could explain a fencing drill. That was setting the bar awfully low for someone of her stature, but then again, most fencers were used to having to explain their sport to people who only managed to be easily impressed every four years. Lauren was infinitely better than most. She was magnetic, confident, compelling, and affable. She put people at ease and made them feel like they were the most important thing in the room, which was why Jess suffered a surge of mixed emotions as she watched Lauren walk Avery through another set of offensive moves in slow motion.

On one hand, she resented this interloper for intruding on the little time they had left together. On the other, she managed to summon a great deal of gratitude that Lauren carried more than her share of the weight on this little publicity spin. She had no doubt Lauren was winning her points both on and off the strip these days, and in doing so, she left Jess to focus on what really mattered.

Or at least what should matter most.

"Have you ever thought about doing sports commentary?" Avery asked. "I think you'd be good."

"This may surprise you, but there's not a lot of press kicking down the door to a small, rust belt fencing club."

Avery laughed lightly. "Maybe you could change that. I'd happily place a call to our local affiliate and drop a hint about an Olympian training in town. Small market stations are always chomping at the bit to get access to local feel-good stories. I'm sure you can trade that for more coverage of your club."

Lauren's eyes got a little gleam Jess hadn't seen since fight night, but she shook it off quickly. "Don't get me wrong, I'd love to entice more people out here, but I'm not willing to leverage Jess's Olympic run as bait."

Avery finally glanced at Jess. "Where did you find this woman?"

Her chest expanded with pride. "She found me originally, but I wouldn't mind her cashing in a little more. She's earned it, and honestly there's no such thing as bad publicity. What's good for her is good for me, and good for the sport we both love."

Lauren's cheeks tinged pink with pleasure, and Jess used the excuse of talking to someone else to bank shot all the praise she hadn't been able to lavish on her directly. "And if my name or image can get people through the door in droves, it still won't be enough to pay her back for all the things she's given me over the years."

"I suspect getting them through the door is all you'd really have to do," Avery added before turning to encompass Lauren in her comments once more. "Once you have their attention, you won't have any trouble keeping it. I've already looked at some of the footage we shot this morning. You're a natural on screen."

Lauren shook her head and laughed, but Jess couldn't imagine anyone mounting an argument against anything Avery had said. She hadn't seen the footage, but if it captured even a hint of who

Lauren had been all morning, everyone would be able to see what she'd known for years. Lauren was good at everything and with everyone.

"Do you want us to run through the exercise one more time?" Lauren asked, shifting the attention away from herself and back toward the work as she so often did.

Avery took the bait. "I'd like to get some shots angled toward Jess's attack, and selfishly, I'd also like to see if I can refine my own fencing eye in the process, if you don't mind."

"We'd love to," Lauren said with one of her big, unencumbered smiles Jess hadn't quite been able to inspire over the last few days, and she lost all her will to push for more.

Lauren gave Jess a playful little tap on the shoulder and pulled on her mask. Jess followed her like she always did, and at least once they got into position, all the conflict fled her mind. They went through their paces again, the movements and decisions both flowing naturally in ways they hadn't in any other area. When they both lunged at the same time, she felt a lift of assurance that not everything had gone off-balance between them.

Jess would've gladly reset and gone again and again and again in order to stay in this perfect place where only the two of them existed, if Avery hadn't reinserted herself into their moment by becoming a one-woman cheering section.

"Brava!" She piled on the praise. "I can't believe I actually followed along. The first round, I couldn't see anything but a blur, and now I feel like I've become a fencing fan. I guess it's true. You should never underestimate the value of a great teacher, right, Jess?"

"Lauren's the best in the business."

Lauren rolled her eyes playfully, but that didn't undercut the blush rising in her cheeks.

"I take it that's why you're back here at your old stomping grounds instead of training at one of the bigger fencing clubs in New York, Chicago, or California."

She nodded. She might be able to overlook the fact that this woman seemed to think they'd reinvented the wheel if she kept

174

reaffirming Lauren as the fencing ambassador she'd always believed her to be. "There are so many distractions and competing agendas in those places, so many people vying for prestige or influence, but in Lauren, I knew I could have a partner."

Avery's eyebrows twitched at her word choice, but she kept her game face on and her voice neutral as she pushed on. "That's quite a compliment. Did your shared history play a role in building trust?"

"Absolutely," Jess said quickly. "Just as Lauren taught you the steps and details that gave you your first real jolt of excitement about this sport, she did those things for me when we were younger. Only for me, she gave me the same excitement times three thousand along with a passion and confidence. And you can't overstate the value of confidence in my career path. Confident fencers take risks that give them the edge, and confident fencers have the fortitude to keep coming back every time they get their butts kicked along the way."

"Well, from what I hear, that hasn't happened very often over the last few years."

She shook her head. "It happens plenty. We fight so many bouts in such large and diverse pools of fencers, even the best in the world get beat as much as they win. You have to have a resilience born from something bigger than any one bout or tournament or even season. For me, Lauren planted those seeds when I was thirteen. She was the first person who believed I'd be here right now."

This time Avery turned to Lauren, and the camera naturally followed. "Did you know Jess felt that way?"

"She's mentioned it a time or two." Lauren's little grin seemed more reflective than reactive. "But she's so special, someone was bound to point it out eventually."

"But you got there first," Avery pushed. "What did you see in her at such a young age to make you believe she had what it takes to be an Olympian?"

"Just look at her." Lauren shot back. "She's the total package, smart and fast and fierce. She goes harder than anyone I've ever known, and she's never once compromised her sense of self. That's impressive enough in your twenties, but she was the exact same person as a kid, only shorter."

Avery smiled, but Jess felt the compliment hit her square in the chest. Lauren thought of her as the total package. Lauren was talking about Jess the way Jess always talked about her, and she'd just done so to a national sports reporter. If she could've kissed her right there, she would have.

"What a great description," Avery continued, oblivious to Jess's paralysis from pride. "So, it wasn't hard for you to see her potential?"

"No, and even the term 'potential' feels insincere because it sort of implies it was hidden or somehow raw. Of course, she's still growing technically, but the things that make her successful today were always there. She's turned heads in every room she's ever entered." Lauren held her gaze for a few electric seconds, as all the things they hadn't been able to say to each other crackled along the current arcing between them.

Then, she seemed to remember they were on camera and locked her professional face back into place. "I appreciate the credit she gives me and the trust she continues to put in my abilities as a training partner, but if you're looking for me to claim some sort of prophetic abilities for recognizing Jessie's talent, I can't. The Kid was blatantly built for greatness."

The last sentence hit Jess like a blow to her chest protector, only she wasn't wearing one.

"The Kid?" Avery did nothing to hide her glee as she pounced on the personal. "Like Jessie 'The Kid' Kidman. What a perfect name for you."

Jess clenched her jaw and struggled to summon every skill she'd ever honed to hide the emotions screaming through her brain at the moniker she'd spent years trying to shake and the easy way it rolled off Lauren's tongue. "Did you get all the footage you need?"

Avery turned to the cameraman who nodded. "I guess so, and I think now we've got a title to market it all with. Jessie the Kid. I love it."

176

Jess put her hands on the small of her own back in an attempt to hold herself up as all the hope and happiness that buoyed her moments ago deflated.

The Kid.

That's all she'd ever be. In every sports report, in every bout for the entirety of the Olympics, and worst of all, in every exchange with Lauren. The realization settled over her like a weighted blanket, suffocating and restricting. Cool water swirled around her ankles and the cold air tousled her curls as she fell back into the moment where she understood she was kissing Lauren, but Lauren wasn't kissing her back.

All the years, all the work, all the progress she thought they'd made floated away, disintegrating like ash. She'd never escape the awfulness of chasing someone who didn't want to be caught and would never reach for her in return.

Lauren sat in her car outside a house she'd never been inside. She couldn't make out all the details in the darkness, but the home seemed big without being ostentatious, and the lights shone from several different windows, suggesting multiple people were home and moving about. It had taken a good bit of research and a couple of awkward phone calls to high school teammates' younger siblings to even get the address, but she'd made every one of them against her better judgement. Then, she'd spent the entire drive across town and out of the city telling herself to turn around, but she hadn't yet. She should've called or texted, and in theory she still could, but no amount of faceless communication would offer her the peace of mind she needed to erase the memory of blue eyes clouded with pain, so she got out of her car and walked slowly to the front door.

Soothing sounds of the lakeshore wafted in on the warm breeze, and she gave herself a few seconds to soak up the rhythm of waves lapping the land somewhere nearby. She wished she could carry their serenity with her, to offer herself something calming, steady, and certain, or at least project those things to

Jess. She had no idea what she was going to say, or even what she'd come all this way hoping to convey. She only knew she couldn't stay away.

With that thought, she lifted her hand and knocked.

Mercifully, she didn't have to wait in her conflicted state for long. Footsteps fell quickly to the door, and it opened wide to the concerned faces of two people she hadn't seen in over a decade.

They examined her features in the same way she did theirs, and memories rushed forward to collide with years of change. Jess's parents had both begun to gray, and her father's face had rounded while her mother's had thinned with time, but their eyes were just as warm as they'd ever been.

"Lauren?" Jess's mother finally asked. "Lauren Standish?"

"Yes. Hi, Ms. Kidman. I'm sorry to drop by unannounced and so late, but I hoped I might speak with Jess."

"Of course," Mr. Kidman said quickly. "Come in. Come in."

They stepped back and beckoned her into a brightly lit foyer with high ceilings. She glanced around at the little touches of home. Shoes on the floor by the door, a coatrack overflowing with jackets and hats, a large family photo in a wooden frame. She stepped forward to examine the shot. Jess looked about eighteen. Lauren hadn't known her then. She hadn't known her for so many long, important years between the present and the time that kept pulling them back.

She turned to Jess's parents again. "Is she home?"

They smiled and nodded, a hint of nervousness hovering around them for a few seconds before Jess's dad blurted out, "Did she fire you?"

Lauren gasped. "No. Did she say she wanted to?"

"No." Ms. Kidman placed a gentle hand on her husband's arm and gave him a warning glance with dark, expressive eyes. "She's said nothing of the sort, and we're so incredibly grateful she's worked so well with you over the last month."

"Oh." Lauren turned the comment over in her mind. "But you've been waiting for the other shoe to drop?"

Mr. Kidman laughed lightly. "Can you blame us? She goes through coaches the way I go through golf balls."

"Ronald," Ms. Kidman scolded gently. "What he means is our daughter has very high standards and expectations."

He rolled his eyes as if that hadn't been exactly what he'd meant, but his wife forged on. "It takes a special kind of person to keep pace with Jess, and we've long ago stopped trying to micromanage, but we've so loved having her close and happy for a change."

"Happy," Lauren repeated as the word tugged at her chest. She wanted to see her happy, too.

Ms. Kidman's expression softened into something so sympathetic, Lauren had to fight the urge to hug her. Instead she said, "Would you mind if I talked to her alone?"

"Not at all." Mr. Kidman pointed to two sets of stairs off to the side of the foyer. "She's taken over our whole basement. Why don't you go on down?"

"Yes," Ms. Kidman said. "We were just headed out to see a late movie."

"We were?" Mr. Kidman seemed surprised by this news, but his wife merely smiled.

"Yes, dear, get your jacket, and you—" she turned back to give Lauren a little squeeze "—are welcome here any time."

She smiled genuinely, if a little sadly, as a million memories of simpler times threatened to overtake her. She managed to hold them at bay only by sheer will and the strongest suspicion she'd need every ounce of her remaining fortitude to face what came next.

She clung to those priorities as she descended the stairs into a fully finished and beautifully furnished basement. Calming tans and grays made for a tasteful, casual living area larger than her entire apartment at Princeton. A long wet bar lined one wall, highlighted by Buffalo Sabres memorabilia, and large glass doors flooded with darkness now that must offer stunning lake views during the daylight hours, but she couldn't manage to process much else as she turned the corner toward a large TV in front of a plush, gray couch with a pair of sock-covered feet hanging over one end.

She smiled in spite of her nerves at the sight of Jess with her guard down. She wished she could keep her loose and relaxed and safe, always. Instead, she cleared her throat loudly and watched those long legs stiffen.

"Hi, Jess," she said softly. "Your parents let me in. I hope that's okay."

Silence for a few seconds made her stomach clench, but eventually she heard a small, "Sure. I mean, yeah, it's fine."

Jess sat up and rubbed her hands over her face, then through her hair. A navy-blue compression shirt hugged her frame, and her gray sweatpants didn't make it all the way to her ankles, suggesting they might have been a leftover from the last time she'd lived with her parents. Lauren's heart twisted from the mix of impulses the sight of her inspired.

"What do you need?" Jess asked without meeting her eyes.

She shrugged. "I wanted to ask you the same thing."

The muscles at the side of her strong jaw clenched. "I'm fine."

She walked over to the couch but didn't dare sit next to her. "Really?"

"Yeah."

"It seemed like I upset you today."

Jess shook her head, but no words came.

"Please don't close me out."

"What do you want me to say?" Her voice cracked.

"Tell me what you're feeling. Honestly."

"Sure, sounds easy enough, right? I feel like an idiot. An idiotic fool."

"You're not."

"Okay, then I'm insane, because I keep doing the same thing and hoping for a different result, but no matter how hard I work or how much I try to change, you aren't ever going to see me as anything other than The Kid."

"Jess, you are so many things—"

"No!" Jess shot off the couch. "Don't take that patronizing tone with me. I'm not a teenager anymore. I don't need you to manage my emotions or let me down easy. I'm an adult. God, I don't know why I can't convey that to you."

"You have."

"I haven't. No matter how stable and strong I try to be, you still talk to me like I'm some adorable puppy who follows you around, and now I feel like one, too." Anguish raked across her vocal cords as the words poured out. "I came back to Buffalo feeling like the triumph you said I could be. I've stood on stages around the world and owned them all. I've carved my own path in every world I've ever entered. I didn't think anyone could ever make me doubt myself again."

"Good. I don't want you to ever doubt who you are or what you can accomplish."

"You make me doubt everything." She raised her voice as her whole face contorted. "And that's really freaking uncomfortable because you were the person who told me I could be what I wanted. You made me believe I could grow into a person I was so proud to be. But now that I actually am that person, you can't stop seeing me as The Kid."

"I don't," she defended weakly.

"You do. You still see me as a kid."

"I can't," she shot back more forcefully. "God, I keep trying to, but I can't. You won't let me. Every time I assert my boundaries and tell myself I can keep them, you look at me with that intensity of yours, and all my walls crumble."

Jess eyed her suspiciously. "They didn't crumble today."

"They did," she shouted. "I was holding pieces of them in my hands and trying to put them all back into place in front of you, in front of a stranger, on camera. Do you have any idea how hard it was for me to stand there pretending I couldn't feel your eyes all over me?"

"No."

"Good." She laughed bitterly. "I'm glad I fooled one of us, but

181

it's not easy when you insist on talking to me like I'm some hero one minute, then look at me like you can't keep your mouth off mine the next."

Jess stared at her, eyes wide now, open and vulnerable in a way that made Lauren light-headed.

"I'm trying to walk that line for you, but when you get so close, I feel like I'm going to fall, and it scares me. You never scared me when you were a kid, but you scare me now, which is why I said it today. Not because I saw you as The Kid, but because I desperately needed to."

All the fight left Jess's expression as those blue eyes filled with new emotions and a deeper understanding Lauren had never wanted her to have.

"I'm sorry." She backed away. "I shouldn't have come over. I shouldn't have said any of that."

"Was it true?" Jess asked softly.

"Yes." She hung her head.

"You're actively trying to see me as The Kid, so you . . ." She shook her head. "So you don't see me as an adult?"

"I know it's not very mature," she admitted, "but I'm grasping at straws around you, and I didn't want to be that person. I wanted to be what you needed. I wanted to be the person who sparked those dreams you're chasing, but I'm barely hanging on by the tips of my fingers here."

"Hey." Jess stepped close and reached for her, but Lauren shook her off. "It's okay."

"Don't try to calm me down. That's not your job. You're not the coach. You're not the mentor, and if I were better or stronger in either of those roles, we wouldn't be having this conversation."

"Why are we having this conversation then?"

"Because I think, in my attempt to not let you down as a coach, I ended up hurting you as a person, and I needed you to know I'd never purposely hurt you, Jess." Her throat tightened, but she had to push forward even if every word felt like a swallowed shard of glass. "I meant everything I told the reporter today. I'm in awe of you, but I also feel a tremendous weight of responsibility to you. You've put so much trust in me, and I should've been able to focus on what we mean to each other right here and now instead of clinging to the things that tied us to the past."

"So, you, when you say . . ." Jess started, then seemed to lose her train of thought, or maybe she lost the nerve to give voice to her hope yet again. "You swear you don't think of me as The Kid anymore?"

Lauren allowed her eyes to run over the stellar body in front of her, from the powerful thighs to the firm core rippling beneath the tight shirt to the strong line of Jess's jaw. She sighed, a dreamy sound so discordant with the battle raging inside of her. "I wish I could. As much as I've tried to remember the kid you used to be, I haven't been able to do so with any regularity since you got back, and not at all since you kissed me."

"You kissed me."

Lauren bit her lip and stared at Jess. "I didn't mean that time. I meant the first time."

Jess stepped closer. "The first night outside the club?"

"Yes," she whispered.

Jess glanced skyward as if saying a rushed, wordless prayer, asking God some question or request, but when she met Lauren's gaze once more, there were no more questions that mattered.

Jess stepped toward Lauren and right off the cliff.

They collided, and every ounce of the reserve she'd tried so desperately to summon melted on Lauren's lips, like sugar in the rain. Who was she kidding? She'd disintegrated the moment she'd seen Lauren here in her space, wearing those low-slung jeans with her hair down and an intimacy in her eyes that hadn't been there before. The only thing that kept her from jumping into her arms on sight was the throbbing fear she wasn't welcome there. As Lauren unraveled before her, offering all the explanation she'd been too afraid to even fathom in her most fantastical justifications, she'd nearly crumbled under the weight of her relief. Lauren wanted her. Lauren wanted her badly enough to fight against her desire by clinging to the same memories Jess had sought to erase.

And she had.

They'd set it all aside for each other, for this moment, and if their last stolen moments had taught her anything, it was to never take this one for granted. They wrapped around each other instantly and completely until they blended together, lips, hips, and legs. She had her arms completely around Lauren, holding her close, clutching her tightly muscled shoulders, fingers tangled in her hair. Lauren's hands were more mobile, brushing her back, her arms, and wandering up to cradle the back of her head.

They breathed in shaky gasps, or they didn't breathe at all in the moments when suffocation seemed superior to separation. She didn't hold back. The time to savor had passed. She wanted to consume, and she no longer suffered any insecurity about her right to do so. Lauren had come to her. Lauren had opened up emotionally and admitted she'd been driven to distraction by her physically. Jess felt no smugness over those facts, only an assurance she'd lacked before. Certainty amplified her desire and emboldened her to deepen the kiss as she lowered both her hands to cup Lauren's amazing ass.

Lauren pressed into her, and sliding her lips to the corner of Jess's mouth managed to mumble. "Where's your bedroom?"

Jess's mind swam at all the wonderful implications of the question, but she didn't have it in her to tell so much as show. Shifting her hands a little lower, she lifted Lauren off the ground and guided her legs up until they wrapped around her waist.

They continued to kiss as Jess managed to make her brain and legs work in tandem, at least enough to back Lauren down a short hallway and up against an unlatched door, applying enough pressure to push it open. Then, still holding two handfuls of Lauren's denim-clad thighs, she crossed the room to set her atop the edge of the bed and began to ease her back, only this time Lauren didn't cooperate, and instead of lying down, she caught hold of Jess's shirt as she muttered, "Show off."

Jess chuckled, a happy little sound that died in her throat as

Lauren snaked both of her hands up under her shirt to the band of her sports bra.

"You feel so amazing." Lauren pushed all the clothing up along the trail her fingers had already blazed, and then followed them with her mouth.

Her breath came fast and sharp as Lauren's lips closed around one nipple while she drew tantalizing circles around the other. Jess threaded her fingers through long strands of hair as her chin fell to her chest, her head heavy and loose. She shrouded herself in the scent of Lauren's shampoo, growing dizzy with the desire this woman immersed her in.

When she could no longer withstand the sensations coiling at her core, she eased Lauren up off the bed once more and pulled off her shirt before unclasping her bra. It had barely fallen to the floor behind her before their mouths met once more. As their tongues tangled, Jess took her turn cupping firm breasts in her palms, testing the weight of them, and sliding along the smooth skin until her thumb brushed across the contrast of her straining nipples.

Lauren gasped in her mouth, triggering a surge of wetness between Jess's own legs and confirming she didn't have it in her to drag this out. Breaking away only long enough to unbutton the jeans in her way, she pushed them down roughly, then went back for the pair of simple, black bikini briefs. Before she could peel them away, Lauren asserted her own desires again. Flattening her palm against Jess's abs, she slid down under the waistband of her sweats and right into the arousal waiting for her there.

They both moaned when strong fingers slipped along sensitive skin, and Lauren thew her head back in satisfaction. Jess couldn't resist the open arc of her throat, and fastened her lips to the curve of that elegant neck, sucking harder than she'd dared to before.

Lauren's knees buckled, but Jess caught her with an arm around her waist, then eased her onto the bed in the same motion as she pulled down on the last little black barrier between her and everything she'd dreamed of. Then, shedding the remainder of her own clothing, she climbed over the beautiful body laid bare before her. Settling down lightly atop Lauren, her nerve endings burned as skin met skin in a myriad of mirrored combinations. She slid her knee between Lauren's legs and felt the press of breasts against her chest, but even the length of passive connection couldn't satisfy years of longing, and she ran her hand over every place she couldn't cover completely.

Kissing deeply, passionately, she skimmed her hands over the side of Lauren's legs, the curve of her hips, the ridges of her ribs, and the edges of her breasts. Then using the tips of her fingers, she traced across her collarbone and over strong shoulders before turning back down her arms all the way until Lauren's hands caught hold of hers and intertwined their fingers with clutching need.

Accepting the hold on her hand and the emotional tug on her heart, a surge of protectiveness laced through her lust. She wanted to know this woman in every possible way, and to live up to the promise she'd always longed to make. They had the potential to set each other's world alight, and she had no intention of settling for anything less. Jess adjusted her knees to fit between both of Lauren's, and rose up enough to see the space between them. She wanted to imprint this image into her mind, but Lauren clearly didn't want to wait. Lifting her hips off the bed and twisting beneath her in a beautiful arc, she reached up to thread her free hand in Jess's hair and direct her back down.

It wasn't that she didn't want to grant that wish so much as she wanted to grant all of them, so she used both her speed and dexterity to catch Lauren's hand in the same one already holding the other and pinned them both over her head. Lauren could've broken away if she'd really wanted to, but the ease with which she accepted the pressure on her wrists while opening her knees a little wider told Jess everything she needed to know.

She slipped her unoccupied hand into the space between them as she stared down at the kaleidoscope eyes that always captivated her. "You're beautiful."

Then she memorized each detail of the breathtaking body beneath her as she slipped inside.

Every part of Lauren pulled her deeper, and Jess's brain had no capacity for determining what she found more intoxicating, the way her body yielded, or the openness she showed by holding Jess's gaze as they began to move together.

Liquid heat spread between them, creating the sweetest, hottest friction. Jess used her hand and her hips to push deeper, and Lauren's lips parted on a heavy breath as she arched up to each thrust, her face flush with the most delicious blend of arousal and exertion. Everything about her screamed perfection and heightened Jess's near-frantic desire to claim her completely. She wanted to possess her and free her all at once. She wanted to be here with her and for her with an almost frightening totality that made her heart pound through her ears, her chest, and the apex of her thighs.

"Jess, Jess, yes Jess," Lauren mumbled, and the sound of her own name on those lips made her dizzy.

She ran her thumb in small circles as she continued to work in and out, and Lauren tightened around her fingers in the most erotic of physiological reactions. She pulled out, then pushed forward in strong, steady strokes.

"Jess, yes." Lauren's chest rose dramatically off the bed then fell, her fingernails digging into the hand holding both of hers.

The next time Jess pulled back, Lauren's legs closed around her, pinning her in place, and the pleading in her eyes found its voice. "Please, Jess, please."

God, how long had she waited to hear those words? How much of her life had she spent poised to answer that call? She curled her fingers inside her, precious pressure against every point where slick skin met its equal, and Lauren lost control.

Throwing her head back and constricting every muscle, she finally closed her eyes and surrendered in the most beautiful quaking arc of pleasure. She rose, shook, collapsed, and rose again on the next wave. Jess hovered above her, transfixed, overwhelmed, on the edge of unraveling. The only thing holding her together was the purest desire not to miss even a sliver of a second that confirmed everything she'd known in the deepest, most primal reaches of her psyche.

The years of waiting, wondering, and fantasizing hadn't been wasted or unwarranted.

* * *

Lauren felt warmer than she had all spring. There'd been plenty of moments over the long, dark frozen months where she'd exerted herself enough to sweat, and over the last few hours she'd felt a fire inside her she didn't even know she could survive, but those swings from hot to cold had only made her feel feverish. The warmth enveloping her now went all the way to her bones and spread outward again in concentric circles. She might not have had her full wits about her yet, but it didn't take a great deal of mental clarity to understand she owed that change to the body, firm and hot, curled around her.

She hadn't exactly fallen asleep so much as eased onto a more subconscious plane as her climax crested and crumbled her coherency. As she drifted slowly down deeper into the mattress Jess crawled up beside her, kissed her into a dreamlike state, then rolled her onto her side and pulled the comforter sideways up around them both.

Lauren didn't know how long they'd stayed that way. Time ceased to matter or even exist the moment Jess's mouth had met hers. There was no past and future here, and for the first time, that felt like freedom instead of fear.

Jess shifted against her, wrapping her more snugly in strong arms that carried her both literally and figuratively. Images floated through her mind. Jess's hand holding both of hers, Jess's legs spreading her open, Jess's eyes as they raked over her body in the most vulnerable moments, fierce, proprietary, passionate, and as powerful as any touch. And the things she'd done inside her. She had no way to picture the points where Jess had most left her mark, but she experienced those memories just as viscerally, as the warmth she'd rested in grew too hot to be considered comfortable any longer.

Rolling over, she faced Jess, those blue eyes meeting hers with the most alluring blend of satisfaction and need. Lauren worked her hand up from under the thick comforter and cupped that flawless face in her palm. She wanted to say something perfect.

Something to convey her wonder or her appreciation, or simply how impressed she was, but mostly she wanted to convey her desire to inspire the same things in Jess.

For so long, she'd held her at bay, so afraid of what it would mean to let herself be wanted, and to allow herself to want something in return. But now that those boundaries had been blurred, she wanted to apply the same urgency she'd felt in defending them to obliterating them.

There were no words, only actions.

Leaning forward, she kissed Jess with all the purpose of someone saying thank you and please simultaneously. Their mouths moved together, open and eager as adrenaline pushed exhaustion out of the way.

She worked one of her knees between Jess's legs and her hand from the soft skin of her cheek over a tightly knotted shoulder, and then paused to flatten her palm across the spot where hard pecs blended into soft breasts. She couldn't imagine any more emblematic illustration of the woman straining against her now, strong and smooth, solid yet yielding.

She slid her knee a little higher, searching unthinkingly for another spot to offer the same sort of all-encompassing contrast, only to find this one soaked in need.

Jess gasped and bit Lauren's lip as she painted her thigh with desire. A sharp surge of power cracked like dashed flint, and the spark that jumped inside her caught hold. She pushed back hard on the spot that had tantalized her and sent Jess sprawling onto her back. Jess's eyes flew open, but before she could even process the separation or form a protest, Lauren pounced.

Straddling Jess's waist, she kissed her again quickly on the mouth before sliding down along her neck, then bit the spot where it met shoulder. Why hadn't she noticed Jess's sexy shoulder muscles until this moment? She could've blamed the high-collared fencing uniforms or her own worthlessly enforced obliviousness, but she had no capacity for blame any more than she could summon regret or guilt with Jess's body firm and flexing beneath her. She continued her path down to the hollow of her throat, pressing her tongue to the indent before dragging it down between her breasts and pausing in her indecision of where to travel next.

Jess made the decision for her by tangling her fingers in the hair at the base of Lauren's scalp and guiding her to a hard nipple straining for attention. She sucked it between her lips, and Jess's hips jerked underneath her hard enough to rock her forward. She kept her mouth where Jess had put it, but seeking better balance and a more extravagant expanse of contact, she worked the lower part of her body down along Jess's ripped thighs until she settled between them.

When she brushed her own core against the newly exposed heat between them, another overwhelming set of sensory cues caused her to gasp and scrape her teeth along Jess's sensitive skin.

Jess released a sound of pleasurable pain and held her closer, fingers tugging her hair in an uncontrolled quest for more.

More was something they could agree on with a sureness that defied verbal clarity.

She used every part of her body she could control to melt into the curves and planes of Jess, soaking up every sensation with a voracity that would've scared her in any other context. Tonight, though, there was no room for doubt. The desire claimed her entirely and consumed her awareness.

She worked her hand lower along the periphery of the pressure pinning them together, down over cut obliques, the dip of Jess's navel, the rise of soft curls, and over the edge into saturated folds.

Teasing Jess's openness, she marveled at the way they reacted to each other on such a primal level, their anatomy knowing things she hadn't even let herself guess at.

"You're so wet." She murmured against the breast in her mouth.

Jess managed a strangled scoff at the blunt statement of the obvious.

Lauren pushed inside with two fingers and little prelude, causing Jess to groan. She brought her palm to rest firmly against the hard center of Jess's need and reveled in the pulse radiating there.

"Lauren, I'm—" Jess gritted her teeth.

"Not yet," she whispered, rising up to kiss the underside of her jaw.

"I can't hold off."

Lauren slid her tongue up the line to her ear and rasped, "I want to taste you."

All the air left Jess's lungs in a hot rush against Lauren's skin. "I'm not going to last."

Lauren smiled at the desperation in the confession, and then ran the heel of her hand in a steady grinding motion.

Jess's little growl grew into a shout of release as the climax ripped through her. The muscles that made her so inspiring on the strip did even more to spark awe as she lay bare and shaking beneath her. Lauren sucked on her neck, but tasting the sweat that pricked there as she rode the waves of release only managed to whet her thirst without satisfying it.

As the aftershocks rolled through Jess's impressive form, Lauren descended along her languid frame, kissing a quick, wet path to where she most wanted to be.

Jess tried to sit up, those amazing abs sparking a million washboard allusions, but Lauren merely used her tongue to trace a cascading route ever lower. The scent of sex filled her senses, and she worked her shoulders between those powerful thighs. Jess's torso fell back with a muffled thump as Lauren drew her tongue through wetness she'd ached to taste.

"Fuck." Jess strained up against her mouth, and Lauren worked to cover as much of her as she could in varied, teasing slides and broad, flat strokes. Large, lazy circles steeped in the luxury of a woman trembling beneath her followed the primal press against places she'd been born to push. Then, slipping lower to coat herself once more, she savored the feel and taste, uniquely Jess.

"Lauren." Jess's voice grew thick once more. "I need—"

The words were choked off as Lauren closed around her fully.

This time, the release wasn't wondrous or clutching or quiet. It racked Jess's body with a violent, careening crash. Lauren had to wrap her arm around Jess's leg to hold on as she twisted, triggering every torsional muscle and the sheets beneath them. Lauren offered no mercy as she soaked and sucked and thrilled at the power she held over the most amazing body she'd ever touched.

Jess's convulsions subsided to shivers once more, and she moaned. Lauren ignored the incoherent plea as she enjoyed herself a little longer, but Jess caught her by the shoulder and pulled her up.

They both laughed a little, matching almost maniacal sounds as their eyes met, and then they collapsed.

Chapter Eight

Jess lay staring at the ceiling of her parents' guest room, trying to catalogue every detail of the woman sprawled half on top of her. They'd assumed a myriad of positions over the course of hazy, sleepless hours, and she'd yet to find one that didn't work for her on a fundamental level. At one point, they'd even made use of the shower to clean up, only to fall back into bed and get sweaty once more. Nothing sated her craving for Lauren's skin, her mouth, her vulnerability, but the closeness she felt with Lauren curled against her side, head on her chest, leg thrown across her midsection at least offered her a few moments of peace.

"Do you remember the night you kissed me by the pool?" Lauren asked from the crook of Jess's arm.

"Um, yeah," Jess managed despite the way her stomach tightened at the contrast of the memory against all the things she felt in this moment. "Pretty much every day of my life."

"But do you remember you asked me what the best part of being queer was?"

"Yes. You gave an awe-inspiring answer about the sense of community I would come to feel and be part of."

"You're very sweet to remember it that way, but I was full of shit."

"Oh yeah?"

"Yeah." Lauren smiled against her skin. "You saw me as the older woman, but I was still just a teenager myself. Don't get me wrong, the community is great when you're just finding yourself, but if you asked me the same question again, I'd give a very different answer."

"Okay." She looked down to meet her eyes. "What's the best part of being queer?"

The corner of her mouth gave a little twitch before she said, "Kissing girls."

Jess laughed. "Good to know my hopes weren't misplaced."

"Do you still agree?"

She shrugged lightly. "I think that's in the running, along with a couple of other things we did last night. There's a lot of really good options to choose from."

"So many."

"It's hard to choose just one of them, but—"

A shrill ring of the phone stopped her, mid-sentence.

"Uh-oh," Lauren said, "the outside world is coming for you."

"They can wait," Jess grumbled.

"What time is it?"

"I don't wanna know. Why do you think I sleep in a room with no windows?"

"Because you're broke and living in your parents' basement?"

"Ouch," she said, but she couldn't hide the humor in her voice any more than she could stop the phone from ringing.

"Either someone is calling you in the middle of the night, or it's morning." Lauren piled on the heap of things threatening to shatter their little cocoon. "Either way, you're probably going to have to face it."

She growled, unable to think of any other argument, but she threw the bunched-up comforter to the side and felt for her phone on the bedside table. Pulling the screen within view, she managed to confirm two unpleasant things at once. It was after seven o'clock in the morning, and Haley was calling her.

Lauren must've seen the same thing as she eased herself up to a seated position. "You better answer while I find my clothes and steal some of your toothpaste."

She didn't want to accept any of those things as her body

mourned the lost warmth of their combined heat. She wanted to throw the phone across the room and hear it crack against the wall, then pull Lauren back to her and the covers back over their heads, but Haley wouldn't call this early unless she needed to. As a sense of dread and responsibility settled over her, she pressed the "accept call" button. "This better be so freaking important."

"Oren's out," Haley said flatly.

"What?" It was a pretty vague statement compounded by the distraction of Lauren's naked body exiting the room.

"Oren McAfee's out of the Olympics. All of it. Men's saber team competition and individual. He's not even taking the trip."

She sat up and rubbed her face. This was bad news for the world of saber fencing, no doubt. Oren was the top American in his discipline and extremely well-liked by everyone, including her, even though she wasn't as susceptible to his boyish charm as many of the other female fencers. This would no doubt send shock waves through their community, but it shouldn't affect her or Haley directly, which made her suspect there must be something else behind the gravity of her friend's tone.

"What happened?"

"Um, remember when I mentioned he might have a stress fracture last week when you were here?"

"Yeah."

"Well, Ansel went against the recommendations of the trainer."

She groaned.

"He, um"—Haley swallowed audibly—"he tore into him yesterday at the gym, about how this was the biggest moment of his life, and he either needed to step up or step aside. And you know Oren. He doesn't ever back down."

"He's a champion," she confirmed, feeling sick to her stomach.

"Ansel had him in open bouting, and he'd faced like five guys in a row when he jumped. You know the high kick-lunge thing he does? Well, when he came down, he went all the way down to the ground."

"Shit. Were you there?"

"We all were. Both saber teams, men and women. I've just been sitting up all night remembering him screaming when the bones broke."

She suffered a wave of nausea at the thought, but it quickly burned into anger. "What the fuck was Ansel thinking? And why did Oren listen to him over the doctors?"

"Ansel's the coach. We're leaving in less than two weeks. We're all out of time and out of options, and none of us are going to get another chance for four more years if we even get one at all."

"Hey," she said softly. "Calm down. Take a deep breath."

"Calm down? Are you, of all people, seriously telling me to calm down?" Haley reacted the same way most women do after being told to calm down, and actually ratcheted up several more notches. "My coach, the person who's supposed to prepare me for the biggest event in my life, the person we're supposed to be able to trust more than anyone else in the sport, just hobbled the top fencer in the country, and now he's got no one left to prey on but me."

"Don't let him." Jess's voice had absorbed some of Haley's panic. "You have to stand up for yourself. You can't let him railroad you."

"It's not that simple."

"It literally is. You're in charge of your body. You're in charge of your career. He works for you."

"You're not here. You don't know what it's been like the last couple of days. The closer we get to the leave date, the more things escalate. We're all barreling down the highway, continuing to pick up speed, and there's no off-ramp in sight, but even if there was, it would mean giving up on everything we've worked for our whole lives. Everyone's cracking under the pressure."

"Come here," she said quickly. "Come to Buffalo. We'll train together with Lauren."

Haley's laugher didn't carry any joy or humor. "I'm legit scared of Ansel right now, but I'm not going to throw away my shot by leaving everything to work out with your middle school girlfriend."

"She wasn't my girlfriend in middle school."

"No, she was just your Mrs. Robinson style—wait a second. You said that all past tense, like she wasn't in middle school but might be now."

"Things got . . ." She didn't know how to summarize what had happened over the last twenty-four hours. "Complicated."

"You slept with her."

"Uh, yep."

Lauren chose that moment to return from the bathroom, fully dressed in the clothes she'd arrived in, looking fresh and stunning enough to lasso Jess's heart and give it a firm tug.

"Was it everything you ever dreamed of and more?" Haley asked in her ear.

"Yep," she managed to squeak out.

"Oh, my Lord, is she still there?"

"Affirmative."

"Shit. Dude, I'm hanging up now."

"Thank you."

She wasn't sure if she was more grateful for her friend's quick release or the little chuckle she heard in her voice as she disconnected. She'd have to check in with her again later, but she got the sense that Haley's ability to be amused in this moment at least meant she'd be okay long enough for Jess to focus on Lauren a little longer.

"What's going on?" Lauren asked as she walked to the edge of the bed.

"Ugh, Oren McAfee tried to fence with a stress fracture, and it went badly."

"Why?" Lauren shook her head. "I mean, not why did it end badly, but why did he fight with a fracture?"

"Because he let the national coach goad him into playing war hero for good ol' Team USA, and he fucking died on that sword. He's not going to be an Olympian anymore."

"How awful." Lauren stepped closer and wrapped her in her arms, resting her chin on her head. "I'm so sorry."

She shrugged. "Haley's shaken up. She doesn't trust Ansel anymore, and I feel bad for her, but I never really trusted Ansel, and

197

you're here with me, so I can't find it in me to feel depressed. Does that make me a bad person?"

"No." Lauren kissed her forehead. "You're a good person who's juggling a lot, and I'm afraid I didn't make things any easier for you last night."

"You made things very easy for me last night." She placed her hands on the curve of Lauren's hips. "I think you're more afraid things aren't going to be easy from here on out, but I don't want you to worry. We don't have to have all the answers this morning."

"It's my job to worry, so you don't have to. We have a lot to figure out." Lauren's voice went low and tinged with a hint of exhaustion, but she managed to smile slightly as she stepped back. "But if you want to take things one step at a time, please help me figure out how I'll find the poise to walk past your parents this morning on my way to work."

"Oh Lord," Jess grimaced. "My mom and dad know you spent the night."

Lauren covered her face with her hands and laughed into her palms. "Also, I was supposed to text Kristie when I got home, and I didn't get home yet, so not on the same level as your parents, but she totally knows."

"Fair. And yeah, awkward, but I'm not bothered about any aspect of last night with you."

"Me neither. That part was . . . perfect." Lauren blew out a slow, steady breath. "I just thought I'd be past sneaking out of girls' rooms at dawn by this point in my life."

"You and me both." She picked up her T-shirt off the floor and pulled it on, feeling a little lighter at the confirmation that Lauren's concern stemmed from logistics rather than regret. "We can do this though. I'm going to walk you upstairs and out to your car, then I'll come back in and face the firing squad. You do the same at your house. We'll both try to get a little sleep and meet at the club after lunch to figure out what the rest of the day needs to entail."

"Okay."

"Okay?" she asked, a little surprised by the quick agreement.

"Okay," Lauren repeated.

"You're just going to let me set a plan and run with it? What a novel idea."

"Well," Lauren drew out the word playfully. "I mean, I did have one step to add before I go."

Jess's grin turned cocky, and she raised an eyebrow playfully. "Oh yeah?"

"Yeah." Lauren leaned close enough to whisper right into her ear. "You might want to put on some pants before you go talk to your parents."

Then, she stepped away, breaking all contact between them, as Jess fell back onto the bed in a heap of her own thwarted arousal, a little relieved to know not everything had changed between them.

Lauren's phone buzzed just as she stepped out of the shower. She reached for a towel and sopped the water off her arm before checking the message.

Of course it was Kristie announcing her imminent arrival with donuts and a bazillion questions. She smiled at her friend's enthusiasm even while suspecting she didn't have anywhere near a bazillion answers for her. She'd texted her when she got home simply saying she'd been out all night. She hadn't known what else to say. Everything seemed too big for a text. Honestly, it seemed too big for her brain. The only part of her capable of processing what happened with Jess was her body. Her body totally understood how a conversation about firming up her boundaries had ended with the two of them in bed. As if to accentuate the point, her thighs gave a pleasant little ache as she stepped into a clean pair of yoga pants and grinned at the memory of being wrapped around Jess's body.

The doorbell rang, alerting her to Kristie's arrival. She must've driven seventy miles an hour through residential neighborhoods, no doubt fueled by her own burning curiosity.

She tugged on a long-sleeve T-shirt with her old high school emblem and gave her still-damp hair one more tousle with the towel before padding barefoot into the dining room, where Kristie was already offering her mother one of the donuts she'd promised.

"You look ravishing as always, Ms. Standish," Kristie said as Lauren entered the room.

"Uh, thanks?"

Kristie laughed "I was speaking to your mom. You look exhausted and confused. Shall we take the rest of our donuts to the porch?"

She rolled her eyes. "Sure."

"Don't leave on my account." Her mother poured coffee into a mug and handed it to her. "I'm well aware my daughter didn't make it home last night, and I'm also aware she wasn't with you, plus she's been obsessing over Jess Kidman for weeks."

"I'm not obsessing. I'm working."

Her mom gave her the same look she'd given her at seventeen when she'd tried to convince her she'd been out late studying.

"When you got in at nearly three o'clock in the morning two weekends ago, I googled your new workout buddy."

"Mom!" she exclaimed. Her face grew warm.

"What? A quick image search made it abundantly clear Jessie Kidman is no longer the hotheaded pip-squeak I remember from your school days, but rather a hotheaded, lesbian, fencing supermodel, and I say good for you."

Kristie held up her hand. "Ms. Standish. Up top."

Her mom gave Kristie a high five before turning back to her. "Now, sit down and tell us what's going on."

She sagged into a chair and rested her elbows on the table. Kristie pushed the pastry box over to her. She opened it and pretended to debate her choices even though they all knew she would pick the maple-glazed Long John.

She needed more time. She needed space to clear her head, but she didn't have the luxury of either. Two of the three most important people in her life stared at her expectantly, and she was going to have to offer them some sort of explanation, which meant she had to face the questions she'd avoided since the moment Jess's lips met hers.

"So, I know you might not be ready to share all the epic details," Kristie started first, "but you said the kissing was the best you'd ever had, and I need to know if whatever happened last night also rose to the same very high bar."

She nodded.

"Yeah?"

"Hurdled the bar . . . by a lot," she admitted, then shoved a rather large bite of donut into her mouth.

"And Jess had a good time, too. I presume?"

"Umm-hmm." She swallowed.

Kristie raised an eyebrow. "I get that we're trying to be tactful here, but I'd hoped for more clarity."

"Join the club. I'm not big on clarity at the moment. There are so many things up in the air, and I can't even begin to sort them all out. I'm her coach, at least for the moment, which makes things ethically complex. She's under an incredible amount of pressure, which puts me under pressure. She's so beautifully open and vulnerable beneath the cocky shell, and I want to protect her at all costs, but I'm also freaking turned on by her, which makes me feel like I need to work a little harder at protecting myself as well."

Both women stared at her, a bit agog at the outburst, before Kristie finally spoke. "Okay, yeah, that's a lot. I think we should talk about everything, but just to be clear, when I said I wanted clarity, I just meant about how much of a good time you two had last night."

"Oh." She tried to take a sip of her coffee, but her hand shook too much to get the mug to her mouth neatly, so she set it back down. "I, um, well, we both had several good times over the course of the night, and then again this morning."

Kristie grinned suggestively. "Several as in . . ."

"Yep, multiple great times. Can't we leave it at that?"

"I'm actually fine at leaving it at that," her mom cut back in, "but I think we need to go back to your mini-meltdown, because you seem to think you need to have everything figured out this morning, and while that's on par for your personality, love doesn't work the same way as settling an estate or running a fencing club."

"Love?" She pushed back from the table, then immediately regretted the distance from her donut. "I'm not in love with Jess Kidman. I'm just wrapping my head around being attracted to her, and caring about her, and trying to figure out how to be there for her without losing myself in the process."

"Yeah, that doesn't sound like love at all." Kristie exchanged a knowing expression with Lauren's mom.

"No." Lauren snapped her fingers to break them out of their mind meld. "Don't look at each other like that."

"Like what?" Her mom feigned innocence.

"Like you know what I'm feeling better than I do."

"Then, tell us," Kristie urged, a new seriousness in her voice.

"Conflicted. Okay?" She leaned forward enough to grab her donut once more and jammed another third of it into her mouth.

"Okay."

This time the full-on sugary goodness didn't stop her from talking. "I'm trying to be a coach and a friend and a red-blooded woman, and obviously I can be all those things at once, but I'm not sure I can do them all well, and I don't have a lot of hope that I can do any of them to the level she deserves in the next ten days."

"Would you feel differently if she weren't leaving in ten days?"

"Hypotheticals aren't helpful right now because she *is* leaving. Honestly, the thought of her *not* leaving is even worse than her going, because it would mean I screwed up in a big way. She's destined for greatness, and yet this morning she got a call that a coach ended another Olympian's dream with one terrible decision."

"Shit," Kristie said, then grimaced. "Sorry, Ms. Standish."

Her mom patted her friend's hand. "We're past the point of worrying about profanity, dear."

202

Lauren pulled a more manageable piece off her remaining donut, but couldn't bring herself to eat it as the earlier bites had turned to lead in her stomach. "The stakes are so high on every level. I couldn't live with myself if I hurt her, but I worry that in order to give her everything I have in me for the time we have left, I'm going to get hurt when she goes."

"You're in a complex situation very few people can even begin to relate to," Kristie said calmly, "but I think it bears mentioning that Jess is one of those people. She knows herself and she knows you. She understands the stakes. If you're looking for someone to talk to, she's the obvious choice."

"Ugh." She sagged so far, she rested her forehead on the edge of the table. "In a perfect world, you'd be right. I'm not trying to be coy or obtuse. I want to have so many conversations with her, but there are just so many other things we need to focus on. I feel like I'm balancing on breaking branches, and it's not fair to add my confusion to everything else she's carrying right now. I promised I would stay strong for her. I want to keep my word."

Her phone buzzed before either of them could answer, and she grabbed it, eager for the distraction, only to find a text from Jess. "*I never got to finish telling you what I think is the best part of being queer.*"

The corners of her mouth lifted even as the familiar pressure built in her chest. She typed quickly. "*What's that?*"

She waited for what felt like a very long time to hold a breath until the response came and took it right out of her lungs.

"*I love the way a woman's scent clings to you. The way it stays on your hands and in your hair like smoke, but richer, smoother. The way she permeates your senses with little wisps of her curling through your airways even after she leaves your bed.*"

She sat there, staring at the text until her eyes blurred the words together, but it didn't matter because never in the rest of her life would she forget the perfection of that answer, or the feeling it sent spiraling through her.

When she finally managed to look up, the others must've clearly read every one of those emotions in her eyes, because neither of them even asked to see the text. Kristie merely closed the box of donuts and held it out to her, before saying, "Go."

She turned helplessly to her mom, who squeezed her hand. "My good, strong, levelheaded girl, I love you, but I'm with Kristie on this one. Go talk to her!"

Jess pulled into the gravel parking lot outside the Nickle City Fencing Club at almost the exact same time as Lauren and parked her mom's Volvo next to the little red Subaru. They smiled at each other through their respective windows before getting out with offerings in hand.

She held out a large carton of cookies and cream ice cream while Lauren turned around with a box of Paula's donuts in her outstretched arms. They each stared at the other's gifts, then their eyes met, and they both burst out laughing.

"I guess great minds think alike," she said, near giddy at the ease of Lauren's amusement. "Great minds or deprived sweet tooths. Or is it 'sweet teeth' when it's both of us?"

Lauren leaned in over the sugary substances between them and kissed her, slow and languid, running her tongue along the top row of Jess's teeth before leaning back. "Yeah, 'sweet teeth,' plural."

Jess stared at her, light-headed and mystified such a thing could happen in their world now.

Lauren blanched a little bit. "Oh my God, did I just say that out loud?"

"You did, and it was the second-most amazing thing that's ever happened to me, the first being last night, so please don't backtrack now."

"I think we've both seen how terrible I am at pulling back around you, so let's plow forward, and tell me about this ice cream melting between us."

"Well," Jess started, then took a deep breath. She didn't want the nerves tingling through her stomach to show. She wanted to sound calm and logical, but a genuine desire apparently did nothing to actually convey those attributes as her words poured out. "Haley told me how tense everyone was, and how no one wants to mess up after a lifetime of work, but that panic also led to Oren doing exactly the thing he was afraid of, and even if I didn't crack a bone, what if I crack under the pressure? Haley doesn't know how to jump off the manic merry-go-round, but maybe you and I could, or maybe that's a terrible idea because I really should be fighting fifteen hours a day, six days a week. I'm worried I don't know where the lines are. Maybe you've noticed, I'm not great with boundaries."

"I may've noticed a time or two, yes." Lauren laughed again, the most beautiful sound in the whole world, and it had come twice in that many minutes.

The thought that Jess could make this woman happy gave her the fortitude to continue at a less frantic pace. "I don't want to stop training. I don't want to throw away my shot, and I certainly don't want you to think what happened between us last night took me off course, but maybe it helped me realize I don't want to lose myself either."

"Jess, I could never think you're lazy or lack motivation. You've worked harder over the last few weeks than anyone I've ever known. Honestly, I'm not sure how you haven't collapsed yet."

"I haven't even considered the possibility, and that sort of scares me now. I've never been in this position before, but I got a literal wake-up call this morning after an amazing night where neither of us got much sleep." She couldn't contain a satisfied smile. "Again, I don't want to make excuses, but I just wondered if maybe we could take a mental health day, or like, even a mental health couple of hours."

"Mental health hours." Lauren nodded slowly, then pulled out her phone and tapped the screen a few times before lifting it to her ear.

Jess waited, watching and wondering what she thought of her, and trying not to wilt under the realization of how much more her opinion mattered today than it ever had before, which was a lot.

"Hey," Lauren finally said into the phone. "You're going to cover my classes at the club tonight."

A voice on the other end said something indistinguishable, but the tone clearly suggested protest.

"I don't know. You're the owner, Enrico. You taught me and about three other generations of fencers. You can handle a middle school group and high school open bouts."

More grumbling came down the line, but Lauren cut him off. "Well, you'll have to figure it out because I haven't taken a personal day in four years, and I'm taking one now."

Then she hung up.

Jess stared at her in shock. "Really? You're going to miss your classes? You won't be mad or stressed out?"

Lauren shook her head and smiled. "The only thing that bothers me about this idea is I didn't think of it first."

Then, before Jess could so much as offer her a chance to second-guess anything else, Lauren grabbed her hand, fingers soft and strong. "Come on."

Thirty minutes later, they were pushing a rowboat out from the dock into Hoyt Lake, and any remaining doubts wafted away on a gentle breeze that stirred Lauren's long hair as she watched Jess row.

"I'd offer to help with the oars," Lauren said, "but since it's supposed to be arm day for you anyway, I figure paddling me across the pond will at least counteract the calories we're about to consume." Then she opened up the donuts and set the slightly melted ice cream on the bench seat between them. "Shall we divvy them up?"

"I want the chocolate one with chocolate icing and M&M's," she said with a long, steady pull on the oars.

"Of course you do," Lauren said.

"What's that supposed to mean?"

"You're so extra, and it suits you."

"So, if this is a personality test"—Jess eyed the remaining donuts—"you're going to choose the cake donut with sour cream glaze."

"Maybe," she said coyly. "Why do you think so?"

"Classic and satisfying with just a little bit of bite."

"Nicely done, but also you forgot to mention it holds up under pressure, like when I dip it in the ice cream."

"Oh, that's good thinking." Jess hauled the oars into the boat and stared at the remaining options. "Is that one red velvet? That seems like it could be great dipped in ice cream."

"Oh wow, yeah, now that you mention it—"

"Nope. Too late for take backs. I called it." She shot her hand forward with her signature quickness, but Lauren caught her. "No fair. This needs to be a democracy. There have to be checks and balances. What about a meritocracy?"

"Are you saying I lack merit?" Jess tried to sound offended, but it came out more amused. "You want to arm wrestle for it?"

"Not a chance," Lauren said firmly, then added a little more suggestively, "not after I saw how easily you carried me to bed last night."

"Oh yeah?" Her ego soared. "You liked that?"

"I might have enjoyed it more than I would've expected"— a new hint of color rose in Lauren's complexion—"but that won't earn you a red velvet donut. How about rock, paper, scissors?"

"Good call." She lifted one hand in a fist and the other one palm up. "On guard."

Lauren mimicked the starting position, and they tapped out their count in unison. "One. Two. Three."

Jess threw scissors just as Lauren showed rock.

"I win!" Lauren reached for the donut.

"No. Best of three. We never do one and done. It's not in our nature."

Lauren's grin suggested she got every nuance of that comment. "Fair."

They went again, and this time Lauren beat Jess with the exact same pairing.

"You went back-to-back rock?" Jess asked incredulously. "Who does that?"

"A woman trying to beat the person who throws back-to-back scissors. Is that a lesbian thing, or are you really just Stabby McStabberson?"

Jess shook her head as her competitive spirit rose. "Let's do three out of five."

"No, I want my donut."

"Three out of five, Standish."

Lauren eyed her suspiciously. "Do you seriously want the donut that bad? Or is this just a competition thing."

"Does it matter?" Jess asked.

"I think it might, but sure, let's go again."

They counted in unison once more. Jess showed rock while Lauren threw paper.

She let loose a roar that bounced off the still lake and echoed through the surrounding trees.

"Wow." Lauren's eyes went wide. "I think you just let me know this wasn't really about the donut."

Her face flamed, this time from embarrassment instead of arousal, and she mentally kicked herself for losing her cool. "Sorry, I just don't like to feel outmatched."

"Yeah, I've gotten that from you, both in person and in the videos."

She grimaced. This wasn't going as well as she'd hoped. "So, you did watch it?"

Lauren nodded.

"Should I apologize again?"

"No." Lauren sighed. "Should I?"

"You? What for?"

"For not knowing how to fix it?"

Her chest tightened at the shame undercutting Lauren's voice, and she reached for her instinctually. "It's not your fault."

"A more experienced coach might—"

"I've had more experienced coaches." Jess cut her off, placing a hand on her knee. "I have access to the top coaches in the world. None of them could fix it either. Some of them actually made it worse. Hell, the guy leading the national team made it infinitely worse."

Lauren didn't argue, but she didn't look completely convinced, so Jess forged on. "And none of those other coaches ever blamed themselves. They all dumped everything on me. They never cared enough to worry on my behalf. They never came to my house to check on me after they hurt my feelings, and they never gave me the freedom or sense of security that comes from a day off."

"Okay." Lauren breathed a heavy sigh of relief.

"You know what else they never did?"

"What?"

"They never gave me half of a red velvet donut to dip in ice cream."

Lauren's smile turned from tense to genuine in no seconds flat, and Jess's world righted itself. "I see what you did there."

"And?"

"And . . ." She tried to make her wait for it, but her eyes sparkled too brightly for the answer to be no. "I find it very charming."

Lauren picked up the donut and tore it in half before handing one of the pieces over.

Jess accepted the gift, feeling more grateful for it and what it symbolized than she had ever felt for any trophy she'd ever won.

They returned the boat after an hour on the water and an inordinate amount of junk food, but Lauren felt relatively certain the sugar high didn't compare to the joy she felt at just walking beside Jess along a curving path, with nowhere to go and no one else to be but themselves. She couldn't help but wonder if this was how they could've been together if they'd met at different times under different circumstances.

"What are you thinking about?" Jess asked as they continued

walking past the end of the lake and into a more wooded section of the trail.

She paused, not sure she wanted to give voice to something so wistful and intimate, but when she met Jess's blue eyes, so open and hopeful, she was reminded how little she managed to withhold from this woman. Taking her hand and starting forward once more, she admitted, "I was wondering if one or two things had been different, would everything have been different between us?"

"How so?"

"Like, if I hadn't known you when you were thirteen. If we'd just met now, at a tournament, what would that have been like?"

"I imagine I'd see you from across the room and become so totally distracted by your beauty, I'd get run through and lose my match."

"Oh no, I wouldn't want that."

"I'm not sure it could be avoided," Jess said with play solemnity, "but then I could put on my most endearing smile and come over to explain you'd just cost me the win, and it would be only fair for you to go out to dinner with me to make up for it."

She shook her head. "I'm not sure that would work on me. I'd think you were entirely too smooth to be trusted."

"Then I suppose it's lucky you knew me before I learned how to be smooth."

"You were always smooth. I think you must've been born with it, or you were just some youth prodigy in that area like you were with everything."

Jess wrapped an arm around her waist and pulled her so close their hips bumped lightly as they strolled. "If you keep talking to me that way, my ego is going to become so unbearable you might not want to be around me anymore."

"I'm not sure I can stop." All the playfulness drained from her tone as the truth of the statement settled over her. "I don't want to keep harping on something we both know, but I've tried to be reasonable with you. I've tried to be professional. I've tried to be responsible."

"All the attributes you've fallen back on since you were a teen," Jess mused. "You've carried all of them so well your whole life. Do you ever just want to let them fall?"

Her breath caught as an unfamiliar ache welled up in her. "Only when I'm with you."

Jess stared at her for a few heavy seconds, her lips parted as they let the words reverberate between them, and then Jess's mouth was on hers.

Kissing her was everything Lauren had ever known and more. She could be fast and strong. She could be light and teasing. This time she was tender and soulful, and Lauren didn't just melt into her, she slipped away from herself. In that moment and place, there wasn't anything else but Jess. No responsibilities, no conflicts, no future, and no past.

Without breaking apart even far enough to draw a deep breath, Jess guided them off the trail and deeper into the woods. With strong hands on her hips, Lauren let herself be led, or at least directed, farther from everything that had anchored her before.

She felt Jess glance away quickly, then shifted their trajectory subtly, until the brush of branches across her jeans drew her own attention to their surroundings. They'd stepped into a small clearing between some trees with their green leaves begging for summer sun. The setting wasn't entirely private, but that seemed like such a fine distinction with the thrum of her own pulse drowning out any ambient noise.

"What did I tell you about being smooth?"

Jess smiled against her mouth and kissed a path along her jaw until she reached her neck. Lauren eased her head back in a delicious mix of pleasure and surrender.

"I feel like I'm not smooth until you tell me I am," Jess murmured into her skin between wet kisses, "just like I wasn't an Olympian until you said I could be."

"I think you would've figured that out on your own." The last word came out as more of a moan as Jess ran her tongue up to her ear and bit the lobe lightly. "You seem to have figured out a lot of things on your own."

As if to demonstrate her point, Jess unbuttoned Lauren's jeans and then walked her back a few more steps until she butted up against a sturdy tree. The rough bark on the nape of her neck offered a stark, sensual contrast to the softness of Jess's fingers skimming her stomach when she pressed the zipper out of the way.

She spread her legs just a little, taking a wider stance for both balance and access, and Jess did what she always did, by taking what Lauren offered and turning it into something more. Running expert hands lower, skimming her need, she curled right inside her.

Lauren gasped at the swift perfection, then turned her head sharply to claim Jess's mouth for her own again. They kissed frantically to keep from screaming as Jess moved in and out with the most deliciously constrained movements. The weight of her body pinned Lauren to the tree, holding her up with an urgency that surged through them both.

Her vision blurred with lust, and she utterly lost herself in this woman who made her feel things that should've terrified her. Instead, those emotions managed only to make her rush faster, harder, more completely toward the edge of a precipice, the bottom of which she couldn't even imagine, much less see.

She was ready, willing, aching to throw herself off the cliff, as her desire made her soar so high she might've been able to take flight, but even if she fell, she would only sink endlessly into the woman already inside her.

Then something crashed, small and hard, rolling across the ground, and in her lustful disorientation, she thought it might be a part of herself, but Jess startled out of the kiss and stared at the object. Then, thankfully, her superior processing skills jumped several steps ahead, and she reacted with all the speed and valor burned deep into her DNA.

Kicking the object to the side, she withdrew her hand and covered Lauren's mouth completely, just as a golden retriever broke through their ring of trees. Lauren's startled squeak was completely muffled by Jess's fingers, coated in the scent of her own arousal.

The dog snatched up the ball and stopped to give them a curious stare. She held her breath as footsteps fell along the path that suddenly felt so much closer than it had before.

"Findley," someone called, "get the ball, boy."

The dog forgot about them instantly in the joy of a task completed, scrambled back under low branches and bounded away, taking with him any need for his human to come any deeper into the woods.

When the sounds of scuffling faded, Jess eased back and slowly removed her hand, allowing Lauren the freedom of movement to let her head drop onto a tightly muscled shoulder.

"That was close." Jess laughed, but her voice trembled.

"Too close." Lauren sighed. "I don't know what came over me."

"Really? I sort of hoped it had something to do with me."

She lifted her head to see the hints of her cocky smile return and gave Jess a little shove before she tugged up her zipper. "Totally you. You're a dangerous woman. What am I going to do with you?"

Jess arched her eyebrow playfully. "Is that a real question, because I have a few suggestions."

"Stop," she said, then undercut the order by laughing again. "Do you really want to wake up to newspaper headlines like 'Olympian arrested for indecent exposure'?"

"They say there's no such thing as bad press."

"Oh my God, you're incorrigible."

"Does that turn you on?"

She threw her hands in the air, as if asking help from heaven. "Actually, I think it does."

Jess was on her again in an instant. Their bodies collided, flush and hot. They kissed passionately enough that when Lauren did manage to work her hands between them, it still took her too much time and energy to push back even a little way. "We can't do this here."

"Then where?" Jess asked, returning to sucking on her neck.

"Are your parents home?"

Jess glanced at her watch. "Any minute."

She only managed to whimper, half in frustration and half at the scrape of Jess's teeth against her throat.

"What about your place?"

Her head swam with images of her mother and Kristie around the table this morning, and it managed to cool her blood just enough for her to shiver. "I live with my mother."

"Why?" Jess whined and sagged against her. "What's wrong with us? We're adults, aren't we?"

"I thought we were until this moment. It never occurred to me that the ability to have sex in the middle of the day was a marker of adulthood."

"Well, I'm not going to lie and say I'm not thrilled I'm the first person to raise the issue for you. Seriously though, I know why I'm living at home, but you're supposed to be the responsible one. I really thought you'd have a mortgage by now."

Lauren grimaced, and the expression must've registered through the rest of her body because Jess stood back slowly.

"What is it?"

She shook her head.

"What did I say?"

"Nothing."

Jess's expression took on the earnestness that always weakened Lauren's resolve.

"It's just, I thought I'd be a lot farther along by now," she admitted. "It's not like I planned to be living with my mom as I closed in on thirty. Things happened, and I'd made peace with that until, like, today. Not everyone gets to chase their dreams."

"What stopped you from chasing yours?"

"It's not a big deal. We should go."

"Please." Jess caught hold of her hand and intertwined their fingers gently. "I know it's not nothing. Don't think I haven't noticed all the things that don't exactly add up."

"I don't know what you mean."

"I followed your career at Princeton. You were going international, and then you just didn't. For a while, I thought maybe you threw in the towel because something better came along. We

214

both know fencing isn't likely to get you the things an Ivy League education can."

She snorted softly. "Apparently both of them get you a decade of living with your mother."

"And don't forget the crushing debt, but you're smarter than that. You think through problems and make plans that outstrip anyone I've ever met. When you left the competition circuit, I thought maybe you went to law school or med school."

"Is this a really long-winded way to ask why I haven't lived up to my potential?"

"Seriously?" Jess asked, hurt creeping in her voice. "That's what you heard there?"

She shook her head. She'd heard the concern, the curiosity, the desire to know her. The old pain wormed its way up from the depths.

"When I heard you were coaching in Buffalo, it didn't make sense, and then I got back here and saw you at work." Jess stepped close again, angling her body toward the answers Lauren didn't want to give. "There's nothing your mind can't do, Lauren."

"Not true." She tried to back away, but only managed to bump up against the tree.

"It is, and I've wanted to ask so many times why you're not doing more, but I didn't know if I had the right." She gave a crooked little smile. "But, seeing as how we've both been inside each other, I thought maybe we were getting a little closer, so I'm asking now. Please don't let me near your body but lock me out of your thoughts."

Lauren had to lean back on the tree to steady herself against the onslaught of emotions. The echoes of the people she trusted most rattled through her memory, both of them imploring her to talk to Jess. A part of her wanted to, but she also wanted to protect them both from reality. She wanted to hold onto the fever dream they were both existing in for a little longer. She wasn't ready to see pity in the eyes that had always been filled with awe when they looked at her.

The weight of it all pressed down on her so hard, she slowly

215

eased herself to the ground. Sitting with her back against the tree, she stared up at the woman who so clearly wanted to know her so much more deeply than she'd wanted to be known. Something about Jess's presence now tore at her. Something about how she'd already curled inside her, something about her insolent stance, the way she demanded more, always more. No, it was something in the way those blue eyes followed her all the way down that made the decision for her.

She patted the sparse grass beside her and simply said, "Okay."

Jess dropped down next to Lauren like a child or a puppy who'd merely been beckoned, but she got the sense easy acquiescence would no longer be enough to sustain them through what came next. She struggled against the twin urges to lunge forward and to shield them both. And still, she didn't even know why.

"You know I'd rather die than hurt you?" she asked solemnly.

Lauren nodded.

"I just didn't know it would be too much for me to ask how you ended up back in Buffalo."

Lauren bit her lip. "It's actually a lot, but you've put so much trust in me in so many different ways, I guess it's not too much to ask me to put a little in you."

She eyed her seriously and silently, trying to read any cue from her body or her expression, but Lauren seemed only to slip further into herself as she began to talk.

"I didn't mean for my life to turn out this way. I had bigger dreams. I didn't plan to come back to Buffalo after school. I got a job in New York, a good one at a great fencing academy. I had a girlfriend who'd been with me for two years, and we'd dreamed all these dreams. I had a business degree, she was going to study physical therapy, and we were so close, we'd paid the first months' rent on a cool Bohemian loft when my dad died."

Jess reached for her instinctually, and Lauren allowed herself to be pulled into the crook of her arm. "I didn't know."

"We kept the services private."

216

"I'm so sorry I wasn't here. I would've been here."

Lauren nodded against her shoulder. "We didn't want people around. We kept it really quiet given the circumstances of his death."

The phrase struck her, but she didn't want to push anymore. She gave her the space silence offered, and after another shaky breath, Lauren continued.

"He died in a car crash. Actually, when the coroner called, he told me both of my parents had been killed in the crash."

"But your mom, you said—"

"Yeah. It was a horrible, grief-stricken couple of hours before I got hold of my aunt, who was actually with my mom, and then I got so hopeful the whole thing had just been one awful mistake, but my dad's phone rang and rang and rang, so we went to the police station, and then the morgue." Lauren shuddered against her. "And it was him."

Jess kissed the top of her head and waited, suspended in the heartbreak she would've so gladly borne if she could've taken it from the woman in her arms.

"Then they showed us this beaten-up body of some woman neither me nor my mom recognized. And the car was in my dad's name, but it wasn't one we'd ever seen before. And then all the papers came in. The estate was a mess. I mean, we had money. We never wanted for money, but there were all these credit cards, and a mortgage on a condo in Miami.

"Oh my God."

"He'd had this whole other life for years. All his business trips. All his golf trips. Even weekends he said he was visiting his brother. And I just started going back through my mind and all the things he missed, like one Thanksgiving he said he got stuck in Colorado. And he always sent my mom and me to tournaments together. He only came to a handful of my biggest college bouts, but when he showed up, he was sweet and attentive and funny. We had amazing conversations, and he supported me so much when I came out."

Her voice broke, and Jess held her a little tighter.

217

"I just thought he worked too much, but I also thought he worked so much because he loved us. When he died, I had to face losing him and all the love I had for him, but I also had to face the reality that my mom and I had never been enough for him."

Jess wanted to argue. She wanted to rage and scream that Lauren would be enough for anyone and she was more wonderful and amazing than most people could handle if they really let themselves see her clearly. She wanted to call anyone who didn't get that a worthless idiot, but doing so would also be a horrible slight against her dead father, and in that dilemma, she experienced the tiniest sliver of the conflict ripping Lauren apart.

"And as bad as it was for me, as much as the grief drove me insane and twisted me into someone else, it just destroyed my mom completely." Lauren's voice lost all its affect. "She shattered into a million pieces. She didn't sleep or eat or shower for weeks. She went catatonic. I worried she might just surrender, or worse, actually hurt herself. And after that first phone call where I thought I'd lost her, I knew I couldn't take it if I really did."

"And that's why you moved back to Buffalo," Jess surmised.

Lauren nodded against her shoulder. I spent two years putting the pieces together. I got my mom a counselor, and I saw one, too, for a while, but mostly I buried myself in the work and wills and the estate and settling the things he'd left up in the air."

"Because you've always been the responsible one." Jess remembered a comment from so many years ago in a past that hardly felt like theirs anymore. "It's exhausting, but if you weren't, you wouldn't be you."

Lauren looked up at her with red-rimmed eyes as if the words burned through the haze of grief. "But I didn't feel like me anymore, not who I'd been, and not who I thought I'd become. I wasn't competition ready. I'd lost my shot at my dream job. My girlfriend had already left me and was living with someone else in the apartment I picked out."

"Motherfucker." Jess's fist clenched automatically.

"It was fine."

"Look, I'm glad for my sake that it didn't work out with some other woman, but it is most certainly not fine. Anyone worth keeping would've been there for you. She would've fought for you."

"She tried for a while," Lauren said sadly. "In some ways that was harder, because I knew I'd never be what she wanted again. When she found someone else, it took the pressure off me to be more exciting or have less baggage. She got to be in love again, and I didn't have to live in fear that I'd drag her into a situation where . . ."

Her voice trailed off, but Jess's brain filled in the blanks. Lauren would rather lose someone early on than live the rest of her life worrying she'd drive that person to do what her dad had done.

Her heart felt like it was literally breaking as pain stabbed her chest and wriggled its way under her ribs like the sharpest blade she'd ever faced. She couldn't stand it. She didn't know how Lauren had ever managed to stand again, and the fact that she had served only to strengthen Jess's already intense admiration for her. "You're a fucking hero."

"What?"

"You." She kissed her forehead, her temple, her tear-stained cheek. "You're the strongest, most amazing, most breathtaking human I've ever met. You're a fighter and a winner and a champion in ways I could never imagine becoming."

"Jess." She pulled back to stare at her. "Did you hear anything I just told you?"

"Yes. You told me someone else's demons dragged you into actual hell, and you clawed your way back, pulling your mother behind you. You came out the other side, and instead of collapsing in bitterness and resentment, you found it in yourself to wish the best for the people who failed you. Then, you started over, building a life you can hang your hat on, step-by-step, from scratch."

"It doesn't feel that way. It feels like I'm still paddling upstream. I've only learned to dream safe and small. I was so broken for so long, and I think deep down inside I still am."

219

"You are not broken." She gave her shoulder a little shake. "You took every strength and every positive attribute you possess, and you used them to survive. You're still brilliant and steady and caring. You still give so much of yourself to the people who depend on you. You're still so inspiring to me." Jess rose on shaking legs. "Come on. Let me show you."

"What?"

She extended her hand, and Lauren took it.

"What are you going to show me?"

Jess pulled her up and wrapped her in a tight hug before stepping back. "Fence me?"

"Fence you?"

"Left-handed," Jess offered quickly.

Lauren gave a mystified laugh. "Why?"

"Because . . ." Jess took a huge breath, then blew it out slowly. "Because we like fencing?"

"We do," Lauren admitted, her eyes holding a tentative hint of amusement. "But it's only like 6:30. There are students at the club."

Jess shrugged and hoped it looked nonchalant instead of noncommittal. "Maybe it'll be good for them to see some Olympic-level training."

"Is that what's about to happen? I thought you were going to show me something."

"I am," she said, a little more confidently. "I'm going to show you that you've got everything you need to move forward in any direction you want, and if some other people see that at the same time, the more the merrier. Do you trust me?"

Her eyes swirled with flecks of green and gold. "I think I just proved I do."

Jess kissed her again, soft and quick. "Good, then let's go."

By the time they made it back to the car, then back to the club and got changed, the last set of students for the night were already in their lessons. Lauren smiled at the sound of Enrico shouting, "No, no, you wild banshees," over the clang of sabers clattering and teenagers laughing. It was good for him to flex the old muscles, and she fleetingly wondered why she hadn't made him cover his own business more often. Then she entered the Elites' gym to the sight of Jess bent in half, stretching her back and straining the seat of her knickers over those impressive glutes, and she realized she'd never had such a tempting excuse to knock off work for a night.

Jess twisted to the side, still upside down, and grinned when she caught Lauren looking. "Whatcha thinking about?"

"I think you already know, and I think you like it."

Jess straightened and lifted her arms above her head in a way that elongated her torso in a delicious arc. She'd borrowed a left-handed lamé and glove, but still managed to look completely alluring, even in club clothes. "Can you tell me again why we decided to come back here?"

"You!" Lauren pointed at her. "You did this. You wanted to fence."

"To be fair, I wanted to do something else, but we both live at home with our parents, and some random dog had something to say about us doing the thing outside. But, in retrospect, I'm not sure that had to be a dealbreaker."

Lauren laughed, a genuine laugh she wouldn't have thought herself capable of an hour ago. "Okay, fine. You wanted to do something else, and for what it's worth, I wanted the same, but not outside. So, apparently with that off the table, the only other thing either of us know how to do is work."

"Right, except I know how to do other things. I just don't like any of them as much as I like to fence with you." Jess plugged herself into the wall cords. "And this is not work. This is joy."

Whatever was left of Lauren's confusion or resistance evaporated. Every moment with Jess carried a myriad of emotions, but there was no denying joy ranked very high among them. And as much as she didn't want to let herself look too far ahead, she hadn't completely lost sight of the fact that her days with Jess in this gym were numbered. "You're right. It's been a long time since I've gotten to beat an Olympic athlete."

"Beat?" Jess's pitch rose.

"You said you were fighting left-handed. I may not be as good as I once was, but I'm relatively confident I can still beat your weak hand."

Jess threw back her head and laughed. "I don't have a weak hand."

Her face flushed as a few vivid memories of Jess using those hands on her flashed through her mind, and she snagged the nearest mask to cover up her arousal. She wasn't the type of person who usually suffered these little lapses, and judging from the competitive glint in Jess's eyes, she did so now at her own peril.

They ran through a couple of warm-up passes, each of them stretching out muscles they'd worked in new ways the night before, and finding their feet after a day spent doing other things. Still, she could've used a little more time to get her mind right before Jess resolutely declared, "I'm good. Let's go."

From there, things sort of exploded. Lauren took the first point, but only by flailing. The next time she was ready, but still had to take a defensive stance as Jess came out swinging. She won only on the second counterattack.

"Yes." Jess cheered. "Go again."

She didn't have any time to argue or offer critique as several more points flew by in rapid succession. Jess finally snagged one of them to Lauren's seven, but she let fly a shout that rattled the rusty old rafters.

Lauren heard shuffling behind her and saw several of her high school fencers watching from the doorway.

"Again," Jess commanded.

This time, a real battle ensued. They traded attacks, and Jess pushed her back several steps before something kicked into a higher gear for Lauren, and she lunged for an unanswered touch.

Jess didn't even flinch as the buzzer sounded, she just stalked back to her starting position as she called, "Beautiful. Do it again."

"What?"

"On guard," Jess said, and Lauren lifted her saber automatically. "Do that same lunge again. Go."

They established a frantic pace, this time whirring blades and blocking, but Lauren stayed with her, not just reacting, but pressing forward when she got the chance, timing her steps, two fast, one slow and short. Then, when Jess faltered, she lunged once more and hit her right in the ribs.

A little cheer went up from the teens, and Jess lifted her helmet.

The room fell silent for several stunned seconds, then whooshed in a rush of gasps and whispers. Jess didn't seem to notice them though, her intense gaze still trained on Lauren.

"Lauren, you're phenomenal. You still have so much grace and timing, and if I can learn to defend you left-handed, then I shouldn't have any . . ."

Her voice trailed off as she spotted the kids at the door, then glanced to the window, which was also filled with stunned faces.

"I think you drew an audience," Lauren said.

"I think we did, together." Jess gave a little salute to the onlookers.

"It's Jess Kidman." One of the kids stated what the others had already surmised.

"I think they're here to see you," Lauren laughed, but when she lifted her mask, a loud cheer went up from the small crowd, and multiple conversations broke out.

"It's Lauren."

"It's Coach."

"Coach Lauren is fighting Jess Kidman."

"Go Coach!"

Jess turned to her with a huge grin. "Are you so sure, Coach?"

She smoothed a gloved hand over her hair as a little something giddy bubbled up in her chest.

"Did you beat her, Coach?" someone called.

"No," she answered at the same time Jess said, "Yes."

"We're just practicing."

"She's teaching me some new tricks," Jess added.

"Can we stay and watch?" one of her peppiest girls pleaded.

Her chest tightened. She didn't want an audience for several reasons, privacy, focus, and a completely unprofessional desire to be alone with Jess.

"How about you watch one more point tonight," Jess offered. "Then we'll set up an event sometime, where you can watch for real. Maybe we can raise a little money for your club to get cameras hooked up to the ginormous TV your coach got you."

Another peal of applause went up through the crowd again.

"What do you say, Coach? What about the weekend before I leave for the Olympics?" Jess flashed Lauren one of those smiles that suggested she knew exactly how amazing she was.

She couldn't argue with the sentiment or the woman who wore it so well. "Seems like a fitting send-off."

She managed to smile before she pulled her mask back on. There was no need for anyone else to see how the idea of them saying goodbye hit her harder than any blow Jess had landed that night.

"Fuck." Jess jumped back again. Lauren had landed hit after hit, and Jess battled a myriad of emotions from frustration to appreciation. She loved having this woman push her, and yet she wanted to win. She was used to winning. The only times she didn't win were against . . . no. She shook her head. This wasn't that.

"Again," she called.

"Jess." Lauren slipped into her placating tone.

"Again."

Lauren shook her head, but she reset, and off they went.

Her right hand still twitched each time Lauren lunged. Even though she saw her coming, her brain split into a million little processing pieces. The attack, the adrenaline, the awe, and then her own reaction fractured from anticipation, form, movement. She had all the pieces there, but they didn't merge the way she needed them to.

Again, she was left with incompetent rage as Lauren's saber bit into the lamé covering her ribs and sounded a quick beep.

"Son of a mother—" She bit her tongue, but it was a useless sort of restraint as all the others had left an hour ago, and Lauren had heard her say far worse over the course of that same period. "Sorry. I'm fine. Go again."

"Come here."

"No. Reset."

"Come here." It wasn't a request this time, so she sullenly shuffled forward.

Lauren unplugged her own saber and set it down lightly. Then, she did the same with her helmet.

"No. Don't stop." Jess tried not to whine, but she didn't want this to end. Not until she could make her brain work the right way.

"We don't have to, but I need to see your eyes."

"You can see them through the mask." Okay, she sounded whiny, and she hated it enough to pull herself together a bit. "I mean, what do you need to see?"

"I need to see you, Jess." Lauren spoke calmly but firmly as she lifted the mask from her face and met her gaze.

She fought the urge to look away from the inspection. It wasn't that she didn't want to live up to it, so much as she wanted it more than anything she'd wanted in a long time. She wanted it desperately enough to fear she would fail, and she had no capacity for processing something she'd spent her whole life refusing to feel.

"Okay," Lauren said.

"Okay?"

"I just needed to check in and make sure it's still you behind those baby blues."

"What do you mean?" she asked softly.

"Sometimes when you pull down the mask, it's like you forget who you are, or you actually become someone else, and I don't mean just competitively. You're competitive all the time. Your

225

mind races all the time. You see openings and possibilities, whole worlds of them, and it's so beautiful to watch, but I can't see the whole picture."

"You see me all the time."

Lauren's smile picked up a hint of sadness. "I'm here with you all the time, but sometimes it's like you're throwing yourself against the bars of a cage I can't see."

Her teeth clenched. "I'm not."

"You just did it."

She pressed her lips into a tight line to keep from shooting back a sharp retort.

"Jess, you're the top fencer in the country. Why do you have such a chip on your shoulder?" Lauren skimmed the back of her knuckles down the back of her tight jaw. "What are you trying to prove?"

She wanted to look away, but she also burned with the desire to lean into her touch. "Yelena is smarter than me."

"What?"

Her heart pounded against her ribs. "I'm not the best fencer in the world."

"You're right up there."

"I should be at the top. I'm faster. I have better form. I'm stronger. I have better hands. I have more passion and guts, and she's just stone cold. I should be better than her, but . . ." Her voice cracked with anguish. "She's smarter than me."

"No one is smarter than you."

Jess jumped back. "She is. God, don't tell me I don't know. I know it in a way that's ripping me apart."

"No."

"Yes. I wake up in cold sweats with the knowledge sitting on my chest so heavy I can't breathe. And there's no answer, there's never—"

Lauren held up a hand. "Stop, Jess. For one second, please, just shut up!"

And she did. Shocked, mouth open, eyes wide. Lauren had

never spoken to her like that, and it cut straight through her panic.

Lauren began to pace like the caged lion Jess had always been, only she didn't roar so much as growl. She kept one palm up as if holding her back, but she lifted the other one to massage her temple as she muttered, her gaze soft and unfocused toward the window into the lobby. "She's not smarter than you. Smart, but not smart*er*. You're maxed out. She's . . . maxed out. She's as smart as you. She's *as smart as* you."

She dropped her hand and lifted her eyes. They shone with a confetti of colors every bit as dynamic as the revelation she was experiencing.

"What is it?" Jess asked breathlessly.

"Yelena isn't smarter than you. She's exactly the same level as smart as you. You are the smartest. You always do the smartest possible thing, so she only has to figure out what's the smartest possible move and defend it." Lauren laughed, a sharp, triumphant shot, then pointed through the window to the coffee table she'd recently fitted with a chessboard for Jess's non-video days. "Don't you see?"

"See what?"

"You're playing chess, but she's just playing rock paper scissors."

A niggling wiggle of hope wormed its way through her core. "What do you mean?"

"When we were playing rock paper scissors earlier, I had no strategy of my own. I didn't sit there thinking about the best possible move. I just thought about what you'd do, and I threw the thing to beat it." As Lauren spoke faster, the more excited she got. "But in that game, there are only three choices, and in fencing, the combinations are infinite. Any person with an average mind could never calculate for all the possibilities. That takes a superior mind, and you have that kind of mind."

Jess nodded and made a rolling motion with her hand. "Keep going. Get to the point where I beat her."

"That is the point! She's just skipping to the point where she beats you. She waits until you make the smartest possible choice, and then she defends against that. Think about the video. Almost every one of her points is defensive."

She ran through the footage in her mind. She'd certainly watched it enough to relive each scene in detail, but this time, instead of surrendering to the despair of her own futility, she analyzed the attacks. They were all hers, or at least the points she lost on. Lauren was right. Every point that depended on speed or strength went to Jess, but the longer they fought, the more Yelena became the counterattack queen. "She knows what's coming."

Lauren nodded. "And don't get me wrong. That's flipping impressive. She's no slouch, but she's not your better, just your equal."

"If she gets one step ahead of me, she's my better"—Jess rubbed her face—"but she's not actually going a step farther, is she? She's just meeting my step."

"And what's more, as she pushes you, the more predictable you become. Confident fencers take risks, which makes them harder to anticipate, but the more she enrages you, the more you sink back into textbook attacks. She's only got to anticipate you a few times, make you second-guess yourself, make you afraid, and then you make her job infinitely easier."

"Because every coach I've ever had told me I lose my temper too much. They swore I needed to calm down and not be so erratic." The defensiveness in Jess's tone didn't even come close to the resentment pulsing through her veins.

"And maybe that's true for a normal fencer, or against normal fencers, but not you, and not against her. You said yourself, the others tried to turn you into someone else, but the more they turn you into a different fencer, the more easily she'll read your playbook."

Jess shook her head, unable to summon any of Lauren's optimism. So far, the news was all bad. "She's got my number."

"Exactly!" Lauren shot back and tossed Jess's helmet to her, "and that's why you can learn to beat her."

"I'm not sure I see what you see yet."

Lauren's smile turned smug. "Then maybe you actually did choose the right coach this time, because I can absolutely show you. Lose the left-handed lamé and put your saber back in your right hand."

Jess did as instructed, her heart pounding in anticipation. Lauren readied herself, then turned to face her on the strip.

"Now, assume your normal stance like you and I are going to have a totally competitive bout. You know me well. You know you have me beat out of the gate. What are you going to do?"

"Three quick steps, then a high kick-lunge."

"Do that." Lauren nodded. "Go."

Jess did just as planned, but before she even got to her third step, Lauren angled to the side and flicked her saber across Jess's arm, setting up an unanswered buzz.

Jess sighed at how easily the point had been made, but Lauren immediately reset. "Okay, I beat you on the attack. What would you do next?"

"I'm going to lunge at you, low and tight, right out of the box."

She could see Lauren's smile through her mask and got the strong sense she found the idea both fun and funny. Still, as she got her cue, Jess did just as she said and flung herself across the center of the strip, only Lauren wasn't there to make contact with. She merely took a sharp leap backward completely out of range. With Jess off-balance, she brought her saber down lightly across the top of her helmet.

"See," she said gleefully, "you don't have to be a better fencer if you know what's coming. And you would never let me get into your head or under your skin by thinking I was. But that's exactly what you let Yelena do. She's been living rent-free inside of your brain for years, but it's time to change the locks on her."

Jess nodded as the implications of what Lauren had just so aptly revealed made her brain too busy to speak right away. She felt like all the microscopic puzzle pieces that floated in unclaimed spaces of her mind had magnetized and were being pulled slowly toward each other.

229

"What's next?" Lauren pushed.

"Um, I'm going to take two quick steps, but instead of a low lunge, I'll go for a high attack inside."

Lauren nodded resolutely, then gave the command to go.

Only this time, Jess didn't do what she'd said. She flinched forward, drawing Lauren into a position to defend a high attack, then dropping her saber low to her side, she swung upward in an arc before flicking her wrist to smack the bottom of Lauren's lamé at the last second.

Lauren's mask lit up like a flash-bang as the buzzer sounded.

"Yes!" she screamed.

"Yes!" Lauren echoed. "That's it . . . wait, what was that?"

Jess removed her mask and took in a deep draw of fresh air that went further into her chest than anything had in ages. "I modified Kristie's slap shot."

Lauren laughed. "You're both insane."

"Maybe, but there's no way to predict against crazy, right?"

"Exactly!"

The tension loosened its grip on her lungs, and she felt lighter in every sense of the word. She wouldn't get a chance to test their theory against Yelena before the Olympics, but for the first time, she felt like she had a viable game plan. She had a workable strategy. She had something to practice, something to hone, something to keep her from feeling hopeless.

Lauren had given her that. She didn't think it was possible for her to love this woman any more than she had at thirteen, with the earnest sincerity of her age and the passion of a first awakening, but as she watched Lauren pull off her own mask and shake out her long hair, she knew with a certainty her younger self could've only marveled at that this woman's destiny was tied to her own.

"What is it?" Lauren asked, her exuberant smile turning curious.

"I . . ." She swallowed the word. "I'm so . . . Lord, I can't even talk right now."

"It's okay." Lauren stepped closer. "You don't have to say anything."

"But I want to," Jess rasped. "I want to tell you so many things, too many things. You don't even know what this means to me, but I want you to."

Lauren cupped her cheek in her palm, so soft and hot and strong, like all the other feelings she inspired. Then, she leaned close and whispered, "Then show me."

Chapter Nine

Lauren stared down at the sleeping form next to her. She wouldn't have thought Jess could look so innocent sprawled half off a broken-down couch in the club lobby, especially after all the guilty pleasures they'd extracted from each other the night before.

She hadn't intended to sleep there. The sofa merely offered the softest surface on which to crash after all the unholy ways they'd used the Elites' gym. That space had seen generations of collisions and decades of exertion, but she felt relatively certain those walls had never borne witness to the types of things they'd done to one another against the padding, on the mats, in front of the mirrors. They'd grown high on their intellectual triumph, emotional enmeshment, and the raw physicality of each other. She hadn't even recognized herself in those moments, but she'd never lost sight of Jess, and she couldn't take her eyes off her now.

Somewhere along the way they'd snagged a beach towel from God only knew where, and Jess had it pulled up to her chin. Smooth skin, paler in the dim light, only seemed to accentuate the burgundy of her lips and the rusty red curl that had fallen across her forehead. Lauren fought the urge to push it back, not because she didn't want to wake her, but because she didn't want to do anything to add order to the chaos they'd fallen into over the last few days. If she started putting things back in their place, eventually she might have to ask where she belonged, and she wasn't ready to face that reality.

Not yet.

Instead, she lay half on her side and half across the strong body radiating heat against her. She watched her sleep and let her mind wander. When Jess had brought her back to this place last night, it had been under the guise of showing her something important, and in true Jess fashion she'd not only lived up to her promise, she'd expanded it several times. The moment when the cheer went up from her students would've been enough to remind her that she did matter, and she'd built something that mattered to others, but Jess didn't stop there. She also made her feel brilliant as they cracked the code to her strongest competitor. In the moment, she felt like they could hurdle any obstacle together. She hadn't felt that way in years. Useful, smart, strong, and all the other attributes Jess had sworn she still possessed.

Jess made her point over and over. She made plans for them. She made progress. She made love to her. She made Lauren feel like she'd left a mark on her career, her body, her future.

She shivered at the last thought, the one that went too far, the one she had a harder time compartmentalizing with each moment she spent wrapped around this woman.

"Are you cold?" Jess mumbled in a half sleep.

"No." She stifled a laugh at the idea. "Never with you around."

The corner of that enticing mouth twitched up. "Is it morning?"

"Yes. And while I'd love to promise no one ever comes here in the morning, occasionally people do stop by."

"Are you trying to imply we need to move?"

"As much as it pains me."

"Oh, it's going to pain both of us," Jess groaned as she wriggled herself a little more fully onto the couch. "I don't think I'm in an Olympic-training-approved sleeping position."

"No. And neither of us got a proper wind-down last night either," Lauren agreed. "We're going to need extra yoga today. So. Much. Stretching."

Jess scrunched up her face as if she found the idea unsavory. "I wish we could just take the day off, but we kind of tried yesterday, didn't we?"

"We tried. I don't think we succeeded because our day off left my muscles more sore than most of my actual workouts, but I also think we found the start of some really important break-throughs, and I don't want to lose momentum."

Jess's eyes fluttered open, a shot of azure under thick lashes. "My body wants to argue, but no other part of me does. You were a revelation last night, even when you still had your clothes on."

She smiled down at her. "Thanks. You weren't so bad yourself."

Jess closed her eyes again with a contented grin. "Maybe we could just snuggle into that sentiment a little bit longer?"

"Sorry, champ." She kissed her on her lips and started to climb over her, but as soon as she was straddling her, Jess found her reflexes and took hold of her. Lifting her hips up off the couch, she managed to shake Lauren's balance and force her to settle across her abdomen.

"Hey now," she warned without managing to sound stern.

"Did you know you're beautiful?" Jess asked, as if that were an acceptable conversational shift.

"I know you look at me like I am."

Jess ran her hands up and down Lauren's sides. "Maybe I could do more than look at you."

"You can." Lauren swung her leg over and stepped out of her reach. "You can follow me to the locker room and take a shower in your own stall while I take one in mine."

Jess laughed from behind her as she walked quickly down the hall. "Can we compromise on a couple of those details?"

She didn't answer. She knew how futile it would be, and she didn't hate that. In fact, the anticipation pulsing through her veins felt every bit as awesome as the warm water soon cascading over her shoulders. She'd managed to soak her hair and work up a substantial lather when Jess slipped through the curtain behind her.

"So, the term 'own shower' was one of those details you wanted to compromise on?"

"See?" Jess asked playfully. "You're brilliant at analyzing the situation and anticipating my next move. That's what made you such a great fencer, and also, if I may say so, a truly spectacular lover."

"Hmm." Lauren closed her eyes and tilted her head back so it ran under the stream of warm water. "I'd like to say flattery will get you nowhere, but seeing as how it's gotten you into the shower with me, I think I'll save my breath."

"Save it for other, more pressing things?" Jess asked as she snaked an arm around her waist and began to kiss along her neck.

Lauren met her mouth on its upward trajectory. She could've argued. At least that's what she told herself, but she wasn't sure she believed her. And anyway, what was the use? Even if she put up a good showing, Jess would win. It's what Jess did, and Lauren had been the beneficiary of that attribute many times. She had plenty of reasons to step back, but the reason she held on was the simplest of them all.

She wanted to.

Jess broke the kiss and pulled back only far enough for water to pool between them. "Want me to wash your back?"

"Sounds heavenly." She turned in her embrace, and Jess kissed across her shoulders, pushing her wet hair out the way to run her tongue along the nape of her neck. "Were you planning to wash my back with your mouth?"

"Maybe," Jess murmured, but she did manage to grab some shower gel and form a lather in her hands before rubbing it up and down her spine. Then branching out, she massaged tight muscles into submission, working from the center all the way to her sides.

Her hands were amazing, strong and skilled in ways Lauren no longer found surprising, and yet hadn't quite come to expect. They worked each knot loose before traveling on in search of the next one to subdue. Lauren might have been willing to stay like that forever, no matter how much time passed or who might find them there, but Jess had never been one to simply accept a dream without reaching for more, and this time her reach worked its way around to cup her breasts.

Lauren bit her lip as a thumb rolled over her nipple before

circling around to tease the other. Jess seemed to take the lack of protest as encouragement, but she was also too smart to give her more responsible nature any chance to rebound, and while still palming her breast with one hand, slid the other lower. She ran expert fingers through wet curls and into wetter folds.

Lauren sighed and leaned back into the strong body encircling her as Jess started slow and soft. She wouldn't have thought herself capable of responding again, but Jess didn't just know that she would, she understood how to draw everything she had left out of her with such delicious, deliberate strokes. Lauren allowed her head to grow heavy and drop so it rested on Jess's shoulder.

Jess kissed her neck, her cheek, her ear as she whispered the sexiest sounds in low, intimate tones. "God, you feel so amazing in my arms. I love the way you can be so soft against me, and so hard under my fingers all at the same time."

"It shouldn't be possible," Lauren said as she closed her eyes and surrendered to the sensations surrounding them once again.

"What?"

"All of it," she managed before the words faded into a moan as Jess increased the pressure on the circles she was drawing around Lauren's need.

She had no idea how she was doing any of this, and not just having morning sex in a shower at work, though that would've been enough to make her mind swim on any other day. It shouldn't have been so easy for her to relax in someone's arms. It shouldn't be this easy to forget all the history between them or the pressure and conflicts inherent in their very imminent futures. It shouldn't be easy to let the water wash away all the fear and insecurity she'd carried for so long. Then again, as her body began to climb once more, she knew it wasn't just the water wiping away the worry. That was Jess.

All Jess.

Her hips rocked forward and resettled so her body molded to Jess's completely, slick skin between them sliding smooth and hot. Jess picked up speed, her own increasing arousal evidenced by the hard press of her nipples against Lauren's back and the thrust of her hips against Lauren's ass. They were both too wet in too many ways to create much friction, but Jess's hands never missed their mark even as their movements grew erratic, and Lauren's mind faded into incoherency.

The orgasm grew quickly out of control and ripped through her body. She bit her lip to keep from shouting, but the sharp pinch of her own teeth did little to contain her cry. At last, Jess's magnificent body absorbed the quick convulsion and kept her upright through the aftershocks.

As she stabilized and the high whine of her most sensitive nerve endings settled into a low hum, Jess turned her gently until they faced each other once more. Softly, she kissed her chin, her cheek, her lips, her temple, and in a low, sultry voice managed to say, "Good morning."

"See, this is why I could never become an elite athlete," Kristie said as she skated backward in circles while Jess took a more leisurely route around the empty ice rink. "I mean, I'm good at hockey. I used to be really good. At one point, I was in the running for the national team, but that stuff will consume your entire life."

"Yeah, well it's not like I'm known for being all work and no play." Jess grinned at a few recent memories. "But we're in the homestretch now, plus Lauren and I had multiple breakthroughs in the last few days."

"I sorta got that, seeing as how I haven't heard from her once since y'all started having sleepovers." She gave her a sly grin. "Which I approve of by the way, but I have to admit I'm surprised she let you out of her sight this afternoon. I also got the feeling that despite whatever else you all have gotten up to, you'd also been locked in the club for days."

"Well, you're not wrong. We've been working nonstop, and she might not love it if she knew I was here right now, which is why I simply told her I needed a leg workout."

Kristie laughed and took a lazy loop, or at least it looked lazy, but it didn't escape Jess that she covered more ground than she did at her moderate exertion levels.

"Besides, a deal is a deal, and honestly, the way we've been working out lately is just as risky as me skating a few laps." She thought of the panicked tinge in Haley's voice over the phone. "One of the top fencers in the world just broke his foot in a regular bout, and I'm heartbroken for him, but everyone's risking something right now. I can't live my life in a bubble."

Kristie nodded. "You play with swords for a living. You can't be too risk-averse."

"I like the way you think. And you're right, I put my body on the line all the time. I go 100 percent in everything I do, but that's also when I feel my best. I'm happiest when I'm pushing and being pushed, which is what's made the last few days so amazing. I feel like a little kid again. I'm just a ball of hope and energy."

"It's kind of crazy that you're working harder right now and under more pressure than you've had at any time since you've been back in town, but you seem less broody than at any point since I've known you."

She couldn't disagree, even if she'd never really thought of herself as broody. She did feel mentally and physically stronger than she had in years. She and Lauren had worked through a million scenarios and strategies in the gym. She'd spent hours every day developing a more nuanced approach that still felt more natural than any she'd employed in maybe ever. She certainly hadn't had this kind of a mind meld with any coach or training partner in her professional career, and she had plenty of coaches to compare Lauren to.

When it came to their personal relationship, though, there was no comparison to be made. There was only Lauren, and at times she found it hard to remember there had ever been anyone but Lauren in her life, in her arms, in her bed. Despite all the early anguish, once the dam had broken between them, everything had rushed toward its rightful place. For the first time, she felt like she was where she needed to be in every area of her life simultaneously.

The joy welling up in her overflowed. "Wanna race?"

Kristie laughed. "I'm not sure that's a great idea."

"Because you're afraid I'll overdo it and get hurt?"

"No, because I'm afraid I'll overdo it and hurt your pride."

"Fair, but like, I have all this energy bursting out of me right now, and I want to do something big."

Kristie's eyes danced with amusement. "Like what? Go to the Olympics in a couple of days?"

"Touché." She was being silly and over-the-top. "I'm just so amped up, I'm splitting in two. I want to go now, but I also want to keep training like this forever, and I want Lauren to—" She caught herself and drew up just short of saying the thing she'd agreed to let go of.

"You want Lauren to what?"

She shook her head. "I don't know, I want her to feel as happy as I do right now. What if I did something nice for her?"

"I don't mean to sound crude, but I get the sense you've already done some pretty nice things for her lately."

Her face warmed. "Yeah, well, I like to think so, but we're actually pretty even on that particular count, and she's also working insanely hard for me in other areas. I'd like to do something to tip the scales in my favor."

Kristie slowed her skates gradually as she seemed to ponder the statement. "Okay."

"Okay?"

"I'm all for you doing something great for my best friend. She takes care of everyone else all the time and rarely takes anything for herself."

"She's always been like that," Jess agreed, "but I think it's gotten stronger as she grew up."

Kristie nodded with a seriousness Jess had yet to see out of her. "And I want to help, but I kind of have to step into protective mode a little bit here, which, believe me, is awkward for both of us. These scales you want to tip in your favor? I'm not sure what all that entails for you in the long run."

It was the million-dollar question and the answer that had

died on her lips a moment earlier. She'd agreed she could do without it, and she could if she had to, but living without something and living without wanting something were very different things. "I'd really like her to come to the Olympics with me, but even if she can't, I want her to stay on with me after I get back, and well, indefinitely."

"Stay on with you indefinitely how? Like as your coach or as your girlfriend?"

"Um, I feel like the answer is both. Is both an option?"

Kristie shrugged. "Don't ask me. I don't know the rules in your line of work."

"I looked into the official rules after she mentioned some ethics concerns, but I couldn't find anything pertaining to us in any meaningful way," Jess said, not sure if she should be relieved or annoyed to even have to question her own right to consent. "Everything out there is about relationships between coaches and youth or collegiate athletes, or like, if the relationship started before the fencer turned eighteen, or maybe if the coach had some kind of power over funding or national ranking, and I totally get why people would be squeamish, but it's not us."

"Okay. So, no official policies is good, but do you worry people might look down on Lauren?"

"I can't say some people won't look down on her, or me, or anything that shakes up their boys' club, but choosing this battle would make them horrible hypocrites. Our relationship is more equal on every level than the vast majority of theirs." The more Jess talked, the more she picked up steam, and the faster she skated. "We met as teammates, not as coach and client. We didn't start a physical relationship until after I had the right to hire and fire her at will. And I doubt anyone in this business would really believe I'm afraid to fire a coach who pushed me in any way I didn't consent to."

Kristie laughed. "I got the sense you run through coaches almost as fast as you run through opponents, and, to be honest, that probably scares Lauren."

"Lauren's different."

"You and I both know it, but I'm not sure she does." Kristie skated beside her now instead of around her. "She still thinks of herself as a pit stop on your path to greatness, and don't get me wrong, she's come to life while playing that role for you, but she's not going to let herself get swept up in some long-term adventure."

"Ugh, I don't know what kind of long-term adventure she's imagining. It's not like I'm about to get my break in show business or become a pop star. Most fencers I know end up in major debt and living in tiny studio apartments over the clubs they fence at. Seriously, how many fencers do you think most Americans can name?"

"Zero."

"Right, so best-case scenario, if I win big in a couple weeks, and that's still a huge 'if,' I'll get, at most, fifteen minutes of mild fame. I'll score a nice hunk of metal and a couple months of press, which I'll try to use to secure a few more deals, maybe a big sponsorship."

"How big are we talking?"

"Not big enough to become a lifelong high roller. Something like an endorsement for Nike's fencing shoes could be a moon shot, but even then, I'd use the money to fund another few years of training in the hopes of doing this all over again in four years."

"Wow, you sure know how to party."

She snorted. "I actually do, but I like fencing more. Also, I have no other discernible skills. And I'm just as likely to go under as I am to go on to big things. Honestly, I've had many older fencers tell me to just get out while I can."

"So, why don't you?"

"Maybe I'm not as smart as I think I am. Or maybe I'm prone to fits of passion and visions of grandeur."

"Seems like a legit possibility for you."

"Thanks." She smiled in spite of the ribbing, or perhaps because of it. "I think, probably, though, I stay in for the same reason Lauren keeps working at a club that's beneath her. The sport is in our blood, and there's no way out that doesn't feel like bleeding dry."

"First of all, I knew you stabby women had a screw loose, but also, you know that's not the only reason Lauren's still here, right?"

Jess slid to a stop, her chest suddenly too tight to exert herself anymore. "She told me about what happened with her dad, and I've been thinking about it, but something still doesn't add up."

"What?"

"I get coming back to Buffalo. I would've done the same for my mom, but even in Buffalo, she could've made other choices. She has a business degree from Princeton. She could've gone to work for any number of corporations or banks. She chose fencing. She stayed in the sport that has her heart and has always had her back. Fencing is where she feels strongest and most secure. Shouldn't that indicate it's also the place where she can begin to branch out and build back to greatness again?"

"I think she's afraid to dream even that big," Kristie said quickly. "I'm not sure she lets herself dream too much at all. But you're right about the first part. She does love the sport, and she loves the club and all those geeky kids who roll through there."

"Hey, I was one of those geeky kids."

"Yeah, and that's how you got your foot in the door with her in the first place. I think you need to stick with what works. If you convince her one of those dreams you're talking about is bigger than both of you, you might have something." Kristie sighed. "Her better angels are stronger than anyone I've ever met, but you'll still have a real uphill battle."

Jess nodded as a few ideas started to form, each one jostling for its chance to rise to the forefront, but before any one of them succeeded, Kristie grabbed her by the shoulder. "And you have to mean it."

"Whoa." She wobbled on the skates.

"Sorry, but that's a sticking point. If you sell her on a dream, you better mean it for real."

"Sure, I will."

"No, seriously," Kristie said. "I get that you're a good person and you don't want to hurt her, but I also think you're the kind of person who makes decisions on the fly."

She didn't argue.

"And don't get me wrong. Lauren could use a little more impulsiveness in her world," Kristie plowed on. "But you've been chasing her for, like, half your life. You need to really stop and think about what it would mean for both of you if you catch her."

Jess opened her mouth only to find her heart stuck in her throat. Even when she realized how much her quest to win Lauren had fueled her entire fencing career, she'd only ever feared what it might be like to lose her. She'd never once considered what it would be like to actually catch, and more importantly, hold Lauren in her life.

"Wow, Coach Lauren, I didn't know you were famous," one the boys from the high school group said as he passed by with a red, white, and blue cupcake in each hand.

"I'm not famous," she called after him, causing one of the local reporters to laugh.

"Maybe not yet, but with all the press here today, you're going to see a bump," the woman said. "I didn't even know there was a club in this old warehouse."

"I get that a lot."

"Maybe you'll get it less after today. I can't vouch for your training methods. It's all still too fast and elaborate for me to follow, but at least I can say you throw a great party."

"Thanks." Lauren smiled as she looked around the full club and had to admit, even if only to herself, things had come together nicely for Jess's official Olympic send-off. The event served as equal parts bon voyage party, local press junket, and open house for the club. They'd spent the last three hours running fencing demos for first-timers, showing Jess's classic bouts on the big screen TV, and serving enough food to provide a sugar high for a small army. For their showstopper, they'd even set up a mock bout between her and Jess, with Enrico officiating.

She caught sight of him still holding court through the big window into the Elites' gym, and he gave her a broad smile. She hadn't seen him this animated in years, and she suspected he might have even awarded her a couple of home-cooked points during the bout because he enjoyed the action so much.

"What are you grinning at?" Kristie asked, strolling up with her fishbowl full of cash. She'd apparently enjoyed her job at fight night so much she'd appointed herself to the same role at the open house and spent much of the event walking around trying to drum up donations.

"I'm just having so much fun," Lauren said. "I love how everyone showed up, all my kids, my mom, Jess's parents, and so many people I don't even know."

"It's like fight night without all the aggressive pheromones steaming up the place."

"Oh yeah, that reminds me—" she grabbed a piece of paper and a pen off the reception desk. "The head coach from Rochester wants to set up a time to talk about some more official interclub competitions and some under-the-table fight nights."

"Like a secret I-90 roving grudge match?" Kristie made her fiercest face. "We can take 'em."

She shook her head as she scribbled a note to herself and set it atop her computer. "Actually, without Jess, they'll crush us, but it'll offer our fencers some better competition and hopefully make everyone feel a little less isolated from the larger sport."

"Including you," Kristie said.

Her heart tightened. She hadn't wanted to think about that today. She hadn't wanted to think about it all week. She'd been living like a woman who didn't know the expiration date on her happiness, but of course, she had never fully forgotten.

Jess was leaving in under forty-eight hours.

Lauren turned her focus almost subconsciously to the far side of the lobby, where Jess sat at a table signing autographs and taking pictures with a steady stream of kids and parents. She was in her element, chatting with them and hamming it up for the camera by flexing her biceps or making comically fierce faces. Everyone loved her, and none of that would change as her circle of exposure got wider over the next few weeks. Once the world got a chance to see her on prime time, the larger audience would no doubt fall in love with her as well.

A dad with a young girl Lauren had known only a few months stepped forward, and while Jess gave the daughter an autograph, the father cleared his throat. "It's been really good for Amy to see an Olympian training here over the last week. I know you're very busy, but do you ever give any private lessons?"

Jess smiled up at him. "Not really. I don't rule it out for someday when things mellow, but between my schedule and my hypercompetitive streak, I'm not suited to it at the moment."

"Not even for a professional rate?" the man prodded.

Jess laughed. "There's no need to throw good money down the drain when you already have the best coach in the business on staff here. I mean really, if you want your kid to move up in the sport, you don't want to just chase random Olympians. You should go after the people who train Olympians."

Lauren's face flushed as Jess glanced pointedly in her direction before adding, "But I do suspect her rates might go up when word gets out she's an Olympic-caliber coach, so you might want to lock her down for some private lessons soon."

Kristie elbowed her in the ribs. "She just upped your income."

She shook her head. "She's very good at upping the stakes, and I have to admit that's been very good for the club."

"And what's good for the club is good for you," Kristie pressed. "You need to let yourself start thinking about a future where you capitalize on that."

She sighed, knowing she was right, but not quite sure she was ready to do so. Jess had given her endless opportunities to take advantage of, and the bowl of money in her best friend's arms said they were at least on their way to starting the next phase of innovations for the club. Cameras were just the beginning of what she could do with more students and better, private rates. She could give her kids all the opportunities they currently had to leave Buffalo to pursue. She could create a community here for them and for herself. She could up the level of competition and give so many more people a shot at the type of hopes she'd helped foster in Jess.

A month ago, all of those things would've sent her over the top with excitement, and while she did feel a good bit of exuberance at all the possibilities, now they were tempered with the realization Jess wouldn't be around to share them with her.

"Ah, there you are, Lauren," Jess's dad called as he strode over, hand extended. "Or should I call you 'Coach Standish'?"

She smiled and shook his hand. "Please, just Lauren, and have you met my friend Kristie?"

"We spoke earlier," he said, "but if she keeps collecting money like that, I might have to hire her for our community foundation over at General Mills."

Kristie laughed. "I'm not one of those lesbians who looks good in a suit, but I do really like Lucky Charms, so you might be able to get me on board."

He laughed heartily. "Good to know."

"Oh hey, some people who haven't donated yet are getting ready to leave," Kristie said with the enthusiasm of a shark who smelled blood. Then, she bolted.

Mr. Kidman watched her go. "She's tenacious, and you have a knack for surrounding yourself with good people."

She smiled sadly. "I learned that lesson the hard way, but I'm glad I have a small circle I can trust."

He nodded. "I know we don't know each other well yet, but I appreciate you including my daughter in your circle, and I hope you know if you ever need anything, you can call on our family."

"Thank you." Her throat constricted a little. "That means a lot."

"Well, so far it's pure sentiment, but to prove how much I mean it, I also wanted to let you know I sit on the board for the charitable foundation at work. We're always looking for community organizations worthy of development grants, and I think you could write a very compelling application for those closed-circuit cameras you're raising money for."

Her heartbeat accelerated. "Are you serious?"

"Absolutely. We love projects that up the profile of Buffalo, and we have a soft spot for applications around youth engagement. Plus, I could speak personally to the positive effects youth fencing had on the life of our family."

Her head spun with all the implications of what his endorsement at one of the city's biggest employers could do for the club. "And you really mean that? You're not just saying it because I've been, um, working with Jess."

He smiled. "Not at all. I would've said the same thing if you'd talked to me before she got back to town. I remember what it's like to be one of these parents, sitting in a cramped lobby praying your kid is doing okay and wondering if you'll get a happy ride home or have to mop up tears."

Lauren smiled at the image of him wringing his hands nervously while his little redheaded daughter diced up her competitors. "I can't imagine you had to mop up many tears while Jess zoomed up the ladder."

He grimaced. "You'd be surprised. She'd cry more after a win she didn't deserve than over a loss she did." He shook his head slowly. "The winning never mattered to Jess as much as being able to find some sort of peace in the chaos."

"She's not someone who seems to settle into peace easily."

He smiled down at her, his expression more introspective than it had been before. "No, never easily, and yet she has settled in this last week. I expected her to be a nervous wreck in the final lead-up to her departure, but she's been more at peace than I've seen her since . . . well, honestly, since she was a child. I thought maybe you'd been the one to figure out the magic formula."

Her cheeks flushed at a few key memories she hoped he didn't know enough to factor into that magic formula she and Jess had found over the last few days. She couldn't even take much credit for those, as Jess had been in the driver's seat for much of those encounters. "I'm not sure I deserve much credit. I don't think I did anything special. I think it's just who she is."

He patted her shoulder. "I didn't mean to make you uncomfortable or monopolize your time. I'll let you go, but don't sell yourself short. She's had a lot of coaches and a lot of friends over the years, and none of them had the effect your presence has had, so maybe you don't have to do anything more special than just being you."

Her heart kicked her ribs at the observation and the love with which it was delivered. Jess was so much more than her win-loss record. Strong and driven and deeply committed to what she knew in her core. Jess wouldn't rest until she was happy with herself, and Jess had a better understanding of what that would take than any person Lauren had ever met.

She glanced across the room again to see Jess's smile, broad, unrestrained, and directed solely at her.

A shiver ran up the back of her neck as a wash of something strong filled her chest. She had to force herself to look away, or she'd have no choice but to pin a name to that emotion.

"Thank you so much for today," Jess said, catching hold of Lauren's hand and pulling her down onto the sofa beside her as soon as the door closed behind the last of the party guests. Lauren had shed her jacket and her breastplate, leaving her in an alluringly tight white shirt atop her fencing knickers, giving her an elegantly disheveled appeal.

"It wasn't just me. A lot of people helped arrange the food, and the kids all got the word out. Your parents handled a lot of the invites, and Kristie harangued so many people out of their wallets."

"Yes, and I thanked them all as well, but none of them would've had anything to support unless you pulled them together."

"Well, technically it was your idea. I would've just let the youth group watch us practice, but you turned it into an event."

"And you turned that event into a success." Jess kissed her quickly to stop her from arguing. "We built on each other's vision. We do that well. We're good together, and not just in bed or on couches or in showers. We make a good team."

Lauren touched her forehead to Jess's, resting there a moment with her eyes closed before easing back with a small smile on her beautifully serene features. "Okay."

"Okay?" she asked tentatively.

"Okay. I'm starting to believe you . . . a little bit."

"A little bit is a start." She laughed, a bubble of joy that rose out of her unexpectedly. "I'll take what I can get."

"You've gotten a lot of me this week."

"Too much?"

Lauren's smile grew. "No, you have a tremendous knack for pushing your toe right up to the line and nudging it forward without actually crossing it."

"Any objection to me doing so again?"

Lauren shook her head and caught Jess by the scruff of her shirt, then leaned back, taking Jess with her as she sank onto the couch.

A hum of pleasure escaped Jess's lips as she settled her body weight against this woman who'd refused to be pinned down. "I've been thinking of doing this all day."

"What a coincidence. I, too, have thought about this several times when I shouldn't have."

She kissed her with the slow deliberateness of their budding familiarity. "Like when?"

"Like when we were fencing during the demo bout."

"Oh, me too," Jess murmured, "especially when you hit my chest on that beautiful riposte. So sexy."

"I love how good form turns you on," Lauren whispered as she scraped her teeth along Jess's earlobe.

She shuddered. "Everything you do turns me on."

They kissed again, this time deepening the sweep of tongues as their bodies melded together more fully. Lauren slipped one knee between Jess's legs, teasing at the kind of friction they were headed toward. She ground her hips into the contact and internally cursed the sheer amount of clothing their sport of choice required. She had absolutely no smooth way to undress in this position, and as much as she really wanted fewer barriers between them, she couldn't bring herself to pull away yet. She might never move if only she could stay pinned against Lauren forever, always entangled.

A warning bell went off in her brain. No, not her brain, her pocket. Her phone. It took her entirely too long to process the shrill ring of her phone, and for someone who prided herself on mental quickness, she probably should've found that more disconcerting.

"You need to check that," Lauren said, then ran her tongue along Jess's neck, sending a decidedly mixed message.

"It's in my pants. I can't reach it."

"Then, get up, and while you're there, lose the pants."

Now that sounded like a great way to multitask, but she still released a stifled groan as she rolled off Lauren and pushed herself up to standing. Fishing in her pocket with one hand, she shrugged off her suspenders, then glanced at her phone screen. She must've made the kind of face that poker opponents would love to see, because Lauren sat up as well.

"Uh-oh. Who is it?"

"Ansel," she snarled.

"Answer. You're leaving for the Olympics in two days."

She nodded and accepted the call, then did nothing to hide the resentment in her voice. "What do you need?"

"Hello to you, too," Ansel said evenly. "I got your coach a floor pass."

"Oh." Her shoulders fell.

"Oh? Seriously, that's all you have to say? You have no idea the strings I had to pull to make this happen on such short notice."

"Thank you?"

"You're welcome. I won't say it didn't pain me. I still think you're making a mistake to throw her to the lions, but it's on you, at least for the individual competition. You fight with me for the team competition."

"Yeah. Okay. That's fair."

"Nothing about this is fair, Jess." He sounded more tired and resentful than angry. "Not to you. Not the national team. Not her. And while we're at it, I looked her up. She's got a stellar record. I'm sure if we got her in a training program, she could be a legitimate coach someday, but this time she's going to be in over her head."

"It's my decision to make."

"And, like usual, you're going to make the selfish one. You'll risk all of our careers when you don't have a real advocate at your side," he snapped, then caught himself and reasserted his professionalism through clenched teeth. "When is she traveling?"

Her jaw tensed, both at his accusations and at the question. "I don't know yet."

"What do you mean you don't know?" Ansel's voice shot into a high whine.

"I didn't even know about the pass until ten seconds ago."

"Yeah, for the floor, not the training center. She always had access to the training center. Does she seriously not have a flight booked?"

Her defenses rose. "Why do you care?"

"Because I'm the national coach, and I've given you a long leash, but you told me you had this worked out, and now you're acting like—"

"Like nothing." Jess cut him off, more out of her own panic than actual anger. "I've got everything under control."

He blew out a frustrated breath right into the phone. "We haven't transferred Oren's plane ticket. His alternate is stuck in LA. If you need a ticket from New York, have your coach call me tonight, and we'll try to get her information into the system."

"We'll talk it over." Jess glanced at Lauren, whose eyes were full of questions.

"You're still going to have to get her on a connection from Buffalo."

"I said I had it under control."

"You don't sound like it."

"I'm hanging up."

"Have this woman call me, Jess."

She clicked the disconnect button, then stared at the phone

as if wanting to be double sure it had actually obeyed her command.

"Hey," Lauren said softly, "everything okay?"

She nodded, not sure how to start speaking just yet.

Lauren patted the couch cushion beside her.

She sat, resting her elbows on her knees and her head in her hand. "Okay. That was Ansel."

Lauren put a hand on her back. "Is someone else hurt?"

"No," she said quickly, "everything's fine. It could even be great, but I think you're going to be mad at me when I tell you what he said, and I don't want you to be mad at me, because you're in control, and I respect you completely, but remember how you said I pushed my toe right up to the line?"

"What did you do?"

"It's not what I did so much as what I didn't do." Her stomach clenched with a horrible mix of hope and dread. She wanted so much for Lauren to hear her out, but if she pushed too hard, she could lose more than an Olympic coach, which made her queasy.

"What didn't you do?"

"I didn't call and ask Ansel to coach me in the individual competition."

"Okay," Lauren said slowly, "so he called to ask you himself?"

"No." She tried to swallow, but it felt like something stuck in her throat. "He called to tell me he got a floor pass for you."

"For me?" Lauren's brow furrowed. "Oh Jess, what did you tell him?"

"I didn't tell him anything. He sounded so smug and condescending, and you heard me. I didn't commit you to anything, but I didn't tell him you weren't coming either."

"You know I can't."

"No." She stood. "I know you won't, and I'm trying to respect that, but it's hard because I think you should. There, I said it. I think you could, and you should, come with me."

"Jess." Lauren reached for her, but she stepped away.

"Ansel wants you to call him about a flight. You can leave with me the day after tomorrow, and I know it's short notice, but

252

Enrico can run the club, or hell, cancel classes, because three weeks at the Olympics would mean more for the future of this place than three weeks of kindercamp for tiny fencers. We could secure a future for this club together."

Lauren sat very still for a few moments, still and quiet and pensive until Jess couldn't take the tension anymore.

"Oh God, are you really mad at me?"

"No," she said softly, "just overwhelmed."

"I'm sorry." Jess sank onto the worn-out couch.

"No. I'm sorry. I wasn't prepared. Not for anything that's happened for the last two months." Lauren's voice shook. "I have no frame of reference, and I got swept up in your passion and all your ideas, and your eyes and your body, and everything but your future. I always knew I wasn't a part of your future."

She clenched her teeth against the pain that surged in her. "I want you to be."

"I'm trying to make sense of that. Can you see how hard I'm trying for you?"

She nodded. "I do, but I don't understand why it's so hard. It's just a couple of weeks of missed classes."

"Except it's not." Lauren cupped her cheek in her hand. "I'm being honest with you right now, and you need to do the same. You're not talking about a three-week vacation. You're talking about risking your entire career on me and then some unknown future you can barely articulate, much less fully understand."

"It's not a risk."

"It is," Lauren said quickly, "and you pretending like it's not true doesn't change the fact that there are better people to argue for you during competitions. You can't pretend just because I got a floor pass I'll be welcome there."

She glanced away, but Lauren turned her chin so they faced each other once more. "Ansel told you that, didn't he?"

She shrugged. "He's a dick. I'm not going to listen to him."

"Then, listen to me. You've spent your whole life preparing for these Olympics. They are your world, and you earned your spot time and time again. You belong there. I don't."

"You're wrong." She broke free of Lauren's hold this time. "You belong there, too. You're too good for this club, but if this club is your dream, then you could do so much more."

"I don't need anything—"

"Stop!" she shouted. "Stop talking about what you need to get by. You deserve better than the bare minimum. You deserve greatness. You deserve passion. You deserve dreams. You don't deserve to be holed up in a dark warehouse always waiting for the other shoe to drop."

Lauren winced, then took a deep, slow breath and released it. "I know you're trying to do a good thing, and I appreciate how high your emotions are running in this moment."

Something about the calm, centered tone of Lauren's measured response sent a trickle of cold water through Jess's veins and swirling around her feet.

"But you don't even understand what you're asking." Lauren eased deeper into the almost maternal melody she'd used so many years ago. "You just see the next challenge, the next adventure, the next big idea, and I adore that about you."

"Don't do this again," she pleaded.

"Don't do what?"

"Patronize me like I'm thirteen and you're so much older and wiser that you can see some future I can't."

"I don't think we see the same future. You see only possibilities, and through you, I got to see some of them, too. But I also see the possible pitfalls. I see the ways I can hold you back or let you down. I see past the next few weeks and months, and even years."

Something inside of her snapped. "No. You only see what you're afraid of. You see yourself getting left behind. You see the ways I could let you down, but you refuse to see that I have a staying power you've never given me credit for."

"I give you so much credit. I see things ahead of you—"

"I know, I know, I'm bound for greatness. I've heard this speech before, I know how it ends in your world, but you were wrong the first time, and you're going to be wrong about me again if you don't open your eyes."

"I wasn't wrong." Lauren's sweet, measured expression made Jess want to shake her. "You've achieved everything I knew you would."

"But"—a building righteousness gave Jess strength—"you said by the time I was old enough to date you, I wouldn't want to. You said I'd go on to bigger and better things than you. You said I'd leave you behind, but I swore I wouldn't. You were wrong, and I kept my promise. I mean it even more today than I ever have. When do I get credit for that?"

Tears filled Lauren's eyes, and she blinked them away, but she didn't seem to have any more words, so Jess rushed into the void.

"I love you, Lauren. Don't tell me I don't or I can't because I do, and I will keep loving you. You think I don't have the ability to see a full future for us, but I've seen it clearly from the first time I saw you. Every moment since then has involved my dedication to that dream. What is that if not staying power? I fell in love with you when I was thirteen years old."

"You weren't in love with *me*." Lauren found her voice again.

"I was there. I know what I felt."

"You developed a crush, or maybe an infatuation with an eighteen-year-old girl. But I'm not that girl anymore. She had big dreams and big ideas. She had an optimism that makes my heart hurt, and a faith that makes my hands shake to remember. She didn't have any idea of how life would pull the rug out from under her. She didn't even know what she had to fear or how badly she could hurt. I'm never going to be her again. Why can't you see I never actually became the woman I thought I'd become? It was all aspiration."

"You became such an amazing, smart, strong woman. And if you would only—"

"If, if, if, you're still talking about potential." She shook her head. "You fell in love with my potential, but I never lived up to it."

"That's not true, and you don't have the right to tell me what I love. I've always known who you are, and I've always known what you mean to me."

255

"No, you've always seen me through the filter of your first crush. Ever since you came back, you still look at me the same way, and—" her voice cracked "—and it's breaking my heart. God, Jess, you are breaking my heart."

"Why would me loving you cause pain?"

"Because you still look at me like I'm a hero when I know I'm just ordinary." She sagged, her chin dropping to her chest and her arms folding around her waist. "I keep waiting for you to notice I'm not special. A part of me has been bracing myself for that moment since you were thirteen."

"Well, I'm not thirteen anymore. How long do I have to wait before you trust in what I see in you now?"

Lauren shook her head again, this time slowly, as if it cost her a great deal of energy she didn't have. "So much has changed, but so many things haven't. You've still got so much ahead of you, Jess."

She knelt down on the floor in front of her and took her hands. "I want to experience it all with you. I want us to take each step together. I'm not giving up my dreams or asking you to give up yours. I'm asking to chase them all together. I'm asking you to believe in me as a partner the same way you believe in me as a fencer."

"I do believe in you. I don't share your faith in me." Lauren gave another shuddering breath. "And I'm sorrier than you'll ever know that I can't be the person you need. It's ripping me apart, but I cannot go with you."

Her heart folded in on itself, constricting like a crumpled sheet of paper, and she sank to the floor in front of her.

"Please forgive me," Lauren whispered.

She swallowed emotions that felt like razor blades. "It's not your fault."

"This is 100 percent my fault."

"No." Jess leaned forward and kissed her on the top of her bowed head, breathing in the scent of her shampoo, and fighting to hold her own pain at bay in the face of Lauren's anguish. "I couldn't love you enough for both of us."

Lauren took hold of her face. "Listen to me. You shouldn't have to. You deserve someone who loves every bit as fiercely and freely as you do, someone who can meet every challenge and rise to every adventure. I'll spend the rest of my life heartbroken I'm not that person."

She gritted her teeth and backed away.

That was it, the end she'd fought against for the majority of her life. Lauren cared about her enough to give her a part of her heart to break, but not all of the pieces to put back together.

Chapter Ten

Lauren had thought the twenty-four hours between their breakdown and when Jess left would be the hardest part.

She was wrong.

As awful as it had been to try to work with Jess the last day, amid the anguish and sadness at all the ways she'd failed to be the person they both wanted her to be, at least they were still together. They still went through the routines, even though they'd lost their joy. She still got to hear Jess's voice, even though it had grown distant. She could still look into her eyes, even if they were glassy. She could still hug her goodbye, even if she couldn't hold her the way she ached to. At the time, she'd thought the contrast between what they'd been and what they'd become was the saddest thing she'd have to face, but none of it compared to the vast emptiness that consumed her the moment Jess boarded her plane.

And the void hadn't dissipated with time. She knew enough to understand grief didn't heed any clock, but in the past, she'd been able to wrestle it into its place by staying busy, focusing on other things, and setting her purpose toward other people. When her dad had died, it had been her mom first, and then the club kept her attention divided enough to portion off the pain, but now she couldn't shake the feeling that the only work that mattered, and the only person who meant enough to her to offer that kind of purpose was halfway across the world without her.

Only the sense of responsibility she carried for the young fencers in her life kept her moving.

"You are going to teach the classes tonight," Enrico said, probably intending it to be a command, but she heard the question undercutting his assertion.

"Yeah," she croaked, rising from her desk despite the constant weight of the unseen pushing against her. "I know it's time to get ready."

"And no one is going to get hurt?"

"No." *No one but me.* "I've never let a kid get run through yet."

"Okay." He nodded slowly, his gray ponytail bobbing lightly. Then he scrunched up his already wrinkled face. "Eh, maybe I'll teach one?"

She sighed. "Are you implying I can't teach the classes I've taught every week for the last four years?"

"No." He raised his hands and stepped back from the desk. "I thought maybe you would like a night off. You worked very hard with Jessie, and, well, I am not good at this, but I think you are very sad she's gone."

All the defensiveness that had kept her upright crumbled. The comment, though not eloquent, was probably the most thoughtful thing he'd ever said to her. She just cracked and began to cry.

"Oh no." He muttered. "No. No. No. Bella, you can't break an old man's heart and scare all the children."

She sniffed a few times. "I'm sorry. I can pull it together."

"I will hold it together." He patted her shoulder awkwardly. "You go home to your mama."

She shook her head. "I have to take care of the kids."

"You need to take care of you, or you are no good for the kids." He nudged her toward the door. "This is still my club. You're not working tonight."

A little flash of resistance flared up in her at the thought of him pulling rank on her, no matter how well intentioned, but it came followed quickly by another bout of depression at the realization he had the right to do so. It was his club, not hers. None of this was hers. It could all be taken away on the whim of an old man, or a fire, or a flood, or a couple of bad checks from struggling parents, and . . . "Okay, yeah. I can't do this right now."

She didn't even remember driving home. She was too far under. It took every ounce of mental fortitude not to just surrender and sink in all the fear and regret swirling around her now. When she looked up and found herself parked in her own driveway, she could only send a silent prayer of thanks that she hadn't driven into a ditch.

She killed the engine and got out of the car, but before she even made it up the front steps, her mom swung open the door.

"What's wrong?"

"Nothing," she said.

"You're home early. You never come home early. The last time you showed up unexpectedly looking distraught . . ."

The unspoken end of that thought rammed into her with so much force, she actually stumbled back. "No one's dead."

All the air left her mother's lungs in a whoosh of relief. Then she eyed Lauren more carefully. "I didn't mean to jump all over you. Come in."

"Actually, I think I'd like to sit out here for a bit if you don't mind." She pushed herself up onto the porch and let her feet dangle off the edge. The air was warm and the breeze light, as if summer had arrived without her knowledge or permission.

"I hope you don't mind some company." Her mom eased down next to her a little more gingerly. "I'm sorry I overreacted. I keep telling myself I've moved on, but I think part of me is always braced for disaster to strike again."

"No, we both earned that kind of reaction," Lauren said, but the echo of Jess's words rang through her ears. *You can't spend your whole life waiting for the other shoe to drop.*

"I hate that," her mom said. "It's so unfair. He corroded all of our memories. He shouldn't get to undercut our futures, too."

She wanted to argue, to say it wouldn't always feel that way, but she wasn't sure anymore, not after the pain she'd seen rip though Jess when she'd told her she couldn't love her the way she needed her to. "That kind of grief changes a person. It rearranges your insides and clouds the way you see everything outside."

"Is that why you're home early?"

"Maybe." Letting Jess go shouldn't have triggered the same kind of grief, but it had, and she didn't see any reason to lie to either of them.

"And also why you're in Buffalo and not at an Olympic training center?"

"I think that's what started it, and maybe the grief curdled through every other interaction after that, but it's all so mixed up and messed up now. I don't know if I can undo the knot of emotions anymore."

"When you were little, you used to tie your shoes in the most horrible knots. I got really good at untying them. Do you want to know my secret?"

"What?"

"Just start picking at different spots all at once until eventually something gives and shows you some hidden place where the whole thing is connected."

She thought for a moment. She did suspect so many things were connected, and just like a knot where she could only see the ends of all the threads, but a part of her worried if she started picking at them, she might actually come undone. Then again, she already felt like several of her seams had been severed, and coming untied might be better than fighting to hold on and shredding her whole life in the process.

Her mom waited, patiently attentive while she rolled things over in her mind and tried to decide where to even start prying. In her indecision, she went back to Jess, which was probably as telling as anything. "I think I was waiting for the other shoe to drop the whole time. It was just too good to be real, too good, and the last time I felt truly happy was right before Dad died. I had so much potential then, so much love and hope, and all those dreams felt so real, but it wasn't. I think when I realized that, I lost my ability to trust myself. Like I don't believe in 'real' anymore, not on big things, not on intangibles. You know what I mean?"

261

Her mom nodded. "I do."

Of course she did. She knew how it felt to live a beautiful dream only to find it had really been a nightmare all along. "Once you learn to live that way, even the best moments are guarded, and I think I tried to guard myself by just not believing in a future to begin with."

"Because if you don't let yourself hope for something, you can't be hurt when it doesn't happen."

"Yeah. Or at least that's what I thought." The lump returned to her throat. "But I am hurt."

"Oh baby." Her mom wrapped an arm around her shoulder and pulled her close.

"It hurts so bad I can't breathe full breaths. I can't think clearly, and I keep telling myself it was always going to end this way eventually, but it doesn't make me feel any better." She rested her head on her mom's chest. "What if I made a terrible mistake?"

"Do you think you did?"

"I still don't know. It feels so much worse than I expected, but at least she's not wrapped up in it all with me. That's the only thing giving me any peace. At least I didn't drag her down with all my fear and insecurity." She remembered the way Jess crumpled and the light that went out of her eyes. "I pray I didn't drag her down. I don't know what else I could've done for her."

"What did she ask you for?"

"Everything." She laughed a nervous little shiver. "She said she loved me, and she wanted us to chase our dreams together, and to go with her and coach her on the floor of the Olympics."

"Oh, that girl does have a flair for the dramatic."

"Right? Like couldn't she have asked for something more reasonable?"

"I'm not sure that's how love works, but just for a second, let's say she had," her mom suggested evenly. "What if she'd asked you to just wait for her until after the Olympics. What would you have said?"

"I don't know. It would've scared me, but it's not like I had any intention of moving on in three weeks. I'm not sure if I'll be able to look at another woman the same way, for, maybe ever."

"Well that's pretty telling. What if she'd asked you to just come to the Olympics as her friend, or her girlfriend, or someone in her corner at the biggest event of her life?"

"I think I—" her stomach twisted. "Oh, that would've been daunting, but I think maybe if she phrased it like that I might have gone, but she didn't. She wanted a coach on the floor. I'm not ready for something like that. I could never live with myself if she put her trust in me and I buckled under the pressure."

"What if you did believe you could do right by her?"

"I don't think I can."

"But what if you did?" Her mom pushed a little harder.

Lauren shook her head slightly as her brain rebelled against the bigger hypothetical.

"Try to dream just for a second, for argument's sake." Her mom tightened her grip around Lauren, holding her tightly, securely. "What would you have said if she asked you to take on any role you thought you could've actually filled in her life and done well?"

She bit her lip to keep the "yes" from spilling out, and instead let the tears fall.

She knew the answer. If Jess had asked for anything she felt qualified to give, she would've done so, no matter how much it scared her. Still, she couldn't bring herself to say it, not with her half a world away. As much as it hurt not to say the word, it would kill her to say now when she hadn't been able to do so when Jess really needed her to.

"You're a fucking mess." Haley lowered her saber.

Jess grunted her displeasure. She couldn't argue. She was getting her ass handed to her in today's practice session.

"Technically, you're still great. Maybe even stronger than usual," Haley said, grabbing her water bottle, "and no one would ever call you slow, but your decision-making has been shit all week."

263

"Hey, thanks for being such a good friend." Jess mopped sweat off her forehead.

"I am being a good friend," Haley shot back. "Everyone else around here is terrified of you and your temper these days. It's fine for you to be a rage machine on the strip, but everything lights your super-short fuse lately. Someone has to be brave enough to tell you the hard truths."

"Do you think I don't know those truths?" She tossed the towel onto a nearby bench. "Do you honestly think that after more than half of my life in this sport, I can't tell when I'm getting beat mentally? You really think I, of all people, can't tell I'm losing my fucking mind and careening toward a nervous breakdown two days before the opening ceremonies of the freaking Olympics?"

"Whoa." Haley jumped forward, catching her by the arm and jerking her away from the practice area. "Calm down."

"Why?" she practically spat. It's not like calmness brought her any clarity these days. At least the anger burned away some of the pain. She planned to stay angry for as long as she could to hold the despair at bay.

"Because," Haley continued once she dragged her out of earshot of the other fencers, many of whom had stopped to watch them argue, "everyone around here is listening, and they're watching, and they're painting targets on your back because you look weak."

"I feel weak." She exploded, then caught herself and reined in her tone. "I feel weak and helpless. My best wasn't good enough for the only woman I ever wanted to win. Do you know what it's like to give something your entire mind and body and heart and still lose?"

"Yeah," Haley snapped. "I do. God, I am the number two saber fencer in America. I know what it's like to come up short on the thing I want most in the world. I also know what it takes to keep fighting. Why the hell don't you?"

"She doesn't want me to keep fighting for her. She sent me away."

"I'm not talking about her. I'm talking about the weapon in

your hand. You need to pour all your hurt and helplessness into the one dream you can still control."

"I'm trying." She sagged. "I'm working myself to death day and night. I'm not sleeping. I'm not eating. I'm fencing like it's the only thing I have left, but how am I supposed to fight when I can't even breathe?"

Haley's eyes softened.

"I never wanted anything as much as I wanted her," Jess continued sadly. "If I could make a trade right now, you could have the gold medal, and I'd run back to Buffalo."

"For what it's worth, I'd gladly make that trade, too."

She snorted. "Well, too bad. You're stuck with me because Lauren refuses to be. She doesn't love me, or maybe she does, but not completely, not enough to take the risk, not the way either of us need to move forward. And I can't make her. For the first time in my life, I can't work or fight my way out."

"And you have no capacity for dealing with that," Haley finished.

"God help me, I don't."

"You live a charmed life, Kidman," Haley said, but her voice was filled with sympathy. "You've always bowled everyone over with your charm, your speed, your brain. Normally, I'd love to see you maxed out, but not like this. I want to beat you at your best."

"Yeah, well—"

"Kidman, what are you doing over there?" Ansel shouted. "Did you get lazy in Buffalo?"

The tiny modicum of peace she'd felt when talking to Haley like a normal person evaporated in a sea of white-hot rage.

Haley must've seen it and placed a hand on Jess's saber. "Don't kill him."

"We're taking a break," she called through clenching teeth.

"Well, break's over," he pushed. "You're both on my clock now. No lazing around."

"We'll be right there," Haley said in a sickeningly appeasing voice.

"No," Jess said to her, "I'm not going to jump when he snaps his fingers."

"Come on. He's not the enemy. He's a jerk, but he's on our team."

"Is he? Or is he on his own team? What happened with Lauren ended horribly, but she runs circles around him as a coach. There's no legitimate reason she's not at the top of this sport when guys like him thrive on bullying people into submission."

"I don't doubt it, but she's got a vagina, and he drinks vodka with the Russian officials, so they have different doors open to them." Haley shrugged. "It is what it is."

"Yeah, and it'll stay that way until one of us kicks down those doors."

"Well, until then, he's the best we've got."

"Ladies," Ansel called in a patronizing tone, "time and money are wasting while you two are over there adjusting your makeup."

Jess stared at Haley with the most insolent expression she could muster.

"Okay." Haley shrugged. "Go ahead and kill him."

Her fist tightened around the hilt on her saber. It would feel so good to knock him off his feet or just pop him in the mouth, and she could. Even in her depressed state, she could clean his clock, but what would she prove that she didn't already know? He was reckless and dangerous, a schoolyard bully trying to goad her into a fight the same way he'd goaded Oren right out of the Olympics. Ansel would always be Ansel. The system would always be the system, and Jess would always have to fight that alone.

The thought sent a sharp pain through her chest.

"What is it?"

"I had something better."

"What?"

"You said he's the best we've got." She shook her head. "He's not. I had something better than him. I had a plan. I had a future. I had a coach who cared about me as a person. I had someone I trusted who made me better, smarter, stronger, happier as both a human and as a fencer instead of sacrificing one for the other by playing on my fear and insecurity. I had something better."

"Better than the Olympics?"

"Yeah." There was no fire in her voice. No defiance. Nothing but a stated fact. "When I had Lauren, I had a better version of everything."

Haley put a hand on her shoulder and squeezed so tightly it knotted the tight muscle beneath her jacket. "You didn't have her."

Jess glanced up and met those dark eyes, full of compassion.

"I'm sorry, but it has to be said." Haley's mouth twisted into a grimace. "You never had Lauren. You were chasing Lauren, and you got damn close a time or two, but you never caught her. She wasn't really yours. You ran beside each other for a while. You shared a lane. Hell, you bumped into each other a time or two, but you always chased her. It was always you reaching for her. It was always you begging her to trust you enough to shake up her world. You took all the risks."

"It's not like that."

"It is," Haley said firmly. "You said so when you called me after your first date back in Buffalo. You said you'd spent so much of your life chasing her you didn't even know who you were without it. But tell me something, in all the years you spent chasing her, did she ever once return the favor?"

Jess clenched her teeth and closed her eyes against the answer she didn't want to know.

"You spent so much of your life trying to be the person you think she deserves, but what about what you deserve?"

She tried to shrug off Haley's hand. She felt too raw to be touched right now, but Haley held on, giving her a little shake, and then a harder one until Jess opened her eyes to the harsh lights and harsher reality before her.

"You are a catch, Jess," Haley continued. "You're magnetic and amazing and powerful. You have a ferocity that scares me sometimes. You bend the world with your brain, and you defy physics with your hands."

"I wasn't good enough—"

"No!" Haley cut her off. "You idiot. Look around you."

Jess glanced side to side quickly and shrugged.

"Try again." Haley forced her to turn so they faced the vast training hall, all the lights, all the strips, all the clanging and conversation, and, finally, all of her competitors and teammates. Some of them went through the motions, others were lounging around, but all of them had angled themselves to keep an eye on her or inclined their ears as if hoping to hear a snippet of their conversation.

"They're all watching you. They're all listening to you. They're all practicing the skills they think they will need to face *you*," Haley said, close to her ear. "Soak that up. Let it sink in, because I don't think you really get it."

"Get what?"

"While you were chasing her, everyone here was chasing you."

Chapter Eleven

Lauren ignored the distant buzz of her phone as she tried to usher several small kids with overloaded equipment bags out of the lobby.

"Coach Lauren, you have a phone call," one of the others yelled as he hopped up onto the desk.

"Get down, Kolten," she instructed as she held open the door for the others. "Where's your dad?"

"He's golfing. Do you want me to answer your phone?"

"No. Go get your stuff."

The kids had been on break from school for only a couple of weeks, and already they were going feral. Normally, she loved this time of relaxed summer schedules and the unbridled energy the students brought to class with them, but tonight, and every other night for a week, she just didn't have it in her to wrestle their energy enough to mitigate the damage they were capable of doing with sharp objects. By 8:00, she was long past ready to go home, take two Advil, and cry softly into her pillow.

"Okay," Kolten said, jumping down, "but I just thought someone should probably answer it, since it's from Japan."

She froze, then glanced around the room until she saw Enrico through the window to the Elites' gym.

"Okay, everybody without a parent here, go talk to Coach Enrico."

They all stopped and stared at her as if she'd told them to run off a cliff.

"Go, do it right now!"

They must've heard the panic in her voice as they scrambled en masse toward the man who terrified most of them, and she dove for her phone.

"Hello?"

"Hi, I'm sorry to bother you at whatever time it is in Buffalo, but is this Lauren Standish?"

Her heart sank and her stomach went right along with it. It wasn't Jess. She hadn't even understood how badly she'd longed to hear her voice until she thought she would and then had that gift stolen from her.

"Hello, is this Lauren Standish?" the voice asked again.

"May I ask who's calling?"

"This is Haley Ivers."

Her heart rate kicked into overdrive again. "What's wrong? Is it Jess? Is she hurt? Is she . . ." Her voice caught.

"No. God, no. She's okay. I mean she's not okay, but she's not injured, sorry. I didn't realize I needed to lead with that," Haley said, a hint of curiosity in her voice.

"No, I'm sorry. It's not you, it's me. Please go on."

"I don't even know what else to say," Haley admitted, sounding a little lost. "I can't believe I'm saying this at all, and if she beats me in the medal rounds, I may hate myself for the rest of my life, but she's my best friend, and she's going under."

Lauren walked across the room and sank onto the couch. "I don't know what to say."

"Yeah, me neither. I've already given her what I thought was a pretty good speech, but between Ansel and the schedule and the pressure, she's just so sad and lost in the chaos of it all. I know you're not into her the same way she's into you, but I guess I just wanted to know if you really care about her at all."

"I do," she managed to squeak out.

"Well, can't you do something?"

She shook her head. "Even if I could get there in time for her individual bouts, I'm not sure I'd be any good for her in that setting."

"I kind of agree, but I also know she's no good without you here," Haley said sadly, then added, "Maybe I made a mistake in calling, but I thought you had a right to know."

"No." She managed through the pain that tightened its grip around her again. "No. I did need to know. Thank you."

She disconnected the phone and hung her head in her hands. People shuffled by and whispered around her. Doors opened and shut, and still she didn't move until she felt a hand on her shoulder.

She glanced up to see only Enrico there. "You have to go, yes?"

She nodded. "I don't know how. I can't just hop on a plane at the spur of the moment. The opening ceremonies are in a few hours, and even if I could get a flight, it would take longer than that."

"The saber competition doesn't start until the second day." Enrico walked over to the desk, sat down behind the computer, and began to type.

"What are you doing?"

"Let me see what I can find."

She rose on wobbly legs and went to stand behind him. She blinked away her unshed tears to focus on the screen, but when she did, she saw him checking airline tickets.

"I didn't even know you knew how to shop online."

He scoffed. "You know I always save money."

She couldn't argue there.

"You will have to fly out of Toronto to go direct. Can you get there in four hours? You have to be there two hours early for international flights."

"If I pack fast and Kristie drives like hell, but—"

He nodded resolutely and clicked on an option. "Then, call your mama and tell her to start throwing things in your suitcase, and don't forget your passport."

She did a double take at the price on the screen. "I can't afford that."

He waved his bony hands dismissively. "I can."

"You can?" she asked incredulously as he pulled a credit card from his wallet.

"Just because I don't like to spend it doesn't mean I don't have it."

"But why are you spending it on me now?"

She glanced at his dark eyes reflecting emotions she'd never seen before. "Because I am an old man who has no children, and you are a young woman who has no father. I always thought we might just take care of each other."

Her chest constricted, this time with love instead of pain, and she dropped a kiss onto the top of his head.

"Besides," he muttered through the blush spreading on his cheeks, "all the money was going to stay with the club anyway, and the club is going to you."

"What? When?"

He shrugged. "I wanted to wait until I was sure it wouldn't drag you down. I always wanted to leave you a thriving business, but it never got there until now."

"Is it thriving now?"

He chuckled. "Not yet, but with you in charge it can. Especially if you coach an Olympian, but you have to get to the airport fast."

"But even if I make it in time, what will I do when I get there? I don't have tickets."

He ignored her and clicked "Purchase."

"Oh my God, what did you just do?"

He smiled and clicked, "Print boarding pass."

She opened her mouth, then she caught herself. She'd done enough arguing. It was time to act.

She grabbed him by the shoulders and kissed him once on each cheek. Then she snagged the boarding pass as she bolted out the door.

Jess had anticipated this day for so long. She'd trained for it more than half of her life, and visualized it purposefully since she was thirteen. She'd worked and planned and fought, and a couple of weeks ago, she'd even believed herself ready.

She shook her head to try to dislodge the memories of the last week she spent with Lauren in a blur of sabers and sex. She'd felt like she could take on the world then, and a part of her desperately wanted to recapture that confidence, but she couldn't go back there without suffering the pain of how it all ended.

She must've grimaced at the thought because Haley turned to her with a worried expression, but she merely looked out the window. She didn't want her best friend, who also happened to be one of her toughest competitors, to see the uncertainty in her eyes. She'd traded all her confidence for pure, raw adrenaline. As they pulled off the expressway and traffic slowed to a crawl, her hands twitched and her knees bounced in the back seat of the car.

She couldn't read any of the road signs, but she knew they were close as they wound through crowded streets toward the convention center where all the fencing would be held for the entire Olympics. People filled the streets, a teeming mass weaving in and out in a jumble. She fought an almost desperate desire to jump out and join them, and not just because she could walk faster than they were driving at this point. She wanted to move. She wanted to run. She wanted to feel the press of bodies and the heat from something other than the pressure building inside her now.

She turned back to Haley. "When we get out, you gotta leave me behind."

"What?"

"My energy is bad. You gotta get away from me."

"You know I'm going to kick your ass when I get the chance, but we can warm up together."

"No. You gotta break away," Jess said resolutely. "Find Ansel. Stay with him. Stay the course. You've been a good friend to me, the best friend I could've asked for these last few days, but this is your big day, too. I want you to love every minute, and you can't do that if you have to hold my hair while I vomit."

Haley laughed. "Your hair's not long enough to get in vomit."

"You know what I mean. When we get out of the car, you need to square your shoulders, point your eyes forward, and walk away. If you don't, I'll never forgive either of us, and I've already lost enough this week. I don't want to lose my best friend, too."

Haley's jaw twitched as if she wanted to argue, but she was a competitor, too. She'd worked every bit as hard and long as Jess had, and those instincts took over. They hugged each other as tightly as their seat belts would allow. Then Haley said, "I'm going to see you in the finals, okay?"

"You better." Jess forced a smile as the car slowed to a stop. She climbed out and grabbed the roller bag with all her personal equipment from the trunk. By the time she turned around, Haley was already several steps ahead of her and fading into the crowd of people streaming toward the athletes' entrances. To every side, a cacophony of activity and conversations closed in as officials, security personnel, and spectators jostled for better positions.

"Jess," someone called, or maybe that was her imagination.

She glanced around quickly, but she couldn't make out any familiar faces amid the shifting masses. Haley continued forward up ahead, and Ansel was already inside, so she kept walking until the shout came again, distant and muddled. She might have thought she'd started hearing things, except this time Haley stopped, too.

"Jess." Her name came again, or at least something like it, amid the mismatch of languages being spoken.

Haley turned around, her eyes wide. She wasn't close enough for Jess to hear her, but she clearly read her lips as they said, "Oh my God."

A chill ran up Jess's spine as the fog that had enshrouded her for weeks burned away with the warmth of recognition.

This time, when the shout came again, she didn't just recognize it as her name, she knew the voice.

"Lauren?" She called back and searched the crowd with an almost frantic precision. A hundred faces flashed by, each set of eyes empty for her until she landed on the ones she wanted most in the world to see.

Lauren pushed against a metal security rail waving frantically. Jess dropped her bag and ran, her heart breaking and rebuilding itself with each step. She didn't know what it meant, or even what she wanted it to mean, but Lauren was here, and in the moment, nothing else mattered.

"I'm so sorry," Lauren said as soon as she was close enough to reach out and take her hand.

"You're here," Jess managed through all the questions swirling through her brain.

"I should've been here all along." Lauren clutched her hand over the chest-high fence. "God, I made a terrible mistake in letting you go alone. I was so scared to lose you, I threw away my chance to try to keep you, or to even go along with you."

Jess touched her face, running her fingers along the smooth curve of her cheek and into soft strands of her hair. "You're really here."

Lauren smiled. "I'm here, and more importantly, I want to keep being here for you in any way I can, as your friend or coach or lover, because I love you. And I know it hurt you that I couldn't say it when you needed me to, but it doesn't mean I didn't feel it. You're just faster than me at . . . well, everything."

Jess laughed. She couldn't contain the joy splitting her open this time.

"So, what do you say?" Lauren bit her lip.

"Yes," Jess said emphatically.

"'Yes' to what?"

"Whatever your question was."

"I think I was asking if it's okay that I took longer to learn what you've always known."

"Yes."

"And you forgive me for not saying yes to all those shared dreams when I had the chance back in Buffalo, even though I really wanted to?"

"Are you saying yes to them now?"

Lauren nodded.

"Then the answer is definitely 'yes.'" Jess jumped onto the rail and kissed her fully on the mouth, feeling insane and over the moon and drunk from her nearness.

Lauren pulled back only far enough to look her in the eye. "You're not mad at me?"

She shook her head, then laughed. "Mad at you? No."

"Why?" Lauren asked, a seriousness still filling her complex eyes. "I know I hurt you. I was so far from what you needed, we ended up on opposite sides of the globe."

"But we're not anymore, and this time, it's because you chased me." She grew dizzy with that realization and all the complexities she might need the rest of her life to sort out. "I've spent my whole life chasing you, and I never knew what would happen if I stopped, but now I do."

Lauren's smile finally spread, bright and beautiful. "Now we both do. And again, I may not be as fast as you, but I promise I'd chase you to the ends of the earth, Jess Kidman."

"You already did!" Jess shouted. "Oh my God, how did you?"

Lauren laughed this time. "It's a long story. Kristie sped me into Canada, and there was a plane and two trains, and I haven't slept in thirty-six hours, but right now we have more important things to talk about. Like how you're going to get me into this convention center."

Jess's jaw set, and her eyes narrowed. "You leave that to me. Stay right here while I go fire Ansel and come back with your passes."

"Oh my God," Lauren murmured as she and Jess pushed through the door to the locker room. The place was decidedly quieter than it had been earlier in the day. Jess's first bout had been over before nine in the morning, and now at just past three in the afternoon, she'd done her fair share to whittle the field down from sixty-four fencers to three. And when Haley finished her current matchup, for better or worse, there would only be two left standing.

"Jess, you're going to the gold medal bout," Lauren whispered, a hint of awe in her voice.

Jess nodded slowly. She'd been exuberant moments before when she'd jumped into Lauren's arms and spun them both around wildly after winning her semi-final by four points. While it hadn't been a rout, at no point had it ever felt like Jess was losing. She hadn't been losing for more than a few seconds all day. She'd steamrolled through her early rounds, and while her last two bouts hadn't been easy, neither had they been overly tense. Jess rose to each challenge with an aggressive sort of aplomb that kept everyone on their toes, and yet no one would know it from looking at Jess now.

Her face had lost all the pink of exertion. All the blood drained from her face as her gaze fell on the TV monitor where her best friend stood opposite her archnemesis.

Lauren watched helplessly as Jess's expression contorted in sympathy pains when Yelena struck Haley for an unanswered touch.

"Hey," Lauren said more firmly, "you're an Olympic finalist."

Jess nodded a numb sort of acknowledgement.

"You can enjoy this moment," Lauren offered as she slipped her hand into Jess's and intertwined their fingers. "It's a big deal, Jess. This is what you've worked your whole life for."

Jess shook her head, this time turning enough to see her before lifting their hands up to kiss the back of Lauren's. "I'm so glad you're here."

"Me too," Lauren said seriously, "but you have to be here, too. You can't be out there with Haley, and you can't be back at worlds last year. Most importantly, you can't go to some dark part of your mind where you store all your fears about what might happen if this match doesn't go the way you want."

Jess's jaw twitched, confirming for Lauren that she had, in fact, gone there.

"There's no *if*," Jess said as she turned back toward Haley and

Yelena just in time to see Yelena execute a flawless counterattack. "Haley's totally outmatched."

Lauren couldn't argue. Yelena was carving up the poor woman like she planned to serve her on a holiday platter.

"She beat me all week."

"Yelena?"

"No, Haley," Jess said, her voice thick with emotion. "She was better than me in practice, and now she's out there getting ripped to shreds."

Yelena landed another unanswered touch on a beautiful, acrobatic lunge, and Jess jerked her head away as if it physically hurt her to watch. Lauren gave her hand a squeeze, and this time when Jess met her eyes, there was no disguising the fear swirling behind those blue irises.

"She didn't beat you," Lauren said, not sure she quite covered up the fear building in her too. She'd never seen Jess look quite so vulnerable, at least not about fencing. She felt herself slipping into that rushing undercurrent. "You didn't practice this week."

Jess snorted. "I did. I busted my ass in the gym. I went mad with all the—"

"Not *you*," she cut back in. "That wasn't *you*. Haley called me and said you weren't yourself. She said she wanted to beat you at your best, and you weren't at your best."

Jess's lips parted, but no argument came. Did she believe her, or was she trying to find the words amid the cacophony of other things vying for their attention as Ansel's shouts rang through the venue?

They turned toward him once more as he tore into the ref in a barrage of words, some in English, some in Italian, and some that devolved into a guttural jumble that, while not quite articulate, still managed to make his point clear. The ref relented, referring the point to video review, and Lauren's palms began to sweat.

She hadn't had to scream at any refs all day, not like that anyway. What if that was about to change? She didn't speak much Italian. She knew a few phrases she'd heard Enrico shout over

278

the years, but she doubted she'd be able to put much conviction behind them, and anyway, the referees rotated between bouts. She could get one who spoke French or Russian or even English, and she still wouldn't know how to beat them into submission the way Ansel just had.

The video review came back and awarded the point to Haley, confirming for Lauren there was value in pushing the right buttons the right way. Would she be able to do so if the time came?

"Shit," Jess mumbled as Haley took another sharp shot to her side, and this time, Lauren winced with her.

It didn't matter that Jess had been overpowering all day, or that she was faster, stronger, smarter than anyone else in the field. Nothing that came next would be like anything that had come before. As Yelena drove her final touch directly into Haley's chest with a peal of victory loud enough to rattle the windows, it became abundantly clear Jess's unstoppable force was about to meet an immovable object, presenting them both with the test of a lifetime.

"I have to see Haley," Jess said, breaking free and leaving Lauren standing alone while she rushed to her friend and pulled her into a hug.

"I'm sorry," Haley said as she collapsed onto Jess's shoulder. "I tried."

"You did everything you could," Jess said, her usually smooth voice full of gravel.

"She's just . . ."

"Yeah." Jess agreed with the unspoken. "I know."

"And she just . . . I couldn't even . . . it was like she knew . . ."

"I know," Jess said softly. She hugged Haley so fiercely their jackets bunched up around them. Still, even as her body wrapped tightly around her friend, Jess's eyes sought Lauren's, deep, intense, unspoken insecurities and emotions boring into her.

Lauren's chest seized with a deep desire to comfort her, to make promises she couldn't, to become someone better, someone more complete, someone who could carry all the burdens threatening to crush them both.

"What the hell?" Ansel barked as he stomped in their direction. "I have two women about to face medal-round matches they're completely unprepared for, and I come here to find you two cuddling each other?"

Jess's eyes flashed with something bright and dangerous as she released Haley to wheel on him. "You worthless son of a bitch."

Lauren's reflexes kicked in before her brain. She caught hold of Jess's arm and tugged her back. "Don't."

"Yeah, Kidman," Ansel snarled, "get your hands off my fencer. Wouldn't want Little Miss Buffalo to get jealous."

Jess surged at him, and this time it took both Lauren and Haley to restrain her.

Ansel had the good sense to take a couple of steps back, but not enough intelligence to stop talking. "Go ahead and rage, you hothead. I'd prefer it to the way Haley melted out there, but you can't change the facts. You're about to get eaten alive, and your girlfriend can't help you on the strip against Yelena."

"Jess," Lauren commanded, leaving one hand planted firmly on her chest and using the other to gently cup her cheek. She turned her face until their eyes met. When they did, the spark in Jess's gaze jumped right into Lauren's core.

Electricity crackled between them like lightning arcing across the pitch-black sky, carrying with it the scent of impending rain. A crackle of purpose settled through all of Lauren's senses. Every awareness heightened, and the hair on the back of her neck stood on end amid all the static. It wasn't as if her doubts disappeared. She still understood all the ways she could come up short in the storm barreling toward them, but now she knew she wouldn't.

There with Jess's eyes on her, and the true, proud, pure heart beating rapidly under her palm, she knew with a certainty she'd only dreamed of that she'd be whatever this woman needed amid whatever challenges came next. She would move mountains or build fortresses. She would be coach and confidante, accessory and advocate, protector and partner. And no, she might not be able to badger or berate anyone the way Ansel did, but Jess didn't need that to win. Jess needed her to provide peace in the chaos.

"I'm right here," she said directly to Jess. "It's just me and you, and it's time to go. Okay?"

Jess nodded. Her eyes started to wander back across the room, but Lauren held her fast. "Let it all go. No one else matters right now, love. Just be with me."

Jess sighed and sagged until her forehead touched Lauren's lightly.

"There you go," Lauren whispered. "We have a plan. We already cracked the code. We're going to walk out there now. Me and you, together. You're going to do what you were born to do, what we trained to do, and I'm going to stay beside you every step and leap and lunge along the way."

"Okay."

"Ready to take on the world?" she asked, then smiled before adding, "Because for the first time in a long time, I am."

Jess paced at her end of the strip. Sweat ran down her sides in rivers, and she had to blink perspiration out of her eyes, but when her vision cleared, Yelena stood waiting once more. They'd already been trading blows for what felt like a lifetime, but a quick glance at the scoreboard reaffirmed what she knew. They were tied at seven points each.

It felt surreal to put such a reductive scoreline on what had transpired over the last few minutes. Her heart pounded so hard her eardrums ached, and still the referee stepped forward once more.

"Ready?"

She nodded sharply and edged her toe up to the line.

"On guard."

She flexed into position and met the cold, gray slate of Yelena's eyes. The woman was an impressively blank page. She'd yet to so much as flinch when Jess scored a point, and no involuntary ticks had offered up the slightest hint of surprise that the bout remained this close as it neared the halfway point.

Halfway.

If she could win this point, she'd go into the break with a lead for the first time ever against her. Was Yelena doing the same math in her head? Or did she merely try to measure her breath against the searing rasp of her own lungs? Did she want this point as badly as Jess, or did she simply want it to be over? More importantly, did she know Jess's thighs felt the sting of a thousand needles and her throat felt scorched by fire?

Every part of her ached to attack quickly, raw instinct and unabashed power, and yet when the ref called "go," she faded back.

The move had worked twice already, drawing Yelena off-balance, and while she still charged, this time she wasn't surprised Jess didn't.

Two steps, three steps, they progressed steadily, and Jess matched her in retreat, but the more Yelena moved, the more she showed her hand, and when she finally took her leap, Jess blocked it easily. As the tables turned, so did the right-of-way. She pushed forward now. Click, clack, clang, their blades crossed as their feet scuffed beneath them. Then, it was Yelena's turn to shuffle backward before planting her feet. They both blanched, out of easy options. One twitch, another flinch, and they both surged on baser instincts, a gunslinger kind of draw and shoot, both betting the house on a quick-or-dead type of lunge.

Buzzers sang out in unison as both helmets lit up like Christmas trees.

The referee threw up his hand in Yelena's direction, and Jess grabbed for her helmet, but before she even got the screen over her eyebrows, Lauren was leaning over the edge of her box shouting for a video review.

Jess smiled broadly, tension evaporating as the outcome of the point became secondary to the sight of the woman she loved shouting in her corner.

Lauren didn't have Ansel's force or vocabulary, but the sincerity creasing her beautiful features accentuated the swirl of emotions in her complex eyes, and no human could've possibly resisted her appeal.

As if to prove her point, the referee bowed his head in acknowledgement and turned toward the video review. Still, it didn't take him nearly long enough to come back and declare Yelena the winner of that point.

Jess closed her eyes as her shoulders sagged. She'd wanted that one more than she should've let herself. One point out of many shouldn't matter more than the others, but the psychological lift of going into the break with a lead would've meant something she no longer had the energy or coherence to articulate.

"Jess." Lauren's voice called her back.

She opened her eyes to see her holding out a water bottle, and stumbled toward it.

She wanted to drink it and use it to drench herself all at once.

"You got robbed there," Lauren said softly, a quiet anger seething through a whisper before she lifted her chin defiantly, "but it's just one touch. You're pushing her like never before."

"The scoreboard looks that way, but she doesn't seem any different."

"Maybe she's not, but you are."

She shook her head. "My brain feels like it's melting."

"Then let it," Lauren said quickly.

Jess lowered the water bottle and searched her expression for more.

"I'm serious, Jess. You're the best fencer in the world right now. You don't need to be anyone else. Believe in you. Trust in your instincts."

"What if she's got my number?"

"She doesn't. She doesn't know the you that you are today. She only knows you as scared and insecure and on the ropes. She's waiting for you to melt down, to fall back, to tighten up and play it safe, but you're not going to."

"But if I get wild, or reckless, I run the risk of slipping into—"

"You're not going to." Lauren caught her by the shoulder and pulled her close. "Confident fencers take risks, remember?"

"Yeah, but my confidence against her . . ." She shook her head.

"You listen to me right now, before our time is up." Lauren

squeezed her shoulder so tightly it cut through every other sensation clamoring through her adrenaline-saturated body. "You have every reason to be confident. You should be the most confident woman in the world today. Do you hear me?"

Jess nodded slowly.

"You're standing on the biggest stage in the world and winning points you've never won before. You're already guaranteed to win an Olympic medal, and what's more, you've already won the girl."

Jess smiled then, the kind that not only bent her cheeks, but also her mind onto a higher plane.

"Either way this ends, you're going home a hero, and you're going home with me. We're racing toward those big dreams of ours, and we're going to face them together, no matter what. You cannot lose, Jess. You can't lose me, and if you fence like that, you can't lose this bout either."

Jess leaned forward, dizzy on the high surging through her aching limbs. Her heart beat anew, this time with purpose instead of pleasure, as if Lauren had taken a piece of herself and plugged it into the power source that had been failing moments before. She couldn't thank her properly. She didn't have the words, and she needed to conserve this wellspring of energy, but she planted a quick kiss on her cheek before whispering, "Best. Coach. Ever."

Then she pulled on her mask and hopped back toward the piste.

This time, she beat Yelena to the line, and as she assumed her on guard position, she did something she'd never done in this spot before.

She smiled.

Not smirked, not sneered.

She smiled, a genuine show of authentic happiness.

Yelena blanched the moment the ref said "Go."

Jess surged and hit her square in the chest.

The crowd gasped, and the ref looked to Yelena even as he awarded the point to Jess.

The scoreboard said they were even now, but she knew better. She was so much more than equal to the task ahead. She relished it.

She had everything she needed, and everything she wanted.

Glancing over at Lauren as she reset, the understanding passed between them, and she nodded.

"Ready?" the ref asked, a little rise in his tone directed at Yelena.

Jess grinned and sank into the on guard position even before being asked, and when given the cue to go, she worked through a series of steps more akin to a happy jig. Yelena managed to block two blows beautifully, and Jess laughed.

She hadn't meant to, but the joy bubbled up in her. She loved this sport, all the passion and power and prowess, and she got to play at the top of the pile. To prove her point, she landed another textbook touch to Yelena's ribs.

This time, the woman opposite her did flinch, and then she turned quickly away, presumably to hide her confusion.

Jess couldn't blame her. She'd never felt like this during a bout before. She thought maybe the emotion inside her right now, new and unexamined, might be joy, the pure unfettered kind.

She sprang back into position, eager to go again, her mind clear, her breathing steady. She wanted to try everything at once, like a kid in a ginormous candy store, every option before her both sweet and tempting.

This time as she came set, she clearly read the confusion in the gray eyes opposite her. Yelena didn't know what was happening, and Jess felt a little sorry for her inability to process happiness.

They went again and again and again before Yelena finally landed a touch, then stared at Jess as if searching for a crack in the walls she couldn't see through, but instead of crumbling, Jess only smiled more broadly.

"Beautiful riposte," she said, sincerely appreciating the artistry of the move.

Yelena scowled outright at the compliment.

Jess turned to Lauren and gave a little shrug.

Lauren met her with a matching expression of pleasure. Jess's heart pushed against her chest in the best way. Lauren got it. She got her. They got each other.

With that thought filling her core like helium, she floated back to the line, and when the time came, she leapt. She had no other choice. Her body levitated in an acrobatic over-the-top lunge Yelena couldn't have defended even if she'd known it was coming, which she clearly hadn't. 13-9.

The crowd went wild, and Jess turned to face them in surprise. She'd forgotten they were there. Tipping up her mask as she walked back to her position, she scanned the front row and found her parents, eyes beaming with pride, hands clutched together in hope and fear and anticipation.

She winked at them and prayed the move came off as reassuring rather than cocky. She didn't discount Yelena. She'd merely crested on the confidence Lauren had stoked in her. Two more touches. She needed only two more, but this time, when she left the ground again, she caught a saber to the side, like a pinprick to her hot-air balloon.

"Ah." She yelped in surprise as if the thought of getting struck hadn't occurred to her.

Both the referee and Lauren started forward, but she held out a hand to them and then nodded to her opponent. "Well played."

Yelena blinked several times, then her eyes narrowed as Jess quickly assumed the on guard position. If she'd thought one well-placed hit could shatter Jess's confidence, she would surely be disappointed. She wasn't that person anymore.

"Go."

This time they battled back and forth, trading attacks and right-of-way up and down the strip. Yelena became the relentless counterattack queen once again, but the more they traded advances, the more fun Jess had, and by the gasps and grumbles from the stands, the crowd felt the same way. The air was electric, and for the first time in ages, Jess wasn't in a hurry to do something more, to get to some other place, to chase the next thing. She wasn't running toward something or from something. She wasn't even rushing. Then, in the moment when time slowed, she saw her opening and stepped right into the most natural lunge.

The tip of her saber pressed into the thick padding at Yelena's shoulder, and she was one point away. 14-10.

She jumped back, but she didn't shout or pump her fist or even rip off her helmet.

She merely turned to lock eyes with Lauren.

Lauren.

Lauren, who set her on this path all those years ago. Lauren, who believed in her. Lauren, who implored her to believe in herself.

"I love you," Jess called loudly, causing several people, including the referee and Yelena, to turn in her direction, then look to Lauren quizzically.

"I love you, too," Lauren said, ignoring everyone else. "Let's wrap this up so we can go home."

Jess nodded. She'd never had a better plan in her life.

With a deep, cleansing breath and a comfortable lead, she stepped forward.

"Ready?" the ref asked.

She nodded to him, then turned to offer a nod of respect to the adversary who'd tangled and taunted and driven her to the brink of herself.

"On guard."

As she settled into position one more time, she also settled on a move even the best of chess players couldn't have predicted.

"Go."

Yelena fell back and raised her saber, clearly anticipating one of Jess's trademark, over-the-top, acrobatic lunges. Instead, Jess angled to the side, swung her blade low, and then arched up into an uppercut swing.

By the time Yelena processed the unexpected angle, it was entirely too late to block the movement that could only be described as a slap slot.

Epilogue

Six weeks later

Lauren paced alongside the two beginning fencers as they sparred as part of her youth class. The one to her right lunged, unfazed by the considerable height advantage of her opponent, who dodged the attack nimbly. She tried for a riposte, which the little fencer blocked.

"Nice," Lauren murmured as they reset and created some more distance before clashing again. "Mind your feet this time when you come in. Keep those right toes pointed straight ahead."

The smaller competitor made an adjustment, then took three quick steps before launching forward again. This time, the textbook attack landed a hit right to the chest, causing the bigger fencer to lumber backward and shout, "Ouch!"

Lauren rolled her eyes. "Ouch? There's no way you felt that through all the pads, you big baby."

Kristie hopped off the strip and lifted her helmet. "I did too. That kid's a beast."

"She's eight."

"An eight-year-old beast."

The kid giggled, and Kristie cracked a smile. "Okay, so maybe some of my reaction to getting stabbed is still a bit psychological."

"Admitting it is the first step." She clasped her friend on the shoulder. "But I'm glad you're committed to working on it."

"Yeah, well, I was promised sexy women with swords." Kristie made a big show of scanning the room full of elementary school children. "I might need my money back."

"First of all, I comped your lesson," Lauren said, then glanced over her shoulder at the clock. "Second of all, wait for it."

"Wait for what?"

She took a slow breath, leaning into the anticipation as her smile spread.

Then, the lesson bell sounded, and Jess threw open the door to the main gym.

"Jess!" The cheer went up in unison as all the kids dropped their weapons and flooded toward her.

Lauren turned to Kristie with a satisfied grin. "There you go. Sexy woman with a sword."

"This is false advertising," Kristie groaned. "I wanted my own sexy woman with a sword, not yours. And besides, how did you know she was going to be standing there at this exact moment? Have you reached the telepathic stage of your relationship?"

"Maybe a little bit," she admitted, because as Jess met her eyes over the head of her avid but short fan base, she thought they might be thinking the same thing. "Also, she promised she'd be waiting for me as soon as I finished class, and if I'm coming to have faith in anything over the last few months, it's that Jess keeps her promises."

"Can I see your medal?" one of the kids asked as he practically climbed up Jess's leg.

"Sure." She laughed and fished it from her backpack, then passed it around to a great many appreciative "ahhs."

"It's heavy," one of the kids said as he handed it back to her.

"It's shiny," another added.

"Gold is my new favorite color," another said.

"Mine, too," Jess agreed.

"All right everyone," Lauren called, "good practice tonight.

Pick up your foils, put them back in the racks, *carefully*, and then go find your parents."

The students did as instructed, even Kristie, though she didn't leave with the others, and instead stayed to talk to Jess.

"How'd your bout go?"

"I got sliced up by a third grader."

"Happens to the best of us."

"Somehow, I don't believe you." Kristie gestured to the medal. "Do you just carry that thing around with you all the time these days?"

"Pretty much. I have the one from the team competition in a safe at my parents' house, but I keep this one on me. It seems to make people happy, and women swoon for it. Watch this." Jess held it up by the ribbon so it swung in front of Lauren as she approached.

Rolling her eyes, she pushed it out of the way before kissing her hard and fast. She wanted more, wanted to feel the press of her body and sweep of her tongue against her own, but she didn't trust herself not to end up doing something indecent. They'd only been apart three days while Jess made a few stops on her post-Olympics press tour, but as far as she was concerned, that was three days too many.

As she forced herself to step back, Jess grinned at her, then at Kristie. "See what I mean? Tonight, I'm going to wear this and nothing else."

"Oh yeah?" Kristie laughed. "And in which of your parents' houses will that defiling of a sacred international symbol take place?"

"Seriously?" Jess groaned. "You're going to bust me for not having my own place after we've only been home for a month? I spoke to a realtor on the phone Monday, but I've been kind of busy lately."

"You've been busy? You don't even know the half of it." Lauren pointed to the ceiling where a tangled mess of wires for the new camera system dangled between the ductwork. "The electricians were here all day."

Jess grimaced. "That looks expensive."

Both Lauren and Kristie stared at her.

"What are you looking at me for? Lauren's making way more money than I am these days." A healthy dose of pride filled her voice. "She's almost doubled her group lessons, plus she got the community improvement grant from General Mills and private coaching requests out the wazoo, and next week she's doing a training intensive with Haley, so basically I'm about to become her second-favorite client."

Kristie pretended to pout. "I thought I was your second-favorite client."

Lauren shook her head, both in amusement and in wonder. She couldn't believe she'd soon be coaching not just one, but two Olympic medalists. Haley had won bronze in the individual, and then a gold alongside Jess as part of the USA saber team before promptly firing Ansel. She wasn't ready to make the move to Buffalo full-time, but Lauren suspected they'd be seeing a lot more of her in the coming months, and while that excited her, Haley's presence would be one more thing to balance amid the myriad of thrilling changes in her life. "Hey, that reminds me. I had a meeting with the lawyers this morning, and the paperwork is almost done."

"Are you all drawing up your prenups already?" Kristie asked.

Jess shoved her. "Dude, seriously, I haven't even had time to breathe since the games ended. You expect me to find a place, propose, and sign contracts?"

Lauren kissed her cheek. "No worries. I only meant the paper-work for Enrico to transfer the club into my name."

"Whew." Jess sagged onto her shoulder. "Good. Now you will be able to support me financially."

Kristie elbowed her in the ribs. "I thought you were going to be loaded now that you got that Nike endorsement?"

"Yeah, that'll be enough for me to keep paying my stellar coach, whose rates just went through the roof, and afford travel for both of us for a year, maybe two. Hardly loaded."

"Yes," Lauren agreed, letting her own pride shine through for a moment, "but don't forget the modeling deals."

Jess's face flushed. "How could I when you keep reminding me?"

"I just never thought I'd be dating a gold medalist and a fencing fashion model at the same time." Sometimes she had to pinch herself to believe it was real. Even amid the grueling pace of Jess's travel and press obligations, and the strain of keeping up a professional-grade workout regimen, she still felt like she was living in a dream she'd never actually dared to dream.

As if reading her mind, Jess wrapped her arm around Lauren's waist and pulled her close. "I wouldn't have become either of those things without you. We've got a lot of adventures ahead of us, but we can figure it all out together."

"I know." Lauren rested her head on Jess's shoulder. "It's a bit overwhelming, but I feel like now that you opened me up to believing in big ideas again, I have so much lost time to make up for."

"And by making up for lost dream time, you mean planning meticulously, crossing every *t*, and dotting every *i* twice?" Kristie teased.

"Hey now, dreaming doesn't mean throwing all my caution to the wind. I still love to mind the details and take care of the people I love. I've already started a spreadsheet of houses for sale in our price range within a ten-mile radius of the club."

"Of course you have"—Jess kissed her this time— "and I wouldn't have you any other way."

"I think that's my cue to call it a night before the sweetness factor gets any stickier in here."

"It was good to see you," Jess said.

"You too."

"You did good in class, too," Lauren added. "Your footwork is improving."

"Sure it is." Kristie headed for the door but paused to call back, "Promise you'll text me when a sexy single lesbian with a sword shows up looking for a human pincushion?"

"I promise."

"What are the odds of that happening?" Jess asked.

"A month ago, I would've said 'pretty slim,' but we've set up three more fight nights with Rochester, and we're working on one with a club from Toronto, so you never know."

"We're never going to sleep on a normal schedule again, are we?"

"Is sleep really your biggest concern right now?" Lauren pushed her up against the door and kissed her hard, no longer worried about lingering in the task. Anyone who hadn't left yet had overstayed their welcome, and she'd waited too long to be held responsible for her actions where this woman was concerned. She ran her hands over Jess's muscled torso, tracing the lines of her abs through the thin, cotton T-shirt.

They made out like a pair of teenagers, groping, kissing, and stealing heated breaths. Jess cupped Lauren's head in her hand, sinking her fingers into her hair and massaging her scalp before tugging gently to expose Lauren's throat. She then kissed her way down the curve of her neck and back up to nip along her jaw and ear.

Lauren's knees almost gave way and she swayed slightly, but Jess's arm around her waist easily bore the extra weight of her arousal.

She gave a little hum of pleasure. "It's only been a couple of days, but it felt like an eternity without you."

Jess pulled back slightly. "Now you know how I felt for like, I don't know, ten years."

"I don't know how you survived. I meant what I said to Kristie about opening up. I didn't let myself feel any emotions this strongly for so long." She shook her head as her voice caught. "But now it's like the dam has broken, and I'm just completely flooded with a desire to hold you, to touch you, to be wrapped up in you, forever."

Jess's beautiful face lit up with an exuberant smile.

"What?"

Jess cupped her face in her strong hands. "This. Us. You were totally worth the wait."

Lauren's head spun again as it had so many times on this

rollercoaster ride. "You waited, but you also worked, both professionally and personally. When I think of everything you've accomplished—"

Jess interrupted her with another quick kiss. "Everything *we've* accomplished."

"I'm not just talking about us now. Jess, you won a gold medal."

Jess shrugged. "Don't get me wrong. That's cool and all, but what I'll always remember about my first Olympics isn't that I won the gold. It'll be that I finally won you."

A part of her wanted to argue, but that part of her had grown smaller with every day, every kiss, every minute with this wild and wonderful woman. She might not have been able to believe it even six months ago, but as Jess held her tightly, she knew without a doubt that what they were building together was indeed greater than gold.

Acknowledgements

I wrote this book at the height of a global pandemic and in the lead up to the most contentious presidential election of my lifetime. To say the world was not a happy place during those months is a gross understatement. My family, like many of yours, lived under strict quarantine, feared for sick loved ones, carried the communal grief of millions of lives lost, mourned the violence against minorities, and felt the turbulence of protest, progress, and political conflict. As so many artists have done throughout history when faced with loss and destruction, I survived by pouring myself into the act of creation.

I binge-wrote this book in a matter of months, working feverishly in an attempt to finish the first draft before election day, out of a concern for what might happen after that. During those weeks and months, this book and these characters served partially as a happy distraction, partially as an escape to a better place (at least emotionally), and partially as an outlet for my desperate desire to put something good into the world we all inhabit together. It's a tall order to pin to a sports romance, but I hope at least some of those things come through when you read this story. I hope it sparks joy. I hope it entertains you.

I hope it helps you forget yourself and your troubles for a bit. Most of all, I hope this book reminds you that even amid the worst we face both collectively and as individuals, love has the power to sustain, the power to heal, the power to overcome, and the power to transform us all.

Thank you to my wonderful readers, who help me stay present and positive. You give me strength and joy. The number of you who got excited about a fencing romance before you even knew anything else about it both amused me and gave me the fortitude to keep pushing in moments when I worried I'd jumped in over my head. I'm so grateful for every one of you who has ever bought one of my books, written a review, reached out on social media, supported me on Patreon, or sent me an email. You give me the ability to turn my passion into my life's work.

Next, I want to thank two Olympic-caliber fencers who generously shared their time and knowledge during the research stages of this book. Eliza Stone and Iris Zimmerman both spent multiple conversations talking to me, not just about the basics of their sport, but also sharing openly about the culture around it, lending parts of themselves and their stories to these characters. They provided Jess and Lauren with an authenticity I couldn't provide on my own, and anything I got wrong in my portrayal is a reflection of my own artistic license rather than a lack of access.

Furthermore, the fencers I spoke to at every level were deeply aware of the fact that most people don't understand their sport, and that even the best among them will never make enough money at it to live comfortably, much less get rich or famous. These athletes compete for love, and they have a passion burning in them that's contagious. My thoughts are with them, their teammates, their students, and the entire world athletic community as we lead up to an unprecedented Olympics, as the games are being held in the shadow of a global health crisis. After researching and writing several books featuring top athletes, I have developed such an affinity for all those who push themselves in the pursuit of faster, higher, stronger. It breaks my heart that so many of them will not be able to have the type of experience I write about in the later scenes of this book. They will not have their decades of work rewarded by being able share their success with their families and friends, or even an international audience. I sincerely hope the global community and the community of people who read this book will find ways to shower them in support from afar.

As always, I must take time to acknowledge that no book is ever the invention of a single artist. Over many years in publishing, I have collected a team of people who I know I can trust completely to take my work and help make it better. Ann McMan once again showed why she is the best in the business by somehow managing to convey a depth of emotion and a hint of attraction, even with both cover models wearing full masks. Thank you to Lynda Sandoval, who loved these characters and this story so much I had no choice but to share her enthusiasm. I cannot overstate how much it means to an author to work with an editor who believes in them and their story so deeply. Thank you to Barb and Toni, my long-time beta readers who are always quick with probing questions and support. Thank you to my copy editor and colleague, Avery Brooks, who dropped everything on short notice to clean up messes and make this book much more readable. And of course, thank you to my awesome page proofers, Diane, Anna, Marcie, Ann,

Jenn, and Melissa, who stand as the final line of defense between my readers and my most stubborn typos.

I'm grateful to have the benefit of a strong community of friends and colleagues who keep me on track, make me laugh, and remind me that I have the best job in the world. Georgia, Melissa, and Nikki check in constantly and keep me entertained without pulling me too far off track. The Bywater romance authors chat about craft and keep each other accountable. Anna Burke has become a steady writing companion who helps me keep my chin above water, and even on my worst days manages to make me smile by reminding me that "women with swords are sexy!"

I also want to thank my therapist, Leah Eagan. Though I started therapy while writing *Modern English*, this book is my first written while fully in that process. After years of using my writing as the primary vehicle for working through issues, a part of me worried that if I had another, more deliberate space in which to do my grappling, my artistic drive might falter. It turns out the opposite is true. There are several lines in the end of this book that were taken verbatim from a single therapy session. So, while I've always been a big advocate for mental health, now I can also vouch for therapy's value in the creative process as well.

And finally, thank you to my amazing family, without whom I'd have no stories worth telling. To Will Banks, you're the best Big Papi ever. To Jackson, your love and enthusiasm for sports makes me feel young and keeps my curiosity alive. Watching you grow and learn and adapt this year inspired me to keep doing the same. And to Susie, my rock, we both know I would've melted into an utter mess multiple times without your steady hand and constant support.

One of the best things to come out of this year is my renewed certainty that I picked exactly the right person to spend the rest of my life with, come what may.

I am well and truly blessed in every area of my life, and I know that none of what I have or what I do would be possible without the gift of grace from a loving creator, redeemer, and sanctifier.

Soli deo gloria.

Also by Rachel Spangler

Learning Curve
Trails Merge
LoveLife
Spanish Heart
Does She Love You
Heart of the Game
Perfect Pairing
Edge of Glory
In Development
Love All
Full English
Spanish Surrender
Fire & Ice
Straight Up
Modern English

The Darlington Romances

The Long Way Home
Timeless
Close to Home

About The Author

Rachel Spangler never set out to be a *New York Times*-reviewed author. They were just so poor during seven years of college that they had to come up with creative forms of cheap entertainment. Their debut novel, *Learning Curve*, was born out of one such attempt. Since writing is more fun than a real job and so much cheaper than therapy, they continued to type away, leading to the publication of *Timeless*, *The Long Way Home*, *LoveLife*, *Spanish Heart*, *Does She Love You*, *Timeless*, *Heart of The Game*, *Perfect Pairing*, *Close to Home*, *Edge of Glory*, *In Development*, *Love All*, *Full English*, *Spanish Surrender*, *Fire and Ice*, *Straight Up*, *Modern English* and *Thrust*. Now a four-time Lambda Literary Award finalist, an IPPY, Goldie, and Rainbow Award winner, and the 2018 Alice B. Reader recipient, Rachel plans to continue writing as long as anyone, anywhere, will keep reading.

In 2018 Spangler joined the ranks of the Bywater Books substantive editing team. They now hold the title of senior romance editor for the company and love having the opportunity to mentor young authors.

Rachel lives in Western New York with wife, Susan and son, Jackson. Their family spends the long winters curling and skiing. In the summer, they love to travel and watching their beloved St. Louis Cardinals. Regardless of the season, Rachel always makes time for a good romance, whether reading it, writing it, or living it.

For more information, visit Rachel on Instagram, Facebook, Twitter, or Patreon.

You can visit Rachel Spangler on the web at
www.rachelspangler.com